ART SEEN

PJ GRAY

SADDLEBACK
EDUCATIONAL PUBLISHING

MONARCH JUNGLE®

SADDLEBACK
EDUCATIONAL PUBLISHING
www.sdlback.com

ISBN-13: 978-1-68021-481-9
eBook: 978-1-63078-835-3

Printed in Guangzhou, China
NOR/0718/CA21800834

22 21 20 19 18   1 2 3 4 5

MONARCH
JUNGLE®

Chapter 1

It Wasn't Me

Marta Lopez sat with her head down. Her long dark hair fell around her face. If nobody could see her, she wasn't there. She gazed at a loose thread on her sleeve. Suddenly she felt a nudge.

"Huh?" She looked up.

"Are you listening?" her mom asked. "Mr. Dalton is talking to you."

Mr. Dalton was the principal of Stone Brook High School. "I have witnesses," he said. "They saw you do it."

He put his phone in front of Marta and her mom. "And I have more proof."

Someone had taken a picture of a drawing. It was a donkey with words scribbled under it.

Marta shook her head. Seriously? She loved to draw.

But not on bathroom walls. That was kid stuff. Not something a 15-year-old would do.

And she would never call Mr. King an ass. He was the art teacher. Art was the only class she liked. Besides that, the drawing was bad. If she *had* done this drawing? It would have been good.

"I promise you," Mrs. Lopez said. "My daughter would never do that. She knows better." She moved Marta's hair from her face.

"Stop, Mom." Marta pulled away.

"Tell me you didn't do this," Mr. Dalton said.

Marta knew the truth. But she wasn't talking.

"I'm sorry, Mrs. Lopez. It's important that your daughter learns a lesson." He looked at Marta. "I'm suspending you for three days. I've told your teachers. They will email you any homework. And this will go on your record. Do you understand?"

"Yes," she mumbled.

"And, Marta," he said. "There are only a few weeks until summer break. I urge you to make the rest of the year count. Do your best. And try to stay out of trouble."

The meeting with Mr. Dalton was over. But the drama was just beginning. On the drive home, her mom did most of the talking.

"I swear on all that is holy. I don't know what to do with you. Or what to say."

"Then don't say anything," Marta said softly.

"Shut your mouth!" her mom shot back. "Don't you dare say another word. I missed work for this. That's half a day's pay. And for what? To hear good things? No. To hear that you're a vandal."

Here we go, Marta thought. There was nothing she could do. Her mom was not going to stop.

"Your dad and I have tried to be patient. But we're tired of your moods. The way you mope around. You don't even talk to us. All you do is sit in your room and draw. Draw, draw, draw. In that little notepad. Thank God for the A in art. At least you have one good grade."

Marta stared out the window.

"There's no excuse. You're a smart girl. And so pretty. Why do you hide it? Just look at your clothes. That big shirt and baggy pants. And your hair. You never comb it. No wonder you have no friends."

That last comment wasn't fair. It was true that Marta didn't have friends. But it wasn't her fault.

For most of her life, her parents had been farmworkers. That meant they had to move a lot. Her dad had a phrase for it. *Following the harvest*. They picked onions in Texas. Lettuce in California. Berries in Michigan.

With each move, it was like starting over. She was the new girl all over again. It was hard to make friends.

It took time, but her parents got better jobs. Now they worked at a factory that canned fruit.

Both worked the canning line. They washed and peeled fruit and filled containers. Her dad made sure the line was set up properly. He also cleaned the equipment.

The factory canned other foods too. The work was year-round. So far, they'd had the same day shift. But that could always change. It depended on when crops came in. Sometimes one or both of them worked overtime.

Even with extra hours, it didn't add up to much money. But the family could stay in one place. It was a better life for their daughters. "More normal," they had said.

Marta struggled with the idea of "normal." What did that even mean? For her it was still a lonely life. She wasn't able to make friends. But she didn't try either.

Her mom's voice broke through her thoughts.

"Your grades have to get better. Do you hear me?" she said. "It's your only chance for a good life. Don't you get that? Or do you want to work in the fields? I know I don't want that life again."

No, Marta didn't want that life. But she couldn't picture what her life would be.

Chapter 2

House Arrest

The ride home had been one long lecture. The car pulled into the driveway.

Finally!

They got out of the car. Marta hurried ahead of her mom into the house. She just wanted to get to her room and be alone.

Most of the time that was impossible. The room wasn't just Marta's. She was forced to share it with her sister. Elena was 12. Her side was done completely in pink. She thought she was a princess. No room was big enough for the two of them.

A teen Marta's age should have her own bedroom. It was that way in other families, wasn't it?

On her way down the hall, Marta saw Elena. She was at the bedroom door and about to go in.

"Get out of there," Marta shouted. She pushed Elena out of the way. "I have to study."

"Hey!" Elena shouted back. "It's my room too."

"Stay out!" Marta slammed the door and locked it. She fell onto her bed.

Her sister was now crying. Any minute their mom would be at the door.

Marta was used to people being mad at her. Usually they were right. But this time was different. She was in trouble for something she didn't even do.

"You are a vandal," Mr. Dalton had said. She couldn't tell him the truth. That Tina Barber was the real vandal. She drew on the bathroom wall and blamed Marta.

Tina was the most popular girl in tenth grade. Nobody would believe Marta over her. Not even Mr. Dalton.

Saying something would have only made things worse. Tina would find a way to get even. She always had to have the last word. That's how bullies were.

Once, Marta tried to stand up to Tina. But it was hard without friends to back her up. So she decided to just ignore her.

Tina didn't like that either. That's when she became

Tina's target. The drawing in the bathroom was payback. And it worked.

She pulled a little notebook from her back pocket. It was always with her. Kind of like a best friend. Her mom had gotten it for her. She knew Marta loved to draw. Then why had she complained about it in the car?

"All you do is draw," she'd said.

Marta ran her finger across the cover. It gave her a feeling of comfort. That must be how it felt to have a real friend.

She put her hair in a ponytail and opened the notepad. Her pen moved quickly over the page. A line of tall buildings stretched across the paper. It was the scene of a city she didn't know.

"Let me in!" Elena yelled. She started pounding on the door.

Marta kept drawing.

The doorknob turned. "Marta!" her mom yelled. "Open this door right now! Let your sister in!"

"I'm trying to do my homework!" she yelled back.

She turned the page and drew even faster. There were the same buildings as before. But she also drew docks and water. It didn't seem like her work. There were details she'd never even thought about.

"You're being punished, remember? For the next

three days," her mom yelled. "You will keep up with your homework. And when that's done? You will clean this whole house! Every room. From top to bottom. Do you hear me? Now open this door!"

It was going to be a long three days. Marta stared at the drawing. Was this a real place? She wished she could go through the page.

Chapter 3

Draw What You Feel

The alarm went off extra early Monday morning. Marta was already up. She'd gotten dressed in a hurry and left the house. She didn't know which was worse. School or being stuck at home for so long.

Nobody was in art class yet. The room was dark and quiet. This was the time she liked most. She could be alone and think.

It wasn't that she didn't like the kids. If she were to have a friend, they would be in this class. Many of them had talent. And most of them were cool.

In Mr. King's class, the students were artists. The classroom was set up like a studio. There were easels and worktables. A display wall showed off student artwork.

He kept the mood light and fun. Everyone wanted to be there.

She sat at a table in back. As she got ready to draw, students began coming in. Some of them looked at her. It seemed clear from their faces. They knew about the bathroom wall. Tina had probably bragged about it.

She took out her sketchbook. This one was just for art class. Marta liked her small notepad better. Those drawings were private. They didn't get graded.

A group of kids spoke in low voices. She thought she heard her name. She opened the sketchbook. Her eyes stayed focused on the blank page.

As the bell rang, Mr. King came into the room. "Everyone quiet while I call roll. Then we can get to work."

Ugh. She hated having her name called. It just brought attention to her. Today would be even worse. When he got to her name, kids might laugh. They all had to know about the donkey drawing by now.

Did Mr. King know about it? Was he mad at her?

Roll call ended. Nobody had laughed. Mr. King didn't seem mad. Like always, he asked to see their sketchbooks. Students had to draw something new for each class.

"Marta Lopez?" he said. He was walking toward her table.

Oh no, she thought. Mr. King was starting with her. It

wasn't surprising. She'd been out for a few days. He'd be curious to see her new drawings. But there was a problem. She hadn't drawn anything new.

She hated the thought of disappointing him. He always praised her work. Once he even said she was his best student. His opinion meant a lot.

"What can you show me?" he asked. "You should have at least three drawings."

"Um." She didn't know what to say. She'd been doing other homework and cleaning the house. Her mom stayed on her. She inspected the house as soon as she got home. If the work wasn't done right, Marta had to do it again. There hadn't been time for art class.

Now they both looked at the blank page.

"I'm sorry," she said softly. "I was having a hard time. I couldn't think of anything to draw."

"You're required to draw every day," he said. "That's the only way to pass."

"I know." It felt like the whole class was staring at her. She looked down.

Mr. King turned to face the other students. "Class? What is it that I ask of you?"

"Draw what you feel," some kids called out.

"That's right." Then he turned back to Marta.

Couldn't he see how uncomfortable she was? Why didn't he just drop it?

"Do me a favor, Miss Lopez. Think back to your time off. What were you going through?"

Oh, nothing much. Getting kicked out of school because of a bully. My mother and sister screaming at me. Cleaning toilets.

Anger rose up inside her. She felt like she might explode.

"Draw what you feel," he said. "You have five minutes. Go!" He walked away.

Five minutes later, Mr. King was back. He looked at the drawing and nodded. "I get it. Good way to blow off steam." He began to walk away. Then he stopped and looked back. "Very realistic. Nice work."

The drawing was of a bomb with a lit fuse.

Chapter 4

Drawing the Line

The school lunchroom was packed. Laughter and loud voices rang out. For Marta, the happy sounds were annoying. It reminded her that she had no one to talk to.

Being around groups of friends was the worst. It made her feel left out. Not that she would sit with them even if they did ask.

Normally she ate outside. Today it was raining. She found a seat away from everyone. It was near the windows. Watching the rain took her mind off the noise.

Her thoughts drifted. Memories of being a little girl came to mind. It was late summer. The days were warm. At the time, her dad had a job picking grapes. He'd bring a few bunches when he got off work.

She'd sit in the back of his truck. Together they would eat the grapes. Then he'd lift her out of the truck and set her down. One time he handed her a stick. The first drawing she ever made was in the sand.

Thunk!

An object had struck Marta's arm. It was a wad of paper. She looked around. A group of girls was laughing. They were staring at her.

In the center of the group was Tina. A tube of lip gloss was in her hand. Slowly she moved it across her lips. Then she gave Marta the finger. Tina and her friends laughed.

Jerks! Marta looked away. She pulled the notepad from her pocket. Her pen moved quickly over a blank page.

She'd drawn an image of Tina. Flames flew out over her head. There was fire in the background.

Just a few more touches.

Two horns. A mustache and goatee. Perfect! It was Tina the devil.

The bell rang. The sound had made Marta jump. Tina and her friends laughed as they left the lunchroom.

Marta sat there, staring out the window. Instead of feeling angry, she felt nothing. Only an urge to run out into the rain. To go somewhere else. Where, she didn't know.

Chapter 5

Sketchy

A couple of days had passed. Marta was on her way to art class. It seemed like something was different. For one thing, the hallway was quiet.

Wait! Where was Tina? She was nowhere around.

It didn't matter. But it did seem odd. Tina was always around. She made it a point to be the center of attention.

Whatever, Marta thought. *One less bully to worry about.*

The bell rang. She had slid into her seat just in time.

"Okay, class," Mr. King said. "You have 30 minutes to draw. Then I'll come around and look at your work."

Marta opened her sketchbook and started drawing. She forgot all about the time. They'd been drawing for 25 minutes.

Mr. King was walking up and down the aisles. He stopped at each table and made comments. Marta kept drawing.

"Miss Lopez?"

She jumped at the sound of his voice. How long had he been standing there?

"I like what you've done. The buildings. The docks and boats. It's very detailed."

Marta was silent.

"Have you been to this place?" he asked.

She shook her head. "No."

"Can you show me anything else?"

Marta turned the page in her sketchbook. The drawing looked like the first one. There were buildings and water. She'd drawn the same docks and boats.

"May I?" he asked. He turned to the next page. Then the next. And the next. Every drawing was the same. His eyes narrowed. "Wow." He didn't sound excited.

She could feel her face getting hot. Mr. King didn't seem to like her work.

"Why?" he asked. "What made you draw this place over and over?"

She shrugged. "I don't know. That's just what I felt like drawing."

"Well, it looks interesting. Maybe you'll go there someday."

"Maybe."

He smiled. "I like what you've done. But next time, try something else. No boats or docks. And no bombs."

She smiled back.

Chapter 6

Flipping Out

Math was Marta's last class of the day. She'd barely made it there on time. *Why hurry?* she'd thought. It was just another boring hour to sit through. Whenever she tried to focus on the work, her mind drifted. She'd rather be drawing.

She pulled the notepad from her pocket. She flipped past the buildings, boats, and docks. Then she came to her latest drawing. The one of Tina the devil framed in fire. She grinned.

A voice over the speaker made her jump. She quickly put the notepad away.

"Attention. This is not a drill. I repeat. This is not a drill. The school has received a threat. Prepare to leave campus. Follow instructions from your teachers."

Everyone rushed to pack up. The teacher hurried students to the door. On her way out, Marta heard someone talking.

"There's been a bomb threat."

The hallway was packed with students and teachers. They were filing out of the building. Marta moved along with the crowd.

Outside, she made her way to the bus. If she got there first, she could get a seat in the back.

"Miss Lopez!" a man called out.

Someone was calling her name. It was hard to make out over the noise of the crowd.

"Marta!"

She stopped and turned around.

"I'd like to speak with you," Mr. King said.

"I need to catch my bus."

"How about tomorrow?" he said. "After class."

"Sure." She looked back at the bus. "I need to go."

A crowd had formed in front of the bus. Marta was forced to wait. By the time she got on, most of the seats were taken. She had to sit in front.

She pulled out her notepad. At least she could draw. Two girls behind her were talking. Marta wasn't paying attention. Until she heard the words *Tina Barber*.

"Did you hear about it? Her house burned down. And she was in it!"

Marta looked up. She leaned back to listen.

"I heard that too. The police say they think it's arson."

"You mean someone did it on purpose? Who would do that?"

"I don't know. But I heard that Tina was badly burned. All over her body. Her face too. She had such a pretty face."

Marta sat there frozen. She lowered her head. The notepad was open to the drawing of Tina. Flames and fire were around her face.

No way! It can't be. Her hands shook as she closed the notepad. This had to be a joke. The girls saw the drawing. And they made up the story to scare her.

But what if her drawing did lead to a fire? A few days ago, she drew a bomb. Today there was a bomb threat. That's why Mr. King wanted to meet. She put the notepad away.

The girls behind her were silent. Were they watching her? Did they suspect her? Now it seemed like the whole bus had gotten quiet. She was sure everyone could hear her heart pounding. She wanted to run, but she was trapped.

"I bet it was her," one of the girls said.

Chapter 7

What's the Deal?

Today was the meeting with Mr. King. Marta's stomach had been upset all morning. Was she in trouble again? Would she end up in the principal's office?

So far, nobody had said anything about Tina. Maybe the girls on the bus were joking around. Tina hadn't been burned in a fire.

She looked at the clock. Art class was almost over. She eyed the door and then glanced over at her teacher. Maybe she could slip out without his knowing. That's when he looked at her and smiled. There was no getting out of this.

The bell finally rang. Mr. King was walking toward her.

"Thank you for meeting with me, Marta." He sat

at the table next to hers. "I'd like to talk to you about something."

"Okay." *Is this about Tina? I had nothing to do with it. I swear.* She'd almost said it out loud.

"I can't believe how fast this year has gone. Do you have any plans for the summer?"

Was not expecting that. "Not really. My mom wants me to get a job."

"You're one of my best students. Clearly you have talent. But it's more than that. The ideas you come up with. The feeling that comes through your drawings. You're gifted. Do you know that?"

She shrugged.

"Have you ever been to Port City?"

"No." She'd only heard about it. It was one of the largest cities in the state.

Mr. King was excited as he spoke. "They have a high school for the arts. There's a new summer program. Kids from all over the country have applied. I sent them samples of your work." He paused to take a breath. "They want you at their school!"

Marta was confused. She'd been expecting bad news. "Me?"

"Yes. You would live in Port City for a month. I know. I should have asked you first. And of course your parents need to agree. But this opportunity came up. And the deadline is Friday. The program starts in two weeks. I didn't want you to miss out. You don't mind, do you?"

This was good news. She felt bad that she wasn't more excited. But she would have to tell him something.

"You said live in Port City?" she asked.

"That's right. This program is special," he said. "You'll learn so much. Only a few kids will get the chance."

She looked down.

"Marta? What is it?"

"My family doesn't have the money."

"Well," he said. "I have more good news. It won't cost you a thing. Your room, food, and even the bus ticket. It's all paid for."

This sounded too good to be true. "Really?"

"There's just one catch," he said.

Her shoulders drooped.

He quickly explained. Marta was a minor. She would have to live with a sponsor. If she agreed to go, Mr. King knew the perfect person. A retired high school art teacher. She taught classes in her home. Her name was Doris Kolder.

"What's the catch?" she asked. She was trying not to sound excited. She didn't want to get her hopes up.

"You would help Ms. Kolder."

"Help her with what?"

"With her art classes. Little things like sharpening pencils. Cleaning art supplies. But you'd be around other artists. I think you'd have fun."

Fun was a strong word. But it did sound interesting.

"So, do you want to sign up?"

It was all happening so fast. But Marta felt sure that this was right for her. At last there was something to look forward to. "Yes!"

He handed her some papers. "Talk to your parents. If they agree, these are the forms you need. Once they sign them, you'll be set."

Chapter 8

Mixed Feelings

Would Marta's parents let her go to Port City? She tried to imagine what they would say. It could go one of two ways. They would either say no. She didn't deserve the chance. Or they would say yes right away. Anything to have peace in the house.

How could she tell them in way they'd say yes?

It's more than a summer program. It could change my life. That's what you want for me, right? And think about how quiet the house will be. Elena and I won't be fighting. She'll have the room all to herself.

They'd never buy that coming from her. It was way too positive.

When she got home, she went into the kitchen. Her mom and dad were at the table. She pulled the forms from her backpack.

"What?" her mom said. "You're not going straight to your room? What's wrong?"

"There's a summer program for art students," she blurted out. "It's in Port City." She placed the forms in front of them. "My art teacher said it would be good for me. I need your permission." She held her breath and waited.

"Port City?" her mom said. "For how long? How much does it cost? Who would you stay with?"

She's actually thinking about it.

"It's just for one month. And it won't cost anything. I'd stay with a sponsor." She quickly explained everything.

Her parents sat there, staring at each other. It was as though they were having a silent conversation. At last her mom spoke.

"You must go, Marta! You're so talented. This is your chance."

"We all need this," her dad added.

She heard the tone of his voice. It was more relief than happiness. But she knew what he meant.

She'd been unhappy and angry for so long. Everybody in the family felt it. Sending her to the arts program would give them all a break. So her parents gladly signed the forms.

This was really going to happen. On the inside, she

was jumping up and down. She even let her guard down for a second and smiled.

That night, she didn't sleep well. She was too excited.

♔

The next morning, Marta was still in a good mood. There were only two weeks until summer vacation.

When she got to school, kids were gathered in the hallway. *Please. Not another bomb threat.*

As she walked down the hall, she heard Tina's name. It was something about a fire. Tina *had* died!

Then Marta heard the word *drawing.*

"It showed Tina in flames," someone said.

Someone else let out a gasp. "There she is."

Kids turned to look at Marta as she went by.

Who had seen her notepad? She didn't share it with anyone. Then she remembered the day before. Those two girls on the bus. It had to be them.

That day and the next two weeks dragged by. It was hard to deal with the stares and the whispers. She kept her head down and tried to stay out of trouble. Some things never changed.

Chapter 9

Something's Off

The Port City bus depot was packed with people. Any of them could be Marta's sponsor. Her mom and Ms. Kolder had spoken the day before. The woman said she would meet Marta at her gate.

As she waited, she thought about her parents. They were so happy for her to have this chance. It was a big change. One that could lead to a good life, her mom hoped. One that would make her daughter happy.

They didn't know why she was mad all the time. She never told them about the bullying. It was hard to explain. And they probably wouldn't get it anyway. They'd just say it was her fault. She was doing something wrong. Not trying to fit in. Or not getting along on purpose.

Leaving her hometown was an escape. Not only from

the bullying. She was tired of keeping up the tough girl image. It was just a way to protect herself. In the arts program, she'd be like everybody else. Everyone would be the new kid.

Her phone buzzed. She'd forgotten all about it. It was a gift from her mom. She bought it just for the trip. It was much nicer than the one Marta had before.

"Your old phone isn't good enough," her mom had said. "I want to make sure we can get ahold of each other. With this phone, we can text *and* video chat."

Great, Marta had thought.

The phone buzzed again. She looked at the screen. It was her mom. Big surprise. She would be worrying about Marta by now. There would be a lot of questions. *How was the trip? Are you okay? Do you need anything?*

"Marta Lopez!" a voice called out.

She let the call go to voicemail. A woman was coming toward her. One hand waved in the air.

It was hard not to notice her. She wore a brightly colored dress that went to the floor. Her gray hair was long and curly. Layers of chains were around her neck.

"Marta!"

"Ms. Kolder?" she called.

"Yes." Her sponsor smiled and reached out for a hug.

Marta stood straight without hugging back. She didn't

even hug her own family. As the woman held on, Marta smelled perfume. It smelled like flowers. But really old flowers.

"Let's go!" Ms. Kolder said.

Marta thought she smelled beer. *Has she been drinking?*

They walked out to the woman's car. It looked old and dirty. A parking ticket was on the windshield. She acted like she hadn't seen it.

The inside of the car had a bad odor. Like dirty wet dogs.

"Do you have any pets?" Marta asked.

"Not anymore. My dog died two years ago. Buckle up," she said as they drove away.

"So, Marta Lopez. Tell me about yourself. How old are you?"

"Fifteen."

"What a great age! Do you like school?"

"Not really."

The woman glanced over. "No? What *do* you like, then?"

"I like to draw."

"Of course! That's why you're here. Mr. King says you're a very good artist. You know, I'm an artist. I used to teach classes at Port City High. Now I teach at home."

Marta didn't say anything.

"I think this new arts program is great. I'm so pleased to be a sponsor."

She pulled out of the parking lot. A car swerved to keep from hitting her.

The driver laid on the horn. "Watch where you're going!" he yelled out the window.

Ms. Kolder didn't seem to care. She kept driving.

Marta was staring out the window. A billboard caught her eye. It said, "Property for sale. River's Edge."

"Do you live near the river?" Marta asked. She started to reach into her back pocket. Then she stopped herself. She didn't want anyone to see the drawings.

The woman shook her head. "I don't. It's downtown."

"Are there docks?"

"Oh yes. This city used to be a trading port. Ships stopped here all the time. That all changed when the highway was expanded. Trucking took over. It was cheaper. The port was pretty much abandoned. Now the city wants to build a casino. They plan to tear down the old warehouses."

"How far is it from your house?" Marta asked.

"About 10 blocks. But you shouldn't go there. It's a bad place."

Here's the Real Deal

Here we are," Ms. Kolder said. She had stopped in front of a large house. "Your home away from home."

They got out of the car and went inside.

"Set your bags down anywhere. We can take them to your room later. First I'll give you a tour."

The house had three floors and a basement. On the first floor was a living room. It was full of old dusty furniture.

Next was the kitchen. "I'm not a very good cook," the woman said. "But I will make sure that you're fed." She stopped and looked at Marta. "No food in your bedroom. I don't want rats again."

They walked up to the second floor. It was one big room. "I took some walls down," she said. "This is where I teach."

The bedrooms were on the third floor. Marta would stay in the smaller room. It had a twin bed and a desk and one small window.

"My room is off limits," she said. "So is the bathroom. But don't worry. I do have another one. I'll show you where it is."

She took Marta down to the basement. The room was dark and cold. It smelled like dirty wet carpet. The sound of dripping was coming from one corner. That's where the bathroom was.

"I use this space for more art classes. You do know you'll be helping me, right? In exchange for a place to live. That was the deal."

"That's what I was told."

"It'll be after school, of course. In your free time. It will be fun."

Yeah. Fun, Marta thought. She was starting to wonder if this was a good idea.

"People of all ages take my classes. From three to eighty-three. So, are you ready?"

Marta nodded.

"Good! You can help me tomorrow. Now let's get your bags."

They brought the bags to her room.

"Do you need something to eat?" Ms. Kolder asked.

"No, thank you. I had a snack on the bus."

The woman left the room. Before Marta unpacked, she got out her notepad. She sat at the desk and turned to a new page.

First she drew a hand with long fingers. On one of the fingers, she drew a ring. It had a stone in the center. On the stone, she drew the letter *M*.

The drawing seemed to come from nowhere. It was like that with the river and docks. But those things were common. Many cities had them. The hand seemed more real. It belonged to a person. But who? And what would happen to them?

It's just a drawing, she told herself.

She closed the notepad and went over to the bed. It wasn't as soft as hers at home. But right now, she could sleep anywhere.

Chapter 11

A Fine Line

A sign was posted outside the building. "Welcome to the Summer Arts Program."

Today was the first day. Marta had arrived early for a seat in back. But the waiting just made her nervous.

Would the kids like her? Would anyone try to bully her? Would the teacher like her artwork?

Students were entering the room. Seats filled up quickly. There was an empty table next to hers. She hoped nobody would take it.

A guy was coming her way. He was looking straight at her. *No!* She lowered her head. Maybe he'd get the hint and sit somewhere else.

He sat down next to her. She peeked out from behind her hair.

"Hi. I'm Dion." He held out his hand.

She looked up. Marta didn't hug or shake hands with anyone. But there was something about him. He seemed nice.

She shook his hand. "I'm Marta."

"Cool. Do you live in Port City?"

"No. I live in a small town. It's about three hours from here. How about you?"

He took a step back. "Hold on now. I just met you. And you're already in my business?"

Her eyes got wide. She could feel her face getting hot. She should have known he'd be a jerk. "Sorry. I just—"

He smiled. "Girl, I'm just messing with you."

"Oh. Right." She smiled and gave a nervous laugh. The guy was nice after all.

It was time for class to start. The teacher introduced himself. He told them about the program. What the classes would be like. What they would learn. The first day would be easy.

At lunchtime, Marta and Dion sat outside together. They talked the whole time. When they got back to class, a sketchbook was on each table. It was the kind that got graded.

"Artist's choice," the teacher said. "Draw whatever you'd like."

Marta drew a portrait of Ms. Kolder.

Ms. Kolder had been waiting for Marta to get back from class.

"Good! You're here. I need help."

"Okay. Do I have time to—"

"I have a student upstairs. You take the class in the basement."

Take the class? What does that mean? Marta thought. "You mean teach?" she said out loud.

"No time to waste."

This wasn't right. Marta wasn't a teacher. She was only supposed to assist. "What do I do?"

"Show them how to finger paint. You'll be fine. Just try not to bother me."

Finger paint? Isn't that what little kids did? On her way to the basement, she heard shrieks and giggles. At the bottom of the steps, she froze. Little kids were running around the room. They were totally out of control.

This was her signal to run. But she could hear her mom's voice. *You never finish what you start.* Her dad would say to be responsible.

She stayed.

Chapter 12

Dion's Secret

A week had passed since Marta got to Port City. Mr. King was right about the arts program. It was perfect for her. But she hated living with Ms. Kolder. The house was always dirty. She didn't cook like she'd promised. Why even be a sponsor?

The worst part was dealing with those kids. It wasn't fair. The truth was that Marta was just a babysitter. Only the program and Dion kept her there.

Dion had talent. She liked his artwork. And she liked being around him. He was nice and funny. He'd joke with her during class. She was always laughing. That was something she hadn't done in a long time.

One day at lunch, they were both quiet. Marta stared at her sandwich. "Yuck. I hate tuna."

"You're not going to eat it?"

"No. Do you want it?" Marta handed him the sand-wich. She ate her apple.

"Can I tell you something? Just between us?" he said.

A secret, Marta thought. *Something else we have in common.* "Sure."

"How old do you think I am?"

She looked closely at his face. And then at his clothes. "Um, 17?"

He looked around. "I'm 21."

"You are not! There's no way."

He grinned. "I have one of those baby faces."

"How did you get into the arts program?"

"I can trust you, right?"

"Totally."

"I used to live in another state. There were these kids at my high school. They bullied me for being different."

Marta was nodding.

"I was really into drawing," he went on. "Art was my favorite class. My teacher even told me I had talent. But I ended up dropping out. Then I moved here. When I heard about this program, it seemed like my chance. I could show that I'm a real artist. So I got a fake ID and lied on the forms."

"Does your sponsor know?" Marta asked.

"I don't need a sponsor. I live with my, uh, dad. If you know what I mean."

"So he's not really your dad."

Dion shook his head. "No."

He explained. He lived with his older boyfriend, Mike. They met in another state. Then Mike got a job in Port City, so they moved. When Mike became ill, he couldn't work. They lived off his savings. And Dion got a job at a fast-food place. They had to move downtown near the river. It was all they could afford.

"We're the only ones there. Well, us and our land-lord," he said. "The city has plans to build a casino. I'm not sure where we would go."

Marta was shocked at what she heard. She could barely get the words out. "You live near the river? Are there docks?"

"Sure. Why?"

She was about to explain. Then something made her stop. There was a ring on one of his fingers. It had an *M* on the center stone. It was the ring in her drawing!

"Are you okay?" he asked.

Was this a sign? Maybe it was a warning. She wondered if or when she should tell him. "We better get back to class."

Chapter 13

Marta's Secret

A couple of days had gone by. Marta was ready to tell Dion about her drawings. At lunchtime they went outside.

"Do you mind if we walk?" she asked.

They walked in silence for a few minutes.

"Is something wrong?" he asked.

"You know what it's like not to fit in, right?"

Dion smiled. "Girlfriend, please. I told you what high school was like." The smile had left his face. "Look. I'm not sure what you've been through. But it's okay. You just have to be you. Just be who you are."

"I'm not so sure that's a good thing. Let's sit here," she said.

They sat on a bench. Marta held her notepad in her hands. She flipped to the drawing of the river scene. The row of buildings. The docks and water.

"That looks like where I live," Dion said. He pointed. "Hey! That's my building. Have you been there?"

"No! That's the thing. I drew this a while ago. You're not the only one with a secret." She started flipping through pages of the same scene. "This. And this. And this. It was before I came to Port City. Before I met you."

"Other cities have places like it. Right?"

"Yes. But hold on," she said. "It gets worse." She turned to the drawing of Tina. Flames were around her head. "This girl was a bully at my school," she told Dion.

"*Was?*"

"The day after I drew this picture, her house burned down. She died."

"Dang."

It was time for the second half of class. "Do you mind if we don't go back?" Marta asked. "I have more to show you."

"Sure."

"Look at this." She had turned to the bomb. "One day I was really mad."

His eyes got wide. "I'm afraid to ask."

"A few days later? There was a bomb threat at school."

Dion shook his head.

"I also drew this before I met you." Marta had turned to the drawing of the hand.

"Can I see that?" Dion asked.

She passed him the pad. He studied the drawing.

"That's my ring. Mike gave it to me. It was his class ring. But how—"

"That's what I want to know." She noticed how serious Dion looked. "What is it?" she asked.

He shook his head. "I'm just glad you're my friend. And not my enemy."

Marta couldn't tell if he was kidding. She waited for him to say something.

"I'm joking," he said. "You're so easy to tease."

She grinned. "Oh. Right. But really. What do you think?"

"I think it's cool that you can do that. In fact, can you do me a favor? Draw a gun?" He handed the pad back to her.

"What for?"

"Just draw it. Please? And make it big."

Marta began to draw.

"We have a new landlord. His name is Jake," Dion said. "He wants to kick us out."

"Why?" Marta asked.

"He doesn't like us."

"You mean the tenants?"

He shook his head. "No. Like I said before. It's just me and Mike. Nobody else lives there anymore. We stay because the rent is so cheap. It's all we can afford. But the guy is making things hard for us. It's getting worse."

"How?"

"Like we used to do laundry in the basement. Suddenly the door was locked. Jake said it's off-limits. The closest place to wash clothes is six blocks away. We stopped asking about it. We just stay out of his way. He has a real problem with us. I've heard him call us names under his breath. The guy isn't nice."

"He sounds really ignorant," Marta said. "Tell me again. Why am I drawing a gun?"

"I've been wanting one. For protection. Mike won't buy one for me."

Marta turned the pad toward Dion.

"Nice," he said. "Can you draw more of them? I want a whole pile."

He watched as she drew. "You're good. And so fast. Now can you draw some money? Stacks of it. We could use it."

"My family too." She started drawing again. "Like this?"

"Perfect!" Dion said. "I love it!" He reached out and hugged her.

There wasn't time to think about it. Marta hugged him back.

He picked up her notepad and turned to a blank page. "Do you mind?"

"Go ahead." She watched as he scribbled something. Then he closed the pad.

He looked at his phone. "Oh jeez! I've got to go. Mike is waiting. Hey, do you want to come with me? You can meet him."

"I'd like that. But I better not. I already skipped class. And Ms. Kolder said she was cooking tonight. Next time."

Chapter 14

True Colors

Hi, Ms. Kolder," Marta called. "I'm back." There was no answer. She checked the kitchen. There was no sign of her or of any food cooking. *Fine with me*, she thought.

Skipping class hadn't been her plan. But spending that time with Dion was worth it. She finally shared her drawings. The secret she'd been keeping was out. And he hadn't judged her. He even liked them. She set her phone on the counter.

"Where have you been?"

"Huh?" Marta turned around.

"The school called," Ms. Kolder said. "You skipped class?"

"Only half. It's nothing to worry about."

"Well, I *was* worried. I'm in charge of you."

In charge of me? "I made sure I was home for dinner. But you didn't cook anyway. So what does it matter?"

"What if I had a class?"

"Did you?" Marta felt herself getting mad. She started to leave the room.

The woman tried to grab her. Nobody was going to control Marta. She pulled away.

"Leave me alone!" She ran to her room and shut the door. Quickly she locked it. A second later, there was the sound of footsteps.

"Let me in now. I mean it."

The doorknob rattled.

"No locked doors in my house! Do you hear me?"

Now she was pounding on the door.

"I'll call your parents. Is that what you want? They will not be happy."

I'll call them myself, Marta thought. *And tell them what a witch you are.* She waited until the woman left.

Going home was sounding good. She thought about calling her mom. But then she'd miss out on the class. And she wouldn't see Dion anymore.

"Phone. Where's my phone?" She looked around the room. "No!" She'd left it in the kitchen. "I hate that woman!"

She opened her notepad to the portrait of Ms. Kolder. The pen dug into the paper as Marta scribbled. She made thick, harsh lines over the woman's face. Now she looked like a witch.

Marta wasn't going to let her win. She went downstairs. As she was about to go into the kitchen, she saw Ms. Kolder. The woman was putting something into her pocket.

"Where is it? Where's my phone?" Marta asked.

"How would I know?"

"It was right here on the counter. Give it to me."

"Don't raise your voice to me!"

Then there was a buzz. It was coming from Ms. Kolder's pocket.

"Is that my phone?" Marta yelled. She moved toward her.

"Don't you dare. I'll call the cops! I swear I will!"

"I'm out of here," Marta said. She ran outside and started running. She had to find Dion.

♕

Ms. Kolder took Marta's phone from her pocket. She read the text.

"Exciting news! Dad won the lottery. We're rich! Call me."

Chapter 15

Dion's Worst Fears

On his way home from school, Dion had thought about Marta. They'd become close in the last week. It was so good to have a friend. One who didn't judge him. He trusted her. As much as he trusted Mike.

He also thought about Mike and how sick he was. As soon as he got better, they would move. Dealing with the landlord was too hard. Dion didn't feel they were safe.

His good mood had faded. There was a bad feeling in his gut. It was the sight of his building ahead. He knew he might see his landlord, Jake.

Jake lived on the first floor. Dion lived on the floor above. He had to pass the man's apartment to get there. Sometimes he'd be at the window. He would stare with those cold, angry eyes.

Like always, Dion kept his head down. He walked quickly to his apartment. As he put the key in the lock, the door opened. That was odd. Mike always kept it closed and locked.

"Mike?" he called. There was no answer. He stepped into the living room.

He's probably in bed. Dion went to the bedroom. No Mike. He wasn't in the bathroom either.

A noise was coming from the kitchen. Dion ran in. Steam was coming from a teapot. He turned off the heat and looked around.

Mike couldn't have been far. The water wasn't boiling yet. He stepped outside.

"Mike!" he shouted.

Without thinking, he ran downstairs. He stood in front of Jake's apartment. It was a risky move that could get him killed. But he didn't care. He knocked and waited. Nobody answered.

He ran to the back of the building. The alley was dark and quiet. There was no sign of Mike. But he saw one of his slippers. It was on the steps leading down to the basement. A noise came from inside.

The door was locked, but it had a small window. He would have to break in that way.

He found a rock and broke the glass. Carefully he reached inside and turned the knob. The door to the dark room opened. It took a few seconds for his eyes to focus.

"Mike! Are you in here?"

Thud!

Something had fallen. As he moved toward the sound, his foot hit an object. It was a crate. The whole room was filled with crates and boxes.

"Mike?" he called softly. There was no answer. He lifted the lid off a box. Gun barrels gleamed in the darkness. On a nearby table were wires and parts. Dion froze. Someone was making bombs.

Then he saw something on the floor. He bent down. It was Mike's other slipper.

"No!" he cried. Mike's body was slumped to one side. He sat in a pool of blood. His hands and feet were tied with wire. His mouth was taped shut.

"Oh God, Mike. What happened? Who did this to you?" He lifted Mike's head and gently pulled off the tape. "Open your eyes. Say something."

Mike didn't move or speak. Tears ran down Dion's face. He held Mike to him.

"It's going to be okay," he said. He gently let him go. "I'll get help." He wiped his hands on his shirt. It was a mixture of tears and blood.

Jake would be coming after him. He dialed 911. There was no signal. He grabbed a gun from the open box. His hands shook. He wasn't sure he would use it. But at least he could defend himself if he had to.

He ran outside and tried the phone again. Still no signal. "Worthless piece of—"

A noise was coming from down the alley. Someone was headed his way. Jake? It was too dark to tell. The person was walking faster.

Dion would have to leave Mike behind for now. He took off running.

Chapter 16

Tracking Down Dion

Where am I? Marta thought. She'd been running for a while. The fight with Ms. Kolder was replaying in her mind.

The woman had gotten so upset over nothing. She practically attacked Marta. For missing a few hours of class? What would she do if she got really mad?

By now it was dark. All Marta wanted to do was find Dion. The river had to be close. If she had her phone, she could figure it out. But no. Thanks to that witch, she was lost.

A liquor store was on the corner. She could get directions. A chime went off as she pushed the door open. An old man behind the counter looked up.

"I'm looking for the river," she said. "Can you tell me how to get there?"

"You mean down by the docks?"

She nodded. "Yeah."

"Why do you want to go there, kid? Nobody goes down there. Especially when it's dark out."

"I'm looking for a friend of mine."

"There's nothing but old empty warehouses."

"Please. It's important."

He shook his head. "It's your life, kid." He pointed. "Four blocks that way. Turn left. And good luck."

"Thanks," she said on her way out.

After running the four blocks, she stopped to catch her breath. The warm breeze felt good. The river was near. She turned left.

This was the place. Docks and water. Warehouses. Just like in her drawings.

Something caught her gaze. It was the way the moon lit the water. She felt calm. Dion was somewhere around here. She couldn't wait to see him.

The sound of someone running made her jump. She looked around. Dion! Where was he going? By the time she thought to call out, it was too late. He'd turned the corner.

She remembered what he'd said. His landlord was out to get him. Was Dion in some kind of trouble?

Chapter 17

Escape from Jake

Dion was tired from running, but he knew he couldn't stop. Jake would catch up to him. There had to be a place he could hide.

He turned the corner onto a dead-end street. All of the buildings were either boarded up or padlocked. If he turned back, he would die.

Please let one of them be open.

There! A side door to a warehouse was open a crack. He pushed on the heavy steel door. It didn't move. He squeezed his body through the opening and stumbled inside.

Moonlight came in through the tall windows. It was a huge space with a staircase. He looked up to see where it led.

A sound came from outside. Someone was running. The footsteps slowed as they got closer to the door.

Dion raced up the staircase. At the top there was a door. He yanked on the handle. Nothing happened.

A gunshot rang out from below.

He yanked again. This time the door flew open. He was on the roof. There was nowhere to go. He glanced over the edge. The roof of the next building was about six feet below.

Bang!

The shooter was getting closer. Dion crouched down. He remembered the gun he'd taken from the basement. He pulled it from his waistband and prepared to fire.

The door to the roof swung open. Standing in the shadows was a figure. The person took a step forward and looked around. Dion could see it was Jake. He was holding a gun. Who would fire first?

Dion stood and pulled the trigger.

Click.

The gun wasn't loaded. There was only one way out. That was down.

As he leaped from the roof, another gunshot went off. The thought of dying went through his mind.

In the next second, he felt concrete beneath him. The fall had left him stunned but alive. He felt a sensation. His arm felt heavy. It was like he'd been hit with a bat. Then he saw blood. He'd been shot!

There was no time to think about it. He got up and ran into the building. He'd escaped Jake for now. He started down the stairs. Below he could see rows of crates. The room looked like a maze.

Halfway down the steps, he stopped. By now he was feeling pain. It felt like his arm was on fire. He gripped it as tightly as he could. But there was no way to stop the pain or the bleeding.

Just a few more steps and he could rest. He ducked down a row of crates and sunk to the floor.

Chapter 18

Forever Friends

Dion must be in trouble, Marta thought. That had to be why he was running so fast. If he was in danger, she had to help him. She took off running in his direction.

When she turned the corner, there was no sign of him. There were only rundown warehouses. It was just like the man at the liquor store said. He'd tried to warn her. This was no place to hang out.

She slowed her pace. What if it wasn't Dion she'd seen? What if it was Jake? Her life could be at risk right now. She needed a place to hide. Somewhere she could think.

She entered a building through some loose boards. The only light came from the moon. The room was filled with crates.

As she looked around, a shot rang out. It seemed to come from above. She dropped to the floor and froze. Her mind raced. *It can't be Dion. He doesn't have a gun.*

Another shot was fired. Loud noises came from above. It sounded like someone was running across the roof. Then a door slammed. The person was inside. They were coming down the stairs.

Marta sat very still. Then the footsteps came to a stop. She covered her mouth to keep from crying out.

Someone was there. She could hear breathing.

Dion let out a long breath. His head fell back against a crate. As he sat there, he sensed something. Someone was close by. He looked over and saw a figure. They were crouched on the floor.

The person was too small to be Jake. Then Dion saw the long hair. Marta! What was she doing here? He had to get her attention. But how without either of them making noise?

He dug into his pants pocket for his phone. The light would get her attention. He turned it on. When she looked over, he held a finger to his lips. Then he held up his hand. Signals to be quiet and stay where she was.

But it was too late. She had started moving his way. When she got close enough, she reached for him. He shook his head and pulled back. She saw the blood.

"Call 911," he whispered.

Her hands shook as she dialed the phone. There was no signal.

"What happened?" she asked.

He waved her closer. "Mike is dead." A tear rolled down his cheek.

"Who did it?"

He winced in pain. "Jake. He's got guns. Remember how I told you about the basement? He wouldn't let us use it?"

Marta nodded.

"Now I know why. He's been making bombs there. Mike must have found out. And now Jake is after me." He looked around the room. "My God. These crates must belong to Jake. They could all be filled with guns. Explosives too. We have to get out of here."

He looked back at her. "I'm so sorry, Marta. You should never have been part of this."

As Dion spoke, her mind raced. All of her drawings had come to life. They brought her to this place. Mike was dead. Dion had nearly been killed.

Mr. King had said she was gifted. Look where it got them.

Could she undo it? What if she tore up all the drawings? But then she looked at her friend. They never would have met. Life wouldn't be the same without him.

Maybe she could start a fire. Or draw a big bomb with Jake's name on it.

"Hold on," she whispered. She handed Dion his phone. Then she pulled the notepad and pen from her pocket.

His eyes got wide. He shook his head no.

It might not work. But what if it did? She had to try. She quickly sketched a police car.

"I know you're in here!" a voice shouted. "There's no way out."

Chapter 19

Darkness

You're dead!" Jake shouted. "Hear me, pretty boy? Dead! Just like your precious boyfriend."

Dion closed his eyes.

There has to be a way out, Marta thought. Her eyes followed a stream of moonlight. It led to an open window frame. Beneath the window was a chair.

A plan was forming in her mind. She would throw her shoe across the room. That would distract Jake. Dion would have time to get to the window. He had to go first. He'd have a chance to get out.

She nudged Dion with her foot. He opened his eyes. She motioned her plan. He nodded. Then she pointed to him and held up one finger.

He shook his head. He pointed to her and held up his finger.

"No," she mouthed. "You first."

She held up her hand. She'd heard the sound of footsteps. Jake was walking across the room. She kneeled and threw her shoe, using as much force as she could.

Dion ran to the window. After that, it was like slow motion. He started to step up onto the chair.

Bang!

Marta ran. Dion turned and threw himself at her.

Bang!

He grabbed her and pushed her to the floor. Neither of them moved. Sirens were going off. There were the sounds of someone running.

Marta rolled out from under him. He fell to one side.

"Dion! Are you okay?"

Her friend was still. She turned and pulled him to her.

"Talk to me, Dion," Marta begged. "Say something!" She rocked him in her arms. "You can't die. Please don't die!"

His eyes slowly opened. "You have a gift," he said softly.

Tears ran down her face.

He tried to speak again. Marta lowered her head to hear him.

"Like I told you," he said. "You just have to be you. You're perfect the way you are. Don't ever forget that."

Dion closed his eyes for the last time.

Chapter 20

Home

Marta."

Huh? Ms. Kolder? Is it time to teach a class?

"Marta."

"What?" Marta slowly opened her eyes. She looked over at the door. Was someone there?

For a second she didn't know where she was. Then she saw the other side of the room. Everything was pink. *Oh right. Elena.* Marta was home. How long had she been asleep?

A memory came to mind. She was with her best friend, Dion. They were talking and laughing. Then she remembered. He died.

What happened that night was a blur. But one thing was certain. She knew she couldn't stay in Port City.

Somehow the next day, she ended up at the bus depot. Someone called her mom for her.

Now she lay in bed trying to wake up. She thought she'd heard someone calling her name. She got up and went to the door. When she opened it, nobody was there. But something was on the floor.

My notepad? She didn't know it was gone. There was a second pad too. A ribbon was tied around it.

She picked them both up and sat on the bed. The new notepad fell to one side. Seeing the old one was like seeing a friend. She rubbed her finger over the cover.

As she flipped through the pages, she stopped at a drawing. There was a girl and a guy. Below that was a note.

Thank you for being my friend. Remember to be who you are. Love, Dion.

It was such a sweet message. That was so Dion. Even with his problems, he always had something nice to say. Even as he was dying, he'd done that. *You have a gift*, he'd told her.

If only she could speak to him one more time. She would tell him the real truth. That he was the one with a gift.

Maybe there was something she could do. It wouldn't bring him back. But she could honor him. And who knew? Maybe he was watching over her.

She turned to the last page in the notepad. This time, she knew exactly what to draw.

When she was done, she sat back. It was a beautiful home near a river. This was the kind of home Dion had hoped to have. It was also a place Marta could see herself living.

"Knock, knock," a voice called. Her mom stepped into the room.

"You're finally awake. Are you feeling better? Do you want to talk about anything?"

Marta shook her head.

"Someone dropped this off." She handed Marta her phone. "The car left before I could see who it was. There's a note with it. It says, *I'm sorry*. What's that about? Does it have to do with why you came home?"

Marta was silent. She was looking at her phone. There was a missed text.

"Exciting news! Dad won the lottery. We're rich! Call me."

She looked up at her mom. "Really? We're rich?"

Her mom grinned. "Yep. And I just heard some other good news. Our town is going to have a school for the arts. Just like the one in Port City. Someone made a big donation."

"Who?"

"Your father and I. We admire your talent. And we

want to make sure you're able to pursue your goals. What better way to spend our cash. That and a brand-new custom home. You're finally going to have your own bedroom."

Marta smiled.

"Speaking of art. Your art teacher called. That Mr. King is such a nice man. He heard that you left the program early. He'd like to talk to you about your experience. I guess there's a question about Ms. Kolder being a sponsor. He and the school are concerned. Do you know why?"

Marta didn't feel like talking. She had another idea for a drawing. But there were no blank pages.

Her little notepad was full. At first she felt sad. It had been with her through so much. Then she thought about Dion. He was the first person she'd connected to. He'd taught her about real friendship. Her notepad couldn't fill that role.

She wasn't sure she would ever have another friend. Nobody could replace Dion.

Marta imagined him smiling and saying it would be okay. She would go on and have a great life. All she had to do was be herself.

She glanced at the new notepad. It sat beside her on the bed. She slid off the ribbon and opened to the first page.

WANT TO KEEP READING?

9781680214802

Turn the page for a sneak peek
at another book in the Monarch
Jungle series.

Chapter 1

The Big Idea

Hey, Rayna," Cora said. "Can you hand me the popcorn?"

Cora was on her bed reading. Rayna was sitting on the floor. She was staring at her phone. A few seconds of silence went by.

"Rayna! Popcorn?"

"What? Oh, sorry. Here you go." She handed the bowl to Cora.

"Don't you have homework?"

"Yeah," Rayna said. "I'm just reading a story on Twitter. Listen to this. Some guys were hiking. They found an old trunk. There were gold coins inside."

"Like buried treasure? That's so cool," Cora said. "Where were they hiking?"

"Near a dried-up river."

"Did the coins belong to pirates?" Cora laughed.

"Not quite," Rayna said. "It just says the trunk is about 100 years old. If the river had water, it wouldn't have been found."

"The drought is good for something, I guess."

The girls lived in the foothills. There were miles of land around them. There used to be so much green. Now everything was brown and dry. There had been many wildfires.

This was the third year of a drought. There was little water. The town had set limits on using it. That meant taking short showers. People couldn't water their lawns or fill their pools.

"Do you think there's more treasure?" Cora asked. "There are so many dried-up places. Like—"

Before she could finish, Rayna had jumped up. The girls were looking at each other.

"Summer Lake!" they called out.

"Let's talk to Lucas," Cora said. "He may know about this."

Lucas was Cora's older brother. Camping was his hobby. Every chance he got, he'd head for the lake. It made him feel close to their dad. He'd died a few years ago.

He taught Lucas all the basics. What gear to pack. How to set up a tent and make a fire. Mostly how to be safe in nature.

Now Lucas was the one to take his sister camping. He'd taught her all the same things. On these trips, they'd fish and hike. Cora really loved to hike.

One time Rayna went with them. At first she hated to be away from her phone. But she started to love being outdoors. It was good exercise. And the photos were great for social media.

After that trip, the girls set a goal. They would hike the Pacific Crest Trail. Not the whole thing. Just a portion. The entire PCT stretched from Mexico to Canada.

They planned to go after graduating high school. That was still three years away. But hiking to the lake would be good practice.

Rayna was reading again. "Part of Summer Lake is dried up," she said.

"Which part?" Cora asked.

"The eastern region, it says here. I'll pull up a map of the area."

"Here," Cora said. She pulled a box out from under her bed. Inside were a stack of paper maps.

"Not those maps. I mean a map app."

"Too late." Cora had a map spread out on the bed.

Rayna rolled her eyes. "I can't believe we're friends."

"What do you think we'll use on a hike?" Cora said. "An app won't help us if we can't get a signal." She pointed to a spot on the map. "There it is. Summer Lake. Doesn't it look amazing?"

"Oh sure," Rayna said. "If you think the world is flat."

"Whatever. Let's go see if Lucas is home."

PREFACE

I consume horror, horror endures. I began consuming horror at an early age via movie theaters, VHS, specialty shops, magazines like *Fangoria*, comic books, and amusement parks. But before all that I dipped my toe into scary waters through the written word. I learned at an early age to see Jane run and before too long it became see Jane run—from alien invaders stealing human bodies. The works of Poe, James, Bradbury, Koontz, King, Serling, Matheson, Shelley, and so many others infected me like a zombie plague from the first inked pages.

In my years of reading ghoulish tales, there has been much debate about what classifies as horror. To me, if it unsettles, forces me to question reality, makes me see shapes where there are none, or keeps me fearfully awake all night, I file it away as horror. While I like my movies bloody, books need not be so as they have other tools which can cut deeper than sharpened knives—well-chosen words. While in high school, I frequented a local bookstore (who identified me as the resident horror addict). They picked my brain like a zombie on a bender to determine which books they should order. Our collaboration resulted in a wonderfully curated horror section. I was proud of the deep cuts I brought to my local reading spot.

Then the crash. Over time horror fell from favor. Many bookstores eliminated the category, filing the frightful gems away in the oddest of sections. (I don't think books about serial killers should be in the self-help section, but what do I know?) I still sought my fix no matter where employees might have hidden the twisted tales (contingent on any being there at all). As time wore on, the genre went absent altogether in some bookstores. Sometimes horror goes away.

While there is a renaissance now, we must nurture it lest it fade away again. I am finally writing in my favorite genre. My intention is to announce it directly on the book-cover. The words, 'A Horror Novel,' will adorn my front covers so if ever people become too scared to celebrate horror again, if they try to bury the medium like a rotting corpse, it will be a little easier to find. This is my first horror novel, but trust me, there will be more. I hope by my chosen words I will unsettle you, frighten you, unnerve or unmoor you. The ultimate win would be if I created a 'freezer book' for even one reader. (A book which frightens someone so much they hide it in the freezer.)

All authors have access to the same twenty-six letters. The writers I listed above know how to arrange them just right. They are the masters and I am their student. This is the start of my journey into horror. Hang on, because if you ride this out with me, I expect it will be a hell of a ride.

I consume horror, horror endures.

To Mom who started this all and left soon.

CHAPTER 1

The day the house mysteriously appeared in Tether Falls was the same day the local police discovered two bodies and three heads. Sheriff Frank Watkins was the first law enforcement on the scene with the bodies. He would also be the first officer on the scene at the strange house but that would come later after the specific point and time when the sheriff believed he had finally seen it all. He would quickly learn, however, that he had yet to see it all.

"Jesus, Frank, you ever seen anything like this before?" Yankee Joe asked from a spot just below the dangling corpse.

"No, I'd say I've reached the exact point in life where people say they've seen it all," Sheriff Watkins said.

The body in question (ejected from a vehicle only to land atop a large road sign) was that of a young white male, twenties, lean bodied, tatted the full length of both arms. Sleeves, Yankee Joe called them. The crash victim wore a Star Wars T-shirt with dark dress pants, and black polished

1

shoes which Watkins felt would be more appropriate if worn with a tuxedo.

Patent leather was the term if he remembered correctly from attending Deputy Breton's wedding two summers ago at the Old Port in Portland. The sheriff also noticed law enforcement sport similar footwear in the cities, but in Tether Falls a good boot did the trick, thank you very much.

"If his sports coat landed in the street over there, don't you think it's odd that his sunglasses are still on his face?" Joe asked.

"If he was wearing the jacket at the time of the accident, then yes, it's highly odd. If he wasn't, then it's perfectly understandable," Watkins said.

Yankee Joe, an employee at nearby Tucker Lumber, was the lone witness to the crash. Upon arriving at the location, Frank invited the man inside the perimeter to take his statement. A large crowd of looky-loos (mostly customers from the lumberyard or drivers who detoured back after passing the scene so they could catch the show) stood well outside the posted caution tape. The sheriff's cruiser, lights on, partially blocked the road.

Joe's name was unrelated to any war, civil or otherwise. Despite having moved to Maine at an early age and being a diehard Red Sox fan, the employee was born in New York. His place of birth sealed his fate in a workplace known for ribbing at every opportunity. They named him for the dreaded Boston rivalry with the Bronx Bombers and it stuck. Other workers had nicknames too, such as Tree, Pappi, and Breezy, so he never complained about his moniker.

The scene of the accident was a rotary where two local freeways met in the center of town. The intersection formed a circle which, while difficult to enter, was even more difficult to exit if one did not know the area well. The stretch was not a daily problem for residents as traffic was modest in a town with a population of only eighteen thousand. Where the rotary gained its reputation as a renowned mass transit engineering failure was during summer months when the town became a gateway to Tether Falls Lake.

Despite being called Tether Falls Lake, the body of water existed across the border in the town of Willow. That natural confusion led to increased commuting problems whenever tourists flooded their little burg in the quest for a recreation area located in a township different than its namesake. Answers to why someone named it anything other than Willow Lake was long since lost to history.

Many businesses erected banners with variations of 'the Lake's that ways, you're getting warmer.' The verbiage remained posted year-round providing comic fodder for locals offered promises of warmth while driving through blizzards. Summers were short-term guests in Maine while winter was family—family that always overstayed their welcome.

The roadway sign holding the dead man's body aloft was of the large green metal reflective type designed to inform drivers of destination choices. Multiple victims relayed to law enforcement how their attempts to read the direction information while in the turnabout often caused their accidents. Law enforcement nodded knowingly while understanding just as many collided while on cell phones so left the signage in place.

Despite a preponderance of crashes in the 'circle of dents,' none had ever produced a fatality which explained why the sheriff arrived solo at the site. The lack of novelty regarding bumper bangers in the spot drew a regular insouciant police response. The first officer to arrive always managed everything before handing the scene off to the tow trucks. Watkins had not put the word about fatalities over the radio which meant his staff remained oblivious to the severity of the situation.

It was lunch time so most, if not all, of his crew were

enjoying Italian sandwiches at Corsetti's. Despite the severity of the wreck, the sheriff decided for now to leave them to their lunch, content with only Yankee Joe for company. Watkins initially canvassed the wrecked car containing a female DOA, but the novelty of a male dangling twelve feet in the air drew most of his attention. Still, there was a street to clear, so Watkins returned to the female.

Joe stayed tight on the sheriff's heels while relaying the events as best he recalled. Before offering his full account, the lumber employee pleaded to the sheriff not to mention anything to his boss about why he witnessed everything. The company sold picnic tables nestled on the street side of the yard and were deemed off limits for employee use. Yankee Joe ignored the rules using one table to gorge on two Italian sandwiches followed by a package of Funny Bones and a carton of strawberry milk. Watkins had to bring the worker back on point when the man burped before going on about the peanut buttery goodness of the local snack cake.

The yard worker refocused and mentioned everything happened so fast beginning with the vehicle taking the circle at an incredible speed suggesting the driver was unaware he was not on a straightaway. After an epic squealing of tires, (the smell of burnt rubber still wafted in the air) the car decided it was unequipped to make the sharp turn requested of it via the steering wheel. It slid into a rollover, turning two or three times—Joe couldn't recall the exact count—up the embankment off the rotary before giving away its momentum in the form of shredded grass and soil. Eventually it rolled nice and slow back down to street level, far from pristine.

"Shame, she's a beauty," Yankee Joe said.

"The woman or the car?"

"For sure the vehicle. Can't say the same for the lady, I mean, her no longer having her face and all. My wife's niece dated a guy from over in Yarmouth," (which Joe pronounced as Yaahmuth). "He had this same convertible Mustang. Now for me, nothing beats the nineteen sixty-five version. I had one back in the day but became dumb enough to sell it the same time I came to think marriage was a good idea. Anyhow, this kid pulls up, offers me the driver's seat, tells me it has a push-button start. I'm pushing, getting nowhere while he and my so-called kin laugh until their asses are blue. I climb out, he gets in, starts it right away. Know the secret?"

"Have to press the brake?" Watkins asked.

"Have to press the brake." Joe nodded. "Made me feel old, I couldn't figure out a Mustang."

"You are old, Joe."

"Don't tell that to the ladies. You think her tits are real?"

"Yeah, maybe your age hasn't caught up none."

The car had righted itself onto crushed tire wells matching its totaled frame. The Ford was an open convertible yet the seatbelt in the woman's case had done its job, keeping her upright in the passenger seat. She wore khaki Capris with a tank top once a light color based on a small portion of the left strap. To look at any other part of the shirt would lead one to believe it was always blood red.

Her head had interacted with a foreign object during the accident, most likely asphalt. Whatever made her acquaintance decided it would not give the face back. Her eyes, while intact, had rolled up white. Chunks of hair had abandoned her coif though some hangers on remained, enough to verify she was a brunette. Her head lay angled up and to the right of her body giving a clear view of her torso. Her breasts were large and stood out prominently from under the thin material. While Joe could—and would—talk about it for years to come, it was Frank's job to pretend he did not much notice or care.

"I don't have the facts, but I'd reckon our friend here is not entirely bio-degradable," Watkins said and left it at that.

The lawman stepped back to take in the big picture. Clothes lay scattered along the street including her cream-colored Ralph Lauren sports coat spread open on the ground speckled with dirt like a Jackson Pollock painting from where it danced around on the same greenery torn up by the crash. The sheriff eyed the car, noting with interest the open glove compartment. The yard worker caught his gaze.

"What is it, Frank?"

"No document debris anywhere. Airbags, which did not help these poor folks none, should have jettisoned a trail. Here we have a defeated glove compartment combined with an open top convertible, so why no paper?" Watkins asked himself, not Joe, not really.

The pair moved to the back of the vehicle. There was no need to pop the rear since deadly force had opened it permanently. With the car now upright again, the trunk rested in a closed position but remained unlatched. Watkins used his flashlight to lift it. Joe leaped as if to leave his skin. His unexpected movement prompted the officer to do the same.

"What was that for?"

"You made me nervous with the paper thing, then I got a bad feeling," Yankee Joe said.

"Well, knock it off."

Two Samsonite carry-on bags sat nestled alongside the spare tire. The sheriff squinted quizzically at the strange nature of how the rear cargo avoided ejection. He pulled one bag free, setting it down before unzipping it. He yelped and kicked the carryon over, where it fell flat on the ground. Staring straight up at him was the severed head of a young white male.

Yankee Joe's oversized meal came back to haunt him as much as the macabre image did. One look at the decapitated cargo and he ungraciously re-purposed his food onto the pavement near the suitcase. The sheriff leaped back to avoid the stomach sauce, fighting a twinge of an urge to do the same.

"Joe, I brought you in as a witness for a routine accident. Turns out this is now a crime scene. I'm afraid you are contaminating evidence. I need you to leave."

The sheriff did not have to ask Joe a second time. The yard worker was in a hurry to go tell everyone what was in the bag. Once the civilian cleared the area, Watkins removed the next suitcase, setting it down then unzipping it. Inside he found severed hands clasped together as if in prayer wrapped tightly in a cocoon of barbed wire.

The officer grabbed his shoulder mic and ordered his deputies code three. The designation meant full speed, sirens blazing.

"So now, now is when I have officially seen everything."

However, Sheriff Watkins had not seen everything, not even close, not by a mile. Not yet.

CHAPTER 2

River Road ran through the southern end of Tether Falls all the way into the city of Westbrook. No one could remember when the street was last paved, but it was long enough ago sand had since sifted onto borders of a blacktop never edged properly. Cracks littered the asphalt like varicose veins along the entire street. Local kids given to boredom often exploited the fissures, picking at them with sticks until they became full-blown potholes.

There was not much for teens to do in Tether Falls beyond visiting the lake in Willow during the summer contingent on a parent providing a ride. The town was so vast it made travel by bike impractical unless one lived near the border. There was always the Maine Mall or the amusement park at Old Orchard, but each were an hour away by car with no public transportation options available.

Brackish streams (which older folks remembered as once upon a time pristine) were plentiful. Many kids used

8

them as watering holes. However, doing so meant braving underwater mulch which sucked hungrily at feet. Swimming in such places required full body searches when finished, not to mention the need for a carrier of saltshaker and pliers used to remove bloodsuckers in case any made one's acquaintance.

Forests and fields served as alternative playgrounds for those fearful of dark waters of which there were plenty in a state where residents lived as much as a mile apart from one another. Long distances between property lines created unique friendships based on proximity where the closest neighbors became buddies even if personalities clashed. Ricky and Bob were two such friends.

An immense field halfway between their homes was the spot where the young boys would meet. While not overly fond of one another, they lived within walking distance of the other, both were nine, and each had an older sister who drove them crazy leaving them eager to escape from their respective houses. The pasture acted as the gateway to a shared fantasy world where they relived variations of whatever Western their Fathers had most recently watched.

A barrier of thin trees and shrubbery separated the street from their playground. Chokecherries grew liberally within the blanket of foliage. The plentiful tiny bitter fruit offered a satisfying snack which allowed the boys to play for long periods before hunger sent them home to eat.

Copious amounts of trees held ghostly white webs high in their branches. The cotton candy like masses housed tent caterpillars. Dozens of the alien-looking species lived within each silky abode. The furry wormlike beings bled a strange green blood when squished which the boys knew well from extensive experimentation.

They feared the tiny creatures because of warnings from their sisters how if the tendrils of white ever touched their hair it would create a permanent caterpillar condo with no way to get it off. Therefore, they kept a respectable distance from the colonies but were happy to take out their wrath on any green gutted furry worms that strayed from the pack.

Despite minimal traffic on the seldom used street, they checked the road before crossing. Once across, they snacked on the horrible tasting berries in between spitting the pits at each other. Successful face shots elicited excited yells of "score" with double arms raised for added celebration. Once they had their fill, they moved through the well-worn path between bushes and thin saplings, a passageway forged by hunters long before the children were born.

The field comprised hundreds of acres and was expansive enough to hold many football versions placed side by side. Beyond the skirt of trees, Mother Nature begat grass nearly as tall as the youngsters before tapering off in the distance to a browning sward followed by desert style brush anchored by an outcropping of mossy boulders. The large stones signaled the end of the pasture and from there the ground bled into sandy patches which fed into the loam of the massive forest.

They called a race to the clearing, but Bob stopped midway after almost colliding with a garden spider. Garden spiders (sporting massively large black and yellow bodies) spent their days lazily perched on intricate webs anchored between elevated blades of grass. The boys gleefully messed around with other arachnids but were certain these were big enough to eat their faces off, so they always kept a respectable distance. Bob finally crossed the invisible finish line only to find Ricky waiting in full gloat mode.

"Loser is a butt crack," Ricky said.

"Takes one to know one," Bob said.

"I know you are and so am I."

Both laughed even though it made no sense.

"I say there are Indians on the top of that rock outcrop, and they have somebody hostage."

"Who?"

"Your sister."

"Then game over, let them have her," Ricky said. "How about Princess Leia?"

"Indians have Princess Leia? It would be Darth Vader and Stormtroopers," Bob (of only so much imagination) said.

"There could be Indian planets. Leia, in her bikini, crashed here, and they took her hostage. If we save her, she'll kiss us like she did her brother, Luke, in the first movie."

Only the oldest Star Wars movies showed in local rotation. The town remained remote enough that cable was a luxury afforded only the most affluent in the form of satellite dishes. The balance of the population survived on channels carrying national programming weekdays and old films or Westerns all weekend. There was also *Bonanza*, *M.A.S.H.*, and *I Love Lucy* which ran in perpetuity.

The pair played together in the sense they both found sticks and made variations of gun sounds but each lived out individual missions in their heads. Both ran, tumbled, fired as they faced invisible enemies. Their imaginations took them to adventurous places where time passed quickly during their play.

Their adventures often lasted until the sun finished its duty for the day. The nightly onset of darkness would always quickly change the dynamic of the children's time together. Both needed to walk home in different directions alone and the setting sun reminded them how far from home they were when rocks and bushes would take on eerie and unfamiliar shapes not to mention how bats took to the skies at dusk. The flying mammals always appeared aware of the boys' location despite being blind as their namesake. The scary creatures would circle high above them in between dive-bombing for their heads. Keep bats and tent caterpillars away from hair were the golden rules.

The guys found themselves suddenly pulled from their imaginations as familiar signs of the evening's arrival crept into the caveman part of their brain. They sensed more than saw the sky darken. The change in atmosphere confused the pair. The unexpected arrival of night often caught them off guard when playing after school if only because it was already late afternoon to start, but it was now a weekend after lunch. The early hour at which they convened combined with the fact neither had battled long enough to save Princess Leia suggested nighttime should have been many hours away.

At first, they chalked up the surprise change to a sudden storm front rolling in unnoticed. A popular saying in Maine was, "if you don't like the weather wait a minute." It was not hard to imagine a thunder bumper had overtaken their formerly sunny day. Both had experience with summer hailstorms which could bring frozen missiles as large as golf balls. While excited at the prospect of unexpected ice play, (it had been two seasons since it last occurred) their enthusiasm dampened under the sheer oppressiveness of the shadows.

Bob looked to the distance where the sun remained bright beyond the tree line. That was not how summer storms worked. A weather pattern would darken the entire area which meant something else was responsible. Ricky noticed it first, freezing in terror. He gasped but could not articulate what frightened him so. Bob followed Ricky's gaze whereupon his eyes and mouth went wide in fearful solidarity with his friend.

A massive multi story home towered over the boys in the previously empty field!

The house came accompanied by its own isolated weather pattern hanging low in the sky above its ominous architecture. They found themselves under a gloominess deeper than the sudden cloud cover should provide only to suddenly realize they were standing in the enormous structure's shadow. The building rose four stories high and extended out to a length they could not distinguish from their vantage point. It appeared to go on forever.

Large swaths of rot covered the home's exterior in place of whatever color palette ever existed. The balance of the surface was a dry wood gray where truffle layers of black mold had not gained hold. Battered gutters ran its perimeters like exposed bones, many broken, others twisted, with some missing altogether.

Fourth-floor dormers jutted out at random intervals unrelated to the flush windows of the lower stories. If the shutters ever existed in pairs, most had since divorced. Those remaining hung loosely at random angles providing a nonsensical pattern along the face of the building. Despite the decrepit state of many window frames, the glass within each remained intact. Someone inside had drawn shades closed on every second aperture as if by design to provide the illusion of giant pairs of eyes winking.

The previously flat land elevated in a bubble of a hill and held the home on its crest. Gnarled trees curling like an old man's fist grew from the ground along the right side of the house caressing the corner like a groping lover. A porch fronted half the length of the home, shy of a full wraparound. Another tree jutted from the ground where the porch ended, its jagged branches twisting incestuously with the wooden slats of the end-cap. As unsettling as the very nature of the structure's sudden appearance was, the center of the building offered a uniquely disturbing oddity. The very front of the home looked as though a giant monster took a bite from an apple. The 'chomp' began with missing stairs which bled down into some missing earth.

The front porch began a few feet to the left of the front door and ran to the right across half the home. Originally a set of stairs would have run from the ground to the porch providing a passage to the front door except they were missing. Evidence of something having torn them away remained in the form of broken metal handrails, half of which remained anchored to the porch while the other half ended in sharp points where the metal had twisted until snapped. The balance of the rails surely lived in the stomach of whatever took a bite out of the house.

Lending a further otherworldly touch to the locale, someone had excavated a large chunk of earth below the missing stairs as if by an earth mover or by the imagined monster's mouth. Within the excavated zone grass was absent while rich soil flanked the edges of the dig in either direction exposing a section of the foundation. The brick foundation rose around twelve feet from ground up to the porch bottom. The open area at the base of the excavated site comprised jagged rocks which promised a perilous drop were anyone to step off the porch in its current state.

Whatever took a bite out of the front surely must have been hungry Ricky thought, hanging on to the idea of monsters biting the home if only to explain how the house could have appeared in the first place, for surely only the largest of creatures could have deposited the massive structure so stealthily behind them. Ricky pissed his pants in fear under the shadow of the unknown while assuming Bob did the same though neither would ever ask it of the other. They would never go on to inspect the house in its entirety other than in future fevered dreams guaranteed to follow them into adulthood.

Movement from above drew their attention. The boys glanced up to find a woman looking down through a window. She raised her arms and screamed. Then they did what young boys do. They ran.

CHAPTER 3

Amelia downward dogged low enough to look between her legs at Jim Harper. Amelia, at thirty, finally embraced her sexuality after years of—well, she did not want to think about the past. That was why she moved from Oregon to Maine. From Portland to Portland, or Portland adjacent. She purchased a home in Tether Falls and opened the town's first yoga studio.

She quickly learned she had three types of clients. Those happy to have a genuine form of exercise in town that could save them the drive to the city. Those a little long in years and waistline who wanted to spice up their marriages (which for many began immediately after high school). The third type were guys like Jim who were there to look at ass. In his case, she was content to comply. She instructed her class to hold longer than usual in the position, ignoring protesting grunts from those in questionable shape. She used the extended move to bust her student for ogling. When he blanched red over his clumsy indiscretion, she knew she had her next man.

Amelia hit the bars frequently in the Old Port often partaking in long bouts of sex with strangers who spoke in an accent she never found charming but who had the rugged good looks designated liberally amongst much of the general male population. Amelia was currently a one and done gal which was why she always offered a fake name along with the backstory lie of being a tourist. She discovered all too soon, however, that Maine was a small world kind of place when she ran into several of her conquests while out running errands.

Her conquests were usually with their families which limited their ability to ask "WTF" upon spotting her. Their reactions to seeing her were seldom discreet which provided her a twisted form of entertainment where she watched (with some sense of humor mixed with dread) their wives publicly scold them for checking out another woman. If only those women knew the truth. Their husbands had done more than check her out, they had checked her out under the hood.

She felt a certain awkwardness in the face of those encounters but never guilt upon learning of her lovers' families. The sexual trysts served her momentary needs, ones which required physical release, not emotions or ethics. She was taking back a part of herself lost to someone whose name she vowed to never speak again.

Once a former lover (seeing her in a Walmart while with his family) snuck away from his wife to beg for a repeat performance in a nearby restroom. That was the first time Amelia thought she was possibly living life wrong. What seemed right at a hotel bar over drinks on any random night suddenly felt seedy in the light of day, not to mention his pathetic actions made her question her taste in men. Not interested in further self-reflection, she used the moment to deny his request while conveying her intention to never see him again.

The man yelled her name as she walked away. Since he

called out a fake one, she felt no need to respond, leaving that identity behind with the desperate man. This was about her choices, not somebody else's.

Back in her studio, she tried to bury awkward memories of her past while deciding she was ready for Jim. She contemplated her readiness for a longer physical entanglement—one that could lead to more than a single go. Her prized student signed up for classes six months after her grand opening, one of a long line of men who joined only to watch members in yoga pants. Unlike many voyeurs who discovered it was harder than it looked and therefore quit, he flourished in the environment always finding reasons to talk to her while growing bolder over time until his original sidelong glances eventually became straight on stare at her butt sessions. Amelia never discouraged him.

Her potential paramour was a firefighter for the town of Falmouth but lived in Tether Falls. His occupation kept him in great shape to begin with and as the weeks wore on, he became even more so, until becoming positively yummy in her eyes. Amelia harbored fantasies about possibly settling down again, maybe spending life with someone like Jim. The visions of marriage were brief, she would quickly come to her senses, remind herself that as a good-looking fireman in a small community, he likely had lovers in multiple zip codes. She was open to being one, but only if there were a way to maintain some space, ensure they never grew too intimate. She needed distance if she hoped to keep things from growing complicated similar to the situation with the Father of the Year in Walmart.

As part of Amelia's strategy to let go of her history and hold people at bay, she had opened the studio as 'Suzy's Yoga.' That became the name everyone in town knew her by, including Jim. Now anyone who might try to get close to her, Google her, or investigate her, would find nothing because, just like her past, Suzy would prove to be a dead end. People would have no way to connect that random identity she created to that of her real one.

Yes, fake names to all her lovers, even to friends. No, she could not keep track of them all, which is why she lived as Suzy in her daily life. Amelia was on the verge of becoming a faded memory which would not be so bad if it meant losing all the baggage which accompanied her birth name.

The class let out leaving Jim lingering as usual while others paired up to gossip their way out the door. She watched her man towel himself off while thinking the women would have something extra juicy to talk about if they stayed behind just a few minutes longer. When everyone else finally cleared, he approached her.

"Hey, Suzy, great class," Jim said.

"What made it great?"

He turned crimson. For a good-looking guy who most likely scored regularly, he sure blushed a lot, Amelia thought.

"I can't lie, I think you're an excellent teacher," he said.

"You are a good student. You know what would make you even better?"

He shook his head.

"If you concentrated on the moves more instead of staring at the instructor's ass."

Again, with the red face. Jim was five years younger which suited her fine. She observed how in shape he was, considered how much stamina he likely had. He also thought her name was Suzy which would allow Amelia to roleplay from the get-go. Suzy could be anyone, so she deemed her to be a straight shooter who goes after what she wants. If she had been as self-assured of herself as she believed her new alter-ego to be then maybe everything awful that happened in Oregon would never have occurred.

"I, uh," he said.

"It's a good thing I'm not looking for conversation right now. You're a failure with the small talk," Amelia—as

Suzy—said.

She leaned in, kissed him which depleted his shyness. She figured this was where he was most comfortable, in the physical moments, ones where he didn't have to think, could just respond. Respond he did, grabbing the same ass he stared at for months. They moaned into each other, groping toward the inevitable until the ground moved.

Not sexually, it shook for real. The pair pulled apart. Jim grew more confident and mature before her eyes, pushing her towards the back door securely under the frame. "Earthquake," he said while hovering over her protectively. "I will have to check for damage in town, gas leaks and such."

She nodded, not used to losing an object of desire mid-coupling but she understood, in fact, felt pride in him for his immediate change in demeanor. He yelled for her to remain there, while stepping into the rear parking lot only to turn back confused.

"What? What is it?" she asked.

He looked to his feet then to her. "It's not shaking out here."

With the ground still rocking violently where she was, Suzy ran back into her studio. Jim rushed toward her when suddenly the door slammed hard enough to split down the center. He yelled from the other side while trying to open it. Despite the damage, the door held.

The front entrance remained accessible. Panicked, Suzy ran for it only to see it slam harder than the other. She screamed at the explosive sound, understood things were obscenely wrong, that the event was occurring only in her world, not outside. The earth finally settled. She breathed deeply, began to relax until something creaked slowly open somewhere off to her side. There was no third door in her studio, yet she heard the squeal of neglected hinges.

She opened her eyes and spotted an opening in a wall that in theory, based on its location, would lead to the independent bookstore adjacent her shop. Through it, she saw no books, no customers, nothing save a blinding light. Jim continued pounding though the noise of his efforts faded away, replaced by her own pulse throbbing in her head as she wobbled forward on leaden legs towards the bright doorway. She stepped through the mysterious gateway and heard it slam as everything went dark.

Amelia woke on a damp floor finding herself in the hall of an immense structure. Filtered sunlight from open rooms on both sides provided incidental light to a gloomy interior. The air felt oppressive and heavy. The charged atmosphere caused her to feel an esoteric hopelessness pecking like a vulture at her soul while edging its way stealthily into her heart. Her existential discomfort layered atop her budding fear akin to being thrust underwater in a sweater and jeans. The combined weight could easily take her down if she gave into it.

Rising to her feet, she screamed for Jim while circling in the wide-open space. The only answer she received was the pounding of her own heart. Rooms stretched out equidistant in both directions. Tendrils of wallpaper drooped low in some spots while in others, patches went missing altogether like the hairline of a middle-aged man. She entered the closest room in search of answers and peered through the lone dirt-caked window. A field extended well into the distance before merging with a vast forest beyond which she could not see for the trees.

She attempted to open the window, but it would not budge. The very unnatural nature of the situation (abduction?) was terrifying enough on the surface, yet a deeper fear grew inside her. There was nothing available with which to break the glass. A glance across the hall revealed a cloned room except that version contained furniture. She crossed over, trying to lift a different sash to no better luck.

A strange gloom trickled over any sense of self suggesting her internal compass no longer held an option for true North. Reality had transformed into a landscape of abnormality which she feared might be permanent. The new view offered more greenery while appearing less a forest and more a veil of nature behind which a road likely ran parallel. It was challenging to tell given the oppressive shadow cast by the house.

She spotted two young boys below. Their distance from her relative to how high up she was—third floor maybe—made it difficult to see them well. They stared up at the building with an appropriate level of awe on their faces. She pounded at the glass to alert them, but her actions elicited only muffled sounds too soft to signal outsiders. She gave up on the pounding, began instead to wave her arms over her head, frantic. Her motions finally caught their attention.

When their eyes met hers, she watched the pair slide into the realm of hysterical terror. Catching her reflection in the glass, she noticed how in the frazzled aftermath of a yoga class, an earthquake, and abduction, she had taken on the stereotypical visage of any number of famous movie witches. She fluffed her hair before lowering her hands in gestures meant to soothe wild beasts if not humans, but it was too late. The boys turned on their heels to run. She screamed for help in vain until they vanished through the shrubbery.

She grabbed a chair which appeared Victorian, raised it and rushed the window. Her breath shot painfully from her lungs when her momentum came to an unexpected stop against a sheet of glass that might well have been solid concrete. The panes neither broke nor cracked, only produced a strange 'thunk' upon contact. She swung the seat wildly again producing the sound of being trapped in a bubble. Despite adrenaline, she lost the strength to lift the furniture, dropping it to the floor.

Further examination of the world outside offered some clues to her whereabouts. The regional trees combined with the sun's location compared to the time of day she believed it to be, gave her the idea she was still in Maine, if not Tether Falls. That thought provided her some small sense of hope.

She exited the room in search of a way out not yet realizing any sense of hope would be short-lived.

CHAPTER 4

The sheriff drove with his cell phone plugged into the dash. The speakerphone played a boop-be-boop symphony at an uncomfortable volume as he pushed the redial button. A tinny voice of an indeterminate sex answered and confirmed Watkins had reached the Portland Police Department.

Being a summer weekend, nothing much ever happened in the city until nightfall when all hell in a handbasket regularly broke out at the local bars. The unique crime pattern kept the squad staffed light during the day and heavier during third watch for the balance of the season. Watkins supposed many officers were ironically close to Tether Falls, enjoying the lake in Willow. Despite their probable proximity, they were off the clock, so he had no choice but to deal with this peon.

"Portland Police, how may I direct your call?"

"It's the Tether Falls sheriff again, remember me?"

"Ayuh."

"Still looking for the detective," Watkins said.

"I already told you he is very busy. He's aware of your situation and will contact you once available. You need to factor in how long it takes to get to there from here."

"You know what I've got a fix on? A lobstuh roll."

"Sheriff?"

The voice did not question lobster being called 'lobstuh' as that was how locals pronounced it. His inquiry related to the sudden shift in conversation. Watkins allowed an uncomfortable amount of silence before speaking again.

"Old Port Tavern probably close enough to you all, they make a fine one. I prefer drawn butter myself, none of that mayonnaise shit, how about you?"

"Sheriff?"

The voice was a man or woman of few words, apparently. Watkins continued driving.

"Course there's Two Lights, they offer a damn good lobster roll too, ayuh. ('Ayuh' loosely translated to yes north of Boston.) Thing I don't understand though is if I pull up to the docks in the Old Port, I can buy me some live Maine lobster for just about what I can get per a pound of chicken. Besides, shelling is easier than plucking, wouldn't you agree?"

"Sheriff?"

"Never mind—it is—but we do not buy the birds that way, I understand your confusion. Anyway, so maybe I pick up a two-pound one and boil it myself, have a grand ole dinner all for less than the cost of a single lobster roll. So why do folks do it?"

"Sheriff?"

"I mean spend so much for it. Is it the mayo? Can't be. And if you're thinking bun, well yes, browned in butter just right they are a pure delight. But we consume those regularly with ground meat parts we refer to as hot dogs, so what are we really paying for?"

"Sheriff, I…"

"Hear me out. We pay for the convenience, you get

me? It's all in one little package you can carry with you for lunch. I mention this because I'm starving and need to eat. My deputies ate at a reasonable hour, but I got tied up some so decided maybe a drive for a lobstuh roll was in order."

The sheriff pulled up in front of a large brick and marble building where he parked in the red zone and, for courtesy, turned on his turret lights. He grabbed the cell from the cradle, stepped out of the vehicle, then nestled the phone to his ear while he wrestled with something in the trunk. "I'm right starved, ayuh."

The sheriff climbed the cement steps and entered the building. A young male cadet in a police uniform two sizes too large sat behind a desk speaking on a landline. Watkins spoke on his portable as he approached.

"Point being, don't bullshit me how it's a long drive from Portland. I made my way here in no time at all for lunch, and as for things being too busy around here, you have not had to pick up any other calls since we've been talking," he said.

Frank pocketed his cell as he greeted the startled employee who still held a phone to his ear. The cadet went wide-eyed when Sheriff Watkins placed a plastic evidence bag with the severed head onto the front counter. The desk jockey, like Yankee Joe earlier, re-purposed his food into a nearby wastebasket.

"So, I ask again. Can you get me the damn detective now?"

The pale-faced cadet nodded in the affirmative.

CHAPTER 5

Charlie 'Thunder' Raine's life changed forever the day aliens abducted his friends. The small population of Tether Falls meant a single twin classroom building was enough space for the local kindergarteners. If students never moved out of town (and most didn't) they attended classes through high school graduation together. Besides neighborhood proximity, other friendships developed in the dual classrooms based on who they spent their first year with. The artificial border of a hallway became an agent of chance, a lottery ticket where the payout was who would grow to be best friends with whom for a decade.

Young Charlie found his closest friend in the form of Troy Alden, a rambunctious boy from a well-to-do family who sat next to him. Despite them both being six, Charlie felt his buddy was wise beyond his years by a day or two. The kindergartener often showed off unique novelties such as green slime that oozed down walls like snot, or an eight ball which magically answered questions (assuring

Charlie all signs pointed to yes, he would forever remain a townie).

Troy also taught him many tricks, some of which Charlie appropriated as his own and brought home to his little brother, Ryan 'Lightning' Raines. There was the house in the steeple with all the people, for example. Even if he messed up, it was okay because his sibling was only five and marveled at anything his brother showed him.

During one fateful break period, the friends experimented with making a loud noise with a drinking straw. Troy as usual had the master plan which included him grabbing the top end while twisting the other around his finger leaving only an inch exposed. He prompted Charlie to flick it which caused an explosive 'pop' that echoed through the lunchroom. Children screamed. Some attempted to flee they were so startled. The two teachers on lunch duty went into hockey goalie mode, trying to keep all the miniature players from getting into the net that was the exit.

It would not be the last time that milk sprayed out of Charlie's nose, but it was the first, spraying gloriously in a wide arc. Troy called grossness, leaping to his feet before laughing alongside other students who finally got up to speed on how hilarious the straw snap was. The teachers fought to restore order which caused them to miss the milk spew. His wet clothes required cleanup on aisle age six, so he slipped unnoticed to the washroom, a simple act which would change his life.

The house Charlie lived in was red as were the neighboring homes on either side. Over half on his block were crimson. Given the abundance of the color, his section of Tether Falls garnered the nickname, 'Red Town.' Once when asking his parents about the oddity they mentioned citizens rationed supplies for the war effort in the past leaving candy apple the only available option. He wondered why the Army would need pink, purple, and other equally girlie colors but not the one everyone in town ended up using. He chalked it up to the horrors of war and, therefore, beyond his understanding. He wasn't even certain which conflict they referred to.

Rationing supplies was only one byproduct of the times. Fears of coastal invasion created a bunker mentality where people designed structures to serve as de facto bomb shelters. The kindergarten fell into that category. The basement lunchroom was reachable only by a set of concrete steps which had taken out many a shin in its day. They made the entire underground portion of the school out of an immensely dense cement which appeared more than capable of withstanding a blast.

A long hallway snaked off from the breakroom culminating in his and hers restrooms. The pathway served as a snapshot of the fears of the time. The corridor might as well have been an underground cavern considering how the thick mortar ran from floor to curved ceiling. Lead-filled gunmetal gray paint only added to the under siege feel. Bulbs dangled at intervals like a mine shaft making the basement feel seemingly unrelated to the quaint wooden structure above ground.

Teachers usually accompanied students to the john, so with no supervision, it occurred to him he could check out the girl's bathroom. Would there be unicorns? Maybe even rainbows as he expected? A strange feeling filled his stomach related to his isolation, so he bypassed the likely epic female oasis to rush to the boy's room. He needed to sit and dump since nervous cramps had overtaken his bowels.

He dropped to take care of business. While in some ways nervous about feeling so isolated, a part of him enjoyed the break given private time was a commodity back home where his kid brother followed him everywhere. He finished with the toilet before rising to deal with what initially brought him there. A cursory examination of his shirt found the stain already dried which meant mission accomplished (though a sniff suggested he maybe didn't smell so good).

His world changed upon returning to the lunchroom. Everyone had vanished! The only things left behind were open lunchboxes, brown paper bags, and half consumed juice boxes. Students? Nada. Even the teachers disappeared. It made no sense. One-minute dozens were there, the next, none. He grew wide-eyed with wonder while running theories through his mind. Alien abduction was the likeliest culprit. He slowly climbed the steps, mindful to watch out for any creatures that may have stayed behind after the attack.

The kindergarten, like the rotary, was of a poor design. Not structurally, but in the Feng Shui sense. The building itself was traditional on the exterior with a modest set of stairs leading up to heavy wood double push bar doors at the front of the school. Upon stepping through the entryway, one would encounter a small foyer feeding into a hallway with two rooms on either side. The first set of rooms were the admin office and teacher's lounge. Beyond the offices a hall bisected twin classrooms.

A 'stairwell of death' descended at the rear of the corridor. The building was solid, despite its age. While serviceable as an education center, its epic fail was in the views available to the students. Impossible to ignore scenery visible through massive windows was the stuff of childhood torture.

One side overlooked the main road into Tether Falls which while lightly traveled, still distracted bored children with every passing car. The only thing worse than the street view was that which Charlie faced daily—the playground which relentlessly teased a jungle gym, see-saw, slide, and merry-go-round. Most educational buildings designed classrooms to face away from play areas, streets, or sports fields. Tether Falls Kindergarten was the exception. The enticing play zone drew longing gazes from students the duration of every day.

Those same deficiencies in design were Charlie's

planned investigatory targets. The large windows in each room would give him a clear view of the outside world through which he might gain some insight to what happened. Maybe aliens even parked their spaceship outside he thought. While his alien theory could still be wrong, it remained the most plausible idea.

Running scenarios through his mind while climbing the steps, his brain wrestled with the possibility that Troy was playing a joke, had convinced everyone to hide. He pondered whether it might be his birthday and he merely forgot. Perhaps the school planned a surprise party. He was notoriously bad with dates and numbers of any sort.

Upon cresting the stairwell into a further realm of silence, all doubt vanished. Not even Troy could keep dozens of kids quiet. Students were not hiding, and oh yeah, his Nana had disappointingly bought him socks on his birthday two months ago ruling out a surprise party. Glances in both directions proved none had returned to class. He entered a street side room and looked as far as he could. There was no movement, not a single car. Could aliens have abducted everyone in town? Likely.

He crossed over to his class. Belongings remained scattered about which meant not only were his friends taken but they left everything. It all became clear how his trip to a bomb shelter shitter caused him to be the last human on earth. The playground was all his now, no more waiting in lines.

The admin office was next. He would never dare enter the adult land behind the front desk in the old world but did so with impunity. *No more hall passes for this kid*, he thought. The street side view from offered no automobiles. He entered the teacher's lounge crossing another once forbidden barrier. Peering into the dense forest in the distance, he wished the best for his parents and brother, hoping they were okay on their new planet.

Reentering the main corridor, he eyed the front doors with fresh eyes. Pushing through them meant freedom.

Where would he explore first? Where should he go? Home seemed so far without a car, but he had to check there. Suddenly a bell rang impossibly loud. He had never stood so close to the round copper half dome device above the teacher's lounge before. The noise was deafening, forcing him to cover his ears.

The double doors burst open from outside. His teacher stepped into view, followed by a throng of kids eager to return to food. They bumped the shocked boy, brushing by while ignoring him, unaware how mere moments ago he was the last person on earth. Charlie could not comprehend this new reality. The world went back to how it was before as life moved past him with an energetic fury. The strangest of feelings overcame him. He found himself—disappointed.

"Fire drill, butt head. Where the heck were you?" Troy said, leaving his stunned friend behind.

Finding himself alone, everyone back in the lunchroom now, Charlie remembered the drills. Students trained to gather in a straight line at the front of the school until cleared. One bell rang to evacuate while a second signaled return. The concrete fortress of the bathroom must have muted the initial sound. He would have discovered his friends if only he had stepped through the doors. A teacher rose from below, stepping partway back up the rear stairs causing her head to appear disembodied. The floating face ordered him to join them.

Life went on in the lunchroom that day, went back to normal for everyone but him. For a brief period, Charlie 'Thunder' Raines believed in aliens with the entirety of his mind and the fullness of his heart and would ultimately embrace many more outlier concepts as he grew older. No longer the last boy alive, he would spend his life seeking proof of the supernatural, understanding that if one believed—truly believed—anything was possible.

It would not be until his twenty-ninth year before he would finally discover evidence there was more to the world than Heaven and Earth might lead one to believe. Not long after that he would realize Heaven had nothing to do with it.

CHAPTER 6

"Charlie Thunder, as I live and breathe, welcome to my hotel!" Agnes Patterson said.

The owner was a big-boned woman from the South whose words sing-songed when she spoke. Her lilt was as sweet as the apple pie special on the in-house restaurant menu. She mentioned the decadent dessert to him over the phone earlier in the week. The Architect in Freeport, Maine had long been a waystation for people partaking of the upscale outlet stores in town.

Long after kindergarten, Charlie grew into a tall, fit man despite avoiding sports over the years too busy chasing nerdier (the cool kids would call it) pursuits. His fit appearance came about because of how busy he found himself in his daily life, not to mention how often he forgot to eat. The magic eight ball from his youth had proved prescient in that he never left his hometown. Despite never moving away, he made a name for himself beyond the borders of his birthplace.

"Hello, Mrs. Patterson." Charlie extended his hand.

"Oh, please son, the Mrs. is my long dead and buried mother, may her sweet rotting corpse rest in peace."

She brushed past his offer to shake and squeezed him in a bear hug while Luis, his college-aged cameraman looked on with a smile. Charlie's glasses fell partway off his face forcing him to adjust his frames while the woman moved on to her next victim.

"And aren't you as cute as a two-dollar button? Luis, I know you from the TV too."

"Can't breathe," Luis said.

Agnes laughed, released her grip, then shoved him for the 'joke.'

"*Paranormal Predicaments* has gotten me through many a lonely night. A girl's gotta watch something when she works the front desk at all hours since I've no man in my life. None that don't pay nightly rates that is. If I were twenty years younger, I might look sweetly at you two. Oh, who am I kidding? I am anyway. Either of you want some summer loving you just let me know. That, or some apple pie."

"Yes, well, thank you, we'll take that into consideration. Now can we please see the inside?"

"Absolutely, welcome to The Architect, gentlemen."

The hotel, formerly a hub for tourists seeking the Maine experience, had in recent years become a destination for amateur Ghost Hunters. A young couple staying at the resort two seasons ago snapped a shot of "the fanciest place they had ever seen," as they recounted. Upon downloading the pictures, they discovered one contained an image of a ghostly male figure in period garb. The picture went viral branding the hotel as a ghost hotspot. Flocks of spectral seekers, professional and amateur, soon arrived in droves.

Meanwhile, Charlie Thunder was hosting his second season of a cable TV show, *Paranormal Predicaments*. The program covered a cornucopia of outlandish topics from Bigfoot to divining rods, but ghost hunting remained the most frequent topic at the direction of New York producers. He only met the executives in person once (the norm ever since becoming a weekly conference call). Luis was his sole crewmember.

His young assistant interned at the 'Mother Ship,' as local stations called the headquarters in New York. Luis proved himself working on two dreadful reality shows unrelated to his current work. When the company discovered his interest in *Bruja Negro* and *Bruja Blanca*, white and black Magic witches, they assigned him to PA for one of the more famous ghost hunting programs in network history.

During that same time, a local yokel, Charlie Thunder, published a well-received novel on the spirit world which garnered him a general meeting at the Mother Ship. A project based on his book was green-lit. They promoted Luis to head the crew, as in one.

The rookie host did not understand a production team traditionally had multiple people, so took it all in stride. He held his first staff meet and greet at a bar where they got stinking drunk together, forming a quick bond of friendship. Luis moved to Portland where the pair filmed episodes of *PP* (as they called it) while working around Charlie's schedule at the University of Southern Maine. The money was cable versus network, so Charlie kept his day job as a professor of literature. He enjoyed the notoriety he received on campus as the success of the program grew.

That was how the duo came to find themselves at the Architect. When mapping out their new season they considered an episode showcasing the local haunt. If preliminary scouting bore fruit, they would use the notorious place in their next opener. 'If you can't start with a bang, then start with a boo,' was a variation of one of the many useless notes they often received from producers.

They followed Agnes up a long staircase into the old rustic hotel approximating a giant version of a bed-and-breakfast. There was nothing eerie about the exterior, it was simple almost cliched New England charm. Charlie took the grounds to be a nice place to sit and drink iced tea on hot summer days.

The lobby was reminiscent of the eighteenth century. Bergere chairs and a matching velvet love seat sat atop a Persian rug filling the space. Tasseled golden curtain tiebacks held elegant drapes open allowing a soft inviting glow to flood the high ceiling room. One wall, trimmed with elaborate gold-flecked molding and covered in paisley wallpaper, displayed a large painting of an angel kissing the nape of a Rubenesque female who appeared non-plussed to be on the receiving end of an unearthly visitor's affections.

Left of the entrance, a hall fed off to a wide wooden staircase which ascended gently on small rise steps. Miniature wall mounted chandeliers provided ambient light along the windowless corridor. A large doorless entry near the stairs formed a gateway to the restaurant.

"I understand why so many people would take pictures of this lobby, it is beautiful. Yet we have only a single documented photo from this staircase over the years?" Charlie asked.

The woman did not answer, too focused on Luis who opened his camera case and snapped away. Agnes looked on concerned.

"I thought you would have TV cameras," she said.

"We're not filming yet, we're location scouting. Frankly, we need to decide if we film here at all. Now about the picture, there aren't any others?" Charlie asked.

"No, actually, we have tons of visitors who have pictures of orbs. Are you familiar with them?"

"I am."

He walked to a fabric chair striking the padded seat with a palm. On cue, Luis snapped away before turning the view screen toward their host to show off a large orb. Agnes lit up.

"See, you have experienced one already!"

"Dust and pollen are the most common cause of orb pictures, otherwise we couldn't have reproduced one so quickly. Besides the staircase where else have you seen activity?"

"Well, it's not so much me, as it is our guests. They complain of cold spots," she said.

Charlie and crew shared a knowing look. During their initial drunken debauchery meet cute, Luis filled his new boss in on some tricks of the trade from the "reality show" he interned on. If everything else failed, and they captured nothing of note on film, (which was common) the go-to for talent was to talk about cold spots.

Forgetting everything the pair intimately understood about the subject, it was an old place built in a climate not exactly warm year-round. Agnes may have been from the South, but the hotel was pure New England, therefore, by nature, it would have chilled areas even if all the spirits in the building fled for warmer climates. Having already busted one bubble for his host, Charlie was not eager to burst another so soon. He smiled, nodded affably.

"Show me."

Agnes led them up a flight of stairs while cursing about the hotel's lack of elevator. Upon remembering guests were present, she turned her charm back on. They reached the second floor showcasing an impossibly long stretch of suites. Charlie instantly realized he had not taken in the entire size of the hotel from outside, a mistake he occasionally made. A cursory exterior exam of any building was a part of his paranormal toolbox which he too often neglected. A thorough inventory of the outside of a location could help identify any anomalies within. Easy to bang on walls if one had a hidden third chamber in a "two-bedroom home," for example.

Guest quarters lined both sides of the passageway with each ingress trimmed in elaborate period molding. A thin carpet, Persian, in red and gold patterns ran the entire length. Three-pronged light fixtures adorned sections of wall. The bulbs barely bleeding through the nearly opaque glass emulating candlelight. Agnes led them past several guest chambers before finally stopping and using a quaint old-style skeleton key to open twin rooms directly across from one another. She gestured for them to follow.

"I get more of a serial killer vibe than ghosts, how about you?" Luis whispered to his boss while on the move.

"I don't believe we will find enough for an episode here," Charlie replied.

The ghost hunters went to work snapping pictures from every angle. Agnes giggled at the activity. "Ooh felt a cold spot just now. I think our guests have arrived."

The cameraman followed the breeze toward the window, shook his head. "Draft from the window."

"Agnes, I'm both pleased and sorry to report that I do not think the hotel is anything other than a wonderful place to stay. As for it being haunted, I just do not see anything out of the ordinary here…"

A door creaked slowly open somewhere behind Charlie, halting him mid-sentence while turning to the guest room across the hall where he noticed a female standing back to him. She frantically signaled toward someone through a window. Her surroundings appeared absent the accouterments of a hotel, was in fact barren. He noted the thick grime covering the window she gestured through, assumed her efforts to be futile through such filth.

"Is that woman a guest at the hotel?"

"What woman?" Luis/Agnes asked.

Charlie felt a stir in his gut much like the moment as a child when he believed in the alien abduction. A sense of dread built greater than any he had ever known. He worried if he crossed the threshold it would change his life forever, but he also understood it held answers to his lifelong questions. He stepped forward on unsteady feet as adrenaline surged through his body, made him heady with fear.

"Hey Boss, you're freaking me out. What woman are you talking about?" Luis asked.

He didn't answer, only walked away until he found himself a single step away from mystery. As he raised his leg, he understood there would be no turning back. While struggling to understand why he found himself so utterly terrified, he shocked himself by continuing as if a puppet on someone else's string.

Upon stepping over the threshold, the woman vanished. Things returned to normal. Charlie breathed in relief, felt his heartbeat normalize until a door creaked slowly behind him before slamming shut harder than any he ever experienced. Lights flashed briefly before everything went dark.

CHAPTER 7

"How's your day going so far, Sheriff?" his waitress asked while serving him a bottle of Moxie.

"It's been a humdinger, ah…"

"Holly," Holly the waitress said.

"Ayuh, a humdinger all right, Holly. In fact, let's double down on the lobstuh roll, make it two."

"One larger tip for me coming right up." She smiled and winked

Frank returned the smile, sipping his soda while she left to change his previous order. He ordered the food and drink minutes ago in a Tavern near the police headquarters. Even earlier, Portland Detective Scott Foster chewed the sheriff out for delivering evidence from a crime scene straight to the squad. Watkins in return barked at the man for not answering his damn phone while bodies piled up in his town.

They both agreed to be disagreeable before parting ways. As much as the sheriff longed to go back to the accident to find out more about the dead couple and their cargo, his deputies, now at the site, had eaten while he had not. He stopped for lunch to allow himself and the detective time to cool off before speaking again. Despite the macabre nature of the crime scene, a more pressing need came to mind.

"Dang, I forgot to ask for extra drawn butter on the lobstuh rolls."

He rose to look for Holly when his phone rang. It was George from the station, his desk duty deputy. Watkins was not a fan of the officer given how the insufferable squad member caused twin fender benders involving his work vehicle, a feat bordering on impossible in a town with minimal traffic. Even peak summer congestion through to Willow was smooth riding unless one found themselves behind a car with Massachusetts plates then it was a game on. Somehow the employee rear-ended two separate residents whose combined ages totaled a hundred and fifty-nine years, neither of whom—until his deputy struck—had ever been in an accident.

That was the thing about George. Someone could go their whole life experiencing nothing distressingly unpleasant until the miserable officer swooped in with no visible effort to change lives for the worse in a heartbeat. His desk jockey was about to perform a variation of the same to his boss.

"Sheriff, we had a call about a house appearing in the big field over on River Road," George said over the phone.

"A house? You mean someone's trailer broke down?"

"They mentioned it was a full-blown house. Big one."

"Was the caller drunk or sober?"

"I don't understand."

"Are you trying to get yourself fired? No way there's a house in any field on River Road that wasn't already there. When someone suggests there may be, your first question should be how many Budweiser's are missing from their fridge."

"They sounded scared. They say it's a house."

Sheriff Watkins pinched the bridge of his nose, not because it helped his George headache go away but because he saw people do it on TV when frustrated. He hoped it would do something for him, but it did not. He felt aggravated with the city detective, the peon at the front desk in Portland, and now his own employee. At least there was Holly, he liked her—she brought him food.

"Here you are Sheriff, one heavy on claws, one heavy on tails," she said.

Watkins raised his index finger to draw her attention but given his conversation she gave him space and moved on to another table.

"Shit on a shingle, George, you made me miss out on more drawn butter. Now I need to get back to the crash anyway, so I'll swing by this field but if there's anything less than a trailer out there you and I will have words. And if anyone else calls about this so-called house what are you going to ask them?"

"How many bottles of Budweiser?"

"Exactly how many bottles of Budweiser they had."

The sheriff hung up, drank the rest of his Moxie, before grabbing the red basket with the lobster rolls. He dropped bills on the table and scratched a napkin note promising the return of the container. He had yet to understand that soon he would owe George an apology.

CHAPTER 8

Charlie felt certain he went unconscious only briefly. As unsettling as his forced disconnect to consciousness was, he found he preferred the obliviousness of dark stupefaction over the burst of raw emotions that surged through him the moment the mystery door slammed shut. The force with which it closed did the opposite to his heart, ripping it open while shredding psychic shields designed to protect one's self against random acts of deep moral inventory. Something had torn away his sense of well-being as cleanly as pulling off a bandage to reveal a wound not of bloody flesh but one containing the hardened scars of past failures.

It all happened in a single step. There was the hotel, the nice lady with offers of sex and apple pie, then another woman entered the picture. He felt drawn to her, as if she were a ghost but not a ghost, more like someone stuck in between. As he approached her, he reached a point of no return, understood he should stop, yet he could not control himself. The moment he placed his foot forward, layers of his consciousness peeled away one at a time, each exposing thoughts and feelings he long sought to bury.

As the black void enveloped him physically, a much deeper darkness attacked him spiritually. The act of crossing the threshold thrust him into the unknown where he existed in a plane he could only describe as nothingness. While in the 'nowhere' an internal anguish descended upon him as if every loss he ever endured coalesced to swarm him with despair. The onslaught of forced psychic self-reflection delivered upon him a sense of total isolation, his heart giving way to a loneliness beyond any previously imaginable. He felt it too much to bear but mercifully he finally passed out.

The reason he believed his stint into unconsciousness to be brief was because he heard the hollow thump of his own arrival on a wooden floor which woke him from his stupor. The memory of his pain throbbed in his heart anew but the specifics of what occurred quickly began to slip from his grasp like a dream after waking. He only knew he was happy to leave those feelings behind.

For an unknown force to rip one away only to deposit them elsewhere would at any other time be a terrifying endeavor, yet he felt relieved to have escaped the cold blackness of misery initially visited upon him. He breathed slowly touching the wood to anchor himself while taking in his surroundings. It became quickly clear he was in a house, a dilapidated one, but at least it appeared to exist in what he considered the normal world. He pressed his hands against floorboards, making a connection. Any relief over discovering a solid foundation beneath him vanished when the woman he glimpsed in the hotel descended on him with a wild fury.

"Phone! Do you have a cell phone?"

Charlie could not determine if her actions were wildly aggressive, or whether he merely had yet to readjust to his return from an existential plane. To stop her onslaught, he handed it over. Below the surface of her frantic movements, he noticed a sad beauty, but still breathed in relief when she stepped away to tap on the screen.

The air was heavy with mildewed rot which he knew well from filming in a variety of older homes. Yet the smell was stronger—too damp—as if the floors might turn to wash at any moment which he could not understand as the boards felt drier than bone. The woman raced about the room cursing, apparently not happy with his choice of phone provider. He noted she was not unattractive, the opposite, in fact. She had a toned body with stunning features despite the hardened edge of concentration sculpted on her face. He tried not to objectify the stranger, but the yoga pants did not help.

Charlie cursed his lizard brain for checking her out while navigating a changed reality. He speculated, based on where he found himself, that different planes surely existed. The void in which he briefly vanished confirmed the existence of a spiritual realm while his renewed ability to lust after a woman (no matter how inappropriate the situation) signaled a return to the land of the physical. The question suddenly became less about how he got here than where "here" was. He rose on unsteady feet, wishing for a chair where there was none then raised a hand to attract the woman's attention only for her to wave him off.

"No bars, damn!"

She raced out of the room. If for no other reason than not to suffer a stolen phone, Charlie gave chase. "Hey, excuse me, Miss," he said weakly.

Upon entering the hall, he noticed the immense size of the building. Given he had just visited a massive hotel, it surprised him to find his new surroundings larger than those he left behind. The structure felt obscenely dark which disturbed him. He had never considered the possibility of a home giving off feelings. The woman vanished into another chamber. Before he could follow, she reemerged only to launch herself into the next. He gave up on his phone as the crazy person continued down the corridor. He entered a nearby room, looked out the window.

Charlie understood immediately where they were. A familiar pasture leading into the woods loomed in the distance except he was unaware of any house existing in the field. Before he could consider that further, he identified the footpath he and his brother traveled so often before. He knew the exact spot all too well. It had to be more than a coincidence. The forest was where his world fell apart. The happiest times of his life were there but also the worst. The despair from the void threatened to return.

Thinking back to what happened, his breath hitched. Never a day went by he didn't think about it. He had never returned, never once, never planned to again, yet here he was. He felt a pain in his heart he could not bear. He pressed hands against the glass, remembering. Before tears arrived, someone grabbed his shoulder.

A part of him feared who the hand belonged to, afraid of who it might be, here, now, in this place. He searched for words he never had the chance to say the last time he was here—the day when his world crumbled. The individual spun him around. The person he half-expected to see did not appear, instead he faced the crazy woman.

She stood so close he noticed a pain in her eyes possibly matching his own. He wondered what demons were at play in her soul. Did they marionette her internal strings as masterfully as they did his own? She handed his phone over as gently as offering a wedding ring to his I do.

"No bars. You look familiar," she said.

He shook off the fog of memory, checking the reception meter to verify. She looked past him searching for what he saw outside.

"We're in Tether Falls. Is that where you are from?" Charlie asked.

"Recently, yes. You?"

"Born and raised."

"No accent?"

"I do a TV show, had to lose it."

"That's where I've seen you then. I'm... Suzy."

He found it odd the way she hesitated to offer her name. True, they were strangers, but that was what introductions were for. He was a strange man appearing before her in the craziest of circumstances. The more he thought about it, he considered himself lucky she spoke to him at all. He moved past niceties eager for answers.

"How did you get here? How long have you been here?"

"I heard something creak open, went into a light, then—well you know. I arrived shortly before you. I've tried to break windows in several rooms but wasn't strong enough, can you try?"

"Or we could look for the front door," he said.

"Window first please, just so I can know for sure," she said.

Charlie followed her across the hall to the next room where a chair lay upended. He lifted it to thrust a leg at center glass. A soft muffled 'thunk' sounded. He grimaced in confusion before striking again. He shifted the weight, gripping it by two legs and swung repeatedly until too fatigued to continue before gingerly setting the furniture down as if a guest at someone's dinner party.

Suzy gestured to it as he leaned on his knees, took in air. "Need a seat?"

He waved her off. "A portal."

"What does that mean?"

"It means that may be Tether Falls outside, but that's not where we are."

"Then, where are we?"

"Nowhere."

CHAPTER 9

Watkins cursed his deputy's name while driving down River Road. He passed the Correctional Center on his left which was a fancy word for prison. The center was—in his estimation—located too close to the elementary school, but he was only the sheriff, not a town planner so who was he to say what was safe for students?

Most of the inmates came from hardscrabble lives while others were folks who couldn't seem to catch a break. Those down on their luck individuals he did not worry so much about. Truthfully, he rooted for them as *there but for the grace of God go I* he thought in relation to his own youthful indiscretions. He knew when to cut some knuckleheads some slack but also understood when they needed time on the inside to cool their heels, ensure they didn't get ideas of grandiosity with their lawbreaking. Point of fact, the gen-pop of the Correctional Center would say Watkins was fair.

Perhaps his deputy should do a spell there for a while,

he thought. Here he had three dead bodies piled up yet was wasting resources chasing down a non-existent house. Their town contract stipulated law enforcement respond to every call. If his desk jockey called the bluff of the prankster or questioned the soberness of the caller, the sheriff could have avoided the trek and would be back at the crime scene already.

Expectations were low for what he might find, figuring it most likely to be a cow with the word 'house' or some other bullshit painted on it. A local yahoo would have a camera ready to post the prank on social media if this was a goof which was why he responded rather than send someone. Part of his job was to keep his boys off YouTube. Anyone could take any idiot thing his staff might do (even in jest) out of context. The result could stain the whole department. The town paid an obscene amount, by Watkin's estimation, to fly a media guru up from Boston several summers ago for a session on handling citizens with cameras. The issue never arose after the class, yet the same training caused Watkins to ride shotgun with paranoia about it ever since.

He used his pointless drive time to consider the body parts. The Portland detective was on it, but it was Frank's job to keep the community safe. He mulled over what it might mean. Was this a one-off killing? Unlikely. Wrapping a corpse in plastic for disposal was par for the course for murderers, but severing limbs and wrapping them in barbed wire? That was troubling.

Hopefully, they would identify the victim by dental records, perhaps fingerprints. Given that both avenues of identification were in the same vehicle, he wondered if the deceased occupants intended to dispose of the evidence found in their trunk which meant they left a mystery torso somewhere else in the world. If the couple were only 'cleaners' then why the jagged wire? Coiling body parts in such a way could easily draw blood leaving an evidence trail, which ruled out them being pros. Besides acting as a

DNA harvesting tool, the wire wrapping also made no sense as an anchor if the plan was a lake disposal because fishermen would trawl it in no time at all.

More likely, and the part that concerned Watkins the most, was they desired someone to find the parts, which meant they were sending a message. The only people who would do so were the drug cartels. The thought any operated this far from Boston or New York was troubling. All regional trouble had prior to this always been of the homegrown sort. The two in the vehicle looked more like California movie stars, body-wise, hard to tell about their overall looks given the whole face thing with the woman. Neither appeared, on the surface, to be central casting versions of dealers, never mind actual ones.

Tether Falls contracted out for detectives, forensics, and coroner services, leaving investigations entirely in the hands of their law enforcement partners in Portland, which was why the sheriff handed off the scene. It did not mean, however, that he hadn't already called his own contacts while driving to lunch earlier prior to calling to the squad desk peon. His inquiries related to running the plates along with pulling reports of missing white males roughly within the age range of the severed head in the Samsonite. He planned to follow up as soon as he finished with his 'house call.'

He rounded a corner taking him past the local church which fronted a massive cemetery reminding him to touch base with Pastor Graves, a man of the cloth who was a good source of information on troubled souls he liked to keep an eye on. Maybe the preacher would also know of any religious significance to the 'praying' hands in their metal cocoon. The sheriff exited the curve into a straightaway on the lightly populated stretch of road nearing his destination when he recalled a news story about feet washing up in the Washington State area.

Wondering whether there was a connection between his loose appendages and theirs, he decided to add Seattle

PD to his call list. The Pacific Northwest thing had been ongoing for years with no publicly identified suspects, along with no clue who the body parts belonged to. He figured...

Smoke filled the air when Watkins slammed on the brakes. Smoke temporarily obscured his vision—blocking the view of that which caused him to stop so suddenly. He fumbled for his police lights only to leap in fright upon accidentally hitting the siren. He killed the sound. The dancing red and blue atop his vehicle flashed a show against the smoky backdrop which slowly dissipated under a subtle breeze on the warm summer day. The officer threw his door open and stepped out.

Looking through the skirt of thin trees lining the edge of the road, he spied in the field—one he knew for a decade to be empty—an enormous house! He had driven past when? A week ago, maybe. Was it even possible for someone to have built a home this big since he last drove by? The answer he determined as he stood there numbly was a hard no.

Carefully crossing the road, the sheriff remained oblivious to his vehicle blocking a lane, (the lights were on for criminy's sake) but that house, what a house! The day was clear, but the sheriff found himself in a fog. The massive place appeared larger than the Turner farm which was the largest structure in Tether Falls save for the supermarket or lumber yard.

He forced his way through tight brush hoping it to be poison ivy free. Once clear, he halted to take in the dark, ominous monstrosity rising before him. Two townsfolk stared in equal amounts of awe at the sight while patiently awaiting the officer's stunned approach. Ricky Senior, AKA Big Rick, and Calvin were the fathers of the boys who discovered the abomination.

Any ideas, Sheriff?" Rick asked.

The sheriff had none, none at all. The presence of the home was startling on its own, yet the altered landscape offered an even greater sense of mystery. The house sat atop the center of a hill which had somehow impossibly grown above the flatland like a pregnant woman nine months along. Thunderclouds drooped so low in the sky over the roof they threatened to drip their dark cotton onto the peaked stone chimneys jutting upward at intermittent sections of the building.

He could not tell exactly what type of trees jutted from the ground at the corner of the house and the end of the front porch, he only knew they weren't native. He found them unsettling the way leafless branches curled in on themselves like arthritic hands closed tight with palsy. There were laws on transporting flora and fauna across state lines so he had his reason to arrest someone if he could find out just who the heck landscaped the heck out of the local field.

His instincts urged him to pound on the door demanding the owners show themselves. Except not only were stairs missing but someone had mysteriously excavated the vast portion of the hill leading to the front entrance, the ground dug down to an exposed rock bed. There was no way to determine if the stratum of stone originally existed only to be revealed by a dig, or whether the jagged outcropping hitched a ride with its host.

Watkins understood Maine suffered weather extremes. While tornadoes were not common, they occurred occasionally. He belonged to a statewide emergency response team related to natural disasters which required a trip to Augusta annually for certification training. Some first responders told stories of a twister lifting a barn all the way across a street many years ago. The story found fresh legs on local stations whenever a major storm front made the news.

Could a tornado have dropped the massive structure into an otherwise pristine field? He considered it a remote possibility but even if that were the case, it would not account for the mesa under the home. Nor the trimmed lawn which did not match the knee-high grass variant native to the pasture. There were many unanswered questions but perhaps the biggest was how the landscape could have arrived so well-tended. How anyone could have performed such extensive yardwork prior to or after dropping off the cosmic Greyhound bus passenger that was a house seemed to layer impossibility on top of the impossible.

Strange enough a hill (where there damn sure never was one before) somehow served as a perfect-sized base for the architectural monstrosity, but to see a massive hole randomly chomped out of its face made no lick of sense. The excavation ran so deep the stone landing rested at an elevation lower than the original meadow itself. The resultant gap exposed a section of a brick foundation rising until nestling into twin evenly spaced basement windows.

Like most residences, the basement windows would normally rest at ground level and they did as normal along the right and left sides of the home, but the exposed center served as a variant of Superman's x-ray vision, allowing the sheriff to see that which normally remained hidden. Where the two cellar windows appeared in plain view, the brick layer continued a few feet above each until merging at the base of a front porch running half the length of the building. The gap from the elusive front entrance and the pit appeared to be at least a dozen feet or more.

A narrow stone ledge ran the entire length of the house except where interrupted by the front porch. The ledge appeared to serve as a decorative feature more-so than anything functional, a dash of character to an otherwise wooden facade. With no stairs, the slim outcrop looked to be the best route to reach the front of the building.

If one navigated far enough along the brick ledge, they could, in theory, climb the side rail to the deck where they could then enter the structure. Several first-floor windows were within reach before the landscape sloped perilously away at the center, but the sheriff had the gut feeling all roads leading to answers hid behind the looming oak door.

"Either of you attempted to get in yet?"

"Hell no," came the collective response.

The sheriff raised his cell only to pull the phone away to check reception.

"Nothing electronic works. We tried to take pictures, no luck. We sent Calvin across the street to snap one," Rick, a large burly man, said.

Calvin, fifties, who looked older thanks to the bottle, waved meekly while lifting his own cell.

"And?" Watkins asked.

"Could be a house, could be Bigfoot, could be my wife Ellie's grey-haired vagina," Calvin said.

"He means it's blurry."

"I'm not stupid, Big Rick. Now, why don't you two follow me? We'll try to get in," Watkins said.

"Why not, I've lived a long enough life I figure," Calvin said.

"Well I have not, so let's not talk like that. Besides, whatever is going on here, as weird as this may be, it is just a house," Watkins said.

Except the sheriff did not believe that. As he and his two-member posse moved closer to the dark edifice, the officer realized he owed George an apology. But more than that, he decided the body parts along with the dead people in the car likely had nothing to do with drugs and everything to do with this house.

CHAPTER 10

The tables had turned. Suzy now followed Charlie through the unknown as he waved his hands in the air while they walked. The hardwood floor creaked periodically underfoot harmonizing with other odd noises of an old house settling. They moved efficiently while canvassing their surroundings. The layout proved a mix of furnished and empty rooms. Most furniture sat covered under white fabric though one outlier bedchamber stood out as if tidied that morning, the bed crisply made, the environment clean. The paranormal host found the juxtaposition of that lone unit versus others unsettling.

"What are you doing?" Suzy asked.

"Portals. I did an episode on them. I was always highly skeptical of the phenomenon if only because in theory it should be the easiest preternatural concept to prove. Anyone who knows of one should be able to show people where to step through. Easy-peasy."

"Had been a skeptic? What changed?"

"Now a door creaked behind me and I'm here, except

here isn't here. The temperature inside is cooler than the summer day we left out there so with no central air as far as I can tell, we should feel the heat. This place is its own environment. If a portal brought us here, it is not as simple as saying we are in that field, especially since I know there is no building in this area." He started the hand motions again.

"Well there is now, which makes you wrong on that front. Not sure I should trust you on the rest. You really think all the waving will do anything?"

"I'm searching for fluctuations in temperature. People speak of cold spots in haunted houses. On a good day, I would classify that as BS, yet our situation is real. We left the physical world as we knew it only to arrive on a plane which may or may not exist on the land outside. Bottom line, even a portal has a way in and out. I would expect a slight environmental change close to an entrance. This is all speculation which means we should still seek traditional methods to exit."

He lifted a chair and slammed it against the window where it broke apart. Deflated, he turned to leave. With a quickness deserving of the yoga outfit, Suzy grabbed a broken leg from the defeated furniture then blocked his path. The crazy woman Charlie initially met appeared to have returned except armed this time, waving the object like a samurai sword.

"What is going on? One minute I'm in my studio, the next I am here but you say here isn't here? We can't seem to get out and you keep talking about portals and cold spots? Why do you know so much? Maybe you drugged me. Possibly you're doing all this."

Charlie raised his hands in defense. "Look, we're both in the same situation. The only information I've gleaned so far is glass should break yet doesn't and there is no house outside, but also there somehow is. The TV show I mentioned? It's a paranormal program. I have covered many strange things which means I know a little about a lot but trust me, nothing prepared me for this. Our best chance of figuring everything out is to work together."

He noted the look of pain in her eyes once again, a look buried deep inside but fighting for the surface like a drowning swimmer. While he understood she posed a threat, looked more than capable of taking him down, he still recognized the tortured demeanor of the sorrowful beneath the surface of a warrior. He lowered his hands while pleading his case.

"I promise I would never hurt you. I understand if you do not trust a stranger, but that goes both ways. If you can't do that, fine, this place is big enough I can go my way and you yours, never the twain shall meet. I plan to trust you even if you don't me." Charlie took a tentative step forward. She anchored herself, raising the weapon higher. "I hope deep down you know I didn't do this. We're in this mess together. I plan to take that thing from you. If you believe I have bad intentions, then use it on me. For the record, I am hoping you won't."

He stepped closer. Suzy held her ground, gesturing with the club until gingerly—ever so slowly—he grasped one end and pulled. They locked eyes as she held tight before finally letting go.

"My full name is Charlie Thunder Raines."

"Suzy. That's all you get. No offense, Charlie but I wish I never met you."

"None taken, I feel the same. Now can we try the front door?"

She nodded and looked at him questioningly when he handed her the club.

"I have a bad feeling we will need it," he said.

The pair stepped into the hall which seemed to stretch on forever in both directions. Despite the seemingly magical nature of their arrival, Charlie noted how stable their surroundings appeared. Forces were at play for certain, but every home had a door at least he hoped this one did.

A grand staircase curved gently down while the stairs picked up again across the hall leading up. Those rising lacked the elegance of those descending. The lower level offered grandiosity, an awe-inspiring welcome to the building. The upper variant narrowed into a straight shot to other stories, pure utilitarian design.

Suzy shivered while gesturing with the club. "I feel like we shouldn't go up there. Like ever."

"Once out of here I plan to return. Bring my crew and…"

"Can we finish the escape part first? Then do whatever you want."

"Sorry, occupational hazard."

They descended to a massive a high-ceilinged empty hall. Charlie figured at one time the enormous place might have been a calling card mansion for someone richer than anyone from Tether Falls, though he assumed such a tenant would have kept the property in better condition. As it stood, blackened mold covered portions of a wall like a painting made of cancer, a sign of a dream having died somewhere along the way.

Two large doorless entryways opened in both directions. Through the nearest, he spotted a sitting room filled with furniture aplenty under sheets. Immense windows lined the farthest wall. From a distance the enormous panes appeared iced over which should have been impossible given the season. Upon a second look, he realized the 'ice' was only the grime of time.

Charlie would give the oversized window sashes the old college try if a door failed them. It bothered him to even consider such a prospect, that a turned knob should deny them escape. That was what doors did, right, they opened? Yet something inside him told him this place wanted to remain closed forever. They spotted the main entrance through the second archway.

Stepping into a wide-open foyer they found the tall front door made of oak or some other hardwood crowned with elaborate molding. It appeared ancient yet solid despite a tributary of cracks littered across its surface like a river. Charlie reached it first.

Grabbing the handle, he turned, pulled. It did not budge. Suzy assisted him to no avail, so he gave over to pushing, shouldering full body weight against it. Still nothing. In frustration, he resorted to kicking. The initial blow sent a shudder through his bones. He tried again and again, grunting through the effort.

It reminded him of trips to the batting cages with Ryan when they were young. He remembered how awfully painful it could be when the bat connected with the ball. He hid his discomfort (twenty pitches for a quarter at a time) so as not to show weakness in front of his baby brother. Charlie would watch his younger sibling struggle through the pitch count in his own cage fighting back tears under the onslaught because, hey not everybody could be Charlie 'Thunder,' but Ryan 'Lightning' was always damn well going to try.

The woods, we're here by the forest. Why here? What's happening, Ryan? Oh, that's right, you cannot tell me what's going on. You can't tell me anything, anymore can you? Of all the things you did, little brother, why did you look up to me? Why? What did it ever get you?

Suzy gripped his shoulder, halting him, ending a pain which had become unbearable several kicks ago. It was her tight grip of restraint which brought him around enough to realize he had been screaming as he kicked all while thinking about his sibling. He halted his vocal attack but not his physical one when he grabbed the club from her to swing at the door, aiming for cracks, hoping to leverage weakened spots to no avail. Dammit, why wouldn't they give?

"Stop, stop, stop!" Suzy begged.

Breathing hard, he stopped, the chair leg drooped to the floor as he leaned down, arms near useless. Suzy had covered her ears during the violent onslaught, trying to block out something his irrationality evoked. She appeared slightly out of focus as his glasses left his face during the fracas.

She finally settled only to scream anew when someone coughed to announce their presence. Spent, Charlie only half-heartedly lifted the wood in defense. The voice belonged to a white male, with dark bushy hair in his forties wearing a gray suit that would not impress in New York but would pass as high faluting locally. The general population of Tether Falls considered jeans and a sport coat to be formal wear.

"We already tried that," the man said.

"I see you. Who is 'we'?" Charlie asked.

Six more people emerged from the shadows, a diverse group with one commonality—all appeared lost and afraid. An elderly woman in her sixties, reed-thin, grey hair half in a bun, wearing a nightgown of faded blue flannel with black scuffed house slippers, pointed her finger at Charlie. She screamed before attacking.

"Him, we're here because of him!"

CHAPTER 11

T he woman might well have been a ghost, given how thin she appeared, almost bordering on transparency. Charlie—on the receiving end of her wrath—deemed her presence disturbing whether live or spectral. The owner of the snarling wrinkled face rushed him with the speed someone of her age should not possess. Suzy stepped between them while Ethan, a young clean-cut man in his twenties, grabbed the woman's arm.

"Pearl stop!" the young man yelled in her ear.

"Get your hands off me, Ethan, or I'll tell your mother!"

"She died years ago, shortly after we stopped being your next-door neighbor when we moved," he replied.

The old lady halted the onslaught, appearing confused. "You grew up?" As if a feint, she quickly turned her attention back to the accused.

Ethan maintained a firm grip on the accuser. Charlie noted with surprise the prowess of the woman despite her skeletal frame. She finally proved human, huffing in effort while struggling with her captor. One arm remained elongated accusingly towards him.

"He does the show with the ghosts and Bigfoot. It must be him!"

"What is this about you being on TV?" the original stranger asked.

"I host a paranormal cable program under the name Charlie Thunder. I have nothing to do with any of this."

"Are you two together?" The man nodded toward the new guests.

"No, we just now met. I'm Suzy."

"From the yoga studio," Ethan replied.

"How would you know?"

"The coffee shop sits across from your business. I frequent there." He released the old woman who seemed to have spent her energy though her face remained twisted in accusation. "She already announced my name. This is Pearl. I used to be her neighbor back in the day."

"Rotten family. Looks like you've grown into a thug," she replied.

"It's not age-related, she's always been mean," the young man said.

The first stranger identified himself. "I am Martin Richman, the assemblyman for Tether Falls."

"Carpetbagger!" Herb yelled. The middle-aged man in his fifties, sported a grey-haired ponytail with matching salt and pepper beard stained yellow around the mouth from nicotine. He wore a tie-dye tee under an open chamois shirt, aging hippy meets hipster. He moved aggressively toward the assemblyman who stood his ground.

"A carpetbagger comes from out of state, I told you that. I'm from Dover Foxcroft up north, a smaller town than even this but it is in Maine. Born and raised, so stuff it."

"You ain't from Tether Falls then you're a carpetbagger."

"We've been here long enough for Martin and Herb to

take a dislike to each other and to learn Pearl is a real peach," Victor said.

Victor was a bull of a man, appropriate since locals knew him as the enigmatic man who owned actual bulls. He lived in a sizeable home close to their current location, atop a large hill set back from the street. He was the rare local who purchased land on the undeveloped side of River Road. Those driving past his place would be remiss not to notice the wide field surrounded by an electric fence containing two massive animals. Charlie was aware of the man's reputation, believed he even knew his name, but the gruff citizen did not bother with introductions so he could not verify his info.

"Do you know what is going on or not?" The local longhorn owner folded his arms over his barrel chest signaling he was closed off to any answer but the one he wanted to hear.

"Yeah, how about it?" Stan stepped to the front of the crowd.

Charlie did not ask the new person for his name since the blue mechanic's onesie stitched on the pocket made it clear. The lean worker in his late twenties likely arrived straight from his job unless he sported the black greasiness of motor oil as a regular accoutrement.

"I do not. But I haven't even processed what's happening. Suzy worried earlier we might have been drugged. How someone could abduct all of..." Charlie started.

"A door opened then you walked through it, we all did. But there is something we should show you to see if it makes sense to you because it doesn't to us. My name is Beth, a manager at First Bank. I was at work and thought I heard the main vault opening somehow. I ran to investigate and then, well, here I am. The other thing Martin mentioned? How about you follow me?"

She gestured them forward. Beth was an attractive woman in her thirties who wore a professional blue wrap dress with a wide belt and matching heels. Charlie attributed her take charge demeanor to her managerial position. She led them away, moving with a gravitas appropriate to her attire.

The group parted to allow the two new guests passage. They stepped into the shadowy zone from which the others had emerged, traveling along a section of the house more decrepit and in greater disrepair than the balance of what they had seen so far. Multiple floorboards were absent. Through missing slats, Charlie noticed a drop appearing to sink further than a single floor but because it was so dark it was hard to know for sure. Cobwebs dangled everywhere like tinsel off a Christmas tree, the white strands stagnant with no breeze to animate them.

"What's that smell?" Suzy asked as they neared a new doorless entryway.

The bank manager answered by gesturing to an elegant dining room lit by candlelight as they entered an area which appeared to be from a different home altogether, one that may well have leaped from the canvas of a Norman Rockwell painting. An enormous crisp-skinned goose lay spread on a platter, darkened sauce dripped over its flank with more of the same in a gravy boat off to the side atop a large communal table. The goose's head remained intact and stretched an obscene distance from the body on an impossibly long neck. Someone had placed fine china and silver flatware along the entire perimeter in front of each available seat.

"There are nine settings." Charlie inspected the scene.

"We wondered who the other guests were, then you two showed up," Martin said.

"This is crazy," Suzy offered.

Pearl dipped a finger in the gravy which came away black. She licked it before smiling, a smear glistened on a single tooth. "Plum sauce is common for geese, but this is blackberry based like I fed my husband Clayton, may he rest in peace."

"I'm sure he got none when he was alive," the bull guy scoffed.

"He was a nice neighbor who gave me neopolitan ice cream if I did chores around his place," Ethan said.

"Did he now? I believe my spouse kept secrets from me."

"That's what men do," Beth said.

"Not all of them sweetheart, I speak my mind," Victor said.

"Is that a fancy way of saying you're single?" Beth replied.

His face turned a red deep enough to infuriate his animals if it were a waved flag. Fire lit in his eyes as he shot a hard glance at the woman who dared challenge him. The politician worked the stressed crowd, bringing them around to the issue at hand.

"I swear we walked through here once before. The feast was not here," Martin said.

"Horse hockey! It's a huge house, we were in a different room. Food doesn't just appear," Victor said.

"I was hungry, and I thought about the old days with my husband." Pearl looked longingly at the bountiful spread. "Goose and mugwort? Who uses mugwort, it's like I…"

"It has nothing to do with you or us, it was already here. We have inadvertently entered somebody's home," Stan said.

"With nine place settings?" Suzy turned on him, shaking her head.

"Coincidence. We know she's crazy or has Alzheimer's. She thinks this guy over here is still a kid. We're in someone's house, that's all there is to it, absolutely nothing weird at all," Stan said.

"Are you kidding? I was in my yoga studio when shit went down. How did you get here? I didn't take a bus. Don't tell me everything is normal."

Suzy stepped toward the mechanic to—what? Charlie

moved protectively between them. Given how she watched out for him when he lost his cool, he figured it time to return the favor. She leaned in on him as if ready to go back to the intensity of their meet anything but cute moment upstairs earlier but rather than push she gestured to the crowd.

"Tell them what you told me," she said.

Charlie nodded, stepping clear of his new friend to face the group. "I assume you all attempted to get out of here already." Agreements all around mixed with various excuses for why that had not yet occurred. Their words of resignation revealed a sense of fear behind the fact they could not find a way out. The TV host stood tall, trying to offer hope. "Everything I've studied before, my search for answers, my belief in the unbelievable has fallen short until now. This is different, it is real. I believe we all traveled through a portal."

"Portals? You covered that on your show once," Ethan said.

"All bullshit. I spoke to so-called experts on my program but the actual ones? That would be us. I think we collectively stepped through a version, but my bigger point is where there is a way in, we can find an out."

"No worries, guys. If you have ever dropped before, you travel through some weird doors. This is not the weirdest place **I've** been to," Herb said.

Stan got in his face. "This isn't a trip. I don't do drugs you jerk."

"Maybe that's your problem, man."

Martin remained focused on Charlie. "I think you're asking the wrong question. Why us? If someone prepped nine settings—a sign they expected that many—then what do we have in common? Identifying our commonality could be our answer to getting out of here."

"The carpetbagger makes sense," Herb chimed in.

"Horse hockey. There must be a way out. I do not care why or how I got here but I want out now. So, if you are right, ghost boy, how do we do this?" Victor asked.

"I cannot say for certain, but a change in air pressure could signal an out. Otherwise, we can waste time banging on windows that magically do not shatter. The place is huge, I think we should split up," Charlie said.

"Aren't we safer together?" Suzy asked.

"We're slower that way, can't cover as much ground," Stan agreed.

Beth gripped Suzy's shoulder. "I'll stick with you, female power and all that crap." Suzy grasped Beth's hand, nodding a thanks.

"Well, I am not going with the carpetbagger," Herb said.

"Fine, the kid and I will investigate the top floor," Martin said.

"Which fool gets the basement?" Victor asked.

"I will take the cellar since I am used to roaming around dark places, and point of fact, it is our best shot at an out," Charlie said.

"We'll go with you," Suzy said.

"I'm flying solo. No offense but I don't much like people," Victor said.

"Really? Hadn't noticed. Guess it's me and the mechanic," Herb offered.

"Scrapyard employee, not a mechanic," Stan said.

The clank of silverware caught everyone's attention. They looked over to find Pearl settled in a chair opposite the goose. She shook an apron out with aplomb, draping it across her lap before picking up a fork and knife. She poised the utensils above the bird.

"While you all play about, I aim to carve this old fowl. Care to join me? I am ready to eat, too famished to pray first even. Anyone?"

Pearl reacted to all the blank stares by slicing through the goose's throat. She lifted the long appendage into the air on the tip of her blade, brought the end of the neck to her mouth and chewed. Suzy turned away, pale, while the others groaned in disgust.

"The sooner we find a way out, the faster we can get her help," Martin said.

Everyone nodded agreements then exited except for Ethan and the politician. The young neighbor leaned next to his former neighbor, placing his hand on the table. She gnawed hungrily on the neck, moaning in delight as the crispy skin grinded under teeth like crunching bones.

"Pearl, we will look for a way out, do you understand?"

She looked at the man with eyes as soft as a Disney animal before suddenly arcing the blade through the air just shy of Ethan's face! She stabbed alongside where his hand rested then raised the knife holding a potato prize. He fell onto his ass as she lifted the treat towards her mouth before snarling.

"You're interrupting my dinner."

Ethan grabbed Martin's outstretched arm to get back up and the two men left the room.

CHAPTER 12

"I don't like the looks of this at all. Shouldn't we call in the cavalry?" Calvin asked.

"My deputies are busy dealing with the body par..." Watkins stopped himself, covering as best he could. "An accident, tourists, fatalities. We're on our own for now."

"The rotary?" Big Rick asked.

The sheriff nodded prompting the two locals to parrot in understanding. The lawman did not want to share information about the true nature of the crime scene for fear his assistants might lose their nerve, or worse, leave to tell the world. He planned to seek help soon enough but first needed to understand the ties between the structure and the severed limbs.

The two mysteries could be unrelated, the decapitation reeked of a drug deal, but the barbed wire element with the hands felt like ceremony. Was there something he was missing, a message? Beyond the sheriff's curious desire to return to the accident, his job required him to do so. By now the Portland detective would have questions for him as the first cop on the scene. The man was likely hot already that a quick lunch detour turned into a much longer absence. While the city officer had every right not to accept any excuses, there was a bigger mystery left to solve, one bordering on the unreal. Possibly solving the second situation would inform the first.

The neighbors brought him up to speed on everything they knew about the home after hearing about it from their boys. Upon arrival, they initially circled the entire estate and reported no other doors (of which there should have been several in such a massive building). They mentioned the rear branched into twin wings and noted the hill dropped so steeply and quickly at the back that the first-floor windows were too high to reach. He could have canvassed for himself, but the men's recounting was thorough and there was enough for now to keep him occupied.

He figured Rick as the type to have a ladder in his truck, but that could wait. Possibly. Reaching the front door would not be an easy task. Though the equipment might be the best way to gain entry, given his druthers, the sheriff preferred not to anchor the legs of one on a non-grip surface like stone.

Cellar windows, while easily reachable on both ends of the home, were too small for any of them to fit through and the kids were no longer around to climb through for them, maybe unlock the place from inside. No despite the adventurous curiosity of children, the boys were too terrified to return, too freaked at the circumstance they shared with their parents, swearing the field to be empty when they began to play only to suddenly find, within a breath's time, an architectural behemoth appear behind them.

The only thing making any sense—but then again made none—was if the building had raised straight up from the depths of hell. Perhaps demonic workers prefabricated it in the bowels of the earth before pushing it through the ground. It bothered the sheriff to consider that the most logical idea he had. He led his crew up the right side of the elevated front lawn.

The closest windows fell within reach of the hill crest. After that, the others continued along the face of the building in an increasingly steep drop over the center jagged quarry. Reaching the end of the porch would require one to navigate across the narrow ridge of the decorative stone wall for dozens of feet. After arriving at the railing there would be thick tree branches to contend with but after that it would be smooth sailing to the front door. As excited as his posse appeared to be, he planned to remain on point, enter the enclosure first.

Watkins cursed his shortness of breath while climbing the gentle slope. Despite being an officer and a hunter, the hill stole air from his lungs. The neighbors fared no better. The onset of a complaint rose from Big Rick only for it to vanish under a yawn as the man sought oxygen. It relieved the sheriff to discover he was not the only one out of shape.

He considered the raised land itself might not be entirely responsible for his physical malaise as it could have more to do with a decapitated head in a crime lab along with hands wrapped in prayer back at the rotary! If his heart were to race, to skip extra beats given how his day had gone so far, it would explain why oxygen was a little harder to come by. The only thing he felt certain of was it being unrelated to all the drawn butter in his life.

The others hiking alongside him were unaware of the day's prior events so what was their excuse? Oh yeah, someone dropped a massive architectural oddity in their neighborhood which, in theory, could have crushed their boys. No. In shape or not, it was hard to breathe because their hearts all worked overtime. There was a further intangible at work. The place felt—*wrong*.

During traffic stops, the sheriff occasionally

experienced a version of a sixth sense, believing if he took another step, it could be his last. None of his previous 'Spider sense' incidents ever ended in bloodshed so if someone planned violence only to abort at the end, he would never know. Regardless, those earlier fears, at their worst, paled compared to what he was feeling now.

This place provided that weird intuition times ten along with a deeper belief that this time his gut was spot on. It felt bad because it was. Very. Not only that, but he sensed in his mind it desired something specific of him—for him to leave. He could almost hear it in his head.

Sheriff, I require you and the looky-loos to please go away thank you very much. I have many dark secret house things to do today and you, my friends and neighbors, do not fit into my plans.

If this home was a driver pulled over on a desolate road, it would come out shooting before spitting on the body of whoever lay dying. The thing gave him the idea that it was not only alive, but evil. Poppycock, he thought to himself and tried to steel himself as not to make the others wary.

They reached the top of the hill and gathered along the right corner where a tree partially blocked their way. The dead grey trunk leaned into the structure as if a drunk exiting a bar seeking any support to remain on his feet. The pretzel like limbs frustratingly obscured the first set of windows within reach.

Watkins planned to climb across the tree, using the branches as an anchor to keep from tumbling back downhill. He reached over to test the stability when a branch broke so unexpectedly it caused him to fall into the fractured limb which speared straight into his hand.

"Son of a bitch!" he yelled.

Told you, Sheriff, I do not bark, I bite, and I do not want any local-yocals hovering around me. I got work to do here. You all are distracting me, so if you keep it up, I will make things unpleasant. Watkins felt it say within his mind.

Yanking his arm free, blood drooled from the

splintered wood feeding the dirt below their feet. The bleach white color of bone showed through torn muscle and flesh until it faded to red as blood pooled across his open palm. The neighborhood posse took a gander.

"Shit on a shingle, we need to get you to a hospital," Calvin said.

"The cursed place drew first blood. That can't be a good sign," Big Rick said.

It concerned the sheriff how the two men suddenly viewed the place. Their eyes opened in wonder looking at it as more than wood and nails, now viewing it the way he had earlier, as something alive. He could be wrong since he was only reading their faces, but that was what he did for a living and he was skilled at it.

Watkins removed his work coat followed by his shirt and Tee wrapping the undergarment tightly around his palm until the yellowed white fabric turned red. He slipped his oxford back on, struggling to button it closed with his uninjured hand. He painfully managed three before deciding it was good enough for modesty's sake. He left the jacket on the ground while pulling a rubber glove from his pocket to slip it over the wrapped injury. The elastic wrist snapped into place despite the overall triage bulging akin to an elephant limb. The field dressing staunched the bleeding yet still hurt like hell.

"Maybe we should call someone," Calvin said.

"I am the one you would on these things, remember?"

"No offense, but you're cut bad. You need stitches as sure as I'm a love machine. I think this place done chomped your hand. It took a bite," Big Rick said.

"I got careless, broke a branch is all. Now if you two grown men will stop shittin' your pants, can we get a look inside?"

Collectively they decided the blocked window not worth their time since a foliage free version loomed ahead. They gave the tree a wide berth while making their way across only to find any hopes of a quick view dashed upon discovering the next set of windows obstructed, one by an interior curtain, the other with a closed shutter. Normally, the sheriff would never enter a home without a view inside for safety's sake, but this was far from a normal time. All they had to do was lift the sash and crawl in. He deferred the lead to his makeshift posse because of his injury.

"Big Rick, will you do the honors?" Watkins asked.

The man grasped the base attempting to open it with no luck. Whether twisted in the frame or locked from inside, it did not budge.

Calvin yanked the louvered panel. "Dang, this won't move either."

"It has to. One can lock a window but not a shutter without a latch, and I don't see none." Big Rick nudged his friend aside to try it himself. The large man whose biceps lived up to his name strained before grasping the edge with both hands to put his weight into it. Nothing. "How is that possible?" He searched the perimeter of the worn cover for a locking mechanism.

Watkins conducted a cursory search before urging the men on rather than dwell on fresh impossibilities. "Never mind. Onward it is then. This one warped over time is all."

The group moved forward, Calvin in the lead. Thick grime covered the next glass surface, opaque enough to keep any secrets hidden. The ground below them receded to the point it forced them to step onto the rock-wall ledge to reach their destination.

Rick failed in his effort again, a look of worry crossing his face. Upon noticing the others observing him, he visibly shrugged it off, brightened with an idea. "Locked from within I suppose. Maybe we're looking at this wrong, there could be some treasure inside."

"If there is it appears guarded by the world's toughest glass, or the world's weakest neighbor," Calvin suggested.

"Give me your gun," Rick said.

Watkins winced at the thought of handing over his weapon but could think of no alternative. He damn sure would not try to fashion a club from any tree branch. He fumbled to remove the bullets, did not need it going off while smashing their way in. It relieved him to discover full mobility in his injured hand which suggested he suffered no nerve damage even though it still throbbed like an ill-natured son of a bitch. He handed the empty gun to Rick.

The big man swung the butt against the pane, gently, mindful not to allow his arm to join the party through possible jagged edges. Upon contact, the revolver bounced back with a weird "thunk." Calvin laughed at the man's failure as if watching a braggart unable to ring the strongman bell at a county fair. Embarrassed, the man swung harder eliciting another muffled sound. Calvin's sense of dread vanished at the sight of someone nicknamed Big Rick being served by a thin sheet of heated sand.

"Need me to take a shot?" Calvin asked in between chuckles.

"No, I do not. I didn't want my arm slashed, so I went easy on it. Enough of that, so be it then."

Rick slammed harder to no discernible effect. The large man stepped away in surprise. Watkins pressed his hands against Rick's back to keep the man from slipping onto the rocky ground below. Despite his earlier amusement, Calvin's laughter died in his throat.

"I think you are right, Calvin, time to call in the cavalry. Something is way beyond not normal here, and I'm not just talking about the house popping up sudden like," Watkins said.

Calvin looked ahead where he spied the first partially open curtain since they began canvassing the home. The curious man ignored the others, inching across the stone ledge for a peek. Part way to the window he slipped, froze in place until finding his footing again and then moved on. The sheriff watched nervously while trying to make sense of the whole day's course of events, how everything might tie together.

Suddenly the voice sounded so clear he could not chalk it up to imagination any longer. *"Did not receive the message, huh? I have got stuff to do here and you all are as distracting as flees on a mutt, so what say you all mosey along. Or I can force you to leave, yeah, that is it. Lesson time, Sheriff."*

"Calvin, wait!" Watkins yelled.

But it was too late, the local man had already reached his destination unaware the voice in the sheriff's head was about to make good on its threat.

CHAPTER 13

Pearl looked out upon the feast and declared it good. She had set the neck back on the plate where its beak now faced her seat at the head of the table. It was a position attributed to her in their marriage, never to her husband, Clayton. She ran things in the homestead, especially in their later years.

She despised geese as they were ornery creatures prone to nip at her heels or skirt if she strayed too close to them in the backyard pond where she grew up in Oxford. Those days suffering the wrath of the miserable feathered fowl happened during childhood well before she ever moved to Tether Falls. Pearl routinely begged her parents to remove the offensive creatures from their property, but they rebuffed her at every turn. At a certain age she came to understand their true intentions for the animals, the reason her guardians allowed the continued existence of the beasts. It turns out they were not above serving the birds as a main course. Great delight accompanied that first meal featuring a goose staring at her from under a butter blanket atop an oversized platter. She swore from then forward to serve the animal every holiday, considering it frontier justice to find the miserable things on a plate.

Pearl had the strangest feeling she had recently spoken to several people whom she did not know. That could not be could it? Her mornings began fuzzy lately and only grew fuzzier as the day progressed to where remembering what she did moments earlier became an exercise in futility.

Her life now emulated the game Match. The concept was simple, spread cards face down and turn over two at a time until the deck was complete. Easy enough except even in her younger minded clarity there was always a lone troublesome card flipped repeatedly only to become absurdly undiscoverable when needed. That was how her memory worked lately. Every thought was that elusive card keeping her from connecting it to the next.

She fully remembered her hatred for geese though, that memory lingered as fresh as remembering how much she despised dinners with her husband—always him with his cough. He could not sit at a table for more than a moment without hacking. Worse, it was never a one and done exercise, more of a constant hemming, hawing, stopping, repeat, like a cat working out a hairball. It was the most common cause of their disputes. Why wouldn't he just hack it up to get it over with?

"It's not a fuzzball, it is the smoke in the air when you cook!" Clayton would always yell back in between grotesque throat clearings.

Well, that finally ended, Pearl figured. She ate in peace now, could not be happier. The occasional smiles or compliments he threw her way if he believed a certain meal worthy of comment vanished from her life when he did. Any joy she might have gained from such praise was so rare as to be negligible in affecting her daily mood so despite any lost satisfaction related to those fleeting moments of recognition, she found herself relieved to be free of his omnipresent physical failings. There was little happiness regarding Clayton when he was alive.

Pearl knew the room she now sat in well. The couple shared a singularly prosperous period in life once when cash was flush. Back then mortgages were cheap enough it afforded them a beautiful two-story colonial in Norway with ease. Relatives regularly congregated at their home given it was the largest owned by either of their families. It encompassed a sweeping backyard with a pond, (free of geese) lush green lawn, and multiple weeping willows which, in betrayal of their namesake, comforted her when she looked upon them.

How did it get so bad with her and Clayton? When had it gone wrong? She understood she would never pinpoint the exact date their bond fractured since she could not even remember what she had for lunch, or if she had eaten at all that day. And who were those people she spoke to earlier? They seemed upset to be in her dining room. This was her eating area for sure. Her daft husband left the proof behind via his infernal wood burning kit.

He thought it might please her to use his new toy to carve her initials into the head of table chair. While she was happy that he formally recognized her status, she would not give him any satisfaction toward his ill-advised handiwork, outright scolding him for marking their expensive furniture. Years later they held a yard sale, (before moving into their smaller place in Tether Falls) and the autographed arm rest reduced the set's value to a distressingly low price versus what they paid.

Gripping the chair, she rubbed her hand over the indented initials, finding comfort in the memory. She wondered how it came to be she was back in their Norway, Maine house from all those years ago. Or was this the present? Had she only been dreaming of another life recently? Had they never moved from their first place? Did they not hold a yard sale, never sell the chairs at a loss? Was Clayton's fate perhaps only a dream?

Possibly, yet she somehow remembered everything about his death.

Bam!

She startled in the chair as something banged from the next room, deafeningly loud. It repeated. Maybe Clayton was still around. It would be so much like him to interrupt her supper.

"Stop that noise!"

When the banging continued, she left her goose to find out what all the fuss was about.

CHAPTER 14

"It's too dark down there, let's explore the rest of the house," Beth said, gripping Suzy's shoulders.

Whatever strength the bank manager showed in front of the others earlier faded once faced with the unknown. The basement proved easy to find after locating the kitchen just off the dining room. Like in so many homes, the entrance to the cellar was there. Rickety wooden steps stretched down into the dim interior until reaching a dirt floor, something common in the region. Beth was correct in that it was darker than the rest of the house, but soft light bled into view from somewhere, dancing around the edges of uncertainty below. Light meant sunlight, and sunlight meant escape? Where the others saw the beginnings of a slasher film, Charlie saw hope.

"There are windows, plus, we have our cell phones. Our eyes will adjust, I assure you, I've gone through this before," Charlie said.

"My guess is you explored with camera mounted lights,

infrared cameras," Beth said.

The 'ghost host' cringed. She had his number. As frightening as things looked on screen, exploring bleak realms often came with the security blanket of high-tech equipment. The banker appeared to know her stuff.

Like before, Suzy stepped in with the save. "Charlie here is an expert. We're in good hands with you, isn't that right?"

"Crawling around dark spaces and houses, yes, but make no mistakes, I don't understand what we are dealing with. My TV show seems goofy in comparison now. My research was always real, I hold certain beliefs, but this is the first time I have ever experienced anything undeniably paranormal. You have all officially reached the same level of expertise as me."

The opportunity to ease Beth's mind had fluttered away with his candor. He felt it best to prepare them for the creepiness factor he knew all too well from roaming in long-forgotten places. They were about to enter the belly of an unknown beast. He grasped how his uncertainty bred tenuousness in his partners so asserted a veil of authority despite remaining nervous himself.

"So, this is an actual haunted house and we're descending into the cellar?" Suzy asked.

"The likeliest place to discover an exit," Charlie said.

"And dead bodies. I am with Beth on this one, I think we shouldn't go down."

"Look, we all want the same thing, to get out. The sooner we explore, the faster we will find a way. I'm going."

He stepped gingerly, testing the wood while illuminating his progress with the meager light of his cell phone. The steps creaked but held as he moved down.

The women looked at each other before deciding on safety in numbers. They followed, moving quickly to catch up. Charlie felt a shift underfoot, a rumbling vibration. He turned to warn them.

"Wait, stop!"

It was too late. The integrity of the stairs shifted as something snapped. They tumbled, falling in a flood of debris, the wreckage matching their trajectory. Dirt puffed high into the air along with a flutter of disturbed cobwebs until all went still leaving the trio sprawled in a heap. The door above them slammed with the equivalent force that initially brought them all together.

CHAPTER 15

Despite the warning, Calvin inched forward to his destination, arriving at a split pane where one side was blocked by a curtain but the other finally offered a room with a view. Raising a hand instinctively to minimize glare, he quickly lowered it, deeming it unnecessary given how dark the skies above remained. Inside was a grand sized sitting room with generous lofty ceilings appearing as antiquated as the exterior of the home. Furniture covered by white fabric filled out the chamber across from which an entry way led out of view. Based on the covered shapes of the décor there was a loveseat, multiple chairs, a few tables of various kinds. Some pieces offered glimpses of legs like the slight rise of a woman's skirt. Calvin whistled at the possibility they all stumbled upon an antiquities score. One large sheet covered chair faced directly toward the window.

"What the hell do you see?" Rick asked.

Calvin tilted, grasping the sill to keep from falling. A steep drop loomed perilously below him. Regaining his composure along with his footing, he looked accusingly at his oversized neighbor who shrugged an 'oops.'

"You almost made me lose my Snickers Big Rick."

"Stop the squawking. What do you see?" Watkins asked.

"Nothing but some antique furniture. Mighty fine kind, I half-reckon. Otherwise, it's just a regular house." Turning back, he screamed at the sight of an old woman staring directly at him. "Jesus, Mary, and... shit!"

The woman looked past Calvin, seemingly unaware of his presence while furrowing her brow in frustration. Giving up, she moved back into the center of the room. Turning her head in both directions, Calvin thought she looked a little lost.

"Pearl is in there."

"Pearl who?" Big Rick asked.

"Our Pearl from Tether Falls."

"Pearl Fournier?" Watkins asked.

"The same. She doesn't seem to notice me. Hey Pearl! Pearl, it's me, Calvin. What are you doing in the house?"

Inside, she angrily spun in a circle. "If anyone is here, show yourself."

"She's talking but I can't hear her. I'll give it a knock, maybe that will get her attention."

Raising an arm to tap away, he suddenly froze in place, staring wide-eyed ahead. Inside, Pearl turned her back to the front facing chair and as she did so, the white fabric rose as if someone underneath the entire time. The figure stood at least six-foot-tall, its cover long enough to brush the floor with no sign of feet.

Whatever possessed the sheet tilted its neck at Pearl before turning toward the open door nearby. Pearl appeared unaware of the visitor. It was not unlike the ghost from the Charlie Brown cartoon except minus the scissors problem as there were no holes at all, none even for eyes, yet somehow it navigated fine.

The figure exited ahead of Pearl and vanished out of

sight through the doorway to the left. Pearl followed, oblivious, but turned right. Calving sighed in relief once he saw Pearl turn the other way. Then suddenly, the clothed being darted across the opening at an impossible speed in Pearl's direction.

Calvin spun, losing control of his feet and vocal cords as he screamed loudly. Tumbling off the ledge head-first, his skull met stones with a sickening crunch. The other two men rushed down the hill, circling around to discover the rock bed gleaming red. The man jerked in tight little twitches making no discernable sound, spasming while his brain tried to auto-correct whatever just occurred. Rick arrived first, searching for life in his neighbor's eyes. Calvin's pupils suggested lights were on, but nobody was home. The burly man tore off his shirt to stem the bleeding which originated somewhere under the man's hairline.

The sheriff understood full well how bad it was having responded to so many similar accidents for teens who did not clear the rock ledge at Tether Falls Leap (the leap was just over the border, so he got as many calls as Willow PD.) A series of cliffs served as a jump station for the daring and the stupid. While the water was deep enough to dive into, the jump required clearing a cliff-side which sloped outward from the starting point. Many could not make the distance which was when things turned ugly. Some kids made it with simple stitches, others did not make it at all, leaving the balance to come out "special o-kay." Calvin did not look okay though, not by a stretch. Watkins heard the voice in his head again.

"Told you, stupid son of a bitch. Mess with me it will not end well for you. Think this is all I can do? You ain't seen nothing yet. I am on a schedule here, so I would ask you to get off my damn lawn unless you need me to teach you another lesson. That body in that trunk you were dealing with? That is mine too, so what is the holdup there? I am taking a dislike to you, Sheriff. I think just maybe I should do something beyond snacking on your hand. Might open a

door for you here. What can I do to get you into a house like this?"

"Jesus, Sheriff!"

By calling his title, instead of his name, it signaled the citizen was frightened enough to yell instinctively for law enforcement. Watkins turned back to the bloody victim, spotting it just as Rick stated the obvious.

"His hair? It's gone white."

CHAPTER 16

Charlie and Suzy dug through the debris to free Beth who took the brunt of the fall after somehow landing beneath the others. The banker's previously polished look gave way to that of an accident victim. Abrasions covered her body along with some visible bruising though nothing bled heavily. The injured woman mourned aloud over the damage to her pantyhose sporting matching tears across both thighs, mentioning she only recently purchased them.

"Is everyone all right?" Charlie asked.

"No! I'm sitting in the damn bank when a door creaks open then I end up in a weird house in a field? No, I'm far from okay!" Beth pushed the others away only to realize her legs were unsteady as she fell into Suzy who held her up. "I am fine in relation to the fall though, yes, thank you."

"Let's find this way out and quick. Charlie, if you know anything, if you learned information from your show, please use it to get us out of here."

Charlie did not answer, as he was too busy digging through the debris, working methodically at first before growing more frantic. "My cell phone has vanished."

The women found theirs missing too so joined in but soon stopped, figuring the debris field was not that grand, there was not anything left to search. They looked at each other in wonder, a bubble of fear began to flit across their faces. Charlie finally noticed the door had closed.

"None of this is right. Forget horror movies where people do stupid things. In actual haunting cases a common question asked of inhabitants is why they stay as long as they do."

"Like Amityville?" Suzy asked.

"Yes, and many other places I have researched. The circumstances we are in should frighten us, yet to a person, when we stood in the group, we acted curious versus fearful, far calmer than the situation warranted. Take just you, Suzy, so frantic when we met though quite calm ever since. My first impression of you is closer to the truth than what I have seen since. That was the authentic you, the righteously frightened version. I believe something has gotten into our heads and since our cell phones didn't just walk away, it means whatever that thing is it may be with us even now."

"I'm still plenty scared, especially after this fresh bit of bad news," Beth offered.

"Good, stay that way, it may be what saves you. The door above is closed, stairs removed. It's as if we are being kept from the others so we cannot warn them."

"Of what?" Suzy asked.

"That they too should be afraid. Very afraid."

CHAPTER 17

Victor was more annoyed than anything else. Sure, there was something crazy going on, no doubt there. What bothered him most was how a bunch of strangers questioned his sanity based on his decision to go solo, ignoring their pleas for him to join a group until they gave up. Half the troops tramped up the stairs in their safety-in-number pairs while the lucky bastard with the two hot twats went downstairs. He took the second floor by himself. Victor needed no one because he understood that which he had always known—it was his destiny to be alone—a lesson learned back in Boston.

Walking the long hallway in search of an exit, he considered his situation while the others pranced around on different floors. Yes, he would be just fine without the nattering classes nipping at his freewheeling heels. A solitary lifestyle was routine for him one could say, a muscle memory developed while living in a one-bedroom apartment after an "incident" forced him to leave the home he once shared with his wife.

Victor married Cora straight out of high school. Year fifteen together was when it all went to shit. He worked in a shoe store when the pair started dating. Strange how his job outlasted his marriage he thought. Over the years she regularly rode him over his failure to move up the ladder since they both wanted children. It supplied her with an automatic weapon's worth of ammunition with which to hound him about.

Budda, budda, budda! "Kids. Family. Better car," she would say, firing her shots. Budda, budda, budda! "Vacations. Retirement. Rugrats again!" He shuddered at the memory of all the blasts fired in his direction. True, he was the gun enthusiast, but she could shoot off her mouth like the best-trained sniper, each syllable striking its target even if he never heard the bullet coming.

She did not want to start a family until they were better off financially. In that regard she considered him the weak link. Cora worked as a temp at a law firm where she quickly moved up while taking classes toward a degree. Victor, meanwhile, lost traction on his employment status when the store merged with a competitor. After years of greasing wheels at his wife's behest, he suddenly found himself at the mercy of bosses half his age and a pay reduction close to the same as the new owners offered a lesser commission.

Promising they would stick it out together, she suggested he look for a new career after she settled more securely into her own. She already made as much per year as he did—more in fact—but she also went out frequently with her work friends which cost plenty. She often invited him along, but he never felt the need for company which she argued was why she advanced while he flatlined. She spoke of politics behind workplace relationships, and besides, it was something to do, and was fun. She regularly chided his isolationist tendencies.

The most common retort in his repertoire (never delivered at anything other than a high decibel level) came in the form of asking whether she thought buying alcohol for underage bosses would earn him mover and shaker status. She would look at him sadly and ask when he stopped being so social, reminding him they used to have a lot of mutual friends though even those folks eventually faded away.

One night, he noticed something different in Cora's eyes, a stilted mannerism in his presence suggesting she made peace with a decision—one not shared with him. He relentlessly probed while she danced on the edge of answering, twirling like a ballerina around any version of the truth. What he read on her face he chalked up to one word—guilt.

Upon leaving that evening, Victor tore through their home in search of answers, eventually finding what he was looking for in their spare bedroom which acted as her crafts room where a desk used as a workstation sat nestled alongside a single bed and a rocking chair. The evidence was that of a bank statement unrelated to their joint account, one in her name with a balance larger than the amount in their shared account. The bitch had been holding out on him. Why?

She likely had a lover. The only question was which of the chumps in their three-piece outfits was it? The thought angered him further. Who wore suits anymore? He hated the privileged scumbags in her office, who felt they could own anything, including another man's wife. He knew what he had to do.

Later that night, after texting she was on her way home, he turned a favorite chair toward the front door. The same message mentioned a surprise. *Well, honey cheeks I've got one too.* Soon the thump of car doors closing outside sounded followed by encroaching laughter. Two sets of high heels clip-clopped up the driveway. He recognized the second voice as that of Cora's friend Trudy (a looker who could be a hooker he thought). The pair drunkenly stumbled through the door laughing, the friend clutching a bottle of wine, Cora a tinfoil swan. Neither noticed him sitting shotgun in hand.

"I figured it was a guy you were leaving me for, didn't realize it was for a lesbian."

"What the fuck is…" Trudy started.

Victor pulled the trigger. The explosive force launched Trudy off her feet even as her stomach tore open, blossoming red as she pounded into the door and crumpled to the ground, leaning against it. Her right hand held the fractured neck of the wine bottle aloft, the bottom half gone so the alcohol cascaded down mixing indistinguishably with her blood. Guts spilled from the exposed wound, spreading all around her in one large liquid squish. Her glazed eyes locked on her killer as if to repeat the same question she posed a heartbeat ago only she never spoke again.

Cora screamed in shock at the sight of her dead friend. She saw her husband ready the gun in her direction so hurled the leftovers throwing off his aim as the shot hit the ceiling. She rushed the stairs as he gave chase.

"You've been hiding money! You've been lying, you've been cheating!"

Cora struggled to flee in high heels. She crested the top of the stairs only to find escape options limited. She frantically made for the craft room while his footsteps pounded close behind. She slammed the door.

"Baby, please! It's not like that. Listen!"

While searching frantically for a way out, she spied the bank statements on the desk. Those pages had created the monster. She bolted for the window. A thunderous boom exploded behind her, jolting her entire body.

Reaching behind her back, she inspected the damage only to have her hand come away smeared red. The door crunched as Victor kicked what remained open. She pulled a large sliver of wood from her side, shrapnel from the defeated slab. She grabbed scissors off the desk before turning to face her husband who smirked at the sight of her bringing a knife to a gunfight. She waved it toward him, anyway.

"I'm bleeding, baby!"

"You planned to run off. You hid all that money when we were struggling to get by."

"No, no, no. I was saving, yes, for our family. I wasn't running away."

"Why did you bring the whore home?"

She struggled to understand who he meant, so he tilted his head toward the hall and stairs beyond. Turning further ashen upon realizing he meant Trudy, she pleaded with him. "The office party, we were bringing it back to you. The wine, the food, some company, you've been so alone. Honey, it was for you."

Victor kept the weapon trained on his wife, remembering words his father used to say, "*if you ever point a gun at someone you had better plan to use it.*"

"You're lying. You were saving money until you could run away. You were whoring together, finding men at your parties."

"Never, I never cheated, please believe me. We can go back, you know, to how things were, I will add you to the account."

"And what about your friend? You'll keep that secret while we stay married?"

She gave the nod her best effort, but she tightened her grip on the scissors as if to suggest she would stab him given half the chance. He felt he could read her thoughts. And why not? They had been together for so long. He saw through her false pleas, understanding that no, *she sure as shit was not okay with covering up her friend's death, not okay at all.*

He fired. She slammed into the window so hard she bounced back falling onto her knees, grabbing her bloodied stomach. A cascade of red poured over her hands while she pressed instinctively over the wound, looking up at him and wailing.

"Oh, what did you do?"

Victor lowered the rifle, touched her shoulder. She gripped his hand, looking back and forth between him and the fluid nature of her injury.

"Oh Victor, oh, please, oh it's bad."

Her other hand reached out for the floor lazily searching for a soft place to rest. She dropped to her side, her head bouncing once before settling into a wide-open stare, looking straight at him. She muttered one last thing.

"I'm pregnant…"

The words hit as if he were the one shot. He shook her, demanded to know if she was lying but it was too late. He held her in his lap, screamed at the loss of his child. Was he wrong, in his assumptions? Was she saving for a better life for their family? Bettering herself for the two of them?

No, she plotted against him. She planned to run off and take their money, their kid. Was she even going to tell him she was pregnant or just leave before he could find out? There was still a chance for the little one.

He called nine-one-one begging the operator to send someone to save his unborn child. Victor's anguish during the call cost the paramedics precious time though the same frantic conversation eventually got him off at trial. His lawyer crafted a story around Cora's hidden bank account and how she armed herself with scissors. During the trial it came out that Trudy had been having an affair, cheating on her own husband, helping to line up the story she also had an affair with Cora. The jury believed the defense's framework that his wife and her lover intended to kill Victor before running away together with her stashed loot.

The jurors deliberated for only three hours before coming back with a not guilty verdict. He was free. Not only that, he also inherited Cora's nest egg. Life was suddenly looking up when women at work noticed that the older 'dude' was now a bachelor with cache and cash. The widower took his dead wife's advice, becoming social again. He hosted parties that left his house regularly torn up by younger folks leaching off his beer while doing drugs which always appeared from somewhere.

Victor looked at the younger women as nothing more than whores and treated them as exactly that. Random female partygoers, all legal but too young for him, would often spend the night. They had no interest in his life story, nor he theirs. He only cared about the pleasures of their flesh.

It was not long before the partying took a toll on Victor's work performance. He was often late since he could not recover as fast as his younger coworkers. Rumors spread of his dalliances with women in the workplace. Word was that one woman (heck, more of a girl) had gotten an abortion.

That news reached Victor through the same grapevine feeding info to his bosses. It angered him immensely how she gave him no say in the matter. He confronted the young woman, Mary, on the job. Turns out she had a boyfriend—an exceptionally large black one who was none too pleased with Victor harassing her.

Human resources finally fired Victor, forbade him from returning to their store. Still upset about the second loss of a child, he stalked his former workplace until catching the employee alone in the parking lot on a smoke break. She rolled eyes upon his arrival but did not walk away, fidgeting with her cigarette as they spoke.

"You had an abortion?"

She nodded.

"You sure it was mine?" He shrugged when she eyed him harshly. "What, I've seen your boyfriend. How do you know it's not him?"

"We don't do that. We do other stuff, but I'm saving that. We're getting married. I love him not you. So, doing it with you was like, well, okay, you know? Get it out of my system and all that before I settle down. Plus, I was high when we did it."

She went back to fidgeting. Victor ran his hands

through his thin hair, pacing the lot.

"That was my kid? You took my child away without telling me!"

"Your kid? I AM one. I mean eighteen and all but jeez, you're old. I can't have a baby with you. I was in it for the beer, dude. It started cool, but everyone got weirded out. You could be my Dad for shit's sake."

He aged at that moment. His wife kept his family secret from him for unknown reasons. Did she really plan to surprise him that night? Now this woman who would have borne him a child took that from him without consultation. She decided for him just like the other woman in his life had. She also insulted him by saying he was old. He was only in his forties for Christ's sake. Who was she to call him that? There was only one thing he could do.

Plastic and bone crunched when he punched her, obliterating the nose job gifted to her at sixteen. The already shoddy work vanished just that easily. Blood gushed from her nostrils. The cigarette dangled, sticking to her lip by the trail of crimson pouring over and into her mouth. She raised a hand as he struck again catching her on the side of the head. She stumbled, falling, further injuring herself on the asphalt.

The scuffle brought other workers outside—two males and one female. The woman attempted to aid Mary except the injured party rose off the ground and leaped through the air onto Victor's back. He screamed when she bit his ear. The guys shifted from protecting their fellow employee to trying to pull her off him.

Victor spent the day in jail. Upon release, he found her boyfriend lying in wait, so he slipped away to a hotel. Mary had a regular bevy of friends keep watch over his place, breaking many of his windows during their stakeouts and spray-painting variations of the word 'bitch' on HIS home! After a week of checking on his place he realized they were in for the long haul which meant it was time for him to pull up stakes. Under the cover of night, he used a moving company to help him quickly vacate, moving to a one-bedroom apartment in Southie back when the area was affordable. That was the last he would ever see of his house, all because of the "incident" with his wife.

The new "home" didn't last long as it turns out, even the criminal element in the neighborhood did not take kindly to manhandling women. Once they discovered his past, they urged him to extricate himself, hinting strongly that the next ask would not be so polite. He did not consider their first ask entirely courteous given how it came delivered via a no-neck guy with a Boston accent so strong he almost requested a translator. A reconfiguration of all the windows in his car with him still inside accompanied the large man's request.

Victor complied, moving north to Tether Falls in Maine. He lived there for a decade, alone—just how he liked it—until a strange door appeared in his kitchen and delivered him to a wacky funhouse minus any of the fun. The thoughts of his past brought with it anger which he used to his advantage while trying to extricate himself from his current situation by punching at a window in an attempt to escape.

He did not realize how hard he was pounding on the window before him until he felt skin break on his knuckles. Despite the pain, he repeatedly punched the surface, unconcerned about flesh meeting jagged edges consequences if it were to shatter. Why wouldn't it break? It took only one punch for Mary's face to crack. Glass was more fragile than bone, why would it not do the same?

After trying to bury any thoughts of Boston since arriving in Maine, his dormant memories flooded back to him with every strike while his hands abraded just shy of drawn blood. He finally stopped, massaging his knuckles. It was true he had grown accustomed to being alone but on his own terms, not trapped. He would find an exit with no help from the townsfolk he never wanted to meet.

Before he could fully shake off his past life, he heard something. Was that a child's cry? In the door's shadow he saw a tiny figure (or animal?) dart by. If a critter found a way in, surely there was an out. By nature, it would run from him on pure instinct. All Victor had to do was chase it to an escape route. He rushed out into the hall.

Light from alternating rooms shone in a staggered manner along the long corridor much like the interior of a freight truck riddled with bullet holes. The cry sounded again, that of a child (or maybe a baby?) followed by a childish giggle. The tiny figure emerged from shadows only to dash out of sight again. Laughter echoed around him.

"Hello?" Victor understood from experience some animal cries emulated human sounds, but he believed it to be a child's voice. "If you're here show yourself, I won't hurt you."

He glimpsed movement again, from a shape hard to isolate. Whatever it might be, it moved deeper into the house. He refused to give up. After twice losing out on having children, he would not lose this one. He gave chase using the haunting laughter as his GPS.

Victor ran off before noticing the chalk white pair of legs standing behind his own mere moments earlier.

CHAPTER 18

Pearl sat down and shook out a napkin. Whatever banged around outside had stopped. She was pleased to find her meal still warm. Before going off to investigate, she had already made her plate minus one key ingredient. She reached for an oversized gravy boat (which was far heavier than she remembered) containing her famous blackberry sauce. Her hands trembled under the weight of the porcelain overflowing with the heaviness of dense calories. She refused to skimp on the sugar in her savory creation. The vessel almost tipped when she attempted a pour.

Changing course, she set it down safely alongside her plate, determined not to accidently over marinate as a little went a long way. (It did not mean she would not use the same over a scoop of ice cream for dessert later that evening.) Grabbing a large serving spoon, she dipped it into the sauce. Someone cleared their throat. She looked around.

"Clayton?"

There was no one there. A chill enveloped her, which while normal for her age, felt unseasonably colder than the time of year would suggest. The hacking sounded again somewhere behind her.

"Please, stop that right now. It's not funny whoever you are."

Confirming she was alone, she harrumphed over the audible intrusion, fluffed her napkin anew, intent on proceeding with her meal. What better than comfort food to do just that in the face of sudden uneasiness? She lifted a spoonful of the blackberry sauce and sniffed deeply. Someone cleared their throat right in her ear. Startled, she dipped her head forward only for her nose to come back dotted with the black liquid.

"You're not here, Clayton, I know you are not. If you were, I would tell you I did what I did because you were eternally clearing that cursed airway of yours. I could not take it. If you had gotten that damn hairball out, I would never have poisoned you!" She slammed her hands on the table hard enough for the silverware to dance a jig.

Pearl recalled the day she mixed the drain cleaner with the dark condiment to mask the taste. Oh, how he had loved her blackberry sauce! On his last night on earth, she offered her husband Clayton a spoonful prior to pouring it over the goose. A little for the old bird before a lot for the dead bird. The speed with which her husband's hands shot to his throat shocked her as did the violence of his spasms. It was her good fortune that his convulsions broke a disc in his back.

The doctor (a family friend whom she had flirted with over the years, considered leaving her wretched husband for even) declared Clayton died from a seizure causing spinal damage severe enough to stop his breathing. No one ordered an autopsy. Pearl could eat dinners in peace after that. While occasionally feeling guilt, it always faded quickly given over to the relief of finally being free.

She found it odd that while memories of most things

grew foggy over time, the specifics of that night returned with a sudden clarity she had not experienced in years. She chalked it up to the aroma of roasted goose. Wasn't the sense of smell the biggest trigger of recall? She would have preferred to be unencumbered with past events while enjoying her fancy dinner, but she would get over it, she always did.

Since the day her husband left, in such a violent fashion, she had never once cooked a spread like that again. Why be so formal when dining alone? Not to mention how labor intensive the whole thing was. With no small amount of shame, Pearl segued to a stable of frozen dinners for the second act of her life. The sheer elegance on the table now was a welcome sight, a touch of luxury in an oft budgeted lifestyle. Despite her clarity of thought regarding a certain poisoning incident, she could not remember something far more recent. When exactly she prepared the meal eluded her. Still, she must have done so. Why not enjoy it?

Somewhere off to her right, the hacky cough sounded again followed by a thrice-failed attempt to exorcise a throat's demons.

"Stop that! You are dead. Don't tell me that even death didn't clear that damn obstruction!"

Pearl looked around—again finding herself alone. She sniffed the blackberry once more not for enjoyment but to check for the telltale smell of drain cleaner. Confirming the deadly additive absent, she poured liberally over her plated portion of fowl. What the hell, it had been a long time and she had no one to watch her figure for. Why not enjoy all the dressing she wanted? She sliced the goose gingerly with a knife and fork only to find it was so tender under the crunchy skin it did not truly need a blade.

She took a bite, moaning in pleasure, rolling her eyes at the wonderful buttery taste of flesh wrapped in a blanket of sugary goodness. Before she could swallow, she choked. Bringing her napkin to her face, she spit out a black mass of partially chewed food then reached into her mouth producing a single long hair. She held it high to inspect the color.

"Oh Pearl, when did you get old? Grey as a goose's feather. If I don't remember cooking the meal, I'm certain I forgot to pull my coif back when I did so. See, Clayton, is it that damn hard? I managed through the effects of a real hairball, well a strand at least."

She blew it away from the table and took another bite, chewing happily. Then she coughed again, her hands shooting to her throat as she hacked much like her husband used to. She opened wide, reached in and pulled more hair from her mouth only to find it more like a clump.

Fighting her gag reflex, she examined the dangling clotted mess which matched the length of her own locks. "What the...?"

Immediately she gagged again, fighting the urge to vomit while desperately trying to clear a blockage. Pearl dropped the initial mass into the sauce bowl and returned her hands to her gaping maw only to grip the largest batch of strands yet, pulling it from her throat. It kept coming. No matter how much she tugged, there was more behind it. Large masses of her tresses permeated her mouth while she yanked frantically only for it to keep on like a clown trick where the ribbon comes out endlessly. Pearl grasped at her neck as the obstruction quickly expanded beyond what her oral cavity could contain, building faster than she could pull free.

Then she saw it, a figure in a white sheet occupying the adjacent chair. No holes, just a body stiffly upright underneath. While aware of the presence, she could only focus on the hair pouring out of her insides at a startling speed. Pearl turned back to the table gasping for air where, despite the dire situation, her face scrunched in vile disgust.

Maggots crawled over a goose no longer expertly

cooked. The bird sat blackened, decayed with bones showing through patches of absent flesh. The animal's eyes opened and closed repeatedly as though still alive. The balance of the food had spoiled also, dishes gone rusty, silverware tarnished green. The mashed potatoes were a silken mess under molded gravy which floated as a skim over putrefied spuds. Corn showcased black, moldy blue, or missing kernels giving each cob the appearance of a rotten-toothed smile.

The hairy blockage finally reached an end leaving a slick pile as full as a regurgitated wig. She gasped fresh air in fast shallow breaths, still close to passing out. She caught her reflection in a silver spoon and groaned a hollow rattle which pinged about the brittle bones of her chest like a wind chime. The image revealed a bald head splotched with age spots alongside open sores freely weeping blood. Could that be her own hair pooled before her? She gripped the table tightly—fear overtaking the pain of arthritis throbbing through clenched fingers. She turned to the white figure.

"I didn't mean to kill you. Help me, Clayton!"

The sheet shook its head no. Pearl coughed again, tried desperately to clear a fresh blockage. She coughed repeatedly until finally, a large hairball ejected from deep inside, splashing wetly into the gravy boat. Fluid replaced hair in her mouth, and she choked anew, sputtering wetness. She gripped her neck in alarm as a dark liquid poured over her hands. At first, she thought it might be the blackberry sauce until noticing the crimson sheen staining the tablecloth.

Her body stiffened then her face slammed violently forward into the sauceboat legs twitching until a single bubble formed and popped within the black pool before she went still.

The white-sheeted figure rose slowly from the table and left the room.

CHAPTER 19

"Move, move, move!" Watkins yelled as he and Big Rick raced through the field with Calvin in tow.

The duo had wrapped the man's bloody head tight to staunch the flow of blood while hoping the act did not further compound a likely skull fracture. They used the sheriff's jacket as a makeshift gurney with which to transport him. While understanding moving someone with that type of injury to be ill-advised, Calvin required immediate attention which would not be arriving via ambulance because of the strange electronics blackout.

They first rushed toward Rick's parked pickup until Watkins blurted out a change of plan. "Use my vehicle, you'll need the siren."

They loaded Calvin gingerly into the rear of the cruiser, placing the injured man partially into the back seat before Frank ran to the other side to pull him in the rest of the way. The two rescuers conversed through the open doors.

"What do you mean? We both should drive him to the

hospital."

"You heard him. He saw Pearl in there. I won't just leave her."

"And I can't get busted driving a cop car, I've got an outstanding warrant on some parking tickets."

"I hereby deputize you to officer chicken shit and don't give a squat about any warrants."

They slammed the doors. Watkins rushed to the front to check the radio only to receive static.

"Damn. Rick, listen carefully. There was an accident in town which I think relates to this."

"Relates how?"

"Never mind. Get Calvin to a Goddamn hospital. When you reach an area where electronics work again, I need you to call a certain deputy."

"Which?"

"Sheryl Breton. Only her, nobody else."

"Got it."

"Start by telling her to swing by Pearl's place first before coming here but tell her to make it quick."

"Swing by Pearl's place? Why?"

"Because if she's sitting there dead then there's no sense in me trying to save her here now is there?"

"Wait, you think she might be?" Big Rick asked making the sign of the cross on his chest.

"Everyone else should stay on that accident, I don't need them rushing over here. You call Sheryl discreetly and do not breathe a word of this place to anyone until I get a handle on it, you got me?"

Rick nodded, climbing into the vehicle. The sheriff grabbed a first aid kit from the glove compartment and looked to the injured man. Figuring it would not do much good for Calvin, he slipped it under an arm for his own personal use before leaning in to switch the sirens on. Stepping off the road, he made space to allow the cruiser room to U-turn. The nearest hospital, besides Portland, was at the correctional center, their mutually agreed upon destination. The car sped off.

Watkins stood alone roadside, or thought he was at first. Suddenly he heard the voice again.

"That is more like it, Sheriff. Keep that distance so I can do my thing. We are just getting started in here. I gave you fair warning about your friend and look what happened. That is on you. If you cross that tree-line, make no bones about it, things will get extremely uncomfortable for you."

Despite the threat, Watkins crossed over. The moment he set foot back onto the field, he heard the voice more clearly than ever.

"Oh my, this is going to be fun."

CHAPTER 20

"You have the power."

"What did you say?" Beth asked.

"Take this board," Charlie said handing over a plank.

After giving up on their phones, the trio searched the first room they came upon. In it, they discovered a cellar window boarded shut. Charlie immediately went to work pulling the timber free by anchoring a leg against the cement wall and putting his weight into it. He handed a plank to Suzy but when he tried to hand the next to Beth, she squared off against him.

"You said, you have the power."

"No, I didn't."

"Yeah, he only asked you to take a board," Suzy confirmed.

He searched Beth's eyes. "You took that fall hard, but your pupils look okay."

"I am. I thought you said a phrase which I heard before. Something…"

"What?" he asked.

Something I'm sure as shit not going to share with strangers. Jesus, I thought I'd left that all behind, Beth thought. A year ago, when her military boyfriend taught her some self-defense moves, he innocently mentioned she had the power. The words triggered her in such a way she lost it, elbowing him in his eye before striking him harder, repeatedly, intent on inflicting damage.

Her partner was bigger, stronger, so quickly corralled her. The initial elbow to his face almost prompted him to strike back in anger until he noticed her trembling. He would later tell her she had a look akin to what he witnessed on people in combat. Instead of retribution, he pulled her tight even while she struggled to break free.

Beth never married, which brought on rampant rumors of her swinging for the other team. Truth was, while she enjoyed an occasional woman in college, she grew out of that phase by graduation. In recent years she began an affair with a soldier stationed overseas with whom she shared a bed on the rare occasions he returned stateside.

Locals were huge supporters of troops, but their support often ended at their sons or daughters dating the traveling warriors sometimes referred to as 'squids.' Beth would have stood her ground, defended her way of life if she were sure her man was faithful and/or not secretly married. She was uncertain of either, so never offered a defense of her choice in a partner to anyone. She kept her relationship secret from most. During his physical absence, they engaged in sex talk over social media which got her by. She occasionally dreamt of a wedding day but never pushed.

He believed she should be able to protect herself especially since she lived alone. He did his best to teach her self-defense where their sparring often ended in the sheets. The dichotomy of trying to hurt him followed by an intense desire to pleasure him kept her physically satisfied but emotionally unbalanced.

Everything became real though when he said those words. She no longer wanted to please him any longer, wanted only to punish, make certain he never used that phrase again. Only his solid musculature and strength reigned her in, squeezing her too tightly perhaps making a point of his ability to dominate even while offering comfort. What he did not realize was she allowed him to hold her, pretended the moment was over. He never understood how capable Beth was of causing more pain than he could ever imagine. She would never explain the reasons behind the trigger to him or anyone, especially not the police from a different day in her past, the fateful one when the dreadful thing happened.

Now she found herself somewhere else, in a mystical dangerous place deserving of her focus. Yet her mind continued to swim with painful memories as aggressive as sharks. What were the chances someone else would repeat those words? She tried to shake it off. "Nothing. Forget it."

"Beth, this could be important. If you heard something it could mean…"

"What Charlie? What could it mean? That I'm freaking out? I am. We all should be, you said so yourself."

"It could signify undue influence on you. Do the words you believe me to have spoken hold significance to you?"

"Oh, so now you're the paranormal expert? That's rich."

"Beth, calm down," Suzy said.

"No, this shithead knows stuff, then doesn't know stuff. Which is it, Charlie, huh? Are you ghostly street smart or ghostly book smart? Because some of the dumbest people I know are book smart."

"You have the power? I know that holds meaning for you, it does not take an expert to see that. I am also aware that something bigger is happening here."

"What are you saying?" Suzy joined in on the questioning.

"The politician, Martin, I initially knee-jerked a reaction against him because of his profession but I think maybe he's right. It is possible whatever brought us here found its targets through energy, one we all share. The sooner we discover what that is, the faster we can escape which means being honest with each other. Judge me all you want, but you're the person keeping a secret, Beth."

"According to your theory then we all are, so what's yours? And you, Suzy, huh? What are you both hiding?"

Suzy bit her thumb, turning away, suddenly uninterested in the conversation. Beth continued to argue with Charlie while the closest thing she had to an ally in the house found herself distracted by one more window.

Charlie claimed he was in fact educated on the paranormal, thank you very much, while Beth argued he had no business probing into her life. It worried her how quick the TV nerd was to identify she had things to hide. She wanted to run, but to where?

Suzy saved the day by ending the fight with a holler. "There are people out there! Hey!"

They all converged alongside each other, spying two guys carrying an injured man away from the house. Charlie grabbed a plank to strike at the glass. While it did not break, (no surprise there, Beth thought) the purpose this time was to draw attention.

The trio pounded and screamed in unison until the men receded into the distance before vanishing into the trees. The group halted their futile efforts.

"That was Sheriff Frank Watkins. I had him on the show once, for a segment about people trespassing on abandoned houses. He's law enforcement, he knows we're here."

"You mean he is aware a giant fricking house is here." Beth stepped back, defeated.

"One which hurt someone somehow. That should ensure he will return after they take care of the injured guy," Suzy said.

"How could that happen? To injure that person so badly he needs to be carried out, what can this place do?" Charlie asked.

Suzy turned on him. "You don't have to say everything that comes to your mind. How about working out theories versus facts before saying things out loud? We're already plenty scared. This quest you set us on, to look for changes in temperature, are we wasting our time?"

"No. Besides the law out there, it's our best shot."

Beth heard the two continue to argue in the distance, wondering when they would discover she had slipped away. She had no reason to trust anyone, no sister power with Suzy just because chromosomes even. They called her name when they finally noticed her absence. That asshole Victor had the right idea as far as she was concerned. With self-defense training and a secret which she planned to keep away from the nosy Nelly strangers, she felt more comfortable striking out on her own.

Beth continued to walk away from the others. Alone.

CHAPTER 21

"**D**amn kids," Victor thought.

Two boys (he did not know they were the same ones who first discovered the house) used to trespass on his land bothering the two bulls penned in by an electric fence across the road from his house. The inner perimeter of the lot contained an open grazing area with twin crabapple trees at its center. The front of the pen faced the road while the back of the enclosure stretched into a thick forest.

The young knuckleheads in all their wisdom often lured his prized animals to one side of the pasture whereupon they would run to another section, dive under the fence and make for the trees. From their perch they hurled apples at the large beasts, riling them to no end. Although the tossed fruit would eventually become snacks for his stock, the way the little snots delivered them was unappreciated. The raucous children's mere presence drove the bulls to rage. The kids were interlopers, trespassers, and the cattle, like their owner, were territorial.

While Victor could never be certain how many times the snots caused chaos for his pets, once on his radar he would intervene by grabbing a rifle and trudging down the long driveway. Upon spotting the gun, the boys always leaped from branches mindless of the proximity of the horned animals which would chase the twits across the field. Victor never got much farther than the side of the road before the boys made their break under the barbed wire then into the woods. A bull snagged an interloper's pants with a horn once, tossing the screaming kid high into the air over the fence. While not the full-on goring he hoped to witness, he took what he could get.

As the adult, he could have visited the boy's parents to stop the kid's shenanigans permanently though he never did, preferring instead to communicate by firearm. It would bring great joy to his heart if he ever got the chance to aim and fire. Victor felt confident he would get off on trial again—if there even was one since they were on his property. He had rights. He longed to catch them before they escaped into the forest so he could relive the day in Boston, the one where he had held so much power over the woman in his life. He would have done things differently if he knew about the bun in the oven situation back then.

Maybe.

Now it was Victor who found himself trapped like those cocksuckers in his field except his was a more claustrophobic environment—a confined building. Despite his hating the local punks, a child's presence here was welcome as it meant some kids (the same ones from his field?) likely snuck in to rob the place. If they could find a way in, then he could do the opposite. For the first time since his arrival, he felt escape was imminent.

The house had proven to be labyrinthian, the twists and turns of extended hallways seemingly endless. The patter of tiny feet drifted above that of the child's mewling. Odd the child did not appear panicked. If he did not know better the little rug rat even seemed to enjoy their game of hide and seek.

Victor rounded another corner longer than the last where suites stretched as far as he could see. Something small (and bloody?) rushed past appearing not much larger than a racoon. Before he could isolate the shape, it vanished into a room down the hall.

"Come out! I won't hurt you."

It giggled in response. The general dimness combined with his already questionable vision (he was too proud to admit he needed glasses) must have caused the child to appear as a pesky mammal which made no dang sense. He was no expert on children, but he understood basic anatomy. Victor approached the doorway for a better look only to leap as it brushed against his leg before scrambling into another chamber.

No way that was a kid, he thought. It was too small first off. It also ran far too quickly on the tippy toes of impossibly tiny feet. Then there was the skin, if one could call it that because the child (the classification of which was now questionable) appeared covered in a slimy liquid. The thing reminded Victor of a calf birth but smaller with visible deformities. Its overall shape made no sense which he chalked up to be a trick of the gloominess.

He proceeded no longer believing the thing he chased to be human. Animals could mimic human voices which would explain the so-called laughter while injuries would account for the malformations. He needed to tread carefully. Wildlife in such a state could prove highly dangerous, yet the same way in, same way out scenario had not changed. Eventually it would return from where it came, and he would stay with it until it did.

"I won't hurt you. It's okay." *Now show me the exit you son of a bitch*, Victor thought. He stepped through the doorway where he froze, feeling pressure build in his chest. "What the hell?"

The room was one from his old home! He absorbed

the surroundings, noticing how it matched the converted hobby cubby where he took Cora from the Earth. Black mold covered areas in splotches like tuberculosis coughs while spider webs dangled in clumps. Other than its state of decay, it was a perfect match.

Searching the area, he spotted the thing cowering in a corner. Something scuffled behind him. Turning quickly, he caught sight of two pale legs running past the entrance, human sized. The moment he stepped into the hall for a better look the door slammed closed.

The voice inside segued from laughter to a wail, to a baby's cry. Instinct told him to run, but he needed another look to put his mind at ease, to prove the interior did not resemble what he foolishly thought it had. Grabbing the doorknob prompted a scream. The metal grip frosted over so completely it would not have surprised him to find someone exposed it to liquid nitrogen from the opposite side of the barrier. Chilled to the point it burned flesh he yanked his hand away giving over to shouldering the door.

The room could not be a duplicate, was surely only reminiscent of his past. How could he remember what his old place looked like, anyway? It had been decades though the memory flooded him so fresh he could smell the gunpowder. He slammed repeatedly against the wooden slab before giving up only for it to then mysteriously open on its own.

Everything went silent.

It was as if the air pressure changed. A chill emanated from within matching that of the handle earlier causing his breath to steam. Hair on his arms lifted high while gooseflesh pimpled his skin. Understanding something was devastatingly wrong, he focused on what the TV guy said. If dude's spirit mumbo jumbo was correct, the different atmosphere meant freedom.

He crossed the threshold. Was someone humming? Yes, softly from somewhere in a room bathed in grim murkiness. He recognized the tune, and the voice.

"Cora?"

It could only be a recording of some sort or video playing on an unseen TV. He grew defiant as it all crystallized. Somebody brought him there for a shakedown.

"They found me not guilty, whoever you are. You can't blackmail me. My past is over, I…"

He spun around at the sound of sheets rustling. Cora sat in the corner in the rocker, pale white with hair caked in dirt as if fresh from the ground while cradling something. She crooned a tune of solace for her (human?) cargo. She looked sweetly down on the bundle at her bosom, almost angelic until in a flash she jerked her head up smiling with decayed teeth.

Then the thing in her arms, oh God, that which he had seen—but not really—turned to him. A single eye blinked through a slickness of blood as it opened its mouth revealing a set of needle-sharp fangs. It let out another wail, one so loud Victor had to shield his ears. His dead wife began to screech along, perfectly mirroring her tiny bundle. He stumbled to the floor on his ass where a bare sickeningly white blanched leg stepped alongside him!

He scrambled away, looking back to discover Cora's friend standing over him, except this version was not the beautiful lively woman he knew and lusted after. The pallid, morbid blue-grey figure crossed her arms over a stomach distended so far to suggest pregnancy. Had she been? He thought not as surely it would have come out in the trial.

Trudy stumbled towards Victor on unsteady feet, her blanched belly weighing her down, jaundiced eyes fixated on his. He crawled away until colliding with the rear of the rocker and spinning it around suddenly freshly reminded him of the other horror waiting. He glanced over his shoulder as the small red thing leaped into a shadowed corner giggling.

Bony fingers curled over the rear of the furniture

above, slowly, one finger at a time, each snapping as if broken, until the hand fully grasped the seat back. The chair suddenly rocked violently at him as Cora thrust her face into his. Her pungent breath reeked of decayed rats, a smell he knew from catching them in traps—a foul stench of death. Her obscenely long tongue (the muscle separated far enough it lolled about loosely) licked his cheek.

Victor retreated to the window as his dead wife's actions threatened to topple the furniture. She stretched her upper body toward him, flaccid breasts dangling, one spotting blood from feeding. Trudy lifted arms away from her belly as she too reached out to him. Her distended midsection burst, flooding the floor with the gory contents of a long-decayed stomach cavity as if suffering a standing c-section. Victor covered his face from the smell while screaming into his cupped hands.

The forgotten little thing reappeared biting deeply into his leg. He heard more than felt the crunch as he slipped into shock. It could not be his child, this deformed monster. Blood poured from his calf as if eager to merge with Dead Trudy's gore. Losing his balance, he fell into Cora's horribly cold arms. The musk of her former life's perfume could not mask the smell of putrescent flesh.

Trudy launched herself forward grabbing her intestines from the floor before wrapping them tightly around Victor's neck. He clawed at his throat for air while regaining his footing despite the dead child at his leg. As he stood, he found Cora standing before him flicking her tongue in an obscene version of a smile. A tooth fell from her mouth as she smiled wider and then she shoved him with both hands.

To Victor it all happened as if in slow motion. The force of the blow sent him into the sill hard enough to break through the glass even as he fought to loosen intestines from his throat. The unbreakable pane shattered in defeat as he fell through, tumbling over the ledge. While airborne he glimpsed his wife holding Trudy's hand as they watched him fall, while the malformed child peered over the parapet giggling.

Then he saw nothing as the fleshy noose went taught, dangling him by his neck stories above the ground, finally free of the house. Sunlight shone in the distance over Tether Falls, a view he would never see again.

CHAPTER 22

"You know what this place needs? A beanbag chair," Herb said.

"Are you out of your mind?" Stan exclaimed more than asked as he pulled at another window.

"Seriously, throw up a few comfy chairs, some strobe lights and you've got yourself a trip, man."

"It's trippy enough as is. Do they even make strobe lights anymore?"

"I own two."

"Color me shocked."

Herb sat in an old chair gripping the wooden legs on either side. "This is in excellent condition. Why are some rotted while others appear new?"

"The only question I want answered is how do we get out?"

"You need to relax. This is all just a chemical journey which will end in no time. I can't tell you how often I've been here."

Stan turned, leaning into the unkempt man in frustration. "Have any of your journeys ever included an angry mechanic who plans to punch your lights out if you don't help?"

Herb rolled his eyes thinking until Stan yanked him from the chair by his shirt. The older hippy finally came to life, raising his hands.

"Calm down, I was thinking. Thought you said you weren't a mechanic."

Stan released him. "Are you on drugs now?"

"What? No, but why would it matter?"

"It matters because I want to know if I'm with an altered partner or not. You listened to the TV guy about changes in atmosphere. I need to get out. Now."

"We're all stuck here." Herb lit up with realization. "We are all hunting for a way to escape, but you, you're on a clock. Why is that? Where do you have to be?"

Stan's eyes hardened as he turned toward the door. "I want to be out, that's all."

"So, I should wave my hands in the air like I just don't care?"

"Exactly." He stepped into the hall while Herb followed making the motions wildly, exaggerating his participation.

Upon entering the next bedchamber, Stan placed some distance between himself and the other man while trying to figure how such a drug-addled idiot could be on to him. It was true. He had somewhere to be. He needed to return to the wrecker yard and crush a certain car before his coworkers discovered the body in the trunk.

CHAPTER 23

"**D**amn, place should have an elevator," Martin griped as he crested the last of the stairs.

"It seems older than elevators I'd guess. You volunteered us for the high road, remember," Ethan said.

They emerged onto a floor to an immense hallway stretching in both directions, rooms evenly spaced as far as they could see. The doors appeared smaller than the norm and a glimpse inside the nearest answered why, someone had converted attic space into living quarters. The ceiling rested low immediately at the entrance sloping even lower toward the dormer window. Martin tried to open it, shrugged at his partner when he got the expected result of nothing.

Ethan moved past him and pressed his face against a pane looking longingly at the field below before suddenly stiffening in recognition. "This should be cold."

"Why just because it's the attic? A huge ass one but still."

"No, the sheet of glass should feel like the underside of a pillow at night. My neighbor Becky Bailey was a grade up from me at school and one floor above my bedroom in the house next door. If I leaned in and glanced up I could..." He stopped, reddened at the confession but needed to finish his point. He swallowed before continuing. "I might have occasionally seen her in her bra. She was beautiful."

"You ever have sex with her?"

Ethan blanched, turning away but continued. "My point is, even on the hottest summer day the initial contact against a cheek feels cool while this one is warm. What do you make of that?"

Martin frowned. "I think you were an inappropriate neighbor. Beyond that, I still believe we are all here for a reason, and our refusal to collectively consider that option will stymie our efforts to leave. What could you and I possibly have in common?" They performed a cursory search of the room, finding nothing of note. "Why us? Why here? Is there anything you want to tell me?"

Ethan wanted very much to share his secret with someone, and part of him thought a total stranger might be the best one to get it off his chest to. Another side of him longed to brag about what went down with Becky, bloviate over how he finally scored. If he shared, however, then he would have to offer the rest, including the horrible, terrible thing that occurred that night.

The incident prompted him to withdraw from friends and family ever since. In moments of somber reflection, he occasionally wondered whether he would ever be whole again. There was the chance his imprisonment in the house was a penance for that day. He had escaped a regular prison only to find himself in a strange otherworldly variation. Yes, there was a shit storm of information he wished to tell the politician.

"No, I can't think of anything," Ethan said.

All the things he needed to share would have to wait. He was not yet ready to shed himself of his guilt. The older man eyed the younger with a look of doubt—the same expression he remembered on the face of a detective from his past. Shaking himself from a yesteryear fugue, he threw himself into the task assigned by Charlie Thunder. While Ethan was hesitant to confront history, he was eager to search for the elusive air as cold as that which he felt in his heart.

CHAPTER 24

Sheriff Watkins stormed toward the house where he found himself thrust into darkness, considering it disconcerting how an isolated weather pattern hung ominously overhead given the brightness of the sun on his six. He flexed his freshly triaged hand which he redressed using the first aid kit. After cleaning the wound, he wrapped his palm tightly in gauze. The damage was bad in the light of day, would need stitches if not surgery but at least his fingers were now in play. Before he handed off his cruiser, he placed fresh gloves in his pockets. If the wound started to bleed again, he would put one on and secure it at the wrist. All things considered, he felt relatively fine because the adrenaline of the situation acted as a natural pain reliever.

Edging closer to the structure, he instinctively dropped a hand towards his weapon before scanning the area to ensure there were no witnesses to what he planned to do. The gun reach was habit, a move used to assert authority in shifty situations like traffic stops or domestic calls. The plan to establish a semblance of such now was new territory for the seasoned lawman. This was one instance where he was happy the town had no budget for body cams. He looked directly at the massive building and spoke.

"Okay, if I hear your threats in my head, I'll assume you will hear mine. I'm here to tell you two can play at that game. Open the door and let those poor folks out or I burn you down to matchsticks. How's that sound?"

The house did not answer. Watkins immediately felt foolish. Any other time he might have questioned his own damn sanity except the place had appeared out of nowhere, so he figured he earned himself a pass. He also had witnesses to confirm he was not hallucinating, visually at least. Auditory variations remained in play. He tried his cell again before slipping the device into his pocket, but when he glanced up, he staggered. The roof was on fire!

"I do not take kindly to threats, sheriff. If it is a barbecue you want, then it is a barbecue you shall get."

Watkins had bluffed a 'suspect' while never planning to start a blaze, especially with an unknown number of people within. The house, however, did not bluff. It started a rooftop blaze with no qualms about sacrificing an unknown number of souls inside.

The fire continued to grow as Sheriff Watkins realized he made a horrible mistake.

CHAPTER 25

Beth was as intent on fleeing from the strangers as she was from the house itself. In their presence, she developed a growing sense of dread about the couple she initially hitched her wagon to so caused a scene as an excuse to slip away. Flying solo had always been her thing and if she had her way, she would forever be alone. As a child, she watched the Twilight Zone episode where a man who hated people but loved books found himself post apocalyptically isolated. Tragedy struck when his glasses broke causing him to wail how it was unfair. Suzy never felt the twist of that story unsettling because the survivalist could surely raid the nearest optometrist shop— problem solved.

The entirety of the TV episode filled her with a sense of freedom, not loss. Life with others was hard— complicated. Even in the craziness of her current situation, introducing strangers into her world added complexity to the already complex. The pair yelled for her in the distance leaving Beth to wonder about their motives. Were they hoping to help her or finish a plan they put into motion?

Who was to say the two white bread people were not the ones responsible for the whole thing? Maybe they drugged her, brought her to the location. She refused to answer their calls, slipping behind a support column until they passed.

There was every chance the pair were innocent, and if that were the case it meant they were victims of the same circumstance as she. Yet, even if they were not ground zero conductors of her current reality, she feared continued contact with them nearly as much as her confinement. Imprisonment ends at some point, walls break, but if the strangers pried information from her, the damage would be permanent, no amount of cramming would force that genie back into a bottle. The young 'non-couple' had aggressively sought details Beth not only refused to share but had fought so long to forget.

They wanted her secrets. That which occurred was a part of her fabric, a reality she could not deny. But until now it was still **her** secret, one she wished to take to the grave. She waited for the dueling voices to fade before stepping from the shadows and walking away blissfully unaware the house was more than willing to accommodate her wish.

CHAPTER 26

L ike many growing up in Tether Falls, Ethan feared forest fires more than any other natural disaster. Lines between backyards and forests blurred in a part of the country where a single spark could decimate an entire town all too quickly. He heard stories of one such place in California suffering such a fate.

Fortunately, their region offered a tempered climate where winters seasonally refilled lakes. Further, melting snow dampened the earth well into spring limiting the fire season to a few scorching summer months. While lightning strikes were the most common cause of blazes in the country, locally electric storms were always accompanied by heavy rain minimizing chances of any sparks. Despite almost ideal year-round conditions, first responders were quick to arrive at any signs of trouble.

The largest blaze Ethan ever witnessed was on Hemon Cobb Road when he was nine and his friend Scott showed up chirping about smoke. The kids hopped onto their bikes and followed the wispy trail. Hemon Cobb culminated in a massive forest on one end.

They sped to the scene where they leaped off their bicycles still in motion, allowing them to fall where they may. Scott's did a front wheel rider-less wobble for another twenty feet before crashing with aplomb while Ethan's disappointingly obeyed laws of gravity by tipping immediately to the ground. Service vehicles were already present.

Dancing red lights reminded the boys of a TV program *Emergency 51* which aired in regular rotation on Channel Six. The friends decided they would pretend to be the two head actors from the show. One character faced down a rattlesnake once with deadly consequences. Ethan wondered aloud if the fire would drive any rattlers out into the open. Scott deemed it unlikely, reminding his friend that Maine was famous for its absence of poisonous critters.

Firefighters scurried in all directions while the boys advanced deeper into the forest until an older firefighter stopped them. "What are you kids doing?"

Ethan was ready to run from the conflict, fantasies of his TV persona vanished under the hardened gaze of a seasoned professional.

Scott rose to the occasion. "We want to help."

The old man looked around, likely checking for cameras or other firefighters who might bear witness to his actions. Finding neither he nodded at the kids.

"Okay, but if you see anything in the sky get undercover or you'll end up ass over teakettle," the smoke jumper said before hurrying toward the flames.

Scott slapped his buddy on the chest, and they advanced. Ethan was not sure what help looked like in the situation, but they intended to do their part. A plane flew over-head, causing them to eye each other in wonder. Remembering the fire guy's words, they searched for shelter.

Large moss-covered boulders dotted the landscape in

gaps between tree lines. Ethan always found it strange how massive standalone rocks existed in forests, jutting willy-nilly from the ground with no other baby ones or even sand in sight. Still, they appeared the perfect solution. The boys sheltered in place beneath a ledge.

The plane roared away, fading in the distance while the two remained hidden for what felt to them a significant amount of time. When nothing happened, they stepped back into the open in time for a massive flood of water to splash from the sky with enough force to knock them over leaving them covered in a sloppy mess of mulch and leaves.

A tree exploded, timbering close by, startling the boys to their feet. Water steamed under nearby flames feeding into smoke which advanced on their position. They huddled together searching for an out. Any adventurous plans went out the window.

The blaze danced around their perimeter, flames leaping across trees like acrobats at a circus, albeit aerialists set ablaze. Smoke grew dense, the wall of grey sucked air from their lungs, trapping them until nature found a way. The flames did not drive out non-existent Maine rattlesnakes, but it drove out deer. The animals cut through the brush charging past the frightened pair. The boys gave chase, and while they could not keep up, they followed the path until reaching the road. They located their bikes and pedaled home, swearing never to go near another fire.

Ethan had not thought of that day in years. The hard drive of his brain had filed it away to accommodate storage of more recent memories, but an all too familiar smell yanked the memory back to the fore with a clarion call of clarity. He yelled to Martin.

"Fire!"

CHAPTER 27

Frank cursed his lack of cardio stamina while running back to the road. Pearl was in the house or possibly was, he never got the chance to ask follow-up questions from his fallen friend. Time was of the essence, so he hustled as best as his aching body allowed. He discovered that which he hoped for in Rick's truck. The neighborhood man volunteered with the fire department so the industrial extinguisher in the back alongside a ladder made sense.

While excited to discover the much-needed equipment it frustrated him to think how the metal rung tool might have spared poor Calvin's noggin' had they used it rather than scooch across the rock ledge. Unable to carry both items and given he was frantic to stop the blaze from spreading, Watkins leaped into the cab and started the engine (locals always left the keys in the ignition as auto thefts were rare) then roared down the street. He fought to keep his eyes off the house, concentrating on the asphalt, but the flames in the distance continued to draw his attention.

The sheriff was aware hunters frequented these woods, especially given the tragedy with the Raines kid years back, what a horrible thing that was. Hunting meant a gateway existed, and he finally spotted it, a break in the trees through which vehicles could drive out trophies. He navigated the tight opening losing a side-view mirror against a tree.

"Sorry Big Rick, official police business and all that. I'm sure the department will see fit to replace that or under our current budgetary situation at least provide you a roll of duct tape."

Watkins drove onto the field before riding parallel to the road until arriving at the same footpath he initially walked. The familiar route would ensure no hidden boulders or pothole surprises making it the safest way to approach. He lined himself up to the path and drove onward.

He hit the brakes out of surprise when the headlights unexpectedly turned on. The area around the building was so dark it triggered auto lights. He cursed his fearful overreaction to something so mundane then stepped on the gas.

***

"Beth, where the bleep are you!"

"If she doesn't want us to find her, we won't," Charlie said.

Suzy grew more agitated. Everyone trapped inside were strangers, that much was true, yet earlier Beth declared comfort in her presence and vice versa, though it appeared she judged her new friend wrong. Perhaps the woman understood what all Suzy's paramours never did, that she kept secrets, up to and including a false identity. The moment she introduced herself as someone other than Amelia, her female partner likely put up a wall, understanding something was off. The banker looked to have a highly calibrated BS detector.

It was not total bullshit on Suzy's end though. She chose the name as a chance to start over, to forget history, to be a new person. In her mind, her new identity was that of a strong woman, powerful, in control. When she was Amelia, something bad had happened, a thing that—well, she did not want to think about that now lest her armor falter, crack under pressure. She covered by getting into Charlie's face.

"What do you mean? Who would want to be here alone?"

"Not the here part but the solo deal. It is crystal clear she was uninterested in talking," Charlie said.

Suzy turned on him. "I'm with Beth on this. You know stuff then don't. Are you psychic or not?"

He blanched at her attack, tensed before shooting words like daggers. "What I know is I don't want to sleep with you. I think you're hot and in a bar with a few beers I'd maybe look your way, but for now I'm not buying what you are selling. I could give a rat's ass about your likes or dislikes or your fashion sense. There are some things I appreciate about you. For example, I like how you say 'bleep' instead of actual curse words. Well except when it comes to me apparently," Charlie started.

"A FEW beers?"

"Okay, half a beer. The point is, I'm not whichever boyfriend you might be mad at and I am in the same screwed up house out of nowhere boat you are. My only interest is to find my way out. I'd be just as happy to do so with you in tow except, believe it or not, princess, you are not at the top of my list!"

"So, you're not here for the sole purpose of staring at my ass?"

"If I've done so, it's out of pure male instinct. I couldn't tell you if you have the square cell phone shape on the right or left butt cheek or if you are old school and go au natural down there. I don't know because I haven't paid attention, nor do I care. Since we met you've treated me like I'm the one that brought us here. I didn't, and I won't stand for the accusation anymore."

Suzy looked Charlie up and down. "Are you done?"

"You tell me because you keep pushing buttons then I'm just getting started." He simmered.

"Thank you," she said.

"For what?"

"This whole thing is jacked up, but you noticed I didn't trust you. Well now I do, at least as far as this sad group in the house goes. I appreciate you speaking your mind. You are right in that I may have assigned you the attributes of some real crap-heads I have been with lately. For the record, I go au naturel."

Suzy offered the double entendre to help determine whether Charlie was the boy scout he appeared to be or if he would react. Almost instantly his look changed. She stiffened under a recognition, saw the look, the same one too many married men gave her, his eyes seemingly locked on hers, wide-eyed, engaged—lustful? She found herself disappointed but not surprised at his outing as a typical male despite her instigating the flirtation by turning on her charm on a dime. Still, it bothered her how he was suddenly interested only because she floated a welcome sign.

Then she noticed he was not looking at her but past her, seemingly oblivious of her presence even. The guilt train pulled into the station as she realized she misjudged him again. A small part of her began to believe possibly, just possibly, in all their time together he might never have checked out her ass.

"There's a truck coming right at us!" Charlie yelled.

CHAPTER 28

C harlie watched the local sheriff drive toward the front of the house. His frustration at being recently judged by his lone partner faded, giving way to the hope of rescue. Looking out, Charlie noticed a disturbingly precarious drop just outside their window meaning there would be no straight prison break of a truck busting through concrete to free them. While unaware of the exact nature of the exterior he felt certain the officer had at least one avenue of approach available somewhere on the face of the home. No matter the officer's plan, the knowledge someone worked on their behalf was a welcome sight.

"He's not slowing. You think he plans to ram his way in?" Suzy asked.

"Looks so. Too steep below us, he'll need to approach somewhere else but maybe we can let him know we're here." Charlie grabbed a board to bang against the window. Inexplicably, before making contact, the surface fogged over.

"You're breathing too hard. He won't be able to see

us!"

"That's not me, I'm not," he started, trying to wipe it clear. "It's not coming off, must be on the outside. Next room, quick."

Next-door they found themselves situated farther from their potential rescuer making it harder to monitor the truck's trajectory. Charlie could not help but feel something moved them by design, an action instigated by forces he had yet to understand. Despite the roadblock, they did their best to signal the officer by jumping, waving, and shouting.

***

The sheriff drove alongside the house searching for signs of life. The dwelling rose so high above him now he could no longer see the fire burning in the rear. With level field running out from his position parallel to the structure, he turned into it, ready to make his move, hoping his wall of choice would easily collapse under horsepower driven steel.

He gunned the engine for final approach but jerked the wheel when a tree rocketed up from the ground in an explosion of dirt. Narrowly missing the obstacle, he scraped the same mirrorless side of the vehicle. The birch was not overly thick but could be lethal at such a speed.

Earlier, after turning off the familiar footpath to run alongside the house from a distance far enough to peer at windows low and high, he spotted movement near the cellar confirming more people were inside. He worried someone might be positioned behind whatever wall he would eventually crash through but would have to worry about that later if he got close enough.

Another tree exploded upward causing him to yank the wheel again. The second wooden missile missed the truck by inches. Dual right turns reoriented him until he faced back toward the road.

"If I were given to song, Sheriff, I might sing a ballad to your efforts to reach the belly of this beast. But since your actions are sorely lacking in originality, I will forego that tune for now. I am not sure how far your roots go in this town, but it should be clear to you that mine traverse deep."

"Shut up, I know you're not real, none of this is," Watkins said mostly to himself.

He course-corrected, circling back around, until aiming toward the house again and floored it. The tires tore up dirt and grass as the truck found its groove as he sped forward. Driving on pure instinct, he changed his angle of approach, using it as his version of a serpentine running pattern to escape predators in nature. Trees do not explode from the ground, he understood that, but there was a house in front of him which brought a hill with it so who could say what else the cosmic landscaper had in mind? He just needed a little more time to build enough speed to crash through.

The world exploded when a tree cruised like a missile from underground, angled to match his route, designed for maximum carnage. The top of the tree smashed through the windshield exploding shrapnel throughout the jostled cab. The trunk shot onward smashing through the rear window stopping the truck instantly. The momentum lifted the vehicle in the air as if launched on a catapult, but the weight quickly dropped it down in a series of bounces before settling under a layer of smoke pouring from the defeated engine. The horn blared in protest as either branches or the officer's body pressed against it.

All fell silent, save for the unabated honk accompanied by a taunt the sheriff could no longer hear.

"Was that real enough for you?"

CHAPTER 29

Martin struggled to keep pace with the fit, determined youth while the mismatched pair rushed into action. Reluctantly on Martin's part. A weariness settled into his heart so powerful it might as well have been a physical weight, one which was so heavy every step took a Herculean effort.

"A fire? What are the chances?" Martin thought.

"I think it's coming from the corner dormers," Ethan shouted.

"Isn't this where we run the other way?"

The young man looked visibly frustrated at his older partner who shrugged innocently, a dismissive gesture born of so often finding himself on the receiving end of many a constituent's bad day. Hell, even inside a house of suspicious origin the local hippy needled him about his occupation. Ethan pressed on.

Martin never intended to run only out of self-preservation, in fact, he fully understood they were the best line of defense against an element which could quickly turn tragic. No, he was reticent to act because the fire existed at all. Of all things, why a blaze? It was as if his hidden history stalked him for years, deciding to pay a visit during a period where he was most vulnerable. He had to let it go for now, there was too much at stake. He would join forces with the kid, make a stand, save the others, that was it, using process to deal with a situation. Once they solved said problem, he would forget the whole thing. As soon as they put out the flames, he would consider his past finally extinguished along with it.

Deafeningly loud crackling filled the air. A door sat partially open, revealing the burning space to be larger than the previous converted rooms. A glimpse through the lone window inside confirmed the conflagration had spread to the exterior.

"We need to put it out, fast. It's reached the roof," Ethan said.

Smoke cleared enough for Martin to see an oddity in the room which made his blood go cold despite the heat. His plans to remain silent about his past vanished under a sudden awakening. "The radiator…"

"What did you say?"

The politician refocused. "We need something to put it out."

"Agreed. Haven't exactly seen bathrooms or running water anywhere since we arrived. You?"

"The tub, she tried to make it there…" Martin faded off, slipping into his own world again.

"Curtains. The floor below us with the larger windows had massive drapes. We can try to smother the sucker. I'll be right back."

Ethan ran off. The older man reached out, begging the boy not to go. Once alone he turned, freezing at the sight of a beautiful woman engulfed in flames walking across the room trailing ash. She smiled a mouthful of fire before disappearing into a connected bathroom.

How could it be? She was dead.

Martin was certain because he was the one who killed her.

CHAPTER 30

"He's not moving," Suzy said.

Charlie pulled her gently back from the window only to suffer a glare sharp as a dagger. He figured they could use it as a weapon later if needed. She fought him off.

"What are you doing? He has a truck, he could ram the building, he…"

"Hasn't moved, you pointed it out yourself. Nothing has harmed anyone inside so far, we cannot say the same for those outside," Charlie said.

"You forget the stair carnage? We've been attacked so we must hurry, and that man can still…"

"Get in? That's the easy part. We blinked, and we were here. Two of theirs are down. Even if help is on the way we do not know things will work out for any others. We remain our own best chance at escape."

"Good thing you're not trying to hook up with me, Charlie, I don't like you very much." Suzy stepped toward the dark tunnel lining the lowest level of the dwelling, pausing in the doorway. "Just because I don't like you it does not mean I do not want you at my side."

She waved him over. Taking the hint, he joined her as they exited out to a new stretch of the basement where dirt floors blended with patches of exposed concrete at random intervals across the large expanse of floor. Lengthy cavities of open space loomed ahead interrupted only by occasional support beams while tiny rooms extended along the perimeter of the front of the house. The center of the cellar grew into a pitched blackness the farther it got from the incidental filtered daylight.

"There's so much dust and dirt that we should see motes dancing. The tiniest of breezes should float particles, yet nothing has moved except what we have disturbed by foot," Charlie said.

"Meaning?"

"Windows give a false sense of hope. We already learned we can't escape through them. They have proven to be anything but a get out of jail free card. I believe to find a change in atmosphere, we must go into the center."

Suzy gulped at the idea. The expanse was gloaming and to enter the area meant willingly leaving illumination behind for the unknown.

"And here I thought I couldn't like you any less."

Together, they entered the void.

CHAPTER 31

Flickering tips of flame became pointers as if the orange fury were a teacher gesturing wildly to lessons on a chalkboard. Crackle! A whipped tip of the blaze pointed out a familiar Ikea dresser, the one with the bottom drawer that sticks. Snap! Crack! The raging element turned in on itself, balled before lashing a new tendril spreading out as if two hands of a game show model showcasing an all too recognizable bed with the baby blue silk sheets purchased as a joke but used frequently.

Martin understood there was no way it could be the same place until...

Pop! Crackle! Flitting flames raced up the wall opposite the window with such fury and explosive force it almost knocked him over. The fire flowed like an upside-down waterfall pouring from floor upward until highlighting an original print by Jonathan Taylor, removing any doubt who the room belonged to.

Taylor was an up-and-coming artist whose prints—

now priced in the stratosphere—became a favorite target of internet startup millionaires. Savvy collectors like himself bought low when the famous painter was still a starving street merchant. Since there were no mass print runs of the artist's work it meant the one on the wall had to be an original. He wanted to attribute the familiar space before him as a delusion, yet he recognized everything. Even if someone had somehow replicated items, they should have already burned to ash, leading him to believe the universe somehow mysteriously planned for him to bear witness.

"I got it, a heavy son of a bitch. Could have used you on the stairs. Help me out," Ethan said, struggling under the load.

"You shouldn't be here," Martin said.

"Almost wasn't. I nearly tumbled down under the weight of this thing. Now come on, help!"

The politician grabbed an end of the massive textile. "How old are you, exactly?"

"Twenty-one. What does that have to do with anything?"

"That's the age she... Never mind. On three?"

"No count, this shit is heavy, let's go."

They stepped into the inferno batting ends of the fabric until they smothered portions along the outer perimeter. The two worked in unison, battling as a unit prompting Ethan to smile. Martin smiled back wistfully, identifying the look of hope on his youthful partner as one he witnessed all too infrequently from constituents. Platitudes provided comfort even in the worst of times, but now his actions offered actual relief. With each new section of the conflagration extinguished, the young man grinned wider. That was youth, the ability to grin through troubling moments. He could not help someone before, but he planned to today.

The bathroom.

He noticed an open washroom where he spied water

running in the tub. There was nothing to suggest any vestiges of working plumbing existed in the dilapidated structure, yet the faucet poured vigorously. The nude woman stepped into view leaning against the door frame. Her stance appeared sexually inviting despite the horrifying nature of her being alight. Fire spiraled in her mouth, flickered out her nostrils while her bonnet of hair twirled toward the ceiling twisting into a wispy smoke chaser.

"The bathroom. We can use the water inside to put it out," Martin said.

"What bathroom?"

"Right over there. The faucet is already running."

"I don't know what you are talking about, there is nothing there. Hey, why haven't any walls burned through? That might provide an escape route," Ethan said.

The young man finally took note of that which confounded Martin earlier, how destruction was lacking given the enormity of the blaze. The Taylor painting should have been ash before they arrived, yet flames continued bubbling the oils on the canvas. As he tried to understand the seemingly impossible, the woman motioned to him with a curled finger. Even charred she remained stunningly beautiful.

A beam overhead exploded, crashed to the floor. Unlike the rest of the space which appeared frozen in time, the collapse was all too real. Smoke billowed vigorously appearing to target Ethan who coughed violently under the sudden onslaught which brought with it a new revelation. They both should have suffered the effects of particulates right away, but strangely neither had until now. Whatever was at work wanted to separate them.

The politician watched as the burning woman stepped into the washroom. "The tub. If she could reach the bath."

"Too much smoke, we have to leave, close doors, maybe starve it of oxygen."

Martin nodded to his young charge, gesturing him to proceed first. The youth wasted no time running out, coughing through the dense air. Martin followed as far as the room's threshold before stopping.

Ethan turned out of instinct to check on the politician. "What are you doing?"

"You can't see it which means it is meant for me. I did something I cannot forgive myself for. I guess it's my turn to face it. I pray you are too young to have sinned as great as I. Good luck to you."

Martin shot back into the room. Ethan tried to give chase, but the door slammed shut. He grabbed the knob only to scream as the hot metal branded his palm. He yanked the hand away, cradling it while kicking at the obstruction, yelling the older man's name.

Inside, Martin breathed in deeply as oxygen filled his lungs which made no sense given the raging environment. In the distance he heard the kid attacking the barrier between them, but soon even that faded until all he could hear was water gurgling into porcelain.

It was his fault, all those years ago. Now time brought it back around, dancing a second chance in front of his face. Martin wondered if the house had a plan for him. A voice in his head replied with a single word.

"*Yes.*"

CHAPTER 32

"You've never had Maine lobster?" Martin asked the lovely young lady seated in front of him in the fancy Bar Harbor restaurant.

The eatery was a long way from his district in a town hosting a public transportation conference. The weekend getaway provided him a chance to extricate himself from grumbly constituents if even for a short while. His territory comprised a small enough size that voters did not need to call on the phone about their problems, most could yell down the street. There was also the matter of his ten-year marriage. He hoped for a change of scenery from both situations.

Martin initially planned to visit strip clubs in the area since he was unknown there which would allow him to engage his vices anonymously. On the off chance someone recognized him, he would still fair well. Maine's heavy financial hitters frequented the upper crust community, ensuring the employees at the scandalous establishments were discreet about their clientele.

All his plans (which included getting laid) changed when Libby stepped into his office the morning he was to depart. A new intern from Orono, Libby had re-energized his campaign staff made up mostly of blue hairs who while well connected had long since lost the political fire needed to fight for people of his great State.

Martin never spoke much to the young worker, despite her obvious beauty, but took notice after a strong turnout at a barbecue fundraiser she organized, singling her out in his speech. While the woman was the same age as his daughter Tish, his offspring was uninterested in politics, but very into tattoos, drugs, and rock bands. The scandalous antics of his misguided kin kept one of his staffers tasked full time spinning her exploits in the press so as not to reflect poorly on the family values candidate.

Despite the young intern's good looks, Martin was away from the headquarters so often he did not have regular occasion to visit with her which served him well as he understood small towns talked, texted, and tweeted anything remotely smelling of scandal. His piety in the face of temptation faded when she appeared in his office with a carryon.

"What is this?" he asked from behind his desk.

"Everyone who is anyone in the circles I wish to travel in will be there, so I intend to go with you. I have worked hard for you for a scandalously low level of pay and have delivered results. I want to see bigger cities. I deserve this chance." Libby stood stoically before him.

Martin smiled at the woman wearing a tight business skirt and blazer, under which she sported a white blouse opened just enough to showcase cleavage she usually kept hidden. While it pleased him to see such enthusiasm, the situation could open a whole can of worms, so he put his glasses on and returned to paperwork.

"Our campaign can't justify two hotel rooms and I can't afford to have my wife see multiple ones booked on my personal card," he said dismissively before returning to his file.

"Because of the conference, there are no more available which is why I'll be staying in yours. Problem solved," Libby said.

Martin noticed that while the woman stood ramrod straight, she displayed a slight tremor in the hand gripping the handle of her carryon. Leaning back, he studied her.

"I understand you have a boyfriend."

"One who lusts after my best friend. I arranged for her to hook up with him this weekend to keep him busy so now he'll have secrets of his own."

"You're being presumptuous about the status of my relationship with my wife."

"I have had occasion to check your browser history here in the office, sir. If you allow me to tag along and introduce me to the right people, I will keep you far too tired to even think about visiting a strip club which is a bad idea in case someone snaps your picture. Also, I regularly delete those records as part of my official responsibilities. You should be more careful," the young woman said.

"As in not being caught with an intern?"

"Protégé sir. No one will be the wiser. Any who might would find themselves inspired by your choice if I may say so."

The intoxicating fragrance emanating from the woman reached the politician. He could not determine whether it was a well-known perfume or just her natural smell. Her hands finally steadied as he nodded.

Immediately after checking in at the hotel, the two explored each other's bodies. Martin reminisced about his youth while partaking of the coed's physique. Based on her reactions to their love making his age gave him an edge of experience over her younger lover. After the long night of sex, he slept more deeply than any time in years. Upon waking he encountered an uncharacteristic twinge of happiness at finding the beauty tangled in sheets alongside him.

Libby made quite an impression right from the first day of the conference where she proved to be a better study on policy than he. She showed a deep understanding of community and health care issues among other wonkier ones, impressing attendees, especially the younger men. She never displayed a sexual interest to the eager charges around them, showing a remarkable loyalty to him, forsaking others who could help her career as much or more than he could.

After the conference ended for the day, they proceeded to a high-end restaurant in the tony community where he hoped to impress the intern. It worked.

"You're from here, but never had Maine lobster?"

"No, I've never slept with a politician before either," she said.

"How do you like that?"

"Very much, I enjoy your platform."

Martin almost spit out the expensive wine. "So that's what we're calling it?"

"Platform, a code word, to keep you out of trouble. Just let me know whenever you want to have a meeting about your platform, your noticeably big platform." Her eyes twinkled over the top of her wineglass.

"You're beautiful," he said.

"So, about that strip club?"

"I think I've given them up for life."

"Good, an honest family man like yourself needn't take such chances." She returned to her food.

Soon after she showed him how much she appreciated the Maine lobster and she discussed his platform all weekend long.

***

Back in the burning room chaos reigned. Ethan pounded furiously from the other side of the door while the fire crackled and popped in a destructive symphony.

Sound returned to the ombudsman suddenly, the fugue he found himself in fading as reality charged ahead like a monster. The ground shook so hard he struggled to remain on his feet. The floor threatened to collapse under the burn.

Water.

The answer was there.

He watched the young woman (the stunning, intelligent, beauty) engulfed in flames enter the bathroom vanishing from view. Ethan could not see her which meant Martin was the only one who could run to the rescue. If he could get her into the tub, she would be okay. He rushed forward with purpose, toward the washroom with a single thought in mind.

"I'll save you this time, Libby."

CHAPTER 33

The couple continued their affair long after the conference and despite occasional gossip, their relationship remained mostly a secret. To put distance between herself and her former boss, she quit the internship to finish her education. Martin helped her with school costs and using a fake name, he rented an apartment in a rough but affordable part of town where they would rendezvous.

After Libby finally broke up with her boyfriend, she moved full time into the 'budget bungalow' as she called it. The politician despised the idea but accepted it. All was well until a perfect storm of events converged, beginning with Martin finding himself eyed for a bigger office, that of State Senator. The prospect solidified after connecting with a developer tied to the New England mob scene.

Mobsters owned their budget bungalow. Once the landlords—in name only—discovered they had a local politician in their backyard, one took the ombudsman to the same restaurant where Martin first dated Libby. Over the same menu choice, the well-dressed developer talked up Martin's national prospects. Instead of dessert, his host served up a manila envelope containing pictures of Libby naked riding atop Martin at the apartment.

The mobster dropped bills to get them out of there before the scene got out of hand since Martin did not take the news well. Once in the parking lot, the benefactor's driver punched the upset politician in the gut followed by two jabs to the face, the second of which drew blood and rearranged his made for TV good looks nose. They tossed the injured man into the back seat.

Once in the car, they filled him in how Libby played a long con, explaining how she kept dirt on him with plans to use it once he reached a higher office. While he fought tears of betrayal the connected developer scoffed openly about choosing the wrong horse while wondering aloud if Martin had the backbone needed to move up the political ladder.

Thinking of how the young woman played him even though he had grown fond of the intern, fine, loved the hell out of her, he stone-faced himself. In recent weeks he started to dream of bigger things including moving to Washington so the prospect of returning to his old life with his wife and child trapped in a small town brought him around to the previously unthinkable. When his host suggested the wheel man could rectify the problem that was Libby, Martin silently nodded.

The developer dropped the politician off at his own vehicle, tossing a handkerchief at him for the blood.

"Just, please, make it quick," he said.

Grinning wide to show several silver teeth under a scarred lip, the body man nodded before speeding off. Climbing into his own car, Martin slammed fists on the steering wheel, screaming into the night.

Martin woke at three AM to his phone buzzing. Exhausted, he initially mistook his sleeping wife for his young lover. The mistaken image of the younger woman brought on a clarity related to her innocence causing him to question whether Libby ever took the photos. Unscrupulous characters owned her building, was it so hard to believe they were responsible for the hidden cameras?

"Hello?" He spoke soft enough not to wake his wife.

"It's taken care of," a deep voice said on the other end before hanging up.

Martin leaped out of bed, ran into the hall, dialing, not expecting things to happen so quickly. "Pick up, pick up." Taking stairs two at a time, he launched himself forward, stepped onto his front lawn, frantically dialed again. He had no shoes, no keys, wore only boxers, but his instinct was to get in the car, drive to her place to check on her. She answered.

"Oh my God, Martin, it's on fire! Help me!" Libby's voice trembled in a high-pitched fear while gasping for breath. A low moan filled the spaces between jagged staccato rasps of sentences. She informed him she already called 911 but did not think she would make it. The whole place was an inferno, especially outside her door.

Over the line he listened to her struggle to breathe, painfully absorbing her oxygen starved coughing as if blows to his chest. Part of him hoped she would succumb to the smoke, die painlessly, yet he urged her toward survival.

"Get a cloth from the kitchen, soak it, cover your mouth," he instructed while pacing in his elegant front yard.

Initially she yelled there was too much fire, that she could not see but soon he heard water, realizing she did as he asked. He begged her to find a way out, any at all until it became clear she could not, could in fact only scream as the destruction spread.

Martin urged her to get to the bathroom. Through cries of confusion, of utter fear, she told him she reached it. He remembered the large tub in which they had nested together nude so many times, arms wrapped around one another offering more comfort than any tepid liquid ever did.

Submersion would buy precious time, so he urged her to fill the porcelain. Sirens blared in the background—rescue within reach. He closed his eyes in relief when he heard the water running until she cried it was not filling fast enough. He promised her it would but knew from experience part of the cheap rent was insufficient utilities. The low pressure always bothered him and now it became so much worse. He vowed to take her out of there, she would need somewhere new, he would get her a place worthy of her beautiful spirit, one with the best plumbing in the world. He just needed for her to hang on.

Then her voice changed, eliciting a great panic in him. He heard within her timbre, resignation.

"I love you, Martin…"

"Don't say that, don't. I forgive you for the pictures."

Despite her situation, she asked what he meant. Her surroundings acted as a truth detector, the woman was raw, open, in no state to lie. She was unaware nude photos existed. He did not offer an explanation. He had lain down with snakes and now, now the innocent would pay.

"I will miss you," she said.

"Libby, don't. Don't say that. The water can save you…"

An explosion roared through his cell followed by a scream from his young lover. He yelled out her name. She yelled the fire was with her then the screams reached a pitch of agony that would haunt him forever. He listened to the clunk of her cell phone hitting the floor followed by bestial sounds which he could not even recognize as human. Finally, mercifully, the line went dead.

Martin cried out, falling to his knees as the lights in his wife and daughter's rooms turned on. Timer sprinklers kicked in, but he could not hear their gentle swish over the pulse of blood pounding at his ears. His tears mixed with the water as a deluge cascaded down his face. A liquid world sluiced around him, slicked his lawn, saturated his boxers, did everything water does except wash away his sins. Martin thought how there was so much of it around him but not enough to help her. Not enough to save the only woman he had ever truly loved.

CHAPTER 34

The fire closed in on Martin who raised his arms defensively under the overwhelming heat. It would have been easy to run back into the house, rush into the labyrinthian hallways to seek help from the strangers. However, if there was even the slightest chance in this new world (one where people could vanish from some place only to reappear in another) that he had a do-over to change his past he was damn well going to take it.

Martin understood his deportation from his own home into the rotted sitting room several floors below defied natural scientific laws. That led him to question whether the same otherworldly energy could crack open a doorway in time just wide enough for him to slip into the past where he might manipulate a different outcome. Perhaps he was being given a second chance. He rushed into the washroom.

The tight quarters proved far more smoke-filled than the living area. Coughing through tears as particulates obscured his vision, a glance over his shoulder gave him pause. The grey seemed to solidify in the doorframe as if a cement poured and set. Another mystery which would have to wait, he had work to do.

Authorities released crime scene reports to him because of his job which gave him full access to the details of events and photos. All the information confirmed no others came to harm during the tragedy. Many tenants were on the mob dole which garnered them late-night calls ordering them to vamoose. A small contingent of innocent, non-mobbed up renters escaped because the fire began in front of Libby's apartment allowing them time to evacuate. That not a single neighbor attempted a rescue destroyed him.

The photos showed the charred remains of Libby curled tightly fetal save for a single arm arched toward the edge of the tub. In the pictures he saw how the bath eventually overflowed. Water had cascaded over her body leaving a slick sheen glistening over blackened, cracked skin, a testament to the horrors of a heat that stole every inch of her beauty. One side of her skull—the only half visible from her curled position—was bloody, a ruptured surface cooked until it split and stuck to the melted floor.

Now, as Martin examined the bathroom, he feared seeing the same horrific scene play out live until the smoke mysteriously cleared leaving the surroundings undamaged, no different from when he used to visit. Water splashed over his feet. Looking down, he found the tub filled to the brim as wetness gushed over the top pouring in gentle rivulets to the floor. He slipped on the slick linoleum, quickly regaining his footing but not his emotional balance. Where was the fire? Where was his intern?

"Libby?"

Then he saw it, her body submerged, wearing a black slip which Martin gifted her soon after their affair became a regular thing. That she wore it in his absence offered more evidence she thought as much of him as he did her. The dying words she spoke that day had been a truth serum of sorts. Why lie at the end? Not only did she have nothing to do with the pictures, but she loved him. Period.

The black slip rippled around her body which lay too still signaling he was too late. She looked far more peaceful in this death than the one in the photos. Then her eyes shot open as she thrashed violently, drowning.

"Libby!"

Leaping in, he lifted her out. She continued to thrash until choking up voluminous amounts of water. After sucking in air, she began to breathe again before wrapping her arms around his neck. Cradling her protectively, he ignored his own soaked clothes, too stunned at finding her alive to think straight. Any thoughts of having lost her before began to slip from his grasp as he looked upon lost love bringing with it hopes of second chances.

"You're, you, you are…" Martin stammered.

"Freezing, so cold," she said.

Exiting the tub, he ignored the strain on his atrophied biceps struggling under her gentle weight. Immediately he almost lost his footing again once he stepped onto the tile causing her to grip him tighter.

"New at this?" She grinned at her knight.

This was not right, this could not be, he thought, yet somehow here she was, the result of the best-case scenario of what could occur within his magical mystery tour of the house. Having arrived himself in a manner bordering on the supernatural, was it so difficult to believe she did too? Despite their reunion, danger still lurked in the form of a blaze around which they would need to navigate. He carried her into the living quarters.

The wall of intense heat immediately stopped him. While the exit appeared enticingly close, flames licked in that direction. As he calculated an escape route, it occurred to him that Libby felt cool to the touch in his arms.

"You're still cold?"

"The sparks will warm me, I'm sure." She smiled at

him.

"I saw you earlier, the fire, it was on you, in you."

"Don't be silly, do you think I'd be with you if I had burned? The situation terrified me, left me oh so scared, but I always believed someone would rescue me and here you are."

Something bounced off his leg before falling to the floor with a noticeable thump. Glancing down, his eyes grew wide in shocked wonder. A foot from the ankle down lay on the ground! As he watched in horror, it burst into flames. Then her left one 'thunked' down next to the first. Martin looked at the woman, stunned to discover her legs ended in bloody stumps. He might have examined the damage forever except her girlish giggle drew his focus back to her face.

"This is so embarrassing," she said.

"What is happening?"

Her right hand broke off, falling to the floor palm up, the fingers curling in on themselves as it burned to black while her arm slipped away from his neck. Martin struggled to comprehend the situation even while Libby remained effervescent in his arms.

"This is the part where you should probably put me down, sweetie."

He lowered her until her bloody stumped legs squished into the floor. Her limbless arm dangled in a palsy position while she reached out and caressed his cheek with the other.

"I knew you would come for me, that nothing was your fault. I mean, there's no way you could have done this."

Then another snap at her wrist and she lost her remaining appendage. Martin leaped back when the hand burst into flame, giving him a hot foot which he frantically stamped out.

"Christ!" he said, staggering back finally taking in a full view of the woman he loved minus some important parts. "I never meant it, they said it would be quick. I, oh Christ, oh Christ!"

She looked at him questioningly. "Wait, are you saying it was you? Martin, how could you?"

The skin on her face slackened, sliding loose. While it remained affixed it drooped several inches, gravity drawing the flesh down as if melting. Her speech slurred through distorted lips.

"You did this? Why?"

"I mixed up with the wrong people, ended up never moving to the national stage, I became damaged goods. But they still own me."

She stepped toward him with a bloody squish, first one stumped leg, then the other, a slow torturous movement, her full body twitching with each step.

"See, it is a sign we should be together, I never moved forward either. Stay with me, Martin."

"No, I am sorry Libby, so, so sorry but you aren't real, I understand that now."

"Honey, you're wrong, I'm right here, we can be a couple forever."

Her words slurred further as her lips fought to find a foundation on her face. Then her speech grew unintelligible while she attempted to offer the possibility of life together. Her entire body burst into flames as her teeth grew to razor-sharp flickering fangs. Her entire skin charred to black.

Libby moved supernaturally quick, embracing him in a bear hug before he could blink. He struggled to break free as the flames grew, taking on a life of their own dancing in a circle around the couple. The dead woman took the lead, spinning Martin until his back faced the window.

His screams peaked as his own face melted. Soon his voice faded along with his mouth until the only sound was the shatter of glass when the pair crashed through into open air. The fire burst brighter once fed fresh oxygen. Libby burned to ash, fluttering away in the wind while Martin's crispy frame rocketed towards the ground bouncing across the grass in the field.

Rolling over the ground extinguished the flaming body though smoke continued to rise from the corpse of a man unable to celebrate finally escaping the house.

CHAPTER 35

Watkins woke with a start. Blood, which poured down his skull while unconscious, had since clotted into a sticky layer of film plastering his hair to his forehead. He turned to appraise his situation only to bump his head against the tree trunk inside the cab of the truck.

"Shit on a…"

The unspoken word, shingle, brought him back to reality, a grim reminder of what burned on the roof. Though uncertain how long he lay unconscious, he was quite certain he suffered a concussion. The plan became to worry about that later, there was no time for it now.

Reflexes saved him of a fate matching that of the rotary victim in the Samsonite luggage. The crash happened so fast yet appeared as if in slow motion under his adrenaline-fueled vision. A glancing blow on the side of his skull, while not fatal, forced a nap, and brought on a whopper of a headache.

Watkins would have a lot of explaining to do to Big

Rick. On the brighter side, if the burly citizen ever considered trading in his vehicle for a convertible he would not need to do so as he owned one now. Worse, his deputy would no longer be the record holder for claims paid out for vehicular damage. Hail the new budget buster king, Frank Watkins! A strong odor drew the sheriff's attention, but his movement caused a second skull bang against the wooden obstruction.

"Christ on a cracker, my head!"

The smell was awful. Chemical maybe? Assuming it to be from the truck, he wrestled with the door handle to escape a possible inferno. Upon pulling the release, he rolled out onto a heap of shattered windshield pieces.

Small cuts pocked his hands from the sharp crumbs. The sting of the fresh injuries woke him further from his stupor as he embraced the new pain to distract from his previous aches. The odor was burn related, yet he saw nothing alight anywhere near the truck. Looking up at the dwelling (*the house that can't be there, it just can't be*) he noticed the fire not only extinguished but could find no signs of damage anywhere.

The situation confirmed a concussion since there was no way a building so old flanked by brush could have survived a fire unscathed. There was no explanation other than he was seeing things. Even if the blaze somehow extinguished on its own (and weirder things had happened this day) he expected to see blackened timbers along with residual smoke damage.

Watkins rose, wiping his blood speckled fingers on his trousers before walking toward the rear yard. The odor grew bad enough the lawman covered his face with his hands, breathing in the smell of his own blood which he found preferable to whatever lay ahead. As he neared the corner of the structure, the voice suddenly returned.

"Put the fire out myself you see, wouldn't want to draw more of your types here. Not yet. I still have work to do. I hope you enjoyed your nap. In honor of your wakey-wakey time, I left you a pair of

gifts. I wasn't sure which style you prefer so one is regular, the other extra crispy. Enjoy."

The sheriff drew his gun and pressed against the edge of the house. A frigid cold emanated from the structure rushing deep into his bones, a subzero temperature found only in the coldest of Maine winters making no sense it being summer. Watkins peeked around the corner, a glimpse which did not afford him a view of a predator nor any other threat other than smoke wafting from a spot in the high grass and where there was smoke there certainly had to have been a fire.

The sheriff lowered his gun but did not holster it as he approached the back lawn. The house stretched far into the field with windows starting high and going higher, with none close to ground level a fact relayed to him by his assistants earlier. Two wings stretched out at the back where in a normal structure the space between would offer an elegant courtyard with furniture for hosting, yet the cavity contained only waist high grass. The well-groomed grass from the front was not duplicated in the back where the greenery rose waist high, likely that of the original pasture.

The lengthy green strands caressed him as he trudged forward, using the acrid smell as a horrific GPS. He had responded to enough house fires in his career (many ending tragically) to understand what awaited him before he even saw it. Below a shattered window high above, he discovered the charred remains of a large man, burnt so badly dental records would be in order.

His mind raced to figure the situation. The individual was too big to be ole Pearl. Time to check a missing person list he thought. Inches above the corpse, an intricate spiderweb danced to the beat of his approaching footfalls. A garden spider posed dead center of the silk appeared to watch the body, happy to have a snack if it would just cool off first.

"Well, my black and yellow friend, while your size is

imposing, I regret to inform you, that you have moved way down the food chain on my fear list."

A subtle breeze shook the spider on its perch which also produced a slight thump behind him. Remembering how the voice mentioned two gifts, he looked over his shoulder only to glimpse a person dangling from a noose high in the air. (Was the rope bleeding?)

The surprise caused him to discharge his gun before cursing himself for doing so. The sight was startling, yet he was not an amateur, so he chalked the faux pas up to the head injury. This man he recognized even from a distance—Victor. The thought anyone could take down that miserable bulldog of a human being was worrisome enough on a good day.

Watkins needed to regroup, required fresh air and wanted freedom from the macabre sight. As his fear grew over the confluence of unnatural events, as whispers of a world sliding off an axis of reality tickled at his soul, the sheriff found renewed strength in his legs and ran. Upon rounding the corner, something unexpected leaped at the sheriff who let loose a long overdue primal scream.

CHAPTER 36

E than braced himself for a blast that never came. Glass broke inside (finally!) followed by all the smoke in the hall billowing in reverse under the gap beneath the door. He saw the movie 'Backdraft' so expected an explosion of some sort but heard only a strange 'foomp' within. Yelling to Martin got no response, so he covered his hand with his sleeve and tested the knob again, surprised to find it cool to the touch though it still would not open.

When a boom sounded, he quickly realized it came from somewhere outside the house which meant help. Ethan yelled one more time for Martin before giving up and charging down the hall to locate the source of the noise. Based on where the sound originated it was not far from his current location. He rushed along trying to estimate the best distance from which to investigate.

Not wanting to press face against glass again, he hoped to find a view where he could simply look down from a safe distance. When mentioning the mysterious lack of cold to the politician earlier, while also spilling some info about his past love, Ethan chose not to share how the memory of the events of a tragic night flooded back to him upon contact with the pane. Strange he would think about such a thing given how dire their current situation was. Stranger still was how he swore he could smell her perfume when the memories hit him.

Ethan shook off the remembrance of that evening to concentrate on the noise. Was help on the way? While searching for the source he hoped to glimpse the roof blaze. It should have spread by now, yet it seemed to have stopped shortly after Martin locked himself in. He trusted the older guy for some reason. Had the politician extinguished it solo where the two together had failed? He could not imagine how, but the situation appeared resolved meaning the man did something.

Having passed several doorways, he chose a random one from which to peer outside, leaning his hands on the sill but keeping his face shy of touching. Looking down, he noticed an object smoldering below. A sense of unease wracked his brain as he attempted to identify the thing but before he could fully piece it together the sight of a cop drew his attention. Ethan banged furiously. The sheriff would easily see him if he looked up, but the lawman was turning away.

The officer suddenly ran away until he disappeared. Ethan cursed in frustration that he had no time to signal the man, but he breathed in relief at just the thought someone was working on their problem. Ethan raced out to search for the others, eager to inform everyone help was on the way.

CHAPTER 37

"Frank, what the hell?"

"You might be right about that," Watkins said.

Deputy Sheryl Breton rubbed her skull where the two collided. After arriving on scene, she promptly advanced on the house with a shocked sense of awe. Calling Frank's name, she received an answer in the form of a gunshot so drew her gun and rushed to the shooting only for the pair to collide along the side of the dwelling. The collision, while painful, was preferable to fatal. Surprising any officer with a drawn weapon was dangerous enough, startling two? Well, they both got lucky.

The familiar couple looked at each other before turning back to the massive house. Sheryl shared a connection with her commanding officer and in his silence as they stood and stared, she believed she could read his thoughts which just so happened to match her own. The thought? *"We're in the shit now."*

***

Watkins took to Sheryl the day she joined the force. The young woman, of mid five-foot height, wore her auburn hair shoulder length nicely framing a makeup-free but enticing face with brown eyes out of a Disney cartoon. The female rookie favored man-tailored clothing and if glimpsed from a certain direction could be mistaken for a male officer, yet Frank noticed only a simple, elegant beauty from any angle, and he had checked them all.

Temptation was part of the job in law enforcement since recruits needed to pass fitness tests. That many people in fantastic shape crammed into one workplace bred physical attraction. Watkins once upon a time married a fellow cop which did not come with a fairy tale ending. After it crashed and burned, he swore off any further company ink dipping, committing instead to an oath of work celibacy. Despite plenty of attractive rookies, his painful divorce kept his libido in check until Sheryl entered the picture.

Frank's attraction to her was immediate, yet rather than dive in and break his own rules (along with his heart if the younger woman rebuffed him) he bided his time to get to know her better. The deputy proved to be whip-smart, a worker who could put together evidentiary puzzle pieces others in the squad had missed. Despite subcontracting major cases to Portland, there were plenty of petty crimes in their town which they solved locally. The talented officer also had a quick wit which raised its welcome head in unguarded moments when she lowered the gates surrounding the castle comprised of her normal serious nature. Her quickness provided her an edge allowing her to give better than she got from the testosterone factory job.

Yes, she was the perfect one for Frank or so he thought. When it came time for him to make a move, to abandon his oath, he learned she played for the other team. At first, he took it personal figuring it might be her go to for all the fellas which was why it relieved him more than disappointed him to discover it was not a line. Sheryl was engaged to a woman named Rachel.

Frank was happy to find out before he made an old man fool out of himself. Despite the hard stop on any chance of a sexual relationship the pair still grew closer. Everything else that attracted him to her remained, he just could not act on it in any traditional way. Those same desirous traits she had in spades continued being enjoyable even in the awkward corner known as the friend zone. Sheryl confessed she had been with men before, found Watkins attractive, (to his ego's delight) yet relayed the information as background not any type of invitation. Nothing changed how she stayed faithful to her fiancé.

The rookie wanted her boss to meet her future wife so invited him to dinner where they had a humdinger of a meal cooked by Rachel who ran a small bakery in Bridgeton among other side hustles. Sheryl's significant other turned out to be a real renaissance woman.

During the evening, the sheriff watched the couple engage in an intimacy and happiness he never quite achieved in his own relationships. The night together became the final nail in the coffin of his crush. He was a male, given to whatever impulses came with that whole thing so he allowed himself to appreciate her looks while understanding fully she was a woman in love. As for Rachel, she was stunningly, objectively beautiful, yet despite her being tall, athletic, with striking features, it was Sheryl who still rocked his boat.

The idea of being 'the other man,' (while understanding it was not his choice anyway) felt so wrong he backed off as a potential suitor while developing a close friendship with both women. That Rachel was the best chef he had ever met did not hurt. The sheriff was happy to be a frequent guest in their cheerful home.

As a trio they became good friends, drinking buddies, even workout and hiking partners while traveling together occasionally. They enjoyed camping in the north part of the state or down south in New Hampshire. On one of their trips Rachel asked Watkins if he would walk her down the aisle since her own father had disowned her when she came out.

The old fool had teared up, could not answer at first. After some prodding, he shouted, "hell yes!" Word got around the office that the two officers were more than friends and neither corrected the record because it kept other men at a distance in a way that her coming out to the world might not. If the testosterone troopers discovered her lifestyle most would line up to be the one to turn her to the other side. Better to allow them to think she was sleeping with the boss as that would put her off limits at least until her wedding day when everyone would be in the know.

***

Sheryl was the person who Watkins trusted most which was why he asked Rick to call her. She followed the directions by first checking on Pearl's place before driving to the field aware that there was something to do with a house. The sight of a massive structure was startling but as an officer she stuck to her training.

Following fresh tracks to the building, she paused along the way to examine the condition of a pickup which sat mid-pasture as weirdly out of place as the dwelling. The broken glass and blood surrounding the vehicle prompted her to yell for the sheriff. A gunshot fired at the rear of the structure caused her to run to the source which ended in the coworkers colliding.

Now with her boss accounted for, the female officer finally did what instinct begged of her upon arrival, she stared at the house while Watkins placed a hand on her shoulder to steady her, understanding full well the sense of imbalance the strange real estate brought with it.

"Jesus, Frank, how?"

"I can't begin to tell you what we're looking at here, but I need your help."

"That smell. Is it what I think it is?"

There was no reason to show her the ghastly sights, so he nodded hoping she would not wander any farther. She was her own woman though, so he could not stop her if she wanted a gander. "Around the back, two DOA."

"We should call for backup, the state, maybe Feds, perhaps…"

"A house just shat itself onto this field. This was not an overnight church barn building. The clapboards are old and weathered, this puppy has existed elsewhere for a lot longer than it has here. Who do you suggest we dial? HUD? Let them know someone built without a permit?"

"This is crazy."

"Things get crazier. Did you check on Pearl?"

Sheryl remained focused on the home, lost in thought.

"Deputy! Was Pearl's place checked?"

Watkins hated pulling the superior card but occasionally the pair slipped into an almost married pattern. When needed they resorted to calling each other by work titles. It helped them focus.

"Yes, Sheriff. Pearl was not home. Her Pontiac was still in the yard, and like most in these parts, she kept her door unlocked. I entered and searched. Her place was not that big, took minutes, impeccable cleaning skills for an older woman. I assumed it to be a welfare check. When I did not find her, I figured a bus must have arrived and left already even though I didn't hear a call over the radio."

"I never sent an ambulance. I believe Pearl is in this house."

"Here, without her car? Who gave her a lift? No way she could walk this far."

"Let's move past all that. More pressing is how we can get in because I fear everyone inside to be in imminent danger." The sheriff looked at his deputy, those Disney eyes so wide while she tried to understand. "You trust me, right?"

"With my life, Frank. Another time, different place you and I, you know that. Don't insult me by asking."

"I need you to get something for me from the rotary."

Sheryl blinked, once, twice, three times. "As in the crime scene?"

"Ayuh."

"Are you crazy? Portland's already pissed you transported evidence. My understanding it was a head? What were you thinking?"

"Hey, I processed it properly, took all relevant pictures. I needed it to prove a point, and it worked. Now I need certain other items to…" he started.

"What? The hands? You are out of your mind. You want me to go to the scene and steal them?"

"Borrow, deputy. I believe they will allow me to save Pearl."

Sheryl kicked her foot in frustration, dislodging a clod of grass before storming off in a tight circle.

"Shit, Frank."

"Look, you and I both understand you won't be staying on with me. That you've stayed this long is likely due to misguided loyalty. We both know you're too smart, you'll have your own squad someday," he said.

She stopped, looking at him. "I've interviewed, got a position in Portland, was waiting for all the red tape to clear to tell you. I'm on detective come a month from now."

Watkins leaped in joy, hugging the deputy until she pushed him away with tears in her eyes. He looked at her with nothing but pride on his face.

"What? You did it. I'm proud of you. You think I should be sad you are leaving? We'll always be friends, best of," he offered.

"No, I am about to start a new chapter in my life and you ask me this? I could lose my job before it starts."

"I know."

"Yet you're still asking me?"

"Ayuh."

"Dammit, Frank. Dammit! I wish to all hell I didn't love you so fucking much," she said and stormed off.

"Oh Sheriff, you surprise me. Are you willing to sacrifice her career on the off chance you can save my current residents? That ship has sailed, their fates determined. Your plan is a folly, but if your workhorse does what you ask, if she brings me what's mine then you will have your opportunity and I hope you do, I really do. I'd enjoy nothing more than showing you in person what I am capable of," the Voice said.

Watkins watched Sheryl cross the tree-line, silently praying she would come out unscathed regarding her new job. He understood that despite her loyalty she would never do what she was about to if she knew for even a moment that the man who she trusted the most heard voices in his head.

CHAPTER 38

Darkness swallowed Charlie and Suzy as they navigated blindly through the center section of basement. The TV host took point which meant absorbing the brunt of each uneven step and colliding with support columns that, without a light source, were discoverable only through unexpected bodily contact. The position placed him in role of the canary to Suzy's coal mine keeping her safe from the same blindside body checks. Maintaining a grip on her hand while moving at a snail's pace, he found circumstance occasionally caused them to brush against one another while traversing the obsidian expanse. A rush of excitement accompanied every touch of the strange woman and he wondered whether she felt the same.

"So, Suzy, tell me about yourself."

"I ran the Boston marathon in under two hours, prefer taxis over Uber, volunteer at homeless shelters and collect exotic fruits."

"For real?"

"No, none of that because it doesn't matter if I offer you truth or lies right now. Lord knows I've created plenty of false identities lately."

"Okay, so that last part sounded truthful. Look, we share something in common and we need to find out what it is."

"So, you believe the politician?"

"More than ever. At the least I have solidified my belief we entered through a portal, otherwise, the officer would have walked through a front door. The question becomes why?"

She jerked him to a stop, their positioning and proximity to one another uncertain in the pure dark. "Are you for real?"

"What? I host a show on the paranormal, it doesn't mean..."

"No. Are you trying to find answers, really? Or only attempting to pick at my wounds, dig out the scarred woman, offer to fix her then move in for the kill? Are you playing a long game?"

"Suzy, I enjoy your attributes, not you per se since we do not know each other. I don't know how to make it any clearer. Full disclosure, two seconds ago, I thought how it was nice to feel your body against mine. I am not proud to have such thoughts, but I'd like to enter into evidence the fact I told you as much, I'm just being honest. We need to be truthful to figure this all out."

Breathing in resignation, she let go of his arm. "My real name is Amelia. I started a new life here as Suzy."

"Why?"

"Because a bad thing happened, something terrible. I am not so innocent Charlie. I..."

On the floor, a phone lit up, vibrating while playing a snippet of "Enter Sandman."

"That's his ringtone, there is absolutely no freaking way that is possible." The device illuminated her frightened face as she picked it up. "Caller ID shows his number, but

178

it cannot be him."
    "Can't be whom?"
    "The man I killed."

CHAPTER 39

Peering outside to discover nothing but more pasture frustrated Stan. What bothered him more was how the old hippy followed behind at a slug's pace. Even if the slowpoke did not fully understand his urgent need to return to the junkyard, shouldn't the guy at least move faster to escape the unknown?

"You really think this is some bad trip?" Stan asked.

"It's more realistic than most, I'll give it that. But yes, this is just a chemical concoction, I'm sure."

He punched Herb in the stomach causing the man to drop to his knees in a quest for oxygen. Then he kicked the kneeling victim, launching him sideways trailing a spray of blood until the man crashed onto his back with a thud.

"Does that feel like a trip?"

Turning on his side, the hippy vomited from the sudden violence before eyeing his attacker. "Why? Why would you do that?" His hand went to his split lip exploring the damage.

"If I'd known you would do the technicolor yawn, I

might have rethought my plan, but you earned that where I'm concerned. I've got places to be and you're dicking around."

"I am sure this helped your cause, asshole."

"What did you call me?" Stan balled a fist again.

"You heard me. Go ahead, beat me more until I earn a little unconscious time to forget the fact that we're trapped in a freaking house that shouldn't even be here while you prance about waving hands solo. Or, the other possibility is when I'm not being sucker punched you discover a tie-dye doesn't necessarily mean pacifist, and I fight back, clean your clock. Give me your best shot, dickwad, let's see which scenario plays out."

The mechanic hesitated in the off-chance Herb could win but mostly because he glimpsed something in the hippy's face, a look usually reserved for those who dance in certain dark places. A closer examination revealed eyes appearing dead inside which matched those of someone he feared. The gaze of the angry hippy brought back memories of the man in black.

***

Two years ago, a stranger dressed all in black showed up at the junkyard as Stan was about to close for the day. When the employee relayed as much, the visitor lifted his shirt to display a pistol in his waistband which changed the dynamic such that the worker welcomed his guest with a smile and a wide berth offering him to drive on through. Firearms were plentiful in Maine (including one in a desk drawer inside the garage) so Stan plotted how best to retrieve it before the fine gentleman could draw his own.

Unfortunately, the newly arrived vehicle parked between himself and the office. That left him a single option—to stall. The man's imposing size revealed itself when he stepped from the car, making his concealed carry only icing on a scary ass cake. The mountainous figure cast a large shadow in the setting sun, where his combination of muscle and fat amalgamated to where the bruiser appeared minus a neck. A ponytail on the sizeable gentleman provided an identifying mark. Mullets were local, ponytails meant Boston or New York.

"The owner, he ain't here," Stan said.

"Which is why I am."

"I don't understand."

"You're sweet on Theresa."

"Who?"

"Oh, she hasn't given you her real handle. Starla sound familiar?"

He knew that name well. The woman was a stripper in Portland who he routinely shared his measly paycheck with. He considered himself an exotic dancer connoisseur, and Starla was the finest of the bunch, an angel if ever there was one despite her passé tramp stamp not to mention her chosen occupation. His paid paramour refused offers of any real dates but whenever he had enough cash, she would ride his pony outside the club in the front of his SUV (borrowed from the yard as a show car since Stan owned a beat to shit Subaru).

The exotic dancer constantly demurred all his requests to take their relationship next level or at least move the action to a hotel room despite any offers of extra cash. The woman always flashed her pearly whites while suggesting it would only complicate things. Not as complicated as this guy inquiring about her, he thought as he blinked.

"Ah, there's the recognition. She does films too. Did you know? Under the name Sandra Summers. How she keeps track of the lies to all the men she hooks up with has always mystified me. That's her true talent you ask me, well that and her tits."

A shake of Stan's head confirmed he was unaware of her mattress actress status, though he planned quite the Google session right after this if he made it out of whatever "this" was.

"Theresa is my girl," the bruiser started.

"Oh God, I'm sorry, I didn't know, I swear, she said she was single!" Stan begged, suddenly understanding where things were likely heading.

"No, not like that, I mean I'm her boss. She is a married woman though, not that it's important or anything, just wanted to get your dumb ass up to speed. The talented tart helps me out in a multitude of ways besides the cash flow. For example, supplying a nice tidbit of info that one of her regular humps, that being you, works at a local crusher yard, that being this." The large man gestured both arms wide partly to point out the obvious but more likely to knowingly cause a subtle rise of his shirt to showcase the packed heat as a reminder. "Next nearest connected scrapyard is an inconvenient distance away. We're looking to grow so this, my friend, is the perfect opportunity for both of us."

"For me?"

"Yes, you will junk this vehicle no questions asked."

"And if I refuse?"

"I can work the machine fine, got no problem with you being inside while I do so. Understand?"

Gulping audibly, Stan nodded before climbing into the driver's seat at the man's insistence. Slamming the door, Stan grabbed for the keys, hoping to speed away until the bruiser dropped heavily into the passenger seat and waved the key dangling from a purple rabbit's foot. Reluctantly grabbing the tchotchke, Stan started the car and drove them deep into the yard to the compactor.

The man in black stood by calmly while Stan wrecked the vehicle, noting the license plate, reciting it repeatedly in his head. Once complete, he stepped away from the machine to approach the visitor.

"I lifted the plates from another car. Don't need it showing up on toll road cameras. Useless to memorize it," the guy said.

"Jeez, you read minds?"

"Just simple ones. You did good. Now there's no cash in this first one but there is something else in it for you." Reaching into his coat, he retrieved a cell phone, tossing it to Stan who fumbled it, dropping it in the dirt before picking it up. The man rolled his eyes. "Really? You need to develop your nerves."

"I've already got a cell."

"Not a burner like this. Two numbers in it. The first is mine. When I call you answer, I don't care if you're on the shitter. The second is that of the whore."

"Who?"

"Theresa."

Stan stared blankly.

"Jesus, she didn't tell me you were touched. Starla's number is there. Anytime you dial she'll meet you and whoopie your cushion. She doesn't respond promptly, or asks for payment of any sort, you let me know."

"You're giving me Starla?"

"For one month, after which, upon delivery of other vehicles, we will pay you in cash once we have established trust. Capiche?"

Stan eyed the phone.

"Don't tell me you think capiche is something you get at Starbuck's?"

"No, I understand, it's just a single go round with her outside the club and I would have done this."

His new partner smiled, slapping Stan in the face. "Good on you for appreciating what I have to offer, pleasure doing business."

A Lincoln had pulled up at some unknown time. The man in black got in the passenger side and the car drove away, leaving him to look back toward the crushed vehicle. A part of him wondered whether he should investigate, try to figure out what was inside but deep down he knew. There was no other option he told himself. Now that it was over, what he began to fear more than the bruiser who threatened him, was how easily he found it to play along.

There was only one thing that could take his mind off his moral failings, he dialed the phone making the first of many calls to Starla.

***

Rising to his feet from the ground without the aid of his arms, Herb noticed the surprised look on Stan's face. "Yoga, you turd. I can move. You almost found out. Now let's get on with it then. I accept you have a specific reason that time is of the essence to escape but understand you won't have withdrawals like others might if we remain here much longer. So fine, you keep acting as though you got a dead hooker in the trunk. Your urgent need to go home helps me."

Herb exited leaving Stan frozen by the man's words. Had the hippy just used an expression, or did he somehow know about Starla, how her body lay bundled in the rear of a Chevy? He followed the man, deciding he could not take a chance, figuring nobody would notice if a drug-addled resident of their scary ass inn were to go missing.

Though he had crushed multiple corpses since first meeting his benefactor, the only person Stan ever killed directly was his former favorite dancer. He did not know how he would get Herb's body out of the house after completion of his plan, but he knew one thing for certain—there was room enough in the trunk of that Chevy for two.

CHAPTER 40

Earlier, after regrouping from the stair collapse, the basement trio traveled to the right. Beth had since crossed back past their point of entry to walk in the opposite direction, figuring it her best chance to avoid crossing paths with the others. She made one more cursory search through the debris for her phone with no luck.

Hurrying away from wherever the other two might be, she wondered how the ghost nerd knew the phrase about power. Her military boyfriend, Zack once unwittingly used the same verbiage during self-defense training triggering her to attack the man whom she shared a bed with. The handsome, muscular soldier served as both her lover and instructor. While teaching her a new offensive move, he urged her to strike harder, telling her, "she had the power."

Upon hearing those words, Beth more than delivered on his suggestion, striking him repeatedly with a combination of moves which forced him to go on the defensive. While Zack understood he had somehow triggered her, he likely ascribed the issue to abuse in her past. He would be wrong.

It was only after countering her attack, pulling her close and holding her tight, that she finally broke down. While she never told him the why behind her actions—despite his deep concern—she experienced a breakthrough related to her reason for starting a relationship with him. The revelation offered a new clarity regarding her choice in men.

Zack was not what one would call smart. Whenever Beth tried to talk about her job or anything in the financial world, he would say things like, "I'll look into my 401 mmm-kay." She would laugh because he joked with such a good heart but truthfully, she was in the sheets with him for two simple reasons—the genes God gave him and the jeans she enjoyed pulling off him.

Immediately after her breakdown in his arms during their self-defense course she demanded he leave, stating how she needed time alone. He complied. Through her drying tears, she realized she had not chosen Zack and many others she slept with because they were her type, but because they were Janet's. She bedded the men her best friend's mind would leave the planet for.

Janet, sadly, would never get the chance to be with Zack or anyone. Janet could not 'do' anything ever again because she ceased being Janet mere moments after saying four words. "You have the power," Janet said that horrific day.

Beth jerked her head startled. While reminiscing about the phrase, she swore she heard it spoken aloud somewhere in the distance. Looking ahead and finding no one there, she chalked it up to the fall, of which her damn ripped nylons served as a reminder. Pure luck kept her from breaking anything especially since Charlie, despite leading the troop, had somehow fallen on top of her. Likely trying to cop a feel, she thought. Even more reason to remain solo in her mission.

"Fucking ghost hunter is getting in my head. Get it

together, Beth." More than ready to leave behind the horrible memories of that long-ago night, she continued forward.

As a bank manager, she had foreclosed on plenty of rundown houses like this one, knew her way around neglected real estate so was certain she could discover an exit. If the ghost host and his girlfriend try to get into her space again, she would dig out her military training moves. Beth rushed through the basement at a renewed pace determined to put more space between herself and the others. So busy navigating the unknown area, she did not notice the single deathly white hand reach out from the darkness beckoning with a finger.

It whispered, "You have the power."

CHAPTER 41

The phone went to voice mail as the blood rushed from Suzy's face so quickly it made her unsteady on her feet. The glow from her cell spilled over her frightfully pale features. An iciness crept into her limbs, settling center of chest while she gasped in shallow breaths trying to regain the bearings not of her surroundings but of a former reality. Cell reception promised a connection to the outside world which should have brought relief, except her mind could not stop rolling over the other possibilities such a call represented. Thinking of the device as a lifeline did not jibe with the knowledge that death just reached out to her.

"Why didn't you answer?" Charlie asked, frantic.

"Why? Because he's dead. No way he could reach out to me, and even if he did, would you want to deal with roaming charges from Hell?"

"Oh please, someone has his cell is all, unless you buried it with him. Do you still have a signal?"

She looked for a bar, any bar, one with gin would be

nice, she thought. Her hands shook while checking the screen. Noticing her level of struggle, Charlie lifted the phone gently from her grasp.

"Look, Suzy, it's not him. But if you did to him what you say then maybe I've finally found the connection between us."

"Mr. Button Down clean cut? Hard to believe. What did you do, Charlie, what did you do?"

Before he could answer, the same ringtone from the same number sounded again. She watched, waiting for the big brave man to pick up only to notice him hesitate. At the moment, she realized he felt what she did, that there was something distressingly wrong with whatever was on the other end of the line and found herself overcome with a certainty they should never reply, that to do so would bring about a horror from which they could not escape. Still, she had to know.

"Give it to me."

She grabbed it, answering on speaker as a baritone male voice filled the surrounding air.

"Ah, lovely Suzy, so good to hear from you again, I've missed you," the man said.

"Brad?"

"Who else would it be? Were you expecting anyone different? Are you fucking someone else dear, sweet Suzy?"

"Brad, please…" she whimpered.

"You sound so timid baby, nothing to be nervous about well, except my elaborate plans to gut you like a fish!"

The words blasted at a volume louder than should have been possible from the device causing her flight or fight to kick in with flight winning until his next comment caused her to freeze.

"Oh, and that goes for your friend Charlie too!"

The pair turned to each other under the light of the phone, a shared look confirmed it was no auditory hallucination. Her mind raced. Brad had never seen her basement partner so how could he know about him? Suzy spun in a circle searching though was unable to see beyond the few feet of illumination provided by her cell.

"Take a selfie, Baby," the voice said.

Charlie nodded. She did not want to, could not comprehend how such a request could come from someone no longer alive. The TV host was the expert, if he asked her to do so she figured he had a reason, so she raised the camera with shaking hands and snapped a pic. The flash momentarily blinded her. Once her eyes adjusted, she looked at the screen and screamed.

Behind her in the picture her ex-husband stood there photobombing over her shoulder. The man appeared washed out white (or perhaps just deathly pale?) sporting a blood-covered Tee. He stood sickly gaunt with a grin almost too wide to be human with eyes registering an inky black. The flash reflected off a blade in his hand. She dropped the phone which went battery-saver dark, then all hell broke loose.

CHAPTER 42

S heryl had long since stopped suggesting where her eyes were to men. It was easier to realize she would face daily issues in her chosen profession so wrote off the multitude of juvenile sexual innuendos in her life as part of her field training. Sexually immature butt-wads on the street regularly offered creative ideas of things they would like to do to her, begging her to recognize how dashing and charismatic they were. She initially suffered the same from the guys in her squad except they quickly moved beyond such superficialities as she gained their respect. Most everyone on the job felt like family.

She gave as good as she got if pushed too far, could provide wallops of physical discomfort as needed. An infamous story involved her arrest of a guy named Pocked Mark who could no longer pee straight after a ride in the rear of her car. Word spread how he mouthed off until she busted his balls—literally. In actuality, the idiot tried to slide his cuffed hands under his bum and over his legs to attempt some lame-brained escape plan. While performing the act, the chain of the cuffs caught on his kibbled bits.

Screams of pain echoed in her backseat. After hitting the brakes, she examined her passenger who she discovered in a position one could label, uncomfortable. The entire squad watched with wonder as she dragged her whimpering human cargo to the station, the man unable to stand fully erect whimpered and whined all the way to booking. The injured perp felt too embarrassed to share the actual events so when people assumed the female deputy had let loose a half ton of whoop ass, the deputy in question did not bother to correct the record. Whenever the story found fresh legs, Sheryl used hers, walking away so as not to have to lie about what truly went down.

The reputation she garnered from that incident came as a Godsend, minimizing the amount of folks in town brave enough to lay their sexist crap on her metaphysical stoop from that day forward. Despite the small population in Tether Falls, not everyone followed gossip trains, so some men remained unaware of her history, or were beyond redemption in that regard, set in their ways as it were. It was in the presence of those locals and visiting tourists that she most often found herself occasionally ogled. One such ogler was Yankee Joe.

After marrying her wife, the newlywed couple spent months refurbishing their kitchen which required routine supply runs to the lumberyard. The obnoxious yard worker was always quick to approach Sheryl with offers of help work-related and otherwise. He was harmless enough, she figured, even though his line of attack was to announce his interest to turn her to the other team was not because of her looks but her mind, assuring her he respected her intelligence plus all her other "complexi-titties."

While his actions were unacceptable in normal settings, there were things she benefitted from in their toxic relationship. The sad sack of a worker had more knowledge about interior work than all the others in the yard combined, so she picked his feeble brain as needed. A part of her always felt there was a decent human being in there somewhere, shame it was buried Mariana Trench deep.

Portland detectives would be on the scene of the accident at the rotary. Maine was not a hotbed for major crimes so something as epic as a head in a trunk would draw a crowd. It would become a story for a generation within the force, which was why far more cops than required drove to their town. The city detective, coroner, and traffic control were the only officially sanctioned authorities while any others present worked in "support" roles.

Someone would have already bagged the evidence and placed it in a transport vehicle. Upon arrival, Sheryl noticed her fellow deputies directing drivers around the ridiculous circle. Scanning the area as she approached, she quickly found what she came for. A Tether Fall's squad car sat alongside the coroner van. That would be where she would find the item Frank asked her to "borrow."

She parked her cruiser near the others, positioned for a fast getaway then emerged from the front seat to walk the scene, drawing stares from some Portland cops. Just by nature of being a woman introduced into the environment she would not go unnoticed. There was no way to stay invisible, but given the severity of the accident, the novelty of another "chick" on the premises would wear off quickly. There were plenty of other female officers in both squads, but a cursory glance suggested this particular day was a boy's club meeting.

Dashcams were not common in their small State. Portland had some but not in every vehicle and those that did had no reason to run 24-7 wasting resources on endless cloud storage which put the odds in Sheryl's favor she was not being recorded. More worrisome were personal cell phone cameras. No doubt some were breaking protocol, taking selfies with the wreckage.

Police officers were professionals. Most would never

take pictures of victims, but they were human so would not miss an opportunity to be a part of something so unique, albeit macabre. She hoped no one would capture her in any photos.

Deputy Nelson, he of a Dunkin' Donuts physique, approached. "Jesus, Sheryl, you believe how that body landed up there?"

"You'd be surprised at what I believe."

She realized at that moment she still had not had time to process how a house had appeared as it did. That combined with the dead bodies jarred her sense of reality in such a way that were it ordinary times she would question her ideas involving faith, might perform a moral inventory except things were not even close to ordinary. Frank's task gave her something to focus on, a job to complete. The inherent danger related to her career kept her on point.

"The head. You heard about the head?"

"Ayuh." Sheryl said, not nearly as talkative when it was not her wife or Frank.

"So why are you here?"

"Because you and everyone else in the department will talk about this forever while suggesting I don't understand how crazy it was because I missed it. To hold off on that particular annoyance here I am."

"Mm, well, good point I suppose. This sets a bar for sure."

"All that said I do not want to get dragged into the paperwork, so guess I'll be leaving." She started to walk toward her vehicle when the chaos began.

"Stand back, sir, stand back!" Portland officers yelled.

"Shit! What's he doin'? Those city boys are likely to pop poor Joe," Nelson yelped but Sheryl was no longer there to hear him.

She fast walked to the deputy's cruiser, glancing over her shoulder at the commotion, reluctantly admitting the local yokel had a pair. Officer's hands settled on butts of guns as the lumberyard employee charged through police tape.

"Yankee Joe, what are you doing? Everyone stand down, this is my case, dammit!" Nelson barked.

"I'm being framed! I want to speak to Sheriff Watkins!"

The deputy stepped closer, raising his arms in a calm the crazy dude motion. "You drunk by noon or something?"

"I hurled when I saw the head so now you have my DNA. You all will try to frame me for the murder."

The lecher sure knows how to put on a show, Sheryl thought while popping Nelson's trunk. She absconded with the plastic bag. Before she had time to dwell on the contents, she slipped it under her duty windbreaker and slid into her cruiser.

During the chaos she met Joe's gaze and almost facepalmed when he winked at her, the idiot. Luckily no one noticed. She drove away, hands shaking on the wheel. Task completed, she thought of the house again, which brought on a sense of unease far greater than her earlier images of getting caught for theft. The strange appearance of the unknown on a section of real estate in their town was on the surface disturbing but what unmoored her more than that was the consideration of what it took to cause an officer as solid as Frank to beg her to steal the gruesome set of severed limbs.

She yanked the horrific bounty from under her jacket. Despite the bags being designed to hold even the sharpness of a knife, the pronged edges of barbed wire still dimpled the container to the point it threatened to cut through. Tossing the disturbing cargo into the back seat, she hit the gas. Joe would continue to demand to see Sheriff Watkins. The authorities could try to locate him but would fail for only reasons she and Big Rick would understand. The whole scenario would buy time for her boss to do whatever he planned. Hopefully, he would figure a way to take ownership of the theft situation.

Earlier, after leaving Frank but before joining her coworkers at the rotary, Sheryl discreetly pulled into a back entrance to the lumberyard in search of her accomplice. During one of those frequent kitchen repair trips, she drove to the yard in the early AM for supplies. Given the hour, she lazily made the trip in her tank-top and terrycloth shorts, the very clothes she slept in. Yankee Joe's appreciation of her new look went off the charts enough she vowed to cover up ever since when she went there. That day came to mind when she planned her strategy which was built around her offer to wear that outfit twice a month if her one-man fan club would create a little diversion. He agreed.

While Sheryl appreciated the man's commitment to the role, she could have done without his idiotic wink which caused her to regret her deal with the devilish man. She focused on her annoyance of having to fulfill future minimalist clothing visits to Yankee Joe to distract herself from dwelling on the object in the back seat which she came to believe was far more than evidence. The bag contained that which she felt could be of great danger to Frank.

CHAPTER 43

Blackness returned as the phone tumbled into the void, the darkness so complete it appeared as if a veil of thick velvet surrounded them. The newly shadowed reality contained the unfathomable—Suzy's dead husband. She dropped low to the ground minimizing herself as a target while strafing her hands along the dirt floor searching for the device until someone grabbed her arm.

She fought against the grip, breaking free and scrambling away in a flail of arms and legs with accompanying shrieks. A dimly lit support beam in the distance gleamed like a beacon. Once she reached it, she anchored herself before rising then turned to search the abyss from which she had escaped.

A face gradually appeared, emerging from the opaque space, the white orbits of eyes grew clearer with every step until she recognized Charlie. She rushed to embrace him.

"Are you okay?"

"That's a big hell no, I saw Brad. How can he be here?"

"He entered a portal?"

"You're not listening. He couldn't walk into one. I stabbed him through the heart, he's dead."

Hands shaking, she remembered the selfie, the horrible image behind her showing a familiar chest wound. She shivered at memories of years ago, of seconds ago. Charlie gripped her fingers to still them, moving in as close as a lover which she allowed.

"Tell me," he said.

Suzy's eyes brimmed with tears. It had been so long since she thought about it, had tried so badly to forget it, throwing herself first into work, then into multiple beds of different men, all as a salve for raw wounds of memory. She nodded. It was time. After sharing her true name with him (and his sharing surprise and confusion why she would not want to use a beautiful name like Amelia) she demanded he continue calling her Suzy. She did not tell him, but she felt Suzy was stronger than Amelia—by a mile. Suzy she would remain until she could escape her past completely, a task growing increasingly unlikely in her current situation.

"Don't judge me?"

"I didn't see the selfie, but I heard him. I need to know what we're dealing with." Charlie said.

"He's a bad person."

"What she said," a voice matching that from the phone spoke from the darkness.

Brad emerged from the shadows, standing over six feet tall, possessing a lean frame with corded arms suggesting explosive strength. The man was lithe and rigid except for his head which tilted to one side bobbing as he stared at the shocked couple through jet-black eyeballs and an evil Cheshire grin. His teeth appeared too wide for his mouth. The smirk almost artificial, alien, as if he suddenly learned how to smile for the first time, then broke it out for a test run.

Blood drenched Brad's Tee, flowing freely from a

gaping wound in his chest, pulsing through a tear in the shirt. The man's physical presence beyond any supernatural elements warranted a threat while the curved rug cutter blades held in each hand removed all doubt. The bestial man was there to harm.

"I've no beef with you, Charlie, but if you do not step away from my wife, I will gladly slice two."

The strange interference in his voice over the phone revealed itself to be unrelated to a bad line. Brad's vocal cords contained a crackling rasp in person.

"How do you know my name?" Charlie asked.

"He told me. A door opens and suddenly I have a new place to play."

"I don't understand how you can be here," Suzy said finally finding her voice.

"Why? Because you literally broke my heart, bitch?" Brad stepped closer.

"No, this isn't real, it can't be!" She closed her eyes, shaking her head only to find the nightmare still present after reopening them.

Brad attacked, unnaturally fast, slicing her arm with one blade while aiming for Charlie's throat with the other. Charlie ducked just in time and grabbed Suzy by the wrist. She yelped in pain when he yanked her away, but the move kept her clear of a second attempted swipe of her ex's now bloody knife.

"Run!" Charlie yelled.

Suzy complied.

CHAPTER 44

The damn dog bit Stan just below his testicles once. The guard animal lived at the junkyard the entirety of time Stan worked there and despite every worker feeding the beast at some point, it never warmed to anyone on staff, not even its owner. They kept it fenced in during the day leaving whoever closed the yard tasked to release it at night. The process involved hitting a button and running for Timbuktu before a gate opened releasing the furry fury aptly named Dante so it could roam the perimeter overnight.

Opening the shop was a bitch. Upon arriving, the down on his luck early bird worker, whoever that was on any given day, had to corral the miserable creature via a series of code words followed by whistles to lure the reluctant mutt back into its enclosed area. Stan, thinking he could make a pact with the devil, once brought a fresh steak from Shaw's. Dante dove for what the hopeful employee thought was the food only for the animal to sink its teeth deep into his leg nipping the hairs on his balls it got so close. Stan went down, bleeding profusely while the animal let him off the hook at that point to devour the treat while Stan crawled away to safety before making a trip to Maine Medical for stitches.

Scrap metal value had increased so much in recent years that it made overnight canine patrols a necessity. If fools were desperate enough to electrocute themselves stripping copper wire from power poles (and some were) they had no problems robbing a scrapyard. Where someone hoped to unload materials was anyone's guess since the industry was incestuous. The workplaces looked out for each other so would interrogate questionable sellers. Still, criminals stole. Many a morning, workers would find a wannabe thief locked inside a vehicle trapped by the dog.

Stan intended to take care of the body after his shift. No one would object to him being the last on site since it meant it would leave him to deal with the animal from hell. His plan included 'forgetting' to release Dante before spending the night cleaning up any evidence before hiding the compacted vehicle after crushing it with Starla in the trunk. He planned to move the remains as deep in the yard as the Ark of the Covenant at the end of 'Raiders of the Lost Ark' where it would remain undiscovered because there were too many vehicles. Time would become an accomplice to his crime.

Stan's plans folded like a paper airplane when he found himself somehow trapped in a freaking house. If his coworkers got too nosy about where he disappeared to— literally—it increased the chances they would check his vehicle. Even if they did not notice the absence of his worldly, upbeat presence and therefore investigated, the roasting sun beating down on the car with its unique cargo would eventually give off a smell worthy of their attention.

Herb had proven to be lethargic, drug-addled, but also prescient. The hippy appeared aware of the reason behind Stan's need to escape. Everyone in the house wanted out, except Stan assumed he was the only one facing jail if that did not happen soon.

The two men searched a dozen rooms since their tête-à-tête earlier. Herb had plenty of opportunities to turn on him for revenge, yet so far only waved his hands around as requested acting as if nothing happened. The hippy was prone to whistle Grateful Dead songs and while Stan appreciated the renewed cooperation from his portal partner, he was more than ready to offer another beating if the man's incessant mouth noise did not stop soon.

They entered a fresh space containing something non-congruent on the floor, a hammer, ball peen, so new it could have arrived straight from a Tucker Lumber shelf. Yelping with joy, he noted how the object did not stir the loins of good ole' Herb who lazily wandered the perimeter.

Lifting it and testing the heft, he determined it real, not imaginary. Somehow the universe bestowed a gift which was surely their way out. Gripping it with both hands, he raised it over his head and smashed the window. The hammer bounced back so swiftly the claw end struck his forehead with a forceful crack. "Shit!" Yelling expletives, he dropped the tool to cradle his aching skull as he circled in frustration, kicking at the air in anger and pain.

Ambling over to investigate the commotion, Herb noticed the hardware. "A hammer? Where did that come from? House seems too old to have that here."

"You think?" Stan pulled his hand away from his temple finding it to be slick with blood.

"Geez man, you're bleeding."

That was it. The Goober he found himself cooped up with always remained a step behind, was a drag on his world. The humiliation he suffered via the blow to his formerly pristine frontal lobe along with the frustration related to a hammer proving ineffective against glass pushed him to end their forced partnership.

Herb bent down and picked up the hammer only for Stan to yank it free and lift it high in the air. The hippy apparently was on the slow side as his head only tilted in wonder at the actions of his paranormal predicament partner.

"Nobody gives a shit about the Dead anymore, you hear me?"

Whack! He smashed the older man in the skull with a sickening hollow crack. Herb's eyes rolled, reset, searching the room for a sound he could not pinpoint. Stan swung for a round two as blood splashed high into the air before splattering like red paint against the canvas that was the floor. *Finally, some color to the place*, he thought before raising the hammer for another blow.

Herb's brain suddenly caught up. "Ah, no, stop!" The words came out slurred as he raised hands defensively against the onslaught.

"How did you know she was in the trunk you dirty, filthy hippy?" Stan swung again.

"What? No! Please!"

The third time proved the charm by bringing Herb to his knees even while he waved wildly searching for the source of the attack.

"Something's wrong, I can't... What's happening?"

Thunk! Stan brought the hammer down solidly onto the man's skull, dropping him face first onto the ground where he kicked and twitched before going still until the only movement remaining was that of his blood pouring across the floor.

CHAPTER 45

S tan smiled at his handiwork, relieved of his burden and witness. The house was so large, everyone panicked enough, that even if someone discovered the hippy, they could not finger him as the killer. If anyone settled on him as a suspect, he would say good ole Herb suddenly acted like a man on bath salts, it was self-defense, really. He practiced excuses in his head. *Would any of you want your face eaten? The best of men could lose their minds if transported through space and time only to appear in a strange building in a field, right?*

Stan did not much care what the others thought deciding he would eliminate them if necessary. Mere weeks ago, he would never have believed murder to be contagious though he did now. After creating two stiffs he found killing spreads like a virus, a fatal one where people were either susceptible to its symptoms or completely immune acting as only a carrier of the disease. Any worries about his actions being discovered by his unwanted flat mates vanished, he would do what he needed to if anyone pressed him.

That which worried him most remained beyond his control out in the real world. Had the cops already found poor Starla? He had loved her dammit, and she said it back to him though it never stopped the woman from charging for services once his free month expired.

Drugs were never his jam leaving his only vice being his chosen stripper and his poon junky brain burned through money fast after getting hooked. The cash not dropped on the club stage, went for hump sessions later. He thought they had a good thing going until one night when she betrayed him by robbing him. While the details of the event remained sketchy, he knew there was a man involved in the treachery (and remembered the man in black mentioned her marriage once which meant her husband was likely an accomplice).

The exotic entertainment venue demanded a two-drink minimum which at ten dollars a pop made beverages cost prohibitive especially after the hefty cover charge. Because of expenses, Stan always nursed the required twin beers the length of his stay at the club. Double fisted brewskis never got him buzzed spread over several hours which was why growing woozy midway through a single bottle that night worried him.

Rushing to the men's room, staggering on loopy legs, before even reaching the sink, his knees buckled, and he fell back into the arms of a large man. His memories were clear up until the race to the restroom and then things got fuzzy before going blank altogether. The in between time left him with images of a man carrying him through a rear exit.

Waking at home the next day, clothes off, the place ransacked, wallet and credit cards gone, it all became clear someone had drugged and robbed him. As a convicted felon, calling the police was out, but it did not mean there would be no justice. There was only one woman at the venue who knew where he lived.

Revenge served cold was not on the itinerary as he was hot and planned to deliver retribution at the same temperature, no waiting for the right moment. Rather than wait to work out the credit situation, he pawned a few old things (not worth the robber's attention apparently) to garner enough money to return to the scene of the crime where he pretended all was well and swell with the world. Those responsible would assume correctly he could not remember dick even while they exposed his for some unknown reason. The gutless lowlifes robbed, stripped, and did God knows what else to him. Memories were unnecessary, he pieced together events on his own enough to paint a very unpretty picture.

Sitting near a potted plant, (who knew exotic dance halls had such elegant ambience?) he dumped his highway robbery priced drinks into the soil throughout the night growing angrier at Starla while she worked the crowd. After leaving the stage she met him in the back for a private show as per usual.

"What's wrong, Honeybunches?" She stopped mid-grind during a lap dance, aware something was off.

"Just can't wait to get alone with you," he said truthfully, promising a sum guaranteed to lure her to his place. For the longest time she refused to go home with him but in recent months if the money was right, she made the trip.

Throughout the night, Stan canvassed the surroundings in search of the accomplice, but with the fuzzy memory, isolating details about the man proved difficult. After the solo grind in the champagne room, Starla returned to the stage dancing to a bass-heavy signature song (some black music, he never listened to that shit). While not appreciative of the tune, boy howdy he sure enjoyed the way she danced to it. Burying his face behind a big fake smile for the rest of the show, eventually she followed him home.

Back home, Stan dropped hints about the evening prior

whereupon she scolded him for leaving without saying goodbye. Everything about her suggested innocence, but he knew better, no one else knew the address to his place. Starla appeared to pick up that something was wrong. During one of their more intimate moments known as his refractory period, she had discussed with him how instinct kept her alive in a dangerous line of work.

"You're acting weird, honey. I'm going. No charge, sweetie."

She had been down on her knees bobbing on him when he began the interrogation. No reason not to enjoy the process. Penis pills ensured he remained rock hard but there was no way he would finish because boiling anger kept the ultimate pleasure at bay. Starla rose, reaching for her bag.

"Willing to work for free now? Don't need the money? Must have had a real score last night, huh?"

"What are you getting at, Stan? I get enough creeps. I didn't take you for one."

Damn she is beautiful when I'm angry, he thought yet could not forgive what happened. Why did they strip his clothes? In retaliation for him always watching her naked? Did they molest him? Snap pictures for blackmail? Laugh at the size of his sausage? The more scenarios he imagined the angrier he grew until he finally locked the door.

"You're not going anywhere, hot stuff."

Starla reacted, registering an understanding everything turned real as she raised hands to calm the animal. "Whatever you're thinking, I ain't had nothing to do with anything. Let's settle down, why don't you get in the chair and let me finish you off. You're clearly stressed."

"Who is your husband?"

"I ain't got none, Stan. I do my thing but am as sweet on you as any."

"Liar! Who manhandled me last night then? Just another John?"

"You are totally crazy. I went home after the club."

Clenching fists and stretching his neck, he watched Starla bolt before giving chase. Many old Portland homes had narrow halls built when people were more petite which caused the fleeing woman to slam into the walls while attempting to escape despite her relatively diminutive size. Launching herself at the back door in the kitchen, she fumbled with the knob only to abandon it when she heard the footfalls directly behind her.

The two noticed the cupboards at the same time and it became a race. Never sophisticated enough to own a butcher's block, Stan kept knives scattered throughout various drawers, his prey would be familiar with the layout and she found a knife first. He pulled a hammer from his junk drawer.

Starla raised the blade with both hands in the tight quarters, both breathing heavily. "Please, Stan, I didn't do nothin'. Whatever you think, I didn't do it."

"Who is your husband?"

"I don't have one. I'm married to Ruby!"

She noted his confusion. "Scarlett Rose, she dances as Scarlett Rose. She's my wife Stan, there is no husband or boyfriend. You hear what I am saying?"

The revelation stunned him. He knew the tatted dancer well, had received lap action from all the girls in the club. The memory of Scarlett's scent returned, enough to identify it as the perfume which lingered after the robbery. So the stripper and her hell of a surprise marriage partner must have colluded to rob him. He raised the tool above his head.

Starla charged driving the blade into his shoulder slicing through flesh until it chunked into his bone. He screamed and whimpered while she struggled to pull it free. He swung the hammer down on one of her arms. The snap echoed sickeningly in the small room as her arm dropped listlessly to her side.

"Stan, no. I didn't do nothin'!"

"Your girlfriend robbed me. Did you know?"

"No, Ruby wouldn't do that, would not mess with my…"

"With your what?"

Starla looked at him, resigned herself, stood straight. "She wouldn't screw with my stream of income—you sorry son of a bitch," she said sealing her fate.

The hammer came down hard where unlike Herb, she dropped with one strike. That was not enough for him, so he struck repeatedly until eventually realizing dead is dead. He intended to do the same to Ruby and her male accomplice after disposing of Starla's body.

He placed Starla in the back of her car and drove it to the lot in the morning with plans to crush it until he heard a door creak open. Next thing he knew, he was in a dwelling with a bunch of jerks, one of whom now lay in a pool of blood at his feet.

Strange that it was a hammer I found, he thought while watching Herb's body bleed out. There would be no clean up on aisle five as he had not encountered a water source since his arrival. He picked up the murder weapon, but before he could decide whether to dispose of it, a thump sounded in the distance. A solo one at first, then another, until it fell into a familiar rhythm.

When Starla used to hit the stage, he often grew jealous of the attention other men gave her so would retire to the John secure in the knowledge he would score naked time with the stripper later. From the restroom, the tunes the DJ spun became lyric free thumps of bass designed to signal things were hot and happening in the club.

He could not understand how, but the thump in the distance matched Starla's signature song and if someone knew the playlist, it signaled somebody other than Herb knew of what Stan had done. He picked up the hammer before following the music, willing to go wherever it might take him.

CHAPTER 46

The couple raced as silently as possible along the edge of the basement, neither daring to look back fearing what an on the run version of a rear-view mirror might reveal. They traversed the underground level quickly, passing so many identical rooms it was not unreasonable to question whether they existed in a Moebius strip, a loop from which they might never escape.

A dark expanse off to one side promised better cover except the same shadowy world originally provided Suzy's dead ex a haven. Charlie stopped, winded, while Suzy continued running, terrified at being chased by history. Once she realized he fell behind, she reluctantly stopped. Every part of her wanted to flee, longed to escape, yet hoped not to do so alone. She turned back looking at her fear factor partner who held the investigative curiosity on his face she came to know and loathe

"Have you seen any other stairs along the way?" he asked.

"What? No. Brad is behind us, we need to run!"

"To where? Look, we are not even certain if he is corporeal…" Charlie started.

"Whether he's what?"

"Solid. Okay, a ghost might be a stretch, but maybe he isn't dead."

"I attended the funeral. Not out of guilt, but to make sure they put him in the ground. He is worm food."

"Common misconception, worms are not responsible for corpse decomposition, in fact…"

"Seriously?"

"Sorry, this is how my brain works. I'm thinking things through. If we can touch him or not is important information."

Suzy showed off her injury. While the compression of her yoga outfit already staunched the bleeding, she still emphasized the damage. "I need to lose the arm for you to make that determination?"

"Good point. He referred to the house as He."

"Who cares?"

"Beth told me not to speak what comes to mind before I have time to complete my thought process which is why I won't relay the reason I believe the information to be so important. At least not yet."

"Fine, but this thing you're thinking? If it pans out, how bad is it?"

"Very."

"How much so?"

"If what I believe is real, there will be no way to stop him," Charlie said.

Dual blades scraped languorously against walls in the distance. The lackadaisical pace of the effort suggested Brad had all the time in the world to hunt, to cut, to gut. Despite the measured approach the sound grew closer, the metal on wood cacophony remained steady, knives wielded by an expert, one who did not stumble in the dark.

The sharp scraping in another setting might be that of horns announcing the arrival of royalty, or perhaps outsiders approaching. He was an outsider all right—outside the land of the living—nothing more than an interloper trespassing on her already fractured reality. The visitor called out in a playful lilt which once upon a time enticed her, though she could no longer imagine why.

"Suzy, come out to play!"

"Think harder, Charlie." She grabbed his hand, and they ran.

CHAPTER 47

Frank paced in front of the house while calculating his next move. That he had not called in backup immediately to process the dead bodies was a sign all was not well with his world. He was the law so he could bring in a small army with one call. But what then?

The building was a Frankenstein monster, but instead of body parts stitched together, it offered different places and times enmeshed creating an abomination that should not exist yet undeniably did. Like the creature of yore, its mere presence would likely terrify people to action, hell, he was plenty scared himself. Once the populace became frightened, they tended toward the dumbest of shit which he could not afford. Watkins remained in the wind regarding what manner of shenanigans was behind the dwelling, but had seen enough to worry for the safety of any staff he might bring in.

Originally, the plan did not include Sheryl's involvement beyond checking on Pearl especially since he could have left the pasture to chase down that which he needed himself (hands wrapped in barbed wire anyone?) except the mysterious mental link he established with the house could fracture were he to leave. The voice in his head, as menacing as it appeared, could unknowingly supply him with info. Like any perp, talk enough and secrets come out.

It pained him to ask his friend to assist him further, especially after learning of her new job. He hoped to minimize any damage to her career related to his request, but he could not leave. There was no way he would take the chance someone else would mentally link besides him. Despite his plan to probe the voice for info, he understood the very idea of mind melding with a house at all was a sign he possibly had gone plumb mad.

"Don't worry, Sheriff, you're not insane, not yet. But you haven't seen all that I have. Give it time. You have the fissures for crazy, I am just here to help crack them open. Too bad so sad you are still on the outside though, we are having so much fun in here. Won't be long now."

"Long before what?"

"Sheriff?"

Watkins leaped at a voice which did not speak in his head. Sheryl stood behind him which disturbed him. He never noticed her arrival, and he was better than that. A lack of situational awareness could end an officer which caused him to consider whether he might be under an influence clouding all his senses and even his judgment.

"Who were you talking to?" she asked.

Not wanting to lie to his friend, he ignored the question. "Did you bring it?"

"Yes, in the vehicle. The story is you felt that the case was taking too long, the rotary needed clearing, so you wanted someone to hustle the evidence over to precinct. You requested that of me. I began said transport, and that's when we got pulled in another direction."

"Thought of all that on your way over here?"

"Came up with several. I'm sticking to this one."

"I'll cover for you—period. Any other thoughts pop into that brilliant head of yours tell me what to say. In the meantime, I need that bag," he said.

"I transported, I maintained custody, it is your call as my direct superior to break that chain of evidence."

That explained why the hands were still in her vehicle instead of in his presence. Watkins nodded in understanding before walking toward the tree line. He stopped upon realizing Sheryl was no longer at his side.

She stared into the distance. "Holy shit, Frank, it's a damn house."

"Ayuh."

After taking a picture they departed, the sun growing brighter the further they moved from the structure. She checked her screen but the glare after leaving the shadowland of the structure made it difficult to see.

"The place is like a blur," she said.

"You monitor calls on your way over here?"

"Yes. I was particularly interested in an APB on myself. No chatter. None of this is on anyone's radar yet. Everything went cold about a half mile down the road, nothing but static. I assumed it was time for a work order, now my gut tells me this place has something to do with it."

"Bingo," he said regarding both her assessment of the mysterious radio silence and the bag in the back seat of her cruiser. He opened the door, pulled it out.

Sheryl stepped up, blocking him. "Who did you think you were speaking to out there? I'm going out on a limb with my career, so I need to know you are okay, that you aren't..."

"Crazy?"

"You said it, I didn't."

"While I appreciate you noticing something might be wrong with me, this isn't normal circumstances. Time to make this formal again. I order you to get out of my way deputy and to leave now."

She stepped aside. Watkins walked away, severed hands at his side. Looking both ways down the street out of caution he suddenly realized how lightly trafficked the road was. Had the house chosen this location based on that? Sheryl called out.

"Sheriff!" Jogging over, she lifted the phone, spreading the photo larger.

"What am I looking at?"

"The picture looked blurry, but when I looked closer, expanded it, well…" The tiny screen showed a dark mass where the house should be, appearing more mist than solid. High in the pic were two red blotches while a jagged rip in the blackness filled the bottom which combined emulated the look of a massive evil face grinning for the camera. "Maybe I'm crazy too."

"Go, I've got this." The sheriff crossed the street, making a beeline for Rick's truck. Grass rustled behind him though he did not bother to turn around. "I gave you an order, deputy."

"With all due respect, fuck your orders, Frank. I won't work for you much longer and you're too good a friend for me to leave you here alone."

Watkins grimaced. He loved the heck out of the woman, but he also understood he could not change her mind. He feared she was in danger if she remained behind, more so than any previous situations, Frank felt a nagging sixth sense that the house could well be his last case.

The sheriff lowered the tailgate on Rick's truck before setting the bag down. He broke the seal, lifted the clasped body parts out, careful not to prick himself with the barbed wire. Gripping the metal strand where the jumbled wrap ended, he pulled, unravelling the metallic cocoon. As the tension of the wiring released, the hands spread until they faced up cupped together.

Reaching between the palms, he found what he expected, a bloody key. Looking back toward the house he could almost see the same face from the picture grinning.

"What do you know, Sheriff? Looks like we're going to meet after all. My, my, my."

CHAPTER 48

The fleeing couple reached a fork in their desperation road. Charlie ran in one direction, Suzy the other.

"Where are you going?" he asked.

"Far away. This has nothing to do with you. I realize that now."

"Not true. Something brought us to the same place. Your reason for being here is mine too. Our best chance to escape is together."

"There is no escape for me."

"Maybe there is. Any answers lie in the man's mystery, but I can't figure him out on my own. Tell me."

Suzy drooped in resignation. "I've been running from this my whole life. I was young then, he was older, we shared a certain sense of… darkness in the relationship but it turned at some point. Things were hard, I worked a suck job, he did carpets until his boss cut his hours to almost nothing. The more our life together went off track, the more he extended his cruelty beyond the bedroom. My attempt to break it off led to the night he tried to end me."

Charlie reached out, but she waved him off, unable to be near any man as memories flooded her, causing her to shiver under the weight of thoughts long buried.

"Look, if he hurt you, emotionally, or physically that's on him, you were a victim. Walking away to face him alone, differs from before. If you go solo, it becomes your choice to be a victim."

Smells and sounds from that night buzzed in her brain. The fear behind her struggles resurfaced as she remembered pushing and kicking wildly at him to halt bedroom antics which had long since become brutal. His answer was to strike her hard enough that her world switched over to a silent buzz while flashes of white sparkled in her vision, threatening to drop her into a world of blackness. Momentarily too stunned to fight back, she took the abuse repeatedly, bouncing on the bed under each blow, until sound returned along with her senses enough to know she had to escape or her time on earth would be over.

Prior to the fight, she discovered he cheated with a saleswoman on the job which somehow became her problem. According to Brad, he two-timed only because she hassled him so much. In her young heartbreak, (twenty-one was the magic number) she took him back albeit reluctantly.

An immature cocktail of insecurity combined with youthful emotions brought the couple to the bedroom the same night after arguing about the affair. During their session he amped up the normal roughness until what started as exciting breath play became an all too real struggle for oxygen. To stop him, she kicked him in the balls which was when the beating began.

Scrambling from the bed during the battle, she rose to her feet despite abrasions and heavy bruising. Her ability to stand at all after his best efforts enraged him anew, convincing him masculinity was not enough to tamp down the will of the woman, so he grabbed a carpet cutter from the work belt on the floor, flashing it menacingly. Flipping it in the air for effect, he caught it before launching an attack designed to be lethal forcing her to use a college course self-defense training move.

Instructors deemed students only use the dangerous action in the direst of circumstances since it required advancing on the weapon. The armed monster reacted in utter surprise when she advanced quickly and gripped his wrist with one hand then slammed her other down on his extended elbow and pushed. The arm collapsed at the joint shooting his forearm toward his own torso where the blade finally found a home, slicing deep into his chest with a sickening thunk. The shock on his face never faltered even as he looked to his victim with wonder.

She leaped to safety while he tilted like a punch-drunk boxer, bobbing and weaving in place on legs which might well have been on a ship in rough waters. Already confused, he appeared further so upon looking down at the handle jutting out at heart height. He wrapped his hand around the hilt.

"Baby?" Gripping the work tool tightly, he yanked it from his chest, the movement caused him to wobble.

The blade was surprisingly free of blood as was the wound itself which showed a large deep black gash below a rip in his Tee. Then as he continued to examine her handiwork, a crimson liquid made for the surface, gushing in thick pulses down his torso causing him to snort loudly before face planting. Suzy dropped against a wall, slid down to the floor on her ass where she watched former love die.

Ever since that night, she held men at arms-length, trusting none fully despite meeting some great ones along the way. Unfortunately for every great connection there were several turds in the punch bowl, but they were all equal at the end of the day in that the relationships ended quickly even if they were Prince Charming. One and done became her motto.

Then there was Charlie who appeared to be a boy scout (as did several husbands who had no problems cheating on wives). She did not want to trust him, planned to abandon him, as Beth had strategically chosen to, except circumstances kept her from fleeing altogether. What kept her tethered to her partner were all the unanswered questions. Despite her best efforts to compartmentalize her situation, she still could not comprehend how Brad returned and how he did so within an environment she could not escape from. Her new friend knew more than he was letting on which was why she remained while Beth fled. Would she stay forever? Hell no, first sign of an exit and she planned to leave, would think no more of him than the guy in the Walmart.

She had wanted nothing from men in so long other than what they could do for her physically. She never much cared for their needs, figured they got what they desired from her in their bouts together given how she remained fit, healthy, vigorous, and determined in the sheets. But now, with Charlie, things were different. For the first time in recent memory she needed his knowledge which left her battling animosity toward him because of it.

Her longing for answers extended beyond the mystery of her abuser's return. That circumstance alone brought with it a fear that the earth no longer rotated uneventfully on its axis as before. As far as she could tell, every turn now passed through a series of interdimensional curtains each of which lifted to reveal unexpected surprises in a formerly safe existence.

The planet turns, and whoomp! A flutter of one cosmic curtain reveals a door in her studio. Flutter, whoomp! Another pass and suddenly she is in someone else's home, from a time period she cannot determine. The earth continues to turn, getting twisted in the mystical drapes, but when it flits wildly again, the dead somehow return, armed with carpet cutters.

While she survived that night long ago, she worried

how the circumstances now differed from before, feared there was no conceivable scenario where she came out the victor this time. Worse, she spent years feeling guilt over Brad's death despite the part he played in it.

What bothered her the most from that long-ago night was seeing his eyes change when he died, witnessing him transform from the devil incarnate back to someone she once loved. The shift in his features occurred in the seconds before he breathed last leaving her to question whether she killed the monster or the man. Now, in the new version of reality only the beast remained. Brad was a vessel for the dark being visiting her that awful night and it had returned with vengeance in mind.

Despite her misgivings, she decided it was time to trust someone. "I need help, but he's here for me. I won't allow this to become your situation."

"Good, I'm glad you feel that way, because my plan counts on you getting up nice and close with him."

Charlie screamed as a blade slashed his back, the angle off enough that it barely sliced but cut skin. He twisted away from the cutter, turning to his attacker only for Brad to punch him so hard it launched him into a support beam where he bounced off before slamming onto the dirt floor.

"Run, Suzy!"

"Yes, run, Suzy, isn't that what you've been doing ever since you killed me? I had no intentions to harm you that night, only had a temporary break, just lost my, you know… cool. You, however, murdered an innocent man, one I'm mighty fond of. Me," Brad said.

"You broke my eye socket!"

"You liked it rough. You never used the safe word."

"I screamed it over and over."

"Yeah, memories fuzzy, don't remember it that way. What I recall is you driving a blade in my heart. Now time to finish what I started that day!"

The attacker closed the distance swiping both blades in an arc designed to dig into both sides of her neck. Suzy dropped to the ground barely avoiding the weapons. Against twin knives, her original defensive move would not work so she performed another by punching him square between his legs. Rather than drop, he only smiled suggesting the man part was dead and no longer vulnerable.

"Oh good. You want to play," he said.

He struck her below her jaw, with a fist wrapped around the hilt of the blade. His unnatural strength sent her airborne before gravity reclaimed her, brought her down hard onto her back, her breath jolted out of her.

Fighting to breathe, she recognized his deadly intent when he raised both blades over his shoulders. She rolled just in time as he dropped straight down, daggers extended, designed to embed into her prone body. The metal struck dirt as Suzy completed her roll, rising to her feet. Charlie struggled to do the same while favoring his shoulder. Her ex arced the blade, sliced the back of her calf as she limped out of his reach, whimpering.

"Brad, if there's any of you still left, can you please remember how we used to be?"

"Ah, Suzy." He rose, flexing his neck. "I never loved you. You were always a piece of meat to me then and I literally intend to make you one now. Well, more like pieces."

"I get it. You are different, somehow stronger, but I also know something else about you," she said.

"Pray tell, sweetness?"

"To hurt me, you need to be able to stand."

She lunged even as he lashed out again. Leaning low to avoid his reach, she kicked him in the stomach. His arms waved wildly at the ceiling as he tumbled back, shocked to discover his feet leaving the ground after tumbling over Charlie who staged himself on all fours behind the monster. The old playground move was just as effective on adults, or undead former husbands, Suzy thought with some satisfaction.

Charlie rose from his crouch before the fallen man could recover and stomped on his knee. Brad screeched wildly in agony, his whole body shaking in an unexpected pain as if seeking a solution for the damage. Without looking back, Suzy gripped the TV host's hand, and they ran.

"His strength?" she asked.

"Fits into what my worse fear is."

"Which is?"

"This House isn't just a portal. I think it's a demon."

Suzy was liking her friend less and less, but she continued to run away with him.

CHAPTER 49

The frigid floor brought Herb around though lifting his head produced a cry of pain. Touching the throbbing area, he found it spongy versus firm and worse, his hand came away bloody. An island of bone shifting under the hairline confirmed a fracture which would require medical help immediately. He understood the fragile nature of the injury so well because he broke the skulls of many others—eighteen in fact.

The cool crispness of his surroundings signified importance though he struggled to recall what that might be. Despite how much it hurt to think, he finally remembered the damn house with its regulated temperature. Coldness signaled a way out. He needed that exit hasto pronto, before the loose piece of bone doing the Tango around his noggin' brushed against the hippocampus or whatever one called the *better not fuck with it* part of the brain.

How did he break his skull? That remained shady. Strange how his recent past proved fuzzier than memories of many years ago. Someone must have laid down quite the beating. Well played by whoever rocked his clock. How had he, a serial killer (the term graduated from spree after his fourth murder) allowed his defenses down long enough to become a victim?

***

Herb attended his first Grateful Dead concert at age eighteen. The experience exposed him to a larger world even as it ejected him minus a parachute out of a life of suburban complacency. The concert initiated him into the world of recreational drugs. Using them tore open a rift in the space-time continuum revealing a previously unseen universe wrapped in a perfect macrocosm over that of his previous small-minded totality.

The new dimension (reachable by a route called Psychotropics Street) defied normal laws of physics. The revamped arena of existence lived in a place where the tiniest of molecules became visible to the human eye while moving in a constant hyper state dancing jigs atop his former reality.

The combination of pharmaceuticals, plentiful sex, and music changed his life as he followed the band on tour whereupon he dropped out of society, quit college, embraced a bohemian lifestyle. He lived in tents, vehicles, or whatever couches presented themselves. During that time, he also fell in love with Blue.

If she had another name, she did not share it, so he only knew her as the color. The raven-haired beauty was ten years older than him and possessed a wild spirit with an insatiable sexual appetite. Even through their budding romance she was prone to sleep with different men in any city where her feet landed. Initially he accepted her free love ways though eventually her generosity of flesh led him down a path of despair and jealousy despite his own routine dalliances with strangers.

Affairs were standard operating procedure for Heartbreaker Herb in his younger days. He considered monogamy so anathema the term deserved to be double the size of a four-letter word. Still, he sometimes called out Blue's name during sex with others which never went well even if his conquests were only after a one-nighter themselves. The start of his apology tour for his all too regular bedroom faux pas often segued into monologues themed around Blue being the only woman for him. His non-apologies drew similar responses each time from angered lovers who yelled variations of "get the hell out of my bed" (or van, hammock, insert other nonconformist living situation here).

He longed for the day when Blue would change her ways, come to recognize what a catch good old Herb was, but then she fell for a younger man named Cedar. He always suspected the biggest barrier to winning Blue's heart was his youth so his master plan was to remain in her orbit until he could get into bars legally figuring she would no longer worry about any maturity imbalance. The age gap reared its ugly head while traveling to the Southern California venue for the Dead Tour. Herb suggested a side trip to Disneyland as he had never been. The request became the exact moment he lost her. She giggled at the suggestion, subtle at first until—fueled by pot—she erupted into a full-blown laughter, the kind one could not stop once it started. He exited the van red-faced to escape the humility, quickly forgetting all about the 'Happiest Place on Earth.'

He spent the night without her after the show hoping his absence would make her heart grow fonder but mostly because he was too embarrassed to face her. When he returned, he found her in the throes of passion with a guy named Cedar. Once she finished her sexual marathon with her new lover long enough to acknowledge his presence she informed Herb their time was over, that while he was welcome to drive with them to the next show, once there he would be on his own.

Cedar (who names their kid after a tree anyway?) was only eighteen, one year younger than he, but his former love decided her new conquest was her soulmate. She wished for them to settle things down, was how she phrased it. Then like that, he was officially single. Herb spent the rest of the summer following the Dead and while he had no problem finding fresh sexual partners, he mourned the loss of Blue. His anger at his ex-girlfriend summarily dismissing their destiny rose above the mellowing effects of the cornucopia of drugs he existed on.

A month after their breakup, he visited only to find Cedar humping with another male in her van. The 'pitcher' in that scenario amscrayed when Herb came knocking. The heartbreaker hippy backpedaled, putting his clothes on slowly, bumping Herb suggestively while offering his body in trade for silence. When Herb declined the generous offer, the Casanova made excuses about the situation, explaining he did not know the guy, it was a onetime thing, Blue did not need to hear about it and so on.

Sensing an opportunity, Herb offered to smoke out with his replacement for old time's sake while realizing, like the act he just witnessed, he might have found a backdoor in with his lost love. The busted boyfriend eagerly accepted the offer, hoping to secure silence about the dalliance. Mentioning how he was out of bud but had a connection, Herb urged Cedar to follow him toward the fringes of the camps leading them past the crowds into the isolated camping area until reaching an empty tent. While traipsing across the well-worn campgrounds, Herb's anger grew at the thought the younger man had stolen his girl.

The cheater appeared to pick up on the bad vibes Herb was inadvertently throwing down. Cedar grew skeptical of the arrangement, even nervous about their surroundings. Herb did his best to put the young man at ease, playing off how their time together would mean a lot to him as he wanted to hear about what Blue had been up to. Trading some old stories of their time in the sack with the same woman was worth it if it meant his holding back the story about the guy being with another type of sack, no? Cedar agreed with a nod which jiggled his leather necklace. Immediately upon entering the tent, Herb jumped the guy from behind, twisting at the string around the man's throat, yanking it tight.

Limbs flew in all directions as the victim fought his attacker while grasping at his neck desperate to breathe, choking and spitting as Herb pulled hard enough to lift the young man off the ground. Cedar kicked wildly until one leg went slack as the other stomped furiously up and down out of reflex. Eventually Cedar's arms fell to his sides, dangling, so Herb dropped the deceased to the floor, stepping back to examine his handiwork.

The hippy's right eye had exploded blood red which stood out on a bloated purple face, leaving the bohemian body to pay homage to the host band's name minus the grateful part. Footsteps passed by accompanied by odorous clouds of pot, unwashed people, alcoholic fumes, and occasional patchouli. Senses dulled by drugs for so long shocked to life with a rush greater than Herb's first dances with chemical partners and even rivalled that of his relationship with Blue.

Slipping from the tent into the crowd, Herb returned to watch the concert where he experienced the music in a way he never had before. The stimuli of the event swarmed him with a sensory overload, so overwhelming it eclipsed any former experiences tripping on LSD. The familiar grew obscenely unique, all senses heightened while he danced alongside a woman all night before dancing inside her after the show.

Sex with the stranger lasted much longer than normal because if his physical state faltered, he relived his earlier deed in his mind until he found himself ready to go again multiple times over.

He expected the police the next day, but they never came. The murder never appeared to make the news as the only thing in print were stories of ODs which were prevalent on every stop on the tour. He assumed Cedar somehow fell into that category, classified as another unfortunate statistic.

Feeling abandoned, Blue sought Herb out hoping to rekindle their relationship except after his recent experience with his current mistress—Lady Death herself—he found he no longer desired his former flame, even pitied her, frankly. He was a new man who continued to follow the Dead with vigor along with a rising body count as he added fresh victims in every city. During the tour, he perfected his skills, discovered ways to hide bodies better or at least to stage them to suggest drugs had taken another lost soul.

The sheer numbers of fatalities would insinuate not all had overdosed (there were defensive wounds to take into consideration, especially from that bitch, Jade). Several finally made the news as murdered individuals. Herb was surprised to learn of victim's true names through media reports. Most monikers turned out to be pedestrian such as Erika Ellsworth, or Melanie Cooper which did not jibe with what he knew them as. To him, they were Riverbed, Moon-petal, or other hippy-dippy variations.

Voluminous amounts of illegal drugs at shows created roadblocks for police who found witnesses far from cooperative, fearful of stings unrelated to the case in question. Herb limited his kills to one per city to minimize chances that precincts might connect dots to a single killer. High-risk lifestyles of victims along with their nicknames of 'Dead Heads' made squads with minimal resources rank the cases as a low priority. The only good hippy is a deceased hippy, right?

On his journey of self-discovery and mortality thievery, Herb collected trophies with which he could relive the moments where he felt the most alive, ironically by making others very much not so. The tire iron was his preferred weapon of choice given how easy they were to find among a sea of vehicles. The length of heavy metal proved enough to incapacitate a person of any size, and if desired one could use the tool until completion which he sometimes did. When the mood struck not to strike, so to speak, his go to for the 'it was a nice life while it lasted' finale was often a wire, belt, pantyhose, or any variation of a garrote with which he could strangle victims.

Besides keepsakes, Herb also recorded detailed notes of each attack in a journal using coded words for times, places, manners of death, even names. The thrill of his kills occurred in quick furious bursts followed by the extensive workload required to hide evidence. The binder allowed him to relive the memories, and all pleasure associated with the acts in safe spaces, far removed from the killing fields. A cross-country serial killer roamed the land while the world was none the wiser.

It was only when the Dead stopped touring and Herb discovered newer drugs like Molly and Oxy that his desire for extracurricular activities stunted. The pills offered him a kick rivaling the taking of life not to mention his increased age made it more difficult to corral younger victims. Near the end of his streak he sought only young males who were far more agreeable to connect with an older man than women were.

***

Now Herb found himself on a floor, face against tile, struggling to move beyond memories of the past to focus on the previous hour. Lifting himself up prompted another groan of agony. Though his wound was dire, he refused to be a victim as he considered that status to be for lesser people. Rising to his feet brought him to the realization his injury was worse than first imagined for when he examined his surroundings, he saw no evidence of the house, only a morgue.

"No freaking way, a super bad trip, can't even remember what I took."

He waved his hand in front of his face, finding it free of visual trails, no Neo from 'The Matrix' style movement. Behind him was a workstation with a dead body on board, a sheet draped over it.

The other walls housed corpse containers from floor to ceiling. While he found it impossible to believe he could suddenly be in a mortuary, the refrigeration required for such places explained the coldness he felt since waking. Herb searched for a door, saw none. *Those corpses got in here somehow*, he thought, and however they did, it could be a way out.

Yes, that was it. He never left the dwelling, only stumbled into another wing under the confusion of his splitting migraine. It made sense that a house this size would have a funeral home within. Hearses could deliver bodies, plop them onto a conveyor system feeding them into the rear of the drawers. Herb would have to check each for an exit. Before he could search, metal clanged loudly behind him.

He turned to discover a pair of forceps had fallen off the exam table only to land on the cement floor.

"Hello?"

He laughed at his foolishness as he was obviously alone. While bending down to to pick up the object, he glimpsed the toe tag of the body on the table and stumbled back.

"It can't be."

The dangling identification card read Cedar. Herb dropped the forceps where they clanged anew. Pulling the sheet aside he revealed the corpse of his first kill! The young man still had the red eye from the attack along with blanching across his face where blood vessels had burst.

Cedar had died *the prettiest* he often thought because

Herb had not yet used the tire iron which eventually changed the dynamic of how his victims appeared at the end of their lives. The totality of circumstances since waking on the frigid cement floor proved he was beyond concussed. Yes, fine, there was a morgue in the home, and where there is a mortuary there would be a dead body. But Cedar? No, his head trauma had to be responsible, a bad wire in his brain brought on by the attack caused him to overlay the face of his first victim onto that of some other poor sap. Draping the sheet back over the body, he turned in search of an escape.

A fast exit became necessary as he urgently needed a hospital. The cooling unit which refrigerated the bodies would require occasional repairs so locating the device was key to finding a way out. The fact one was not visible suggested they had built it into the rear of the corpse drawers. Technicians needed to work on it from somewhere, he only had to discover where.

Hiss! The air flooded ice particles as he unlatched and yanked open the first drawer to reveal a young nude woman, flowers threaded through her hair and wearing a beaded bracelet he remembered, one which he took as a trophy. Its presence flummoxed him given how it remained locked in a storage shed with all the other items. She appeared identical to a redhead named Sparrow whom he had killed on the last year of the tour. A toe tag confirmed her name.

"What is going on? This can't be!"

There was no clear access to cooling hardware anywhere behind her body even though frigid air continued to escape into the room after opening the corpse cupboard. Herb prayed Charlie was correct that a change in atmosphere meant a way out. He rushed from one to the next, pulling each out while seeking that elusive back door to freedom.

Each exposed body came adorned with familiar objects, a scarf here, a necklace there, items that never could have made it to the room he found himself in. Despite recognizing names on toe tags, they could not be the same people because it was not possible for them to look as fresh as the day Herb killed them. Never mind how they were pushing up daisies in different states making it impossible anyone possessed the capability to bring the dead body band back together. There was no conceivable way all the victims could share the same stage, or in this case, the same charnel house.

His breath crystallized under the frigid temperature which dropped significantly after opening all the drawers. Then he heard it, somewhere behind him, a rustle, subtle but distinct, that of fabric rumpling. He slowly turned.

A scream froze in his throat. Cedar sat up on the table, the cloth draped over him like a ghost. It leaned toward him before swinging legs over the side of the exam table where it pushed off in a small leap and stood up! Scrambling away, Herb fell into the arms of someone. Looking back, he spied Sparrow behind him! He launched himself clear even as he noticed movement from every direction.

"I'm not okay, I'm not okay. My head. I'm not okay!"

A sea of bodies climbed from drawers where those in the highest tombs scrambled straight to the ceiling, defying gravity as they crawled across the surface as if it were floor. Those above looked down with lifeless eyes while others clamored along cold ground, staggering on bent and broken legs. Flap. Flap. Flap. Their steps, awkwardly paced, echoed with the sound of dead meat slapping concrete.

Rushing to the farthest side of the room, he crouched in the corner, placing his hands over his face while curling as small as he could.

Then he felt a tap.

Sparrow stood over him, attempting to look into his eyes though her head could not lock on a position, given how it dangled awkwardly on a broken neck. Taking her bracelet off her wrist, she waved it in front of him as if a hypnotist with a pocket watch.

"I don't understand."

Dropping the item in his lap, she moved her hands to his skull wound, pressing fingers in until one reached his brain. Kicking and spasming wildly, he gasped in agony as jolts of debilitating pain wracked his body.

"Stop, stop, shtop!"

She walked away while he glanced at the bracelet on his thighs, feeling it should mean something, but it was fuzzy now. Why couldn't he remember? Another person appeared before him, a young man, Tuck. One trophy Herb kept in his storage unit was that of this youthful man's necklace, an odd piece akin to a bolo tie. The dead youth dropped it alongside him before reaching into Herb's brain.

He spasmed again, screaming in a pain unbearable, as if lightning burned something internal. Portions of his body went numb. Once his involuntary jerking in place stopped, he found himself confused by the item in his lap. Hadn't he looked at it a moment ago? Didn't he know who that necklace had belonged to?

Standing above him, the line of those long since passed stretched out filling the length of the mortuary. Each held an object in their cold pale gray hands, and it was then he came to understand. He knew those items well, had savored them in the aftermath of his handiwork but now they had returned, intent on stealing his precious memories! Jessica was next, dropping her panties before pressing aggressively on his grey matter.

Something snapped during his spasm paralyzing him below his neck. He lay in a heap, slumped against the corner, items scattered around him like offerings for a God. Was that not what he was? Had he not he risen above the frailties of human flesh by separating souls from their vessels? Had he not come to decide the fates of mere mortals? Yet whatever powers of a superior being he might possess, damned if he could no longer seem to move anything below his shoulders. His head remained mobile which left his pain receptors there still firing overtime.

Glancing at the tiny piece of cloth, he sensed the item was an undergarment though his scrambled brain could not find the word panties in his vocabulary anymore. He could only howl when the memories of every trophy he ever collected paid one last visit before vanishing forever.

Those in the long queue, waiting to greet him after all those years, took their time exploring his inner workings, oblivious to his slurred, drooling protests. As the probes on his cerebrum continued, he quickly lost the ability to scream. As they poked away at his gray matter further, soon he found himself unable to recall the significance of his trophies, even forgot how to beg for his life until finally, he reached the point where he could no longer remember how to breathe.

CHAPTER 50

The pair ran hoping they lost the crazy ex, only to find their hopes dashed upon hearing Brad curse in the near distance. Though the force of evil navigated on a compromised leg, he resumed the scrape of blades against walls with an authority suggesting a broken limb was no problem, nothing to see here. Charlie listened for signs of life overhead surprised at the absence of footsteps. It weighed on him how they had covered so much ground but had yet to encounter a single creaking board, nary a muffled voice besides their own. Had something bad happened up there too?

Maybe the others had found an exit. Perhaps they wisely escaped with no thought of going back for Charlie Company. His curiosity begged him to explore the strange realm they were in but that would come later after finding a way out. The surprise introduction of an outsider, (albeit a dead one) forced him to recalculate their situation.

The non-couple poked heads into various openings in search of a spot from where to make a stand. He opened a door, examined the interior. "This is it, wait here."

"Hurry," Suzy urged.

Rushing off, he yanked boards from a window frame in the next room before returning to drop the planks on the ground.

"So, this is it then, huh?" she asked.

"Yeah, good luck."

They hugged tightly before he walked away, leaving the woman all alone with her past.

CHAPTER 51

Beth finished her one Mississippi style count after reaching thirty minutes which she ticked off from a Lotus position on the floor. Meditation became a part of her life since, well, the incident. Counting fed into her cogitation helping to ground her until enough time passed that she might find her nightmare over. Unfortunately, the bad dream continued unabated when she opened her eyes and found herself still trapped. The practiced breathing which calmed her initially provided no change to her circumstances. Like a fad dieter, her temporarily shed anxiety returned tenfold.

"No, no, no! Why am I here?"

The makeshift concentration room sat off the main corridor. She chose a space without a door to allow a quick escape if needed. The option provided a safe space where she could more easily focus on her breathing. The subterranean darkness of the basement, frightful even when accompanied by the prying couple earlier, proved far more nerve-wracking solo.

A flutter of fabric zipped past the opening, drawing her to her feet. Only a turn of the century frock felt proper in such an old house, yet the garment appeared modern, fashion-forward even. Despite the speed at which it passed she identified it as designer wear, a colorful mini, tight enough to show off curves while easy enough to disrobe if the right guy came along. Gooseflesh wracked her body. The only way she could pick up that much information from such a brief glimpse would be not from recognizing a style of dress but remembering the exact one. And she did, because she lent it to her absolute best friend in the world.

"Janet?"

Beth entered the hall in time to catch another flash of red zip through a blanket of illumination in the distance. She immediately gave chase, noting the footprints in the sandy floor showed the runner wore heals. They looked to be her own size, causing her to remember how she used to swap shoes with her friend all the time.

The pursuit brought her to a hard corner meaning she reached the end of the house. She continued fast walking along the side of the house which grew totally dark as there were no windows along the side, no rooms, just a solid length of wall. She finally came to the next corner which turned out to face the entire length of the opposite side of the house she initially traversed. Learning the dwelling had end points rather than stretching into eternity provided her a level of comfort absent since her incarceration. The minimal relief quickly faded when she realized the entire length of the massive home now lay ahead. She peered nervously into the tenebrosity.

The mystery figure maintained a comfortable lead over herself. A sense of isolation fluttered in her gut as she pondered traversing the grand vastness ahead, the thought of which caused her to consider returning to the very folks she abandoned. No, she left them behind for a reason, she could handle the situation, she only needed to reassert control over it. Steeling her nerves, she shouted out.

"Show yourself!"

Janet could not be running through the corridor. It was exceptionally silly for her to think so. Whoever she was, the woman appeared fitter, younger than the townspeople upstairs, so there was the chance she was a new prisoner. Given her wardrobe she came straight from a nightclub which would account for the flashy clothes. How horrible would that be? Imagine going from such a fun time to... She halted that train of thought on her mental tracks once she realized the juxtaposition of such a transition eerily matched that of the incident involving her friend.

Unlike Janet, who she could not help, Beth planned to aid the newly arrived tenant. Forging onward, she navigated gaps of complete darkness which forced her into a blind defensive using outstretched arms to avoid colliding with any obstacles. A moan emanated in the near distance causing her to worry the woman in a fearful flight might have run headlong into an obstruction.

"Hello? I understand we're in the shit, but don't fear me. My name is Beth, I'm here to help you."

"Beth?"

The voice, though slurred, sounded eerily familiar. Because she had not heard Janet speak in years, it would be easy to mistake another as being her friend's tonal twin, so she shook it off as a crazy thought. The view ahead flummoxed her. Long stretches of pitched darkness gave way to staccato bursts of ambient illumination from cellar windows at irregular intervals. As soon as she started to adjust to the gloom, the re-introduction of light made the return to black appear much darker each time.

"Yes, my name is Beth. I'm stuck here too but I can help you."

The voice suddenly shouted horrendously loud directly into her ear.

"You have the power!"

She spun in a circle trying to locate the perpetrator. The metallic dress reflected briefly in the distance as the person took off. Whoever she was, she could move absurdly fast in heels.

"Stop! How do you know those words?"

Beth chanced a sprint into the blackness only to freeze upon reaching the next arc of ambient sunlight. The word, 'you' painted in large red letters covered the wall exposed by filtered daylight. The figure remained within view in the distance, as if by design, except the shadows cast themselves such she could not single out the woman's facial features nor hair color, leaving nothing to identify her by other than the dress. Beth rushed forward again while the runner scrambled away.

Upon reaching the spot where the woman just now stood, Beth noticed 'have' painted in large block letters, designed for easy discovery in another narrow shaft of illumination. The simple combination of four letters made Beth nauseous. Not only did someone know of her past, but they were messing with her. There was no way the lady could paint so quickly while on the run, could she? More likely an individual painted it earlier, planned it out in advance. But who?

Then it hit her. The ghost whisperer and his accomplice were the only ones who knew she was here. They probed her, asking questions about her history. Had she inadvertently provided personal information? Supplied them insight into her past tragedy? Moments ago, she considered returning to them for comfort only to understand now how her gut had been right. The pair were a toxin. Even after she escaped their clutches, they continued working a master plan.

Hell, Suzy was a yoga instructor which meant she could likely run in heels, and her toned body would fill out the outfit like her friend. Suzy did not have the tits Janet did, (and the mystery woman did, she had noticed that much) but she herself had used padding of various types over the years so why not the downward dog lady? It would be an easy fake versus a deep one.

"Is that you Suzy? Are you the sick fuck painter, Charlie? Upset I didn't want to hang with your sorry asses? This shit is why. I can't figure out how you got it from me, maybe I said things while I was under duress about being in this fucking house! Huh? Is it you? You know those words. How?"

In the distance, the woman faced a wall, even as her visage remained hidden which Beth believed to be deliberate. Keeping her identity in shadows so long required a dedicated effort. The individual's attempts at obfuscation suggested the culprit was the fitness instructor but before Beth could determine for sure, the person vanished again. 'The' showed in full view.

There was no need to read any more of the paintings as she already figured out the pattern, understood what would come next. Combined, they formed the last words Janet ever spoke in the form of a plea to her best friend. They were both drunk that night—dangerously so when they met two cute guys who invited them to an after party.

The pair argued over driving versus taking an Uber because traveling in the hunks' vehicle was out in the chance the guys turned out to be of the genus creepazoid. Beth claimed she would be fine if she followed the red train instead of the white one. Shortly after setting out on the road, Beth drifted across the line and over-corrected. At first, the besties laughed it off but upon entering heavier traffic, Janet grew more concerned.

Another car honked startlingly loud when they listed into traffic. Janet saved them with a yank of the wheel. The event sobered the frightened passenger enough she demanded they pull over. Beth demurred, arguing the remaining distance was minimal (the fact she pronounced it 'mmmimimal' should have been a clue all was not well in their clarity carpool). Janet pleaded for her friend to apply the brakes "right this incident," a Freudian and foreshadowing variation of the word instant.

Janet begged her to stop, saying Beth could ensure their

safety by stopping, finally yelling, "You have the power!"

Then, (oh God) it happened.

Looking ahead in the dark basement, Beth witnessed the woman painting which disproved her theory about the lettering being staged. How someone in heels could remain ahead of her while also carrying equipment and completing tasks made little sense. She was no slouch in the running department yet every attempt to catch the stranger proved fruitless so far. Changing tactics, Beth slowed down, hoping to sneak up on the female before she vanished again.

Stealth was easier said than done as it required Beth to tamp down her building rage over the thought of people messing with her. It angered her how someone was forcing her to relive certain memories, was furious anyone wanted to rub it in that once upon a time she had the power to stop but did not, at least until another car forced her to via a collision.

Steady creeping paid off, as Beth got close enough to witness the woman holding a bucket under one arm while dipping the other into the paint then smearing the words onto the wall. Beth found it strange how any features with which to identify the woman continued to remain hidden. No matter, she finally had her. The word 'power' took longer to write which provided enough time to catch up where she grabbed the painter's shoulder and spun her forcefully around.

Beth staggered in shocked terror. The person had no face! Above the shoulders, the neck ended in a bloody stump. A scream rose in Beth's throat only to turn inward, squeezing at her heart. The woman held not a bucket crooked under an arm but her own decapitated head into which she dipped fingers before writing in blood. The lady in the dress **was** Janet, and her former best friend's upside-down face yelled the horrific deep welled words from earlier.

"You have the power!"

The corpse dropped its ghastly cargo. The lopped off skull rolled to Beth's feet where it looked up and blinked repeatedly.

"Oh God, no!" she screamed.

That night the accident decapitated her passenger while Beth somehow walked away unscathed even as her best friend ended up half inside the vehicle and halfway out. Scrambling back in terror, Beth stumbled through an open door quickly realizing she trapped herself in an enclosed space as the headless body appeared, arms stretched out, searching.

"I didn't mean to. It was an accident!"

Janet marched impossibly fast and in one swift motion gripped Beth forcing her back at the same tremendous rate of speed with a strength beyond this world. Beth could find no foothold, cruising unwillingly under the extended arms of an old friend. Glimpsing over her shoulder, she noticed a cellar window approaching fast at just the right height.

"No Janet, no, pl…"

The basement aperture did not 'thunk' as before but shattered as Beth's skull broke through, the glass slicing the throat deep while the momentum carried her head through the broken pane even as her body remained upright in place against the wall.

Outside, the bloody bundle rolled through the grass, eyes open in shock. It finally stopped in a position where it appeared to stare up at Victor's dangling corpse. Like the others earlier, Beth could not celebrate that she too had finally found a way out of the house.

Inside, Beth's torso slowly slid down the wall while Janet lifted her own decollated crown by the hair before walking away. Upon reaching the doorway, Janet's pendulous face shouted in a horrific voice.

"I have the power!"

CHAPTER 52

"Are you sure about this, Frank?"

"I told you, call me sheriff. And no, I'm not sure, but this is how it has to be."

"Inching along the stone wall to the porch rail could get us to the front door," Sheryl suggested.

"Didn't work out so well for Calvin."

Watkins dragged the ladder from Big Rick's truck over the uneven ground. The renewed proximity to the house placed him on edge, his gut ached like a bad tooth with every tentative step, while trying to hide nerves from his partner.

"You're scared as shit," she said.

"You weren't supposed to notice."

"I know you too well. This isn't normal, us not calling for backup. There are dead bodies out back. Plural."

"I still stand by the idea we are the best resource to rescue anyone inside, but beyond that, yes, I have long since determined the place is exerting influence over our decision making."

"The house is influencing us?"

"Hell, Sheryl, you didn't just steal evidence out of loyalty. I'll take the fall if it comes to that, but it took a mental push, you must understand that."

Planting the claws of the ladder into the ground below the door, he raised the extended length above the stone outcropping to balance against the porch. Sheryl nodded, nervously chewing at a thumb while contemplating.

"You're right. Clarity returned at the accident scene but then the adrenaline of the situation took over and I did what I did without thinking. I'm better than that, would never normally break the chain of evidence."

"And I would normally never ask you to do so. Yet I did, you did, and here we are. So, do we abandon everything, drive away, clear our heads, and get help, or do we enter the house?"

"Let's go in."

"Under mental duress or not, my thoughts exactly."

Watkins climbed the ladder while considering whether to inform his friend, about the voice. While feeling it would be best to tell her the full story, he decided against revealing the information. Before determining if the clouded mind situation was influencing the decision, he reached the top rung. Climbing over the porch rail he expected some new manipulated form of nature to hinder forward momentum. When nothing happened, he pulled the key out.

"Hold position for now," he called down to the deputy who still held the base steady.

Sliding the key into the lock and turning, the tumblers clacked audibly into place. The door opened easily, and he entered, not waiting for backup. A joyful voice filled his mind immediately upon crossing the threshold.

"Here we go Sheriff, here we go…"

CHAPTER 53

The vessel that was Brad, developed a pattern to his wall scraping which audibly pleased him. He conducted his symphony by extending a blade until the metal tip barely touched wall (did not want to cut too deep, it would slow him down and dull his killing tool) before dragging it phlegmatically as he walked. Brad lifted his arm with each pass of a doorway, the abscesses of architecture creating skips in the live time score that was his own personal soundtrack. The makeshift theme song tickled at Brad's brain, hinted at the joy of what was to come—the death of the bitch who killed him.

Brad found it bothersome how Suzy earlier denied him his plan to administer pain (she had grown balls since he last saw her). This was his chance to un-ring the bell, an opportunity to finish that which he failed to do in an earlier life. Each time he fantasized about what he would do to Suzy and her friend, his hands gripped the blades tighter in anticipation longing to puncture flesh.

As he passed one of many doors, it was only a sense of something in his peripheral vision that caused him to lean back and poke his head in. Suzy sat alone in a chair, the boyfriend nowhere in sight. Blocking the exit, he smiled at his former love while flexing his hands. Muscles knotted, and veins bulged under the effort. Stepping inside, he attempted to swing the door closed only for it to bounce back upon striking a plank on the floor leaving it open.

Grimacing at the annoyance, he considered whether to kick the obstruction away until deciding it did not matter. Realizing there was no escape, he ignored the minutia to focus on the task at hand. Revenge.

"Hello, Brad."

"You look delicious."

"Wish I could say the same. Thing is though, I have lived long enough after your dead ass to realize how ugly you truly are. How's the knee?"

Brad gripped the blades. "Only flesh, no need to worry, speaking of, I hoped to slice Charlie's head off before gutting you. Pray tell, where is he?"

"The new boyfriend? The one who really knows how to take care of a woman? Well shit, Brad, he done run off. Figured my bad life choices did not have to be his bad life choices."

Brad erupted in laughter though it came out as if gargling marbles. "Tales of infidelity do not bother me in the least. I always considered you a whore, never loved you, only loved what you allowed me to do to your body. Once I realized that ship was about to set sail, I planned to remove you from my life on my terms, until you stuck me with my work tool!"

Suzy laughed while remaining seated as Brad tilted his head. She flexed her own fists. "Yes, I killed you, but I only intended to stop you, assuming you would have come to your senses eventually, but the knife went where it did. What truly saddens me is the guilt I carried all these years. Took me this long to realize you deserved every inch of metal. I wasted years on regret. But I digress. Now, what was it you were here to do?"

Brad raised both knives.

"Hey, remember my safe word?" Suzy asked.

"Useless here, and I'll still take the head of the boyfriend after taking care of you."

Brad flipped the blades in the air, muscles reaching a fullness, pumped beyond where they had ever gone before. The corners of his mouth threatened to snack on his own eyes the smile reached so high. Then he lashed out. Suzy leaped from the chair. Brad's momentum carried him forward where his arms shot through the open slatted back of the seat. In one swift motion, Suzy lifted the chair and twisted taking Brad's arms along with it forcing him to drop the blades.

"I've had years of self-defense since I last saw you. What have you been up to besides just, you know, sucking on night crawlers?"

Yanking the furniture free from Brad's twisted limbs, she smashed him in the face. The blow staggered him, yet he quickly rose to his feet. Suzy swung at the bad knee which popped loudly. The predator collapsed in a roar of frustration. She slammed the furniture against his head so hard it broke into pieces. Despite the punishment, Brad bit her leg with teeth as sharp as fangs while leaning over her like a wolf on a sheep.

Suzy screamed in agony as Charlie rushed in, grabbing Brad from behind only for him to lash out launching Charlie through the air and back out the door. Blood gushed from Suzy's leg while she flailed her arms across the floor until finding what she searched for. Gripping the blade tight, she stabbed him in the eye. Suzy yanked her leg free as Brad grabbed wildly at the protrusion sticking from his face. Charlie reentered as Suzy drove the second blade into Brad's other eye.

"No guilt this time you son of a bitch!"

Charlie leaned Suzy onto his shoulder, guiding her out while Brad rose unsteady on the damaged leg. Despite multiple injuries, Brad rushed them. Charlie removed the board from the floor, slammed the door closed then used the plank as a wedge pressing one end under the knob, the other into the dirt. Ferocious animalistic grunts sounded from within where the door threatened to shatter but held.

Setting Suzy down, he tore part of his shirt off to tie around her gashed leg.

"Found a room with a chair, check. Found a room that closes from the outside, check. Found wood to block the door from closing completely and then use the same wood to lock the door, check. The part where my ex grew vampire teeth? Did I miss that part of the plan, Charlie?"

"I mentioned he was likely a demon."

"You say a lot of stuff. Ow!" She winced as he tightened cloth.

"Did he know the answer to the personal question?"

"My safe word?" She shook her head no.

"And Brad, the real Brad would have known that?"

"He still knew a lot, remembers things."

"But he would know the word, wouldn't forget it?"

"I was a barista, he was a regular, a man who was forward, dangerous, which I liked then. During one of my breaks we got to know each other. The first conversation we had he goaded me for a safe word, telling me I would need one because he planned for us to do freaky things in bed. The word was Pumpkin Spice, he would never forget that. That was a long way to go to get this info, you better put it to use in that nerdy brain of yours."

"He's obviously not human, that's why two blades to the eyes and dude's still on his feet." He lifted Suzy back to hers. Charlie looked back while leading Suzy away. "Chance he breaks out by himself, but I'm guessing whatever released him here does not want your ex locked up. One way to free him is to open another portal. If it opens for him, it does the same for us."

"But if he gets free? I won't let him harm you, I'm the reason he's here."

"Something dark and evil is the reason he's here. I heard you in there, and the explanation of your

252

relationship. No more guilt, you're not responsible for the monstrous things he did. It's time to find the others, safety in numbers and all that. We can't let this place influence our decisions any longer."

"You think everyone else is okay?"

Charlie refused to answer. They walked away as Brad continued to rage.

CHAPTER 54

The door slammed shut so forcefully behind the sheriff it tipped the top-heavy ladder, wrenching Sheryl's shoulder. She leaped away before it hit the ground. She wrestled to reset it, favoring her strained arm. Without a spotter, she climbed furiously up the rungs then vaulted over the porch rail only to discover the door would not open.

"Frank!"

From inside the foyer, Watkins listened to the muffled cries of his deputy. While he had yet to explore the house and was eager to search for survivors, he wanted to relay to Sheryl that he was okay. He heard her struggle, her voice muddy, distant, as if she stood yards away rather than inches.

"I'm all right. He only wants me here."

"Who wants you in there?"

"I don't rightly know," Watkins said. "But he's been prodding and poking me for some time, thing is he is not aware I have been doing the same to him."

Outside, Sheryl fired at the knob. The shot exploded loudly while somewhere underneath sounded a hollow thump as if a metal rod tapped a tire. Shielding her eyes from shrapnel, she looked back only to discover the knob not only still locked, but unscathed. The deputy took in the barrier with shocked surprise. It should have been impossible to miss from that close. She raised her gun, fired again.

Inside, Frank heard the muffled 'whoomp' twice in a row, fully understanding the source. There was no entryway reinforced enough to muffle a gunshot to such a degree suggesting there was far more than just a slab of oak between them. Whatever it was, it could suppress the sound of bullets while still allowing their voices through, albeit hushed.

"Don't waste your ammunition, you're not getting in. He doesn't want you here."

"Who are you talking about, Frank?"

"I'll let you know when I figure it out. I have to go."

"Wait! Do not do this alone!"

Only a few steps into the dwelling and her protests faded away, leaving him on his own. Before even considering a direction, a foul smell reminiscent to that of the backyard drew his attention, so he followed his nose. The house remained eerily quiet. Watkins found himself tempted to announce his presence. If it was a normal search and rescue that is exactly what he would do. Except now he was uncertain what he was up against, or what lay beyond each doorway, so he kept his mouth shut but gun drawn.

He followed the odor to a stairwell feeding up to other floors and aimed his weapon to clear it before moving on, repeating the exercise for a hallway branching off to his left. Once clear, he stepped through to his destination noticing a smell of death blended with the hint of a sticky sweetness he could not place. He entered a dining area centered by a long table flanked by velvet cushioned chairs. He covered his face with a free hand to block the nauseating smell.

The antiquated furniture sat caked by thick layers of dust. Cobwebs dangled at semi-regular intervals along the entire space while scattered utensils on the tabletop lay tarnished, rusted. The stench of rotten food was thick in the air. An entire banquet appeared to have gone to rot. He wondered where all the flies were as there should have been a swarm of them enjoying a feast the living had long since abandoned. Watkins found some relief to discover the smell of death was only that of decayed food until spying the hand. The chairs had wide upright backs, the fronts of which were all in his view save for one, the head table position. He walked past it upon entering never noticing someone occupied it.

He steadied his gun, feeling foolish and lucky. Not clearing a room was how one got themselves killed. A single hand dangled over the armrest. Whoever it was, they had cover while Watkins stood in the open.

"Hands! Raise them!"

The breaking of silence startled even himself, yet the person did not flinch. Holding his gun aloft, he swiftly arced across the room in a semi-circle until discovering a woman so petite the chair-back initially hid her from view. He holstered his weapon. Though the person's face lay in a bowl of liquid, it was clear it was an aged female. One of her hands rested on the armrest, the other grasped her swollen neck. The sheriff lifted her gently only to leap back in fright.

The body tipped into an upright position, eyes rolled up white, a dark substance covered the dead woman's lips like a child sloppy with spaghetti sauce. Her mouth hung open much too wide for human's normally to manage. A clump of matted hair dangled from her oral cavity. The sheriff wiped his brow which had gone cold with sweat. There was nothing he could do for the woman he now recognized.

"Ah, Pearl."

Stepping out, he reoriented himself and looked through another doorway which appeared to be the sitting area Calvin spoke about before the deadly stumble. Watkins peeked in to clear the space before entering. Once inside, he peered out the window noting the spot where the local man had fallen. The contact point was easily identifiable by the red-brown stain of liquid covering a large swath of ground. Anyone's head would have cracked like an egg from that height.

The room housed chairs and love seats covered in sheets, a home abandoned. The sheriff could identify nothing that might have frightened Calvin so. Place was creepy for sure but saw nothing worthy of turning one's hair as white as the furniture covers. There was no sign of Sheryl outside leaving him to wonder where she had gone, what she planned to do. Whatever it was, he trusted her. Abandoning the view, he returned to examine the surroundings.

Watkins gripped a coverlet and tugged but it did not budge so he checked whether a leg had trapped the sheet. It did not. Pulling again offered continued resistance which took the form of hands gripping from underneath. The clenched hand shapes quickly vanished once it molded to the chair again.

Giving up, he stepped over to a nearby love seat which ceded its cover with a single yank. He exited, unaware how the first cloth he wrestled with suddenly rose. The six-foot ghostly figure appeared to watch the sheriff depart. Sensing movement, Watkins turned finding the space unchanged with one exception—the initial chair he inspected now stood exposed while the sheet covering it earlier lay pooled on the floor.

"Well ain't that a bitch."

Returning to the dining room, he laid the love seat wrap over Pearl's body while noticing bloody strands of hair at her feet as if she received a haircut from a clumsy

Edward Scissorhands. Clumps of blood-matted chunks rounded out the hairy mass. Watkins intended to investigate the cause of the woman's death but figured there would be time for that later because there was still a massive house to search. While Victor and an unidentified male were dead outside, not to mention Pearl inside, he assumed there were more locals present and those alive were his priority.

A thump sounded overhead. The sheriff climbed the stairs in a quest to identify the noise. As Watkins reached the second floor, he did not notice the ghostly white figure looking up from below as it too began to climb.

ı

CHAPTER 55

ypnotic music guided Stan like a GPS. The rhythmic thump-thump of the bass was a welcome sound, a sense of normalcy in an otherwise wacky day stuck in a crazy place. Sure, the club was discordant to the Victorian surroundings, but he felt, in this case, familiarity breeding the opposite of contempt as he welcomed the symphony of a simpler time. Starla loved her songs, telling him they made her want to dance out of her panties, did not matter to her who was on the receiving end of her good graces, she could not help herself when the groove hit just right.

"A *woman needs to move when the music moves her,*" she always said. If it wasn't Stan, some other lucky hump would get her bump when it started. Ah, she was a great gal, he thought.

The context within which he normally absorbed the tunes could not possibly exist in a home in a field in Tether Falls, yet he heard it. The dwelling existed in a permanent twilight of shadows, but Stan's experience informed him that nothing except perhaps cosmic space beyond the heliosphere was as dark as a strip club. Sure enough, his surroundings grew more pitched with every step closer to the beat. Gripping the hammer as a comfort in face of the unknown, he followed the sound thumping so deeply it throbbed from his feet up his legs jolting his penis with muscle memory excitement.

Exotic dance clubs were dark by design to mask imperfections of both the real estate and dancers. Some people found plastic surgery scars, track or stretch marks exciting but most did not. Cheating husbands paid for fantasy, not the same realities awaiting them at home. Lightlessness provided anonymity for men who might otherwise be negatively affected if spotted at 'Whip It Out Wednesday' or other themes nights held on days ending in the letter Y. Stan knew every theme night.

A heavy plush curtain (another familiar staple) dangled over the entry. Stan parted it before stepping inside. The drapes closed tight behind him, making certain the brief influx of light did not scatter cockroaches of the actual or human types. He performed the traditional 'cheating husband freeze' upon entering to allow his eyes to adjust while also searching for anyone he might know.

Stan never married. No one had bitten, not the way he wanted them to. He had a few Beyonce style 'shoulda put a ring on it' situations but nothing ever took. He prided himself on being more respectable than the average titty bar patron in that he was single, so he considered his money clean, not laundered in the cosmic scheme of things.

Once his eyes adjusted, Stan marveled to find himself inside an actual strip club. Round tables surrounded by low back chairs (designed for strippers to turn around and sit backward on to showcase cleavage) overlooked the action. The accommodations served as waystations for dancers to ply men for lap-dances while the balance of seating comprised stage-side furniture crammed together so tight guys' nuts could almost touch one another's. The runway adjacent space was popular given how it offered an up-close look at the talent who had to lean in close to pick up the tips.

An oblong performance platform jutted from a back wall like an erect penis along which ran a narrow bar ledge. If a full club inside a Victorian home had not utterly surprised Stan, (and for the record, it had) the appearance of a frosty cold beer at the cock tip portion of the runway surely did. Alcohol sales required establishments to remain topless only. Once upon a time, he frequented exotic locales offering the whole kitty which forced him to get his drink on in advance. But after stopping by Starla's workplace on a lark, he got over the disappointment at having to suffer the indignity of a woman banned from slipping off panties. His first time drinking whilst pussy shopping sealed the deal for the change in his preferred environment. Shows were more enjoyable with some brewskis.

Now a Budweiser—his brand of choice—dripping condensation at the end of the stage teased him as much as any dancer. He approached the oasis of liquid cautiously. Beyond his angering more than a few people in his day which left him constantly on the lookout for retribution, there was always the drugged beverage which instigated his current situation. Still, despite every reason to be cautious he was pleased as punch to discover a beer. He had been under a lot of stress lately, up to and including his recent interactions with a certain hippy.

The frosty bottle replaced his hammer as a comfort item of choice when he dropped the ball peen to grab the Bud, finding the cold, sweaty twelve-ounces glorious. Earlier upon first hearing the music he assumed himself to be experiencing a dream, albeit a highly lucid one. Beer all but confirmed it. This was La La Land stuff, not wakey, wakey world stuff. And a strip club? Hells yeah.

Stan laughed, figuring things were looking up. All signs

pointed to the fact he remained at the junkyard where he simply drifted off only to find himself in a reverie full of alcohol and strippers. Soon, he would wake to realize the whole strange mess about a mystery house where windows go 'boink,' where hippies and politicians alike gather, was nothing more than a fevered nightmare brought on by a Taco Bell lunch coma. While relieved to discover his existence in the sleeping realm, he hoped to remain there long enough to receive an epic lap dance.

Dream fragments were part of every noon nap. He felt foolish, realized he should have understood sooner the essence of the house. He's sitting in a wreck yard, a door creaks open, then bam! Suddenly he finds himself in a century-old structure as big as the hotel in 'The Shining'? Highly unlikely, sir, no thank you. *There are laws to nature, and you my friend I call the real world, just broke them all.* No, only the dreaming provided answers for all he suffered since the start of his workday. The stress of what hid in a car trunk surely affected his subconscious, throwing a monkey wrench of a monstrous building into an otherwise perfectly wet dream.

The home was a straight up laws of nature outlier. Being a flat-Earther does not make the world a pancake, sorry, Stan thought. *The piece of rock we live on is as round as my balls, people, and only half as blue.* No, the building as he experienced it so far—beyond not making a damn lick of sense—was non-viable. Unless the Devil was real and decided it was time to get off his ass (leaving what was surely the most Bacchanalian of Fests twenty-four-seven in an environment comparable to Florida) to visit good ole' Maine for some mischief, it left only one other alternative. The house: Is. Impossible. Period.

Sorry, El Diablo, I may be your biggest fan in the waking world but I'm also an atheist, so go back to, well, you know where. I have a tit club dream to finish so move along now, nothing to see here except for some double D's, he thought.

Weird how the place felt real though. The strangers

who came with it pushed his buttons so easily which
suggested they might not be a creation of his mind, so
successful were they in annoying him. It wasn't like him to
be a rage sleeper.

Oh well, he never whacked an aged flower child in
waking life then which he considered a wash since the
dreamed character following him around was a slug on
drugs. Stan believed anyone unable to get by on alcohol to
be weak. It was time to thin the herd with the druggies. He
did his part—hippy down, but look out, here come the
calls to the NSPCH.

The only lingering dream fragment which concerned
him, bordered on nightmare, was the whole trapped thing.
Dang, he would be pleased as spiked punch to wake up
from that sooner rather than later because it harshed
heavily on his mellow, detracted from the dance club
atmosphere. There was no way anyone could have
retrofitted the exact establishment he frequented into a
house which he considered the nail in the coffin proof he
had truly consumed 'an undigested bit of beef,' maybe a
'fragment of underdone potato' like a certain Charles
Dickens' character.

Finally accepting his surroundings were a sleep time
fantasy, he tipped a toast to the empty stage before gulping
a beer which had never tasted so good. It was so refreshing
that, for a moment, the idea he existed in a causal reality
bubbled back toward the surface of his awareness. Before
he could contemplate the true nature of his existence any
further, a voice boomed over the music.

"Gentlemen start your engines! Welcome to the stage a
woman born on second base, giving third bases, and
knows you are about to hit a home run. Zip your flies
together for the lovely, naughty, racked and stacked,
Starla!"

A solo handclap echoed somewhere behind Stan. He
turned to locate the fan, but shadows made it difficult to
see. Near as he could tell there was only one other person

in the club besides him, nary a bouncer or bartender in sight. Strange that. He finally isolated the other patron who appeared to be wearing a sheet and sat immobile, erect.

"It's a hell of a dream, huh?" He toasted the man in white who nodded slowly in return. Stan squinted for a better look until the clomp-clomp of heels he knew so well drew his attention and he turned to watch the performance.

Starla slinked through a curtain from behind the stage drawing him to his feet in appreciation of her many stunning attributes: double Ds, bountiful raven hair, pouty lips glossed crimson, and a sparkle of green in eyes that changed color with the weather, yet it was her impossibly long legs which hooked him from day one.

The dancer was prone to stilettos which arched her in such a way to provide the most adorable (by that Stan meant hard-on inducing) lift to her ample ass. The heels lifted her rear to impossible heights, a perfect starting point for her lengthy, toned, spreadable gams. She wore impossibly tight glitter shorts topped off with a black lace bra which barely held in check the second-best thing about her in Stan's estimation.

While generous with his singles when Starla danced, she usually focused on other customers, getting what she could out of them first, knowing full well she would hook up with Stan after. Whenever she finished milking at least wallets dry, she would flash her epic smile before nodding towards the back. There she would meet him for several songs of lap action.

With Stan the lone stage side occupant—maybe the man in the sheet was light on singles—Starla focused solely on him which further confirmed dreaming beyond the obvious fact the stripper was dead in a trunk. He had never been her center of attention during a show before, always focusing on other gents to get what she could before absconding with him and his wallet to the back after. Now she danced only for him.

She spun around the pole on a single arm, body tilted to one side, her smile targeting him. When she flashed her pearly whites, he often forgot her other more obvious features. He silently cursed himself for killing the woman which meant no more real-world dances for him. A wave of nostalgia threatened to ruin the enjoyment of the hardness in his pants. Almost.

Starla came out of her spin, walked directly to the edge of the stage, towering over him. She extended a leg to press her stiletto heel against his chest with vigor. He winced.

"Well, well, well, my number one fan, Stan. I've got quite the show planned for you," she said.

"Bring it on, darlin'."

Pushing off from his torso, forced him back into his seat with a yelp while he checked for broken skin but grinned so as not to look like a wimp. She spun around again before stripping off the glitter shorts and kicking them into Stan's face, leaving her in a black thong. In the waking world, rules required her to leave the butt floss on. Given his lucid excursion, he hoped she would take it all off.

"How do you get them off over the heels?"

"Lots of practice and sheer force of will, Honeybunch."

She lifted her right leg higher than he had ever seen before and latched it high on the pole before dangling from it. Then she arched down toward him in a position causing her breasts to dangle invitingly while threatening to fall out of her skimpy top.

Suddenly remembering the other attendee, he glanced back noticing the sheet still in place, no sign of an erection. Maybe the guy is dead, Stan thought while squinting for a better look. Was the dude sitting a table closer than before? He felt a pain in his chest again, not entirely unwelcome.

Starla stood above him, leg pressed again. He noticed her makeup appeared darker than moments ago, lipstick a charcoal black, eyeliner smudged into the perfect smoky eye. Was that a wisp of real smoke drifting from the same eyes? Unlikely, must be the shitty lighting. She had never danced in a Goth look before.

"Am I losing you? You want me to focus on him? Maybe rock him with a lap-dance?"

"Dude's under a sheet, I think. Weird is all."

"I believe you are all kinds of wrong about him, baby doll, but whatever floats that boat of yours. Watch the audience instead of me, your choice, but you'll miss quite the show."

"Nah, I'm in."

"That's the spirit."

Starla spun around the pole several times before backing up to present her rear assets. He could have enjoyed that view forever, but she raised her arms high, arching her back until her hands planted as if positioned for a backflip. She smiled from an upside-down angle, hair dusting the stage as her chest lifted toward the ceiling offering him an epic view of cleavage. Stan wanted to lose himself in her heavenly globes except an odd movement of her head distracted him as it shifted to one side turning well past a point any normal human could manage unless they belonged to the Cirque du Soleil.

Starla's talents had always fallen into the dirty energy category (as he called it and would know as a connoisseur of the finer arts of coochie hopping). Starla was not the most acrobatic of dancers because her physical attributes kept her from emulating some moves of her more agile coworkers. This time, however, she performed at a skill level heretofore unknown to Stan.

She kicked off to complete the backflip landing on all fours with her bottom facing him. Stretching her feet wide apart, she winked at him through the gap where her wonderful tits dangled toward the floor. He had seen her doggy style plenty before, except now her legs stretched taught, higher than sexually functional, although maybe he could do her standing up from behind, he thought. Stan was full of genius ideas. Though the flip had brought her closer to where he sat, there remained a length of stage to play on.

Kicking feet into the air, she planted in a handstand position facing him upside-down now only standing on hands, another first. Was her grin wider than before? Maybe it was the upturned angle. Her eyes and lips had gone even darker. The smoky eye had vanished as near as he could tell along with her eyelids leaving wide gaping spaces larger than the normal orbs, more like twin mini black holes.

Ever so slowly she lowered her legs behind herself as if to come back down to all fours except her feet stopped shy of contact with the stage, dangling mere inches above. The posture should have been impossible to maintain, yet she managed. Stan thought her lower torso emulated a scorpion's tail the way it dangled. The comparison to such a deadly creature proved apt when suddenly she raced toward him using only her hands!

It was an abomination of a stance, unnatural. She was not in a full handstand, her body remained bowed defying physics, biology or any other number of sciences. He could not remember them all as he was not much on book learning. Starla's face twisted from the natural upside-down position one hundred and eighty degrees until facing him head upright. The movement should have broken her neck long before completing the rotation.

Stan tried to bolt but bumped into the sheeted figure which was solid enough to stop him in his tracks. He lashed out only to have any solidity under the fabric vanish as the sheet enveloped him completely.

Waving arms while trying to dislodge his cover created temporary gaps through which he caught glimpses of the wide-grinned dancer crawling ever closer. Each time he found a slight opening, he spied her moving insanely fast on her hands in his direction.

The cotton swallowed him again with the tightness of twisted bedsheets after a long, tortured sleep. One more brief glimpse showed—oh God—she was so close! He finally grasped the material with both hands, yanking it free. Starla stood perched on the edge of the stage, her broken necked visage looked directly into his own.

With her face so contiguous, he noted she wore no makeup. The strange dark pallor he noticed earlier was that of rotted flesh, skin decomposing. Smiling through piranha style teeth she hissed while lifting a hand (leaving her elevated on a single arm her head twisted unnaturally) and spinning around before planting both hands in a handstand until her back faced him and her dangling legs curved toward him.

As he watched them dance in an almost hypnotic movement, they suddenly struck, one leg then the other, lightning fast. After two quick 'thwips' of motion her limbs returned to their limber position like snakes ready to strike. He looked down to find twin small holes in his shirt. A further examination revealed the stilettos punctured skin. Starla's head dropped low on a loose spaghetti neck, animalistic. Stan turned to run but felt more jerks as the heels added additional punctures to his back.

"Ahhh!"

The exact location of the wounds remained elusive as he waved a hand along his back awkwardly, trying to touch the ache which throbbed the entire length of his torso. A sickening 'thunk' sounded followed by fresh pain in the hand seeking to stem the back pain. Bringing it back around, he found he could see all the way through a hole in his palm.

"No, Starla, no!"

He faced her again, raising hands in defense while she made quick work of both, giving one a new single perforation while the other received a twin so the first puncture would not be lonely. Fingers curled uncontrollably, tendons triggered to full tightness, the pain of which caused him to scream, earning him a stiletto in his mouth for his troubles.

Stan gagged, coughing up blood as the length of her heel stabbed quickly into, then out of, his throat, a precision lightning strike which garbled his screams. Starla punctured his chest two more times unnaturally fast staggering him while he attempted to reconcile the pain and horror with the most beautiful woman he had ever met. A shot under his lip drew a high-pitched whine from his damaged vocal cords, the sensitive area throbbed uncontrollably with agony.

He grew woozy, the collective injuries numbing parts of his body, his head feeling as though it was going somewhere far away. Her legs were a tornado of movement, everywhere at once, impossible to follow, with trails of pain the only way to identify the damage she had visited upon him. The sheet rose from the floor, fully embodied again watching with interest.

Stan reached out to the figure for help, but Starla punctured his arm which twitched in place, spasmed such that he could not pull it back as he fell to his knees.

He looked up at the contortionist horror. A single foot wobbled, waved serpent-like, then 'thunk!' A sharpened stiletto dug deep into his forehead. Suddenly Stan did not have to worry about taking care of the body in the trunk, nor about anything else ever again.

Starla finally left the stage crablike while her bread and butter man remained on his knees with the dazed look of the lobotomized. Once Stan's drooling and full-bodied twitches lost their novelty, the figure under the sheet turned to leave the club. A ghost in the night.

CHAPTER 56

Watkins reached the next floor which brought with it a fresh choice of directions. Clearing each level was what his tactical training taught him to do but what appeared massive outside seemed more so on the inside. One person could not clear such a large structure since targets could remain on the move all around him.

Protocol was not an option. Storming a building like this on the job would only occur once enough officers assembled to assist. Teams would then travel in groups of four to sweep with air and tactical support keeping eyes on every window until someone gave the all clear. With none of that now, not even Sheryl by his side, a thorough search was out, leaving him only with his gut to tell him where to go.

A noise in the distance became his target. Looking down the stairs to ensure his six was safe, he furrowed his brow. Damned if it did not look as if a sheet lay splayed across the floor of the foyer. Must have caught it on a shoe like toilet paper and dragged it, he thought. Upon turning back a figure leaped at him. Despite wind-milling his arms, he lost his balance. The steep jagged stairs appeared eager to catch him.

"Told you, Sheriff, that this would be so much fun," the Voice said as gravity took hold.

CHAPTER 57

I n their hurry to escape, Charlie pulled Suzy too aggressively causing her to grimace under his sudden jerky movements. Jerk was about right, he thought because he found himself behaving like one, not as mindful of Suzy's condition as he should have been. Where he sought his whole life for signs of something beyond the realm of human understanding, it gave him no small amount of shame that the lizard part of his brain turned so quickly to chicken shit run status once he finally secured his proof. No studying prepared him for the real thing.

While he mostly believed they interred Suzy's ex, he also had to admit the supposed dead person now walked these very halls. There were plenty of medical mysteries involving people waking in morgues, so he had to consider his female acquaintance was wrong about her former flame's mortal coil status. Except no matter how hard he tried to ascribe a logical explanation for how Brad could have tracked them down in such unfamiliar surroundings, there was one thing which he could not deny, the supernatural strength the predator possessed. The man easily dispatched Charlie, rocking his clock when he launched him across a basement.

With Suzy occupied in her own fight for her life, she likely missed the display of force. Given her fragile state, he chose not to share his worries how dire he believed their situation to be. No gym fitness regimen would give anyone that much strength. Brad's abilities offered a peek behind a curtain revealing an 'other place' one which shows only when hearts beat fast enough, when time slows under adrenaline, when senses grow heightened, when threats to mortality lift the veil to things previously unknown in the earthly realm. That new place did not just crack a door open to possibilities; it sent an ambassador to negotiate its intentions in the form of an ass kicking.

In all the disquieting developments so far, the least of them related to portals as they were not in and of themselves malicious. Their primary function served as modes of transport. More worrisome was the notion of possession. Demonic spiritual sequestration of human hosts was a well-documented phenomenon recorded even before the written word when people passed down tales of such horrific events through lore over generations, stories too spectacular to succumb to the ashes of time.

If one were to believe history, innocence could give in to darkness of the heart, but most research suggested the ease with which a demon could inhabit someone related directly to a host's moral turpitude. There was no reason to doubt Suzy's tales of abuse which certified her husband began evil. That would leave the dirtbag open to receive a malicious guest of the soul. "*Knock, knock. Who's there? A barrage of butt-fuckery. Oh, well then, step right in, allow me to show you the way,*" Charlie imagined the scenario that allowed her ex to welcome further bleakness into his world.

"Something's wrong," Suzy announced gasping through pain.

"After all that's happened, you'd have to be way more specific."

"You shutting up ever since we left Brad behind means you're silently judging my taste in men, or you are aware of something terrible. Which is it?"

"I would never judge you."

"Can't believe I'm upset with that answer," Suzy said. "So how bad is it exactly, Mr. In the Know?"

Charlie pondered how much to share as earlier his companions declared speculation unwelcome. Enough facts bolstered his theories now that they approached certainty. The strangers in the house might never believe the nature of their plight but he no longer questioned the supernatural underpinnings behind it. He resigned himself to the belief his skeptic muscles would now atrophy over time given they were no longer needed. If Brad could exist and interact with Suzy, there was nothing to stop other lost souls from crossing over.

As if his kid brother could read his mind. Ryan 'Lightning' Raines, called out in the distance. "Help me, Charlie."

Staggering under the sound of a long-forgotten voice, Charlie felt his world warp into a new reality, one offering a direct line to his past. While he could not help his younger sibling back then, in that forest, he was damn sure going to try now, even at the expense of his own life. He bolted away from Suzy leaving her to fall against a wall for support.

"What are you…"

"I'm sorry, I have to go."

"You think this isn't what it wants, to separate us? We made that mistake once, do not make it worse. Don't leave me."

With a despondent look, Charlie turned from his new friend to run off chasing demons of one kind or another.

CHAPTER 58

Frank envisioned a repeat of Calvin's accident with wooden stairs replacing cobblestone as the instrument of injury until the figure responsible for his fall grabbed him by the belt.

"A little help!" Watkins yelped, still not out of the woods.

The young man struggled under the lawman's weight. The officer worried whether the lobster rolls might have been just enough calories to seal his fate as he planted one foot securely then reached out and pushed off from the staircase wall leveling him out onto solid ground. The youthful rescuer fought for breath while shaking out overtaxed arms.

Back on the safety of the landing, Watkins identified his savior. "Ethan DeWitt? What's going on?"

Ethan grabbed the sides of his head frantically, pulling at his hair. "You don't know? I thought you were here to rescue us. You don't even know what is happening? I assumed you had a way to get out. Great, just great!"

The sheriff knew most folks around town personally while others he met through cases. Ethan's next-door neighbor, Becky, had died prompting police to interrogate the milquetoast of a kid who was never an actual suspect. Becky's death was ultimately ruled a tragic accident.

"I know a huge house has appeared in Tucker field," Watkins said. "Who besides you and Pearl are inside is the info I require. I understand your frustration, but I am here to help."

Ethan paced, appearing to forget the man was there. "It's crazy, we can't escape…"

"The 'we' part, that's what I need from you, Ethan."

"Glass. Why doesn't it break? I mean it should break. I've hit a baseball through a window for crying out loud, had to pay it off from my allowance for six months, all because glass freaking shatters, right?"

"Ethan!"

The young man finally stopped ranting long enough to look at the lawman like a deer in headlights. The officer's position of authority appeared to frighten the kid, but Frank needed info, therefore did not have time to coddle someone far better off than poor Pearl downstairs.

"Yes, Sheriff?"

"Clarify we."

"My former neighbor Pearl, as you mentioned. Beth from the bank, the hot woman Suzy from the yoga place, a stoner named Herb. Let's see, a crazy old coot called Victor. Charlie, the guy from TV, and Stan from the garage, and, oh God…"

"What?"

"Martin, a politician. There was a fire which he walked into. Said he saw something, but I swear nothing was there. I don't understand what he was talking about. He refused to walk away from the flames, but he performed some kind of miracle because near as I can tell, the blaze went out. How about that, huh?" Ethan's hands shook recounting the incident.

Watkins nodded while doing mental math. Pearl dead, Victor dangling outside. Martin answered the question of who the crispy critter on the lawn was. That left plenty of people still unaccounted for, some possibly alive.

"We need to do a sweep for the others. What floor should we start on?"

"A few took the basement, the rest climbed up, but it's pointless, we can't get out. Wait, but you got in! How did you find your way in? Did a mysterious door creak open?"

"No, a real son of a bitch taunted me in. Now help me gather everyone up and then we see if this works in the other direction," the sheriff said holding up the key.

Ethan straightened, his face flushing with hope before bounding up steps two at a time as Frank followed.

Not so smug now I am here to rescue folks, are you? Watkins thought while climbing at a pace slower than that of the young lad.

Stopping midway up the climb, he listened intently when suddenly he believed he heard something, not in his head, but an actual voice somewhere below. That which reached his ears was not the soliloquy or taunts he expected, it was instead a hysterical laughter. Shrugging it off, he continued following the distraught young man.

CHAPTER 59

"What comes before Thunder, Charlie?" Ryan Raines asked his brother as they forged through the tall grass.

Hunting season had begun so the young men donned obscenely bright orange vests before grabbing rifles and setting out for a day of sportsmanship. The pasture served as a convenient gateway to an area of forest prime for game. Deer spent many months of the year feeding in the field so their presence in the thick woods abutting the distant edge of flatland were all but guaranteed.

Ryan, at seventeen, had grown into a fine young man who was a better hunter and more athletic than Charlie ever was despite their age difference. Back home on a college break, the vacationing student was happy to trudge through the woodland with his sibling like old times. Most folks in town used a hunt as a fancy excuse for drinking, yet Charlie (ever the protective brother from the same mother) preferred they did so while sober.

The reunited family members talked women, sports, some

life problems, but mostly they busted each other's balls. Ryan took the lead on the ribbing after noticing his hunting partner struggling with the hike. In college, Charlie limited his physical activities to video games and girls, not necessarily in that order. Okay, fine, exactly that order. Point being, a semester's worth of beer and pizza had taken a bigger toll on him than he realized.

Ryan threw taunts over his shoulder at his lagging partner. Charlie loved his baby brother and after some time apart welcomed the return of their old dynamic and familiarity. A large part of the sport required a staged stealth after staking a position so while jabbing and taunting was fun, the silence they would soon impart upon themselves would be the true sign they were a team.

Talking was easy for family but remaining quiet in one another's company for extended periods was the sign of a connected unit. The thunder and lightning combo were more than willing to act opposite what their nicknames suggested if it meant bagging a deer. Silence would come later after they staked out a position, until then there were the jabs at each other.

"You going soft on me, bro? Too much book learnin' not enough squat thrusts, is that it?" Ryan taunted.

"Plenty of thrusting coeds, it uses different muscles, you wouldn't know, virgin twit," Charlie shot back.

"Still need to hunt to get the girls, right? Must be difficult for you."

"Nah, in higher education they come to you. Might want to think about improving them grades of yours given how you are in senior year."

"Like converting to Catholicism on a death-bed? I think it is too late. I believe that ship has sailed on my prospects."

Charlie stopped his brother. "You're smart as shit, smarter than I am, especially with all the computer stuff. Don't rule it out or just blow it off. You could go to college."

Ryan looked at him with a sad smile signaling he was open to suggestions and maybe even redirection. "Not interested in the books. The woman part, I'll consider that."

"Well, I said you could get into a university, didn't say the same for you getting into any pants, you know I got all the looks in the family."

Roaring in laughter, Ryan shoved his brother as they left the field behind for woods quickly falling back into their pattern of riding each other. The deeper they traversed into the woodland the more they lowered their voices and softened the sound of their footsteps. They did not verbally instigate a silence, just fell into it, naturally, as only two brothers can.

Growing up, Thunder and Lightning were always together, forming a lethal combo against anyone who went after the other. A school bully, Jeff Higgins, once challenged Charlie to a three PM brawl in the schoolyard. Charlie had wanted to run but did not want to lose face with everyone so found himself in a parking lot where he and the bully circled each other surrounded by what appeared to be the entire class.

Though it was not his fight, Ryan struck first, breaking through the masses and shoving Jeff while the spectators went wild over the surprise attack. The instigator tried to win people back by protesting about a two against one situation.

"Ain't no two here. Heck, ain't even a crowd here to film this and cheer on some blood. This just became you and me because even thinking about touching my brother means going through me first," Ryan yelled.

"My beef isn't with you, it's with him," Jeff said.

"Then it is with me. Let's call it family beef…"

Jeff attempted to sucker punch the younger student except Ryan tilted his head causing the swing to go wide. Ryan repositioned himself and threw a massive uppercut. The clack of the bully's jaw crunching into itself elicited oohs from the crowd. A piece of flesh rocketed from the bully's mouth.

The upper classman staggered under the blow, his mullet arcing high into the air before dropping back down over his face. When he righted himself, it was clear something was wrong. Blood poured through fingers held over his teeth and when he finally pulled his hand away, it exposed a dripping sea of red.

"My thongue!"

In front of the whole class (minus any teachers who should have been there to stop the fight but were not) young Ryan had brought the lightning, punching the school bully so hard he bit off part of his tongue! Charlie grabbed a fountain soda from a nearby student and loosened the top to filter out the sugary liquid before putting the severed muscle on ice while he and his brother helped the injured stooge to a hospital where a doctor sewed it back on.

The point where Jeff changed his ways, grew to be friends with the Raines Brothers never happened. The bully continued to be a shit and moved to Portland after high school. Someone stabbed and killed him less than a year after graduation.

As the boys settled in waiting for deer, (the day the event happened) Charlie thought of that fight, of how proud it made him that Ryan stood up to a much bigger person all to protect him. He smiled in memory even while crouched uncomfortably in the brush causing his brother to shoot him a questioning look. He could only shake his head suggesting it was nothing. "*Just think you're a pretty good kid is all,*" Charlie thought.

The brothers sat in the bushes for the better part of an hour when Charlie's unpracticed legs cramped until he could not remain crouching any longer, tapping out to his brother. Ryan smiled with understanding and they stood to allow Charlie a stretch.

"I might as well piss since your antics have given us away. Shame you've gone soft," Ryan said with a smile before heading into the nearby brush.

Laughing at the accurate slam, he lifted his rifle high, twisting right and left then felt the twinge in his leg. A bad cramp appeared imminent, forecasting its arrival in tight twinges of muscle that throbbed deeply but were quickly working toward the surface of his calves. Charlie leaned his weapon against a tree to massage the limb while thinking about his brother.

Charlie wondered whether higher education was the best fit for someone who thrived in their home state, had lots of friends, was beloved by so many in town. College did not fully make one who they were, as much as revealed who they were. Little Lightning was a Mainer through and through. Maybe the better option was if he took online courses, stayed near Mom and...

The gunshot sounded so suddenly it dropped Charlie on his ass. He tried to determine where the blast originated from, wondered whether Ryan had stumbled upon a buck. What a story that would be, huh? Went out for a piss and came back with a rack?

Charlie rose to his feet and quickly determined the shot was too close to be from his brother. Then he saw it. Charlie felt an idiot. His rifle had slipped free of the tree only to fire after hitting the ground. Stupid mistake. The amount of ribbing about to come his way would be epic. Then he noticed the direction his fallen gun faced and panic set in.

Crunching brush brought with it a sigh of relief, as it meant Ryan was on his way back. Then he realized the footsteps were too loud, too unpracticed. His brother was better than that, would not make so much noise, unless...

Ryan stepped into the clear, pants down, dragging along the ground caught on a single leg, his underwear twisted between both causing him to stagger in an awkward trajectory. Ryan was pale, oh so pale. His back must have been to Charlie when the gun fell because the crimson red hole in Ryan's chest was the monstrous size of an exit wound.

"Charlie, something weird happened," Ryan said before falling to one knee.

He rushed to his baby brother, lowered him to the ground, pulling open the buttons of Ryan's shirt only to find blood pulsing up and out with every raspy breath the young man took. He ripped off his own vest to press it against the wound.

"Did somebody punch me?" Ryan asked, his eyes moving around as if he could not find something or someone.

There was a glassy look on his face, a confusion.

"Ryan, I'm sorry, I'm so sorry?"

"Why are you sorry? Dad? Is that Dad behind you?" Ryan asked.

Charlie glimpsed back out of instinct, seeing no one there. When he turned back to his ever-paler brother, Ryan's eyes seemed to focus and understand. Ryan looked to his brother one last time.

"Told you lightning always goes before thunder…"

CHAPTER 60

C harlie understood it was not possible for his brother to have called out moments ago, yet he gave chase on legs threatening to wilt under the pain of memory. The world around him blended inexplicably with his past. One moment he was running through the house and the next he was back in the forest screaming for help, for someone to aid a brother he already knew to have passed. He **felt** it when it happened, the part of him holding their connection snapped like a bond broken forever when his sibling breathed his last. Memories bubbled again until he was walking alongside Ryan through the field, both smiling at the prospect of a great hunt, a big future, though it never came to be.

"Ah, no, I, mmm..." Charlie stopped, sucked in a breath, battled the pain coursing through him in crashing waves. It took him so long to get over that day or at least to reach a new normal. He only survived at all by embracing his newfound numbness to life.

He blinked, and the grass vanished returning him to the

decrepit surroundings of the dwelling where floorboards groaned under footfalls and mold thick as lead paint covered walls. A menagerie of spiderwebs dangled at intervals accessorizing with the hideous decor. There was no mistaking the unfortunate nature of his imprisonment. He understood with a clarion call of clarity his inability to escape, but for a moment, the tiniest tick of time, he stood in the field again smiling at a brother who smiled back.

Death claimed Ryan that day, of that there was no doubt. Yet somehow his brother called out for help, of that too he was certain. One circumstance would suggest the other could not exist, except he found himself in a place immune to any concepts related to normal reality. *Abandon all logic, ye who enter here*, he thought the inscription on the welcome mat outside should read. Charlie lost his brother. Fact. Yet, a portal brought Suzy's deceased husband back, so why not his brother?

"Bring the Thunder, Charlie," Ryan called from a distance.

A flash of orange shot past at the end of the hall. It was him. It had to be. After all those years, Ryan was so close. All he had to do was give chase to find his brother—this place allowed that—and maybe he could make things right. This was his chance to save him where he could not before. All he had to do was run a little faster and he could catch up to his past. Guilt returned, weighing heavily as Charlie looked in the distance and whispered, "I'm sorry, Ryan, so sorry."

Charlie ran.

***

Suzy shuffled along as best she could. Her leg had attained a numbness which finally allowed her to increase her speed. The pain had been enough to keep her from running which was all her instincts begged her to do. She longed not just to get further away from a door she feared her ex would soon break through, but to run from a past which had somehow followed her. She would not be a victim anymore, ever again, yet her body betrayed her attempts to avoid being just that by moving too slowly. While she hustled at a brisk pace, a sprint was not in the cards.

Pain meant she was alive, there was that. She had been a solo act for so long she lost faith there could be a balance between those who wanted something from others and those who wanted to help others. She had lost sight of the sheer vigilance required to determine which types of people were which. A part of her began to believe Charlie was there for her until he up and ran off. *Who needs him?* she thought. *Maybe I do*, she also thought. Never mind. There were others in the house, she planned to find them, work with them no matter their motives, use them if she had to. Anything to find a way out of the cursed house.

Something clunked in the distance causing her to turn in fear, spinning wildly to identify the threat, worried Brad escaped. Finding nothing, she turned back and leaped in surprise at seeing Charlie.

"I won't leave without you. I promise. Forgive me?"

Suzy answered by pulling him tight. As he hugged back, she decided this was the man she would trust, that this was a man she would put her faith in.

CHAPTER 61

The officer and civilian climbed two more floors before stopping to get their bearings. During their ascent, Ethan filled Watkins in on all that occurred so far up to the mysterious circumstances in which he believed Martin to have perished. While making it clear he did not witness the politician's demise, Ethan could not imagine a way for anyone to escape the inferno. The sheriff nodded knowingly causing Ethan to feel the officer held something back. The presence of law enforcement put him on edge so to avoid uncomfortable silences, he continued to talk.

"Stan and Herb took this level. Running to find you earlier, I passed by here and swore I heard music which makes no sense. This place has no electricity near as I can tell."

"Okay, this is a start, let's go," the lawman said.

The sheriff led the way. Within a few steps the thump of bass sounded in the distance. Watkins raised an arm signaling Ethan to stay back. There were still several rooms between them and the music. Watkins searched each while Ethan followed at a safe distance peeking his head into several out of curiosity once cleared. With suites running along both sides of the corridor, the process took some time.

Ethan fell behind and was about to rush to catch up when he glimpsed a room different from the others, one which looked out upon another wing, a window looking out into other windows. A level up from where he stood, he glimpsed a flash of something. Silk? Stepping inside, he moved closer for a better view.

Calculating the angle required to get a decent view, he felt a familiarity take hold. He glimpsed motion again, a flurry of fabric moving quickly until it took shape and he realized there was someone in the window above. Ethan's blood ran cold, a shiver wracking his body. He opened his mouth to yell only he could not find his voice. Above he saw that which could not be—his neighbor Becky!

A jaundiced arc of light from an unseen desk lamp cast a glow across the four-post bed he knew so well. In years past, lights on meant showtime. He used to press his face tightly against the glass looking up to see her strip. The angle matched, so he moved into the familiar position where he found her repeating her routine with the only difference being the woman involved should not exist. Becky reached behind herself with practiced precision, unhooking her bra before bringing her hands around to lift the cups away displaying glorious, generous breasts until she turned to reach out of view. She returned holding a red negligee, a silky, sexy version he saw many a night.

Looking back, he realized he lost the sheriff and found himself thankful for not yelling in surprise at his discovery. If he alerted the law and allowed the man to see that which he did now, it could lead to the reopening of a closed case, one in which nobody was the wiser about what truly happened.

It suddenly worried him that Becky had a plan, that

maybe she understood law enforcement to be present and she (someone who somehow found her way back for a fresh show) was ready to tell her story. He was so sorry for that evening, horrified at what he did, but was unwilling to share the information with the sheriff about his neighbor returning. Poking his head out the threshold, he watched the sheriff following protocol by clearing the surroundings on his way toward the music. Ethan ran to the stairs taking steps two at a time, intending to rectify his past.

CHAPTER 62

The bowels of the basement offered no signs of life anywhere above their heads. In any other house (any normal one) the fall of footsteps would traditionally echo from every corner. Returning to the collapsed stairs was a questionable choice, yet they believed it to be the quickest way to reunite with the others if they could reach the door. Together they agreed something beyond their understanding influenced the choice to separate from the group initially. Like bad decisions on alcohol, the one they collectively made earlier appeared the result of a different spirit, not the type that goes down well with a slice of lime.

Returning to the stairs required passing the spot where they engaged the otherworldly, locking it away in a prison not designed to hold anything for eternity, maybe a few hours if lucky. Fearful of waking the Kraken known as Brad, they moved in silence. Any other time evoking such a concept, the awakening of an evil from lore, would serve as a punchline, a button on a joke. These were not normal times. Charlie and Suzy existed in a place proven to facilitate travel to the 'Other' which existed in a world previously known only in the minds of dreamers, writers, madmen. As they passed the scene of their earlier battle, they stepped lightly, mindful of the proximity to the sheer evil trapped behind a thin curtain of wood.

Wham!

The door bulged.

Wham!

The wood slab stretched outward appearing to mold into the shape of the beast contained within. Stretching unnaturally beyond the confines of the threshold, the formerly solid slab could have been mistaken for latex. The frightening image caused the pair to stumble in fright halting their forward progress. The image dropped them into a world of uncertainty, one where the edge of sanity became that of a slippery slope where a descent into madness was no more than a millimeter away on any side.

Wham!

The third blow finally kicked them into gear as they ran from the trapped monster. "Jeez, why come back this way again?" Suzy asked.

"We should never have left the others. Not sure what made us do so, but we did. It is time to rejoin them."

"The stairs collapsed."

"Very convenient and most likely intentional. No point in facilitating such a roadblock unless it prevents our escape. I have grown convinced we could waste hours searching every cranny and nook with no luck. From where we came is likely the only way out of the house."

"What if there is no exit?"

"We got in, we can get out, but we need to strategize, to think more clearly which can be done better in larger numbers. We were safer together. Divided, I believe we are too susceptible to our worst fears, biggest regrets."

"Like Brad? How many variations of him do you think are out there?"

"More than enough to go around and my baby brother is one."

Suzy could almost hear his heart rip open as he uttered those words. Still, her new friend stiffened in resolve as they forged ahead. She agreed with him fully on one point, they would not split again. Charlie and Suzy? They were a team now.

CHAPTER 63

The sheriff took on the trappings of a rat following the Pied Piper except the instrument of the invisible Shepard varied from that of the popular folklore. There were no notes of a pan flute to follow, instead the heavy bass of a modern-day DJ enticed the entranced follower. Frank had his share of drinking years under his belt including visits to strip clubs. There was freedom behind such places he always told himself. Freedom to hate yourself, freedom to be a loser, freedom to disrespect women despite most patrons having wives, daughters, and mothers of their own.

Yes, the sheriff was no fan of the establishments nor a of himself during that disappointing period of his existence. Still, having not been a saint for obnoxiously large chunks of his life was exactly what made him give a break as often as he could to those down on their luck in his town. It also helped him understand when a cell was proper, might be a good motivating tool for someone in need of a little self-reflection—or cell reflection as he

293

called it—versus a formal knock it the 'eff' off and be on your way style conversation.

He pushed the door open to a foyer as dark as some people's souls. The single item in the tight entrance should have been a warning for all—a portable ATM. Stepping through the velvet curtain he discovered a replica of a club he had visited before. Portland maybe? Hard to remember details when alcohol served as the foundation for specific memories or lack thereof. His badge allowed him sex with no payment (clubs wanted friendly cops in hopes they would tip off any vice squad activities) allowing him the loophole to claim he never partook in prostitution. Deep down he understood he put himself into a situation where his badge was a loan for certain dancers to cash in if ever busted.

Watkins swept his gun wide across the room, but he saw no movement. It relieved him to discover no dancers on stage as he was on edge enough, did not want to deal with the rawness of nude women engaged in an industry he had long since left behind. While relieved, he recognized dancers present would have suggested a criminal element erected the house as a makeshift den of illegal activity. That the sheriff would have felt comfortable dealing with. He might have welcomed it in some twisted way. The absence of the same jettisoned the theory which left him with the hard reality he now traipsed on the unearthly.

Frank continued swinging his gun in every direction while hoping the movement might reveal an artificial environment. Perhaps the sweep of an arm would expose a holographic shimmer which could explain so much. He found himself open to the wildest of science fiction concepts if it meant avoiding the reality of living in a world where laws of nature no longer ruled the roost.

The absence of sex workers allowed him to avoid the guilt factor. In his current sober lifestyle, their presence would have brought on a sense of cheating despite there being no one to cheat on. He had every right to partake of certain services as a single man. The problem was, he was improbably in love with a woman who even now was somewhere outside attempting to save his hide so she could finish her shift and go home to her wife—another woman who he loved almost as much.

Too emotional. The place scattered his thoughts in a wind he could not feel. He needed to focus. Finally, he settled on the only thing allowing him to return to work mode, the body on the floor.

"I'll assume you're not going to move." He lowered his gun.

The corpse was of the swiss cheese variety and held a strange look in its open eyes with one staring straight ahead unfocused, while the other looked toward the ceiling. Unsettling. Watkins noted multiple punctures including in the man's forehead. The clean holes were not of the bullet variety yet appeared too small to be the work of a knife. While not recognizing the individual, the name tag identified him as Stan, another name to scratch from Ethan's list. The sheriff suddenly remembered his young companion but did not see him. Ethan's absence was a good thing, meant he was safely out in the hall. Frank continued to examine the body.

Defensive wounds were present and consistent with the others, tiny yet lethal. Ice pick maybe? He made a cursory search of the surrounding floor but did not spy the weapon. The sheriff did not plan to collect evidence, understood he could not magically solve the case with the tools, or lack thereof at hand. But if he did not occupy his mind, did not speculate on motive and cause of death, it would leave him open to think about how in all Hell a freaking strip club popped up in the middle of a freaking house which somehow had dropped into a freaking field in the center of his Goddamn town.

"Fuck!" Watkins yelled at his failure to gloss over the supernatural morass he found himself in.

"*I could tell you the details, Sheriff, all the gory ones, but where would the fun be in that? Keep the mystery afoot and all that, yes? There's plenty more for you to see, plenty more,*" the Voice sounded both in his mind and in the air.

Frank considered yelling back but stopped himself, unwilling to pile crazy on crazy. To answer a voice in one's head, would admit just that, insanity. Something moved near the rear of the club. An individual stood as a silent sentry, covered in a white sheet. He aimed his gun.

"Freeze, or I will put you down!"

The sheeted figure vanished into the back of the club as the sheriff gave chase.

CHAPTER 64

E than raced down the hall in search of a room where light converged with architecture in such a way as to nudge his brain into believing he had glimpsed Becky. There was no reason to think it could really be his former neighbor, was surely only an imaginary figment, one given form by stress brought on by his arrival in the cursed house. Still, if there was even a chance that an echo of her life bounced back, with him somehow serving as the Doppler, then he needed to ensure secrets long buried remained that way. A fleeting image of the familiar face was not the only memory fragment, as the sweet floral perfume he noticed earlier was back, enticing him with all the subtlety of a come-hither finger.

The scent was one with which he was intimately familiar given all the days he slipped into Becky's house on a panties quest. Sometimes after a stealing a pair, he would see her stomping about visibly frustrated while searching for the missing item. Ethan did not consider himself at fault, not really because she was the person who pranced around half naked every night. Despite what he expected was many late dates with various boyfriends, she always returned alone to put on a show. There was no reason not to believe she only undressed for him. Why else would she do so regularly from the same spot, from where he could easily watch?

Well, not too easy. Spying from the angle required to catch the show brought with it a heavy strain on the neck. Never did he fault the sexy neighbor for being unaware of his discomfort because with his lights off to stay invisible on his end, she would be ignorant of the contortions required for him to watch.

Becky's mother was rarely around which made him wonder why the object of his affections never brought her guys back for sex which would have been the real show. With her Mom perma-gone and Becky working an after-school job, Ethan always had plenty of daylight hours to roam the neighbor's home, entering through the never locked back door. The wicker hamper was the spot from which he would abscond with her frilly things, retrieving the most recently worn pair which he would excitedly sniff before placing them back sometimes. Occasionally (by occasionally he meant often) he would take home the trophies.

A shoebox under the bed served as a container for the prizes. While watching each strip show he would often pull one out for a fresh sniff session. Despite all the attention she showed by regularly undressing for him, eventually his anger grew at her refusing to invite him into the bedroom. It made no sense because she frequently invited him over for movies (usually to watch scary ones she dared not view alone). On those date nights, Becky always wore dumpy sweats and frustratingly sat in a chair opposite him rather than share the couch which would easily hold both comfortably.

While thoroughly enjoying the movie nights, he always left upset wondering why she sent him home with no action. Surely there were plans in store when she invited him, yet they never got together no matter how obvious he relayed his intentions. In fact, she made a show of laughing off the advances.

One day he learned of a way to make her more comfortable after overhearing some buddies talking about roofies. Fine, he had no actual friends it was strangers in a public restroom he overheard. With no small effort, he found a place to buy the drug online, figuring it could not be too illegal if the item was available over the internet. Once the package arrived, he awaited the next movie invite which she only offered when her Mom planned to be out extra late.

The second she finally invited him again, Ethan wasted no time. Immediately after settling into their frustratingly separate seating, he volunteered to raid Becky's fridge for sodas. returning from her kitchen, he nervously handed off her spiked beverage while she thanked him with a smile, sipping right away. Smiling back, he thought how she would thank him another way soon.

The movie had been scary from the get-go which was why Ethan leaped in fright when Becky's can hit the coffee table with a clunk. While not asleep per se, (her eyes remained open while sitting listlessly in the chair, arms drooped over the sides) it became clear she was not her normal chipper self. Ethan called out her name only to receive a grunt as an answer, prompting him to stand and wave hands in front of her face though she appeared oblivious to the movement.

"How about we go to your bedroom, huh, Becky?"

Struggling to lift her, he tossed an arm over his shoulder allowing her to half walk alongside him. Drool poured out the corner of her mouth which would have been gross on someone else but with most things involving Becky it was hot on her, Ethan thought. Fumbling up the stairs to the bedroom, Becky grunted approval making him excited how she appeared eager for some time together. Once in the room, he dropped her onto the bed laughing when she bounced up and down off the mattress, the motion of her tits under the Tee exciting him.

Though she lay on the surface of the furniture, her legs hung over the edge, feet still on the floor. He pulled her sweat bottoms off revealing red panties which he knew she usually wore. As the sweats cleared her calves, they dropped with a weighted thud slamming hard against the ground. Ethan winced, feeling like a tool, embarrassed to be so new to all this stuff with women. Despite Becky's condition, she groaned as the heels banged violently.

Rising above her, he shoved her further up on the mattress to where he could stare into her face. He found her so beautiful and moved her hair away from where it had fallen over eyes, hands trembling as he did so. This was the closest he had ever been to a woman before. Her breasts were large and firm, long the envy of many guys at school. Reaching down, he rubbed one through her Tee which felt amazing, better than he could have hoped. Lifting the cotton top slightly confirmed a red bra underneath, the sight of which drove him wild. Tracing a hand down her stomach towards the hidden treasure under silky guard, he froze upon hearing a grunt louder than that elicited by her involuntary foot stomp.

Turning curiously toward her, she spoke, slurred but audible. "Stop."

Ethan rose off the bed panicked, wondering if the drug needed more time. Taking a moment to look down on his own bedroom window from the exact spot she showed off every night, it surprised him to discover the amount of neck gymnastics it took to view it. Glancing about the room he suddenly realized there were many areas elsewhere she could stand which would have made things easier for him to watch.

The craziest idea formed in the back of Ethan's mind that possibly the older, sexier woman did not put on shows specifically for him. Frustrated, he tried to determine why it was she allowed him to touch her breast just a moment ago if she was not that into him. Duh, that was it, things were moving too fast. Women liked men to take time he heard somewhere. Returning to the bed he snuggled alongside the stunning beauty, touching flesh through Tee again, more gently, whispering apologies, suggesting he would go slow even as he kissed her neck.

The kisses excited him again, readied him to bring things to the next level when something salty bathed his tongue. Rising back up, he discovered the taste was that of a tear running from one eyeball in a steady stream down her cheek onto her throat. Another word reached his ears.

"No."

"Why isn't this working? I paid a lot of money!"

Tears rolled from her other eye. Frantic, he tried to determine what was happening, suddenly thankful that at least she still could not move. Something was wrong, exactly what he could not figure out. Too much drug, too little? He was so new at this and could not bear to watch her weep anymore. Frustrated, he did the same.

"Stop! You tease me all the time, then cry when I'm here? That's not fair. Let's forget this all right? You won't be able to remember tomorrow anyway, so let's forget it all, yeah, this never happened, not at all." Ethan ran from the room, clomping down the stairs before racing home to weep over the box of panties, trying to determine what went wrong.

Waking up to sirens the following morning caused him to fear she somehow remembered, became angry at what occurred. But to call the police? Seriously? He called out for his own mother. When she did not reply he knew she had gone to work for the day, leaving him alone to deal with the chaos next door. Emergency lights flashed through windows all while he waited for the knock which was certainly forthcoming. Then he noticed both red and blue flashes, meaning there were more than just cops outside. Putting on clothes, he stepped out in time to see paramedics roll a gurney from Becky's house with a body under the sheet.

"Becky? Becky!"

A cop interceded when he rushed the ambulance. Becky's Mom wailed in grief nearby. The cop told Ethan how the young woman OD'd, sadly noting she was a drug user who choked on her own vomit. Ethan watched with horror as they loaded Becky into a coroner van. For a moment he remembered leaving her on her back thinking if she vomited and could not move, then...

No, Becky was a drug addict. The police said so. Ethan had nothing to do with it, no way, no how. Still, his heart broke as the vehicle drove slowly away with the first woman he had ever been with.

CHAPTER 65

E than found the room exactly as he remembered with a four-post bed, floral touches, purple decor, and Harry Potter memorabilia (which seemed out of place for someone so hot with a penchant for always banging guys). Truthfully, he never witnessed Becky with a man though she would surely keep such indiscretions hidden. For certain there had been plenty, what other reason was there for her to wear such frilly things?

An ensuite bathroom branched off to one side serving as a reminder how that porcelain Goddess had been an option for getting sick. Yes, she must have OD'd unrelated to what he administered to the drink as there were options to vomit somewhere other than the bed. Nothing in the room gave Ethan reason to question his innocence, still, there remained the need to make certain the sheriff did not discover the time capsule location.

Movement flashed in the washroom as fingers wrapped over the door frame from within, before Becky slowly emerged bringing one word to mind.

"Wow."

The former neighbor wore the same red panties from that night with matching bra, no more baggy sweats. The fingernails (in the past always worn bare in a plain Jane style) now glittered under scarlet polish and grown long where they tapered into sharp points. High-heeled pumps completed the outfit. To say she looked sexy was a no brainer even as his departed the cranium station. Not even pretending not to stare, he absorbed everything about her, noting that while utterly enticing, there was something else, she appeared—dangerous.

"Hello, Ethan. So good to see you."

"Really? I expected you to be angry. How did you come to be here?"

Raising a finger to her mouth, she shushed him before moving closer, pressing up tight.

"Ask too many questions and maybe all this goes away."

"No, okay, fine, thought you might be furious is all…"

"Why would I be mad at the one who saw this rendition of myself, do you like?" She moved in even more. "Most people would see a young woman who was studious, bashful, college-bound, a bit nerdy. But not my little nosy neighbor, oh no. You somehow viewed this interpretation of me through all that."

"If everything is cool, why cry that night?"

"Because I could not move, could not do what I wanted. Do you want me to do things to you, Ethan?"

Nodding in place, afraid to break the spell, he fell back when she shoved him. Once on the bed she yanked off his pants causing his heels to slam the floor reminiscent of their previous encounter. He cried out, suddenly aware of how much the soft unprotected part of the body could hurt. The sharp agony caused him to jolt up to massage the ache out of his lower limbs. While sitting erect, she stripped his shirt over his head leaving him clad only in white underwear.

Pushing him back again and rising above him, her sweet-scented proximity allowed him to forgive the feet faux pas, payback and all that anyway, he figured. Somehow worlds aligned in such a way to help him win the lucky bastard lottery. How else to explain someone dropped the chance to relive a failed night the proper way into his half naked lap? Ethan had experienced no success with women after his epic fail evening, developing an inability to handle rejection so debilitating he stopped trying. Becky was almost his first once, now she would be for real.

They kissed, causing him to moan, as she (growled?) responded passionately to their coupling. Frenching immediately shot to the top of his list of life goals as the pair performed an oral Tango he wished would never end until suddenly it did, violently. Jerking suddenly away from his paramour he clasped hands over a throbbing mouth before dropping them away to whine in protest.

"You bit my tongue!"

She laughed. "Sorry, I've waited so long, I'm having a hard time controlling myself."

Moving into him, she kissed his neck eliciting fresh murmurs of pleasure from her lover. Grabbing her hair, he caressed her while she suckled his tender flesh. The earlier transgression now a distant memory, he suddenly pushed her away to nurse an abraded throat.

"You bit me again!"

"This is how you wanted it, right? I should be rough, be a bad girl?"

Ethan nodded with some level of uncertainty as she continued down his chest. The sensations of being touched in places no one ever had before surged pleasure he could never fathom through his whole being. Breathing came in staccato bursts of air as he sought to gain some sense of control over the foreign feelings. Then he screamed anew as she bit his nipple hard enough to draw blood.

"Jesus! What the hell?"

"Which is it, Ethan?"

"Huh?" Confused, he did not connect the contrasting exclamations.

Despite an excitement level off the charts, he grew weary of his boudoir partner, wondered whether he was up to taking part in the world of lovemaking. Besides the whole her being deceased thing, something else was off. Out of caution he rose intent to leave only to freeze, stiffening with resolve to stick it out when she caressed him through his underwear. Gasping under an experience surpassing all others, he involuntarily launched himself back down onto the mattress allowing her to pull off his tighty whities.

"Don't worry, I'll be gentle this time," she said.

Ethan gripped the sheets wildly when she placed her mouth over him drawing an extended moan of pleasure. The sensations were amazing, so soft. Instinct kicked in again and his hands sought her head, massaging it in appreciation of her efforts. This new world had taken too long to arrive. Why had he waited so long? Then something shifted, almost felt like a snap in his hands as they twisted through his lover's hair. Out of curiosity he lifted his hand shocked to find not only his fingers still twirled in her locks, but his hand brought with it her scalp!

Eyes already wide in ecstasy shot open wider as he tried to understand the dreadful development. Remaining hard despite the gruesome image, he felt his waist wracked by a sudden quick pressure. There was something about the tug and jerk at his groin, a sharpness behind it that escaped him. A sense of foreboding filled his gut all while his brain scrambled, attempting to identify the source. Before his thoughts caught up, a hollow pain howitzered across his body causing him to roar in terror.

Becky smiled up through rows of jagged canine style teeth, mouth smeared red (please be lipstick!). Then he noticed the severed meat piece laying nearby on the bed before inspecting his groin only to find an open hole where the most important part of his anatomy used to be. A river of crimson flooded from the wound in thick pulses perfectly matching his lover's lips.

Eyes unblinking in shock, Becky morphed before him suddenly displaying more than just razor teeth. Flesh, partially decayed, hung loosely over a bony frame like a person wearing the wrong-sized suit. A worm wriggled half out of one empty eye socket. A stench of spoiled meat and copper notes of blood overcame him as she leaned in close, a lover's breath away.

"Full disclosure, I've never been with a man before, always planned to get out of this small town and find someone, eventually. Truthfully, never even kissed a guy which means you were my first. Was it good for you too?"

Ethan moaned, pulling legs toward his body which had grown so cold as the room went white under pain so extreme that he found himself unable to reach down to staunch the blood-flow. Curling into a ball, he wondered how he could have been so wrong. How could he have not known who she really was? Growing dizzier, his vision blurred until he could no longer see the neighbor. He whimpered, crying where he lay all while finding he could not seem to get small enough.

Somewhere above, Becky hissed and breathed like an artificial lung at a hospital. Putrid breath filled his nostrils as she whispered gently to her lover. "Look, we've discovered your favorite sexual position. Fetal. I told you I cried when I could not do certain things then. Now you know what I wanted to do that night, you son of a bitch!"

She laughed a long cackle showing a joy Ethan never experienced from her in their past life together. She bellowed so loudly he found he could not bear it, but mercifully it finally faded along with every other sound. A cone of silence enveloped his world until he could not hear much of anything including his own heartbeat.

CHAPTER 66

The curtains danced in the air when Watkins rushed the stage and launched himself into the dressing room. Mirrors dotted the cramped quarters where makeup on tables had faded black with time. The space appeared to age before his eyes as though the memories of the dead man next-door were vanishing along with his life.

Movement flashed off to his right, so he fired shattering a mirror in the remnants of which fluttered the reflection of the ghost. Watkins cursed, understood only fools fire indiscriminately especially with no way to know who might be under the sheet. To take such a shot without absolute certainty of the target could lead to tragedy. Adrenaline be damned, he knew better.

The white image flashed in another reflection, the angle off making it difficult to triangulate the location. Advancing through the room, the figure appeared to follow him from mirror to mirror. Even as he slipped into a jog the ghost matched his pace until he momentarily lost sight upon bursting through an emergency exit only to find himself facing the suspect who somehow got ahead of him.

Using his momentum, he tackled the figure encountering no resistance under the covering. The white fabric enveloped him as he collided painfully into a wall before bouncing off while continuing to struggle with the cloth. Even with no host, the tight sheath strangled him, cocooning tightly. Frantic, and growing increasingly claustrophobic, he ripped it violently away, causing his hair to spread wildly, a variation of bed head. Still on edge, he breathed heavily and figured if he found himself in front of a mirror in the other room he likely would appear as the maddest of men. With no time to collect himself, he glimpsed another figure, corporeal now, so drew down on the perilously close target.

"Don't shoot!"

"Charlie Raines?"

"Yes," Suzy answered, stepping from behind the bookish man holding hands in the air.

"You two have some explaining to do."

CHAPTER 67

After safely bypassing the imprisoned psycho, Charlie and Suzy navigated back to their initial point of entry. Piling the debris provided a base from which to reach the upper floor which they did with old-fashioned hand clasping on Charlie's part. Lifting Suzy brought her to a broken step which remained precariously attached to the doorsill. Years of yoga proved useful as she lifted herself into place anchored in the threshold before pushing the door open with little effort. It swung wide, so she launched herself inside before it could magically close on its own again and planked herself across the ground before reaching down to assist him.

Scrambling with his legs as she pulled him, Charlie crested the doorway falling atop her back in the first story of the home. Breathing heavily, he struggled with his lizard brain all over again given their full body contact. As soon as he realized she caught wind of his renewed moral deficiency, he leaped to his feet then helped her up. She gave the slightest of smiles which surprised him. Less than an hour ago such a move would have resulted in fisticuffs, yet now she—tolerated him. Progress.

Any intimacy quickly faded as they slipped back into argument mode over which direction to go until a gunshot decided for them. While following the concussive noise up a flight of stairs, they spied Ethan sprinting farther up well ahead of them, far enough that he did not hear them call his name. The unexpected sound of club music drew their attention away from the young man.

A heavy beat suggesting a hot party was in full swing drew them curiously forward only to suddenly cover each other protectively in fright as a ghost flew through a doorway. (Then banged into a wall?) The specter appeared drunk and disorderly as it thrashed about in an almost comical manner until the apparition revealed itself to be the sheriff. Charlie parked all questions related to the circumstances in which they discovered the officer, choosing instead to fill the man in on everything they knew. Suzy finished the update on where they left her ex (leaving Frank skeptical about the resurrection part of the story but he let her talk) and that was when it hit Charlie, the ultimate question.

"How did you get in?"

"Truth is, someone goaded me to enter, to a certain extent."

"Who?" Suzy asked.

"Let's not go there. I may have a way out, but I need to account for everyone first. Victor, Pearl, Stan, and Martin are all accounted for, though by that I mean they are no longer with us."

The two looked at each other only mildly surprised the otherworldly had not spared others in their party. Charlie wondered whether Brad was responsible or if they suffered fates at the hands of their own version of a crazy ex-husband.

"I've been piecing together what this place might be. If you found all those folks, then you have more knowledge than we do. Share what you know, don't hold back," Charlie said.

"There's nothing to tell."

"He's lying," Suzy said.

"What are you talking about, young lady?"

"All men have a tell, including you, I'm a bit of an expert on the subject. You're not telling the truth. Only people with secrets get into this house. So, what is yours, Sheriff?"

Watkins cinched up his belt, arched an eye and huffed. "Got a friend outside you should meet, reads me like a book too. There was an accident in town, not just any, this one involves an extra head," Watkins said.

"Extra head?" Suzy asked.

"Two bodies, but three heads, yes Ma'am."

"Tell me about the hands," Charlie said.

The lawman rose to full height, looking inquisitively at the TV host who shrank under the authoritative gaze, suddenly feeling as though he were a suspect.

"How in the devil would you know about that?"

"The head is the proof of sacrifice when someone performs a sacrifice outside the presence of the benefactor of said ritual. Hands represent the gateway between the land of the living and the dead. We did not even do a show on it because the network deemed the subject too controversial. I went down a rabbit hole with the research though, creepy dark web stuff that frankly I abandoned for fear of getting a visit from law enforcement types."

"That is not how that works, severed head and hands are not the hot-words feds would isolate, what killer would use those terms online? But your theory about gateways?"

The sheriff lifted the key from his pocket.

Suzy went wide-eyed with hope. "That's how you got in here?"

"Ayuh. Hoping it gets us out."

"It should. Someone lost their life to get that to us,"

Charlie said.

"We can leave," Suzy said more to herself than the group.

"Not going without the kid."

"And Beth, we lost contact with her in the basement. Ethan ran upstairs, we saw him," Charlie said.

"Let's start there since he was in my charge, dang foolish of me to lose sight of him."

"The house is influencing our choices, nudging them to the not so wise brand of decision making."

Watkins nodded in recognition. "Kid first, then Beth, then get you folks home."

They headed for the stairs and as Frank gripped the banister a familiar voice chimed in his head.

"Now Sheriff, you know nothing is ever that simple. You must understand I have more tricks left in my sleeves and you know full well, tragedy follows you around like a stray dog that's been fed a snack. As fun as my day has been, the best is yet to come!"

CHAPTER 68

B rad felt strength powering his muscles stronger than any he ever reached at the gym before that bitch killed him! Truth is, he found himself grateful for the rebirth since it provided him something formerly inaccessible, the ability to savor the tastes of darkness and evil. While a decayed morality and preponderance of sin previously existed in him, the actual flavors of violence presented in the form of rich textures of foulness eluded him until his current form.

Even the act of plotting how best to dispatch of his past love supplied him a world of dark flavors accompanying every violent thought. Some tasted so bitter they bordered on torture yet still surged him towards an overwhelming ecstasy as the grim flavor profiles poured down his gullet with each bloodthirsty wish.

If he had the same strength when alive his ex would be in a hole in the ground, minus a box, buried so deep no one would ever find her, only to show up occasionally on true crime shows, a mystery for someone to solve. As it stood, she got the best of him so far, but those days were over. Even blind he could sense her presence, smell her fear.

The throbbing power in his veins, brought with it the pump of something richer than blood twitching muscle fibers beyond human capacity. A tiny part of him supposed he should have been grateful to his prey given how she facilitated the transition to his present state, yet the desire to complete what he started raged inside. Suzy existed among the living and to remove the breathing from the earth promised a luxurious taste sweeter than any encountered so far.

While some of his limbs remained crooked and damaged, acting as a sad reminder of the limitations of human vessels, the pain it supplied, like the deeply penetrated eye sockets, felt exquisite.

Despite his blindness, other senses grew enhanced especially his olfactory receptors firing on a scale off the charts. Not even the bittersweet odor of gangrene developing in one of his legs escaped his notice. The rot would metastasize through the entire limb soon and he found himself eager to explore the joys the accompanying pain would visit upon him.

The door exploded off its hinges after he lashed out with flexed arms chuckling while thinking of doing the same to that bitch's boyfriend, wondering whether he could take the head off at the neck with the same swift motion.

To seek the others, he would follow his nose. Another sniff and he separated odors as efficiently as any bloodhound leading him to believe it might be possible to smell the mismatched couple's deaths in advance. Eager to get to work he dragged his bad leg along the dirt floor in a hunt for the ultimate revenge.

CHAPTER 69

The trio arrived on the next floor where they soon discovered Ethan's grisly remains. The males in the group reacted with abject horror to the scene while groaning with sympathy pains. Suzy positioned herself in such a way to control the amount of visual input related to the horrific imagery. Sidelong glimpses of the carnage through the reflection of a nearby vanity mirror were enough for her to understand the fate of the corpse.

Beneath the lingering smell of death, she noted subtle hints of a life very much like her own youth. An inexpensive starter perfume lingered in the air while the more cloying odors of cheap makeup and flavored lip glosses encompassed the vanity providing a welcome respite to the scent of fresh blood.

Taped to the mirror was a strip of photo booth pictures in which a pair of attractive young women mugged for the camera with each pose progressively goofier. Could be best friends, could be lovers, could be both. No matter the relation they were full of life. The snapshots exposed a comfort level between the two suggesting a comfortable intimacy. A Harry Potter Tee on one girl in the pics suggested this was her room based on the matching accoutrements on the wall. She wondered whether Ethan had any ties to the woman. How he came upon his end here in a such a place defied comprehension. She knew Brad was on the loose, but the manner of death here appeared unrelated.

Behind her, the two men argued over the sheriff's insistence on examining the crime scene. Charlie stressed that time was of the essence. They had someone else to find before they could leave. Why was Watkins so intent on remaining when others remained in danger? She turned on him while reading something other than rights regarding the officer.

"Do you recognize this room?" Suzy asked locking eyes with Frank in the mirror, still unwilling to turn around for a full view. The man nodded back at her reflection.

"Ayuh." Watkins lifted out of his crouch, cursing his weight as he did so before stepping over to her and singling a person out in the pictures. "The Harry Potter woman? Her name was Becky. She OD'd in this same room. Ethan was her next-door neighbor, was mighty choked up about it."

"If we get out, might want to reopen that case Detective. At the least he supplied the drugs to her, at worst, something else happened," she said.

"That's a leap wouldn't you say?" Watkins asked.

"Before today, sure. We all are here for a reason which suggests he had a hand in her passing. It is worth a look," she said.

"Seemed like such a good kid, never even got on our radar."

"Ain't none of us here good, Sheriff," Suzy said.

"This room being here should not be possible, nor a certain club scene earlier. None of this should be real but I see it, can touch it, smell it."

"Well, you're so far better off than us because you haven't lived any of it," Suzy said before her head exploded!

There was no blood, just the shatter of mirrored glass exploding. The jagged shrapnel nicked Suzy's arm adding battle scars on top of battle scars. She eyed the remaining piece of reflective fragment left in the frame, shocked to see the bullet hole centered where her forehead reflected a heartbeat ago. She should have been dead, a simple mistake of her image for the real thing saved her. The sheriff hit the ground, pulling Suzy down with him.

Charlie scrambled across the floor to their position shouting for them to move. Scrambling out of the room they crouched against a wall in the corridor. Another shot ripped through punching a hole above their heads.

"Where is that coming from?" Watkins asked.

"My brother. We need to run because he's on the hunt. The first bullet was the one freebie because he doesn't miss."

Running together low down the hall, the sheriff mentioned another round could help isolate the shooter which could help them triangulate a position. Suzy eyed Charlie and could almost hear his thoughts. His brother would not waste another shot, the next move would mean the end for at least one in their small group.

CHAPTER 70

The group rushed down the stairs where they holed up in a room on the opposite side of the hall.

Watkins held his gun aloft, peering out scanning for the shooter. The sheriff felt the bubbling sixth sense of dread creep up his spine.

"If you see him it's too late, he's a great shot," Charlie said.

"While that may be, he messed up on a mirror like yours truly did earlier, I'll take my chances. Now who is it we're facing, again."

"My brother."

"As in your dead brother?"

"It was like I knew he was here all along, the moment I saw the field. You questioned Suzy's claims before about her ex, now you've got your proof. I know he's been tracking us, watching, even asked me for help earlier."

"So why don't you go out there and help him then?" Watkins asked.

"The plan was to lure me out and split me from my

new friend. I hold no fantasies he hasn't found a darkness in his heart if he is here."

"How can this place do this, bring them back? No way you meant to kill your brother," Suzy said.

"Intentions do not change the fact I did and have had to live with it ever since, almost gave up on my life once out of sorrow, only stopped when I thought how it would piss Ryan off if I ended it all. The sheriff is right though, I should step out. No need for you all to suffer for the horrible act I committed."

Charlie moved towards the exit, but Suzy blocked him. "Our thing goes both ways. I'm not leaving here without you."

"And I won't quit empty-handed. Bad suggestion just now about you going out, my sarcasm meter is on high alert. We find Beth and leave," Watkins said.

"That's it. The basement is the one place Ryan wouldn't have higher ground advantage. He could still get to us, sure, but we'd have a fighting chance."

"So, we go for it. Supernatural origin or not, he has yet to discover our position and the stairs are close. Let's bolt straight down into the cellar, grab the woman and take it from there," the officer said feeling relieved to have a semblance of a plan. "On three."

The sheriff counted down then they stomped toward the first floor, thumping down the steps with purpose, hoping the noise would prompt Beth to follow the commotion, meet them halfway. The distance from the shooter was vast enough the clamor would not alert him, only their movements might except the stairwell remained window free.

Watkins reached the main landing first and flew off his feet with a grunt when something smashed him in the face with a force beyond anything he ever felt. Thoughts scrambled like eggs under a seasoned chef, the power of the blow flashing him back to the wreck in the truck. During his brief time in the air, he wondered if he never left the vehicle, remained there trapped in the wreckage. Surely the impact he suffered was equivalent to an accident. Was everything since only a dream?

Any other theories and any other thoughts drifted away when he hit a wall hard enough to crack it before hitting the ground as his world slipped into darkness.

CHAPTER 71

Brad blindsided the sheriff the moment he emerged from the stairwell. Charlie and Suzy watched in horror as the madman easily dispatched their armed protector. The couple gripped each other, frozen in shock at the idea that somehow a man long dead and should be dead a second time over because of two blades in place of his eyes, had found them. Despite a lack of vision, the monster struck with deadly efficiency.

"How did you get here?"

Brad followed Suzy's voice and made a show of pulling one blade slowly out of an eye socket. The sight threatened to draw a scream from her, but to keep from giving him a second audio beacon, she clasped her hands over her mouth.

Charlie put a finger to his lips while she nodded in understanding. Together they sidestepped quietly in a wide arc around the threat. As they passed, he swung wildly causing the knife to stab into a wall shy of the pair. Brad sniffed, wiped his nose then pulled the blade free.

"Limitations, limitations, limitations. It's all good. Watch as I sniff you out, that's how I found your dead friend in the basement," Brad said.

The couple shared a defeated look at the surprising news.

The blind man tilted his head before spinning to face them again. "Your heartbeats spiked with the information. You're already jack-rabbiting, the two of you so I will find you. But first, there is an easier target. The big one sweats. Shame I used a fist instead of a carpet cutter, I'll make up for that now."

Charlie and Suzy crab-walked to the downed officer, each taking an arm. Brad advanced on their vicinity swinging the metal tool wildly but his listless, dead leg dragging behind provided them a chance to remain a step ahead.

A nearby opening led through the foyer into the sitting room. The young couple pantomimed where to go, while also noting the proximity of the front door in the near distance. As they dragged the sheriff, his holster clunked on the wooden floor.

Brad turned, repositioned himself before grabbing the hilt of the other tool, pulling it free of his eye, hissing in ecstasy. Now armed with twin blades, he faced Suzy directly as if he could still see her through the black bloody orbs that used to be eyeballs. Swiping both arms through the air he followed right on the tail of his prey who cleared the opening just as one blade chunked deep into wood molding. The couple stealthily slipped into the next room.

***

Brad struggled to free the knife, momentarily confused because he should have been able to tear it out even if it meant taking the door frame with it. No, he had lost a part of his strength, experienced a sudden weakness like he initially encountered in the basement. It pissed him off how his power vanished earlier only to return later allowing him to escape his makeshift cell that never should have held him in the first place if someone hadn't done fucked with his vigor for fuck's sake! Why had his power waned suddenly? It was his gift, HIS gift dammit! Why leech off it to share it with anyone other than himself?

That had to be the reason, he thought. Being someone so exceptional, so driven, others needed access to that which he possessed given how there were visitors with missions akin to his. Fine, while something diverted some brawn, gave it out on loan, he would make the most of the knives. When he next grew to full power, he would find some way to keep it for good. When the time was right, he would take control of the whole place.

Freeing the blade from the wall with a struggle, he sniffed the air, tracking Suzy by her fear. It was time. Even with no eyes he had her dead in his sights.

CHAPTER 72

The sheriff groaned as they pulled him into the sitting room and propped him up behind a love seat. Watkins opened his eyes, gasping back to awareness. Charlie gestured for silence.

"Get your gun ready, we're going to need it," he whispered to the officer.

"What hit me?"

"Someone who isn't a man, never was. Just less of one than when he was alive if that's possible," Suzy said.

Storming the room with arms swinging, using a slice and dice strategy designed to catch any flesh in his wake, the hunter blocked their path to the exit. Charlie quietly removed a pair of handcuffs from the sheriff's belt and launched them through the air into the foyer. Brad turned, bounced off the door frame before stumbling through on a quest for the noise. The sheriff leaned his head around the seat where he glimpsed the monster scuffling out of view, humming through gargled vocal cords, a man with a plan.

"You sent him toward our exit," Watkins whispered in frustration.

"You're welcome! Look, better that than he finds us. We'll regroup, run for it when you are ready. No need for the basement, Beth didn't make it."

"Guys?"

The men rose from behind their cover squaring off over strategy which quickly brought on a hushed argument over tactics. Suzy remained focused on something else.

"Guys."

Reaching back, she urgently patted at the two who finally turned around. A highly unsettling scene greeted them. A half dozen sheets had taken leave of the furniture and now stood in formation. An army of ghosts.

"I know how many bullets you have left, Sheriff. Do you? Let us play a game, shall we? I am under one. If you guess correctly before running out of ammo you got me. But you choose wrong…"

Watkins did not hesitate. After all the taunting, he shot the nearest. The sheet fluttered to the floor, revealing nothing underneath. He knew how many shots he had left—three. Firing two more times in quick succession caused a pair of sheets to dance on a current of air before drifting to the ground.

With a single bullet remaining, he swung his gun between the targets. One moved slightly, a subtle twitch of a head so he fired at center body mass. Arms flailed underneath the sheet, blood blossomed across the chest as the 'ghost' flew back onto the floor where the cloth spread out as if prefabricated to cover a corpse.

The sheriff grew suddenly cognizant of the protests from the townsfolk. He understood the consequences of his actions, that he just invited the beast in the next room to return, but he needed to take the shot while he could, figuring he might never get a second chance to silence the noises in his head. Knowing the person renting space in his brain was a trickster and might not play entirely fair, he somehow trusted it not to rig the contest like a carnival barker. The damn voice had to be one target, and he felt certain he discovered the bastard's tell.

"What are you doing? Brad's on his way back for sure," Charlie whispered urgently.

"Long story. I played a game. We won."

"Did we? Do you have enough ammo left to stop my ex?"

The sheriff approached the sheet eager to identify the face of that which knew him far too well, that which had crawled into his head. He would explain all to the couple later, they would come to understand why he did what he did.

"Let's see what you look like, you son of a bitch!" Watkins yanked the cloth and staggered, fighting to hold back a howl of fury. At his feet, someone gasped for air through a bubbly blood-stained chest.

Sheryl was bleeding out!

"See, Sheriff, told you this would be oh so much fun!"

CHAPTER 73

Tears poured down the sheriff's face as he used the sheet to apply pressure to the deputy's wound.

Writhing on the floor she kicked her legs in a fight for air while her beautiful innocent eyes sought reason even as she gurgled a question.

"Why, Frank?"

"Sheryl, I didn't know, I..." She threw her head back in mortal agony—the death rattle. Watkins witnessed it once during a domestic call. "Deputy, look at me!"

The barked order focused her for a moment until her gaze danced around the room seeking understanding. Her look suggested her brain tried a reroute only to find no storage space left. Watkins watched as the hard drive that was her life seemed to erase right in front of him.

"No, Sheryl, no! No..."

Suzy wept as it became clear the poor man's friend was beyond any kind of help.

CHAPTER 74

The moment the sheriff fired his weapon, Charlie knew the monster would quickly return. While the others remained preoccupied, Charlie staged himself in the doorway. Brad stalked forward with purpose, arms swinging. Feeling he held only one advantage, that of his foe's blindness, he used it against the predator by surprise tackling him in the foyer.

The pair flew across the room causing a knife to slide away when they crashed to the ground in a heap. *One easy way to kill me down, one easy way to kill me left to go*, Charlie thought as he noticed the blade in the distance.

They struggled over the other weapon until the monster, from his prone position lashed an arm high, finding a home in Charlie's shoulder blade. Brad pushed his advantage, rolling atop his victim burying the metal deeper when the hilt hit floorboards. Charlie gasped silently, unable even to scream until one was ripped from him along with the blade when Brad lifted him up enough to pull it free. Excruciating throbbing radiated from the wound accompanied by a negligent relief the knife no longer pressed against bone.

Laid out writhing, he could only watch as Brad grabbed the hilt with both hands, lifting it high in the air, readying a death strike. Charlie had no strength left to fight back even as the blade reached its apex. Suddenly Brad's head exploded! Charlie gasped under the sudden gore splashing over his face and torso. Pushing the lifeless corpse off himself, he glimpsed the familiar flash of orange vanish down the hall.

"Ryan!"

Staggering on unsteady feet, he noticed Suzy holding the distraught sheriff who continued to rock in place over the body of his fallen comrade. They could wait, he figured and rushed after his brother. The onset of dusk camouflaged the house deeper in shadows until rooms blended into the background. It was as if the home had ceased being a dwelling, had vanished, replaced by a long dark tunnel.

"Ryan!"

The orange stayed ahead of him, moving at a steady pace.

"That was meant for you. You don't know what I'm fighting," Ryan yelled in the distance.

"Let me see you, please, I miss you."

"And I want to kill you. Not sure what's holding me back. Every ounce of me desires to hurt you."

The clicking of bolt action sounded followed by that of a shell popping out, landing on the wood surface. Charlie stumbled upon it, kicking it with his foot, spinning it away. The tiniest gleam of metal allowed him to follow its trajectory. Picking it up, he discovered it to be a bullet rather than a casing. The weapon must have jammed which might be the only reason he was still alive. Having cleared the gun, his brother surely would have re-loaded it by now so he knew he would not get so lucky again.

Rounding the corner, he came upon Ryan moving at a

slower pace, dragging the rifle along by the barrel as if walking in his sleep like when they were kids staying up late to watch scary movies. He approached with the same sense of caution he used to when helping his brother return to bed. "Hard to catch you, lightning is fast."

"You're old, slow, the deer I will put down."

"This isn't you. No way you want to hurt me."

"You have no idea," Ryan said before finally turning around.

Ryan appeared as pale as a corpse with the exit wound from yesteryear no longer bloody but a gnarled, knotted twist of flesh hardened by scars entwined in gangrenous rot. The hole in his chest was enormous with dozens of worms to flutter wildly within, dancing obscenely among tendrils of torn muscle. Snowy white down, blasted free from his vest, served as a contrast against the backdrop of dark, fleshy carnage.

Charlie pulled a fist to his mouth, fighting the urge to be sick. Ryan looked down at his chest before smiling a crooked smile. "That was a hell of a thing you did to me."

"I am so sorry. I have had to live with this…"

"You lived! That is the point! You shot your baby brother in the back! You never answered me that day. Why? Why did you do it?"

Tears streamed down Charlie's face. Ghosts. He had researched them, believed in them, chased them over the years hoping to understand that which, by nature, defied understanding. Never once did he suspect his first actual spirit would be that of Ryan 'Lightning' Raines.

"No! You do not get to call me that! You did this. I owe you for taking everything from me. I can't hold back anymore, Charlie!"

Ryan raised the gun, closed the distance, aimed directly at his brother's chest and fired! Charlie gasped as it clicked empty while Ryan examined it, bewildered.

Charlie held up a bullet. "You ejected them. See, you couldn't do it."

"I was confused. I'm not any longer."

Ryan flipped the rifle in midair, catching it by the barrel before swinging it like a baseball bat against Charlie's chest. The blow knocked Charlie away where he landed with a thump hard enough to knock his breath away. Ryan tossed the weapon and advanced, kicking his sibling so forcefully he crashed through sheetrock into an adjacent room.

Charlie dropped the bullet which rolled across the floor. Scrambling on all fours, he sought to retrieve the fallen object, but Ryan grabbed him by the belt and tossed him through the air. Smashing again with bone crunching force, he coughed up blood from somewhere deep inside.

While his brother had always been fast, he was now unnaturally so, advancing before Charlie could even get his bearings. Ryan lifted him until his feet were off the ground then slammed him down onto knees before pressing Charlie's face against a window. Then he stuck a finger in his shoulder wound causing him to spasm as if electrocuted.

"Uncomfortable? Trust me, you don't know what pain is until your own brother shoots you!"

Were the windows not so impenetrable, his face would surely have smashed through given how hard Ryan pushed him against the pane. A storm brewed outside. In the distance Charlie noticed the edge of the forest where they began their hunt.

"As close a view as I can offer. Now you get to die the way I did, alone in the woods, betrayed by someone you trusted. Sure, lightning goes first, but it is well past the time for Thunder to follow."

Ryan pressed deeper into his sibling's fresh wound. Charlie screamed in agony while finding some comfort knowing at least the pain would soon be over.

CHAPTER 75

Suzy stood over the officer, gripping his shoulder in comfort while simultaneously tugging at him to subtly hint it was time to leave. He pushed her hand away too focused on Sheryl. From the floor, he rocked the deceased woman as if lulling a child to sleep.

"Sheriff, please, let's go."

"Not going anywhere, I can't..." Watkins stopped short of breaking down again, holding the finest person he had ever known lifelessly in his arms.

Pulling out the key, he held it out to the woman who tilted her head. "Sheriff?"

"There ain't no turning back from this. There is another woman out there who I cannot face. Go, just go. No Charlie, no me, just... survive."

Suzy took the key, looked pleadingly at the tortured soul who turned his back on her to make it clear no one was moving this misery mountain of a man. She took the hint and ran.

"Bold move Sheriff, I knew you would like it here, would want to

stay once I let you in. How's my hospitality so far?"

"Son of a bitch! I'm only staying to get you for this. The reason I don't need a key is because I am not going anywhere. Make no mistake, I will find you!"

"So angry, it's a good look on you. Despite all you say, I believe you will not give me a second thought soon enough because as mentioned earlier, I still have a trick up my sleeve. Check your shirt pocket."

Watkins set Sheryl gently down before reaching into the fabric at his chest where, as impossible as anything else in the cursed place so far, he discovered a single bullet matching the make of his service weapon.

Taking the gun with shaky hands, he loaded the ammunition. The voice was correct, he could search the home seeking revenge or could forget all that, forget what he did to the person who mattered more to him than anyone.

He raised the gun to his head.

CHAPTER 76

Suzy reached the front door and threw herself against it, pressing her face onto the solid slab. Finally. She did not know how the key came to be, but did not really care, only hoped it would allow her to escape from the horrific house. Once she turned the lock, she could leave her past behind once and for all.

She looked back to take one last look at the downed body which she identified as Brad based on the poorly inked tattoos. Ignoring the gory state of her ex, she returned her attention to the freedom the door represented, fumbling the key, limbs shaking.

Moving the key toward the lock, she suddenly wondered what happened to Charlie. He had promised he would not leave without her, had proven to be the first man she trusted in so long. Still, he would understand, would likely demand she free herself if given the chance. What better way to send help after all? She slid the key into place.

CHAPTER 77

Another scream. Charlie prayed the pain would at some point subside, would relinquish its hold on his nervous system, except it continued so long he felt certain he would soon pass out from sheer torture. The worst mental anguish he ever experienced had been at the expense of his brother. Now the biggest physical agony came from the same.

"Just end it. Please, I can't take anymore."

"That's not how this works. I have got a lot of time and misery to make up for. Trust me, I will finish on my schedule, not yours."

Rain pelted against the window as a storm took hold outside. In the distance, a flash. Despite all the suffering, Charlie laughed.

"What?" Ryan growled more than asked.

"Look outside—lightning."

Ryan peered out into the storm. Charlie found his own reflection in the glass along with the twisted image of his brother (whom he still loved despite the torture). Charlie roared harder, hysterical while his brother grimaced in frustration at the perceived slight.

"Remember how scared it made you? I had to soothe you, remind you to count after the lightning so you know how far away the storm is. You always felt better once you realized it was farther than it looked."

Electricity crackled again prompting Charlie to count. "One Mississippi, two Mississippi, three Mississippi, four Mississippi..." Thunder rumbled. Ryan met Charlie's eyes in the reflection. "Nothing to be afraid of. Your namesake is four miles away, you're safe."

Ryan dropped his sibling to the floor, clenched his fists while hovering over him.

"No, I'm not, I'm dead! You killed me! I've changed. I need to hurt you. As family, I'll give you the same four-count, that's it. After that, lightning strikes."

It flashed violently again outside. Ryan started, voice rising with each digit. "One Mississippi, two Mississippi..." Ryan screamed the second number directly into Charlie's ear, prompting him to scramble, grabbing the bullet on his way.

"...three Mississippi..."

Charlie flailed out into the hall, grabbing the rifle, struggling with the bolt.

"...four Mississippi. I gave you more of a chance than you ever did me."

Ryan flexed his neck, clenched his fists. Charlie raised the gun.

"Please, I know you're in there somewhere, don't make me do this."

"End me or I end you. I'm feeling it now. No more chances, it's your time to be worm food."

Ryan ambled despite the speed he was capable of. With each step, Ryan's muscles grew larger, distorting, flexed for a fatal blow. Charlie aimed at center body mass before lowering the weapon.

"I can't do it. I can't hurt you ever again," Charlie said.

"But I can." Suzy grabbed the rifle.

Ryan nodded at her as she pulled the trigger, the shot blowing him off his feet across the room where he collapsed in a heap against the windowsill.

"Good seeing you, Charlie," Ryan said before going still.

Suzy dropped the gun, took Charlie's hand, showing him the key. "We need to go, now."

Charlie took one last look at his brother, then the couple ran.

CHAPTER 78

They reached the door when Charlie realized they were down a person, so he rushed into the sitting room. Suzy followed explaining the sheriff's decision. Both cried out upon seeing the gun against his head.

"Sheriff, stop, we made it!" Charlie yelled.

"You did. I done screwed up. Should have known not to fire in anger. This is the best way out for me." He pressed the weapon tighter against his temple.

"It wasn't your fault, this house, it did things to all of us," Charlie said.

"Can't do any more where I'm going."

Suzy looked away to avoid the carnage only to find her gaze fall on the gory sight of her ex in the adjacent room. Suddenly she flailed her arms toward the officer. "Stop, Sheriff. It lies!"

Watkins finger eased off the trigger but kept the gun in place. "What?"

"My name isn't Suzy, it is Amelia. Brad called me Suzy

since I arrived here. I never called myself that when he was alive, it was a creation after his death to allow myself to get away from who I used to be. Calling me that proves he was not truly my ex, or fully him at least. The house somehow had access to what was in my head or what it heard which would include everyone calling me by my alter ego. Not sure why, but it missed my confession to Charlie about my birth name."

"So maybe that wasn't Brad, wasn't really my brother, and maybe—just maybe—that isn't really your deputy," Charlie said.

"It lies." Watkins lowered his gun. "I know it does. I paid attention to all it says, read into its words, got blinded by grief, but yes, it lies."

The sheriff rose to his feet. Suddenly Sheryl's face changed colors, red, black, purple. She aged rapidly, the skin of the body sluicing in fluid motion while large abscesses grew liberally along every appendage. Scraggly dark hairs sprouted wildly from her widening scalp, ears and nose. The hair growing in sharp black spikes as threatening as porcupine quills. Its eyes rolled to pure whites before turning jaundiced yellow. Pupils drained from the eyeballs, spilled down cheeks as if runny mascara until only urine colored orbs remained.

The body turned larger still, bones snapping loudly through the changes like timbers falling. The heinous misshapen form morphed at a pace threatening to fill the entire room.

The sheriff raced towards the couple, pushing them back as the thing on the floor continued to grow, limbs extended impossibly long with patches of insect setae fluttering with every movement. An abomination of a creature showing traits of arachnid mixed with animal grew to a massive size, rising rapidly toward the high ceiling. The trio ran as darkness rose behind them, snuffs of air sounding over their shoulders like a bull ready to charge. The door frame at their rear exploded as a monstrously large evil launched itself at them.

Suzy fumbled with the key as thunderous hoofed footsteps pounded on the floor, so close now. Sharp clawed arms aided the creature's advance, the claws clacking obscenely against the hardwood. The space shook so violently it threatened to knock them off their feet. Suzy fought to remain standing even while trying to work the lock. The beast was almost upon them.

CHAPTER 79

Rain pelted down on Charlie and Suzy. Having grasped hands while at the door, they continued to hold each other even after finding themselves in the deep grass of the pasture. They opened their mouths to take in the rain before sitting up and noticing the sheriff standing nearby. He winked before holstering his gun. The couple rose to their feet only to discover the house had vanished.

Suddenly the grass shook, parting in the distance as something moved in their direction. The height of the grass and the slight angle of landscape offered a view of grass parting like waves. Then Sheryl appeared.

"Frank? The house vanished, I feared you went with it."

Watkins launched himself at her, all aches and pains forgotten, hugging her tightly. Suddenly bright lights flooded down while the massive thump of rotor blades filled the air, whipping the meadow turf in wide circles. Watkins looked up at the helicopter. Sheryl grinned.

"The cavalry. Perks of my upcoming new job. Called in my first favor," Sheryl said.

Officers flooded the field. Sheryl pointed toward the dead bodies in a spot beyond where the house had stood minutes earlier.

"Get any evidence before the rain washes it away," Watkins said.

Sheryl looked at him and he shrugged.

"What? Still my jurisdiction, you don't work for Portland yet," he said.

"Looks like we may step on each other's toes from time to time," Sheryl said.

"Wouldn't have it any other way." Watkins joined the procession of officers.

Suzy and Charlie turned to face each other, close enough for Suzy to see his Lizard Brain at work. He smiled at her. "Amelia? I like it."

"I'm not looking for anything, Charlie. I'm at a unique place in my life where men are concerned."

"Don't worry, you're so totally my type, I could absolutely head over heel it for you in a heartbeat. Putting that out there for full disclosure. Having said that, the only thing you need to expect from me is I'll always be there for you. No matter what."

"You know what, Charlie? I believe you."

They continued to hold hands as rain washed away their pasts.

CHAPTER 80

EPILOGUE

Jeff bounced around in his pickup while roaring down a dirt road in Loden Creek, Washington. Mount Rainier loomed both above, and well beyond his windshield. Considered scenic to tourists, it was a curse for those who lived in its shadow unable to find a way out of their small Podunk burg. Most of Jeff's friends had gone away to college, (if only to Seattle) so he found himself isolated after graduation.

The scarcity of local available women abetted his loneliness, leaving him a bounty of single moms as the only targets for his affections. While he could hook up with some baby mamas if he put half a drink to it, he had to be careful with all the baby daddies floating around as many were armed to the teeth. He needed to reach a level of desperation for some action before bedding down with that type of conquest. The problem was he did so whenever the horny train pulled into town, and that was a train that never seemed to leave the tracks.

He tried his best to find women in the city but that well dried up when all the outsider tech geeks moved in driving up both rents and women's expectations. Heck, outrageous monthly housing costs even reached Loden Creek where rent control became rarer than birth control. Nerds were inheriting the earth. He hated nerds.

Jeff cursed upon nailing a large bump which sent his head into the ceiling. He left the main roads behind to avoid cops who knew him far too well. The more fun he tried to have the more they hassled him to where one more traffic stop guaranteed he would lose his license.

Fog rolled in, as it often did after dusk, making the road treacherous though he still maintained a high-speed figuring there to be no other cars out so late. The mist grew thicker forcing him to adjust the controls on his beat to shit truck dash to clear his windshield. While he waited for the vents to do their thing, he used his flannel shirt sleeve to wipe a circle through which he could see. He bashed the console, trying to urge it into action. When he looked back at the road and hit the brakes, it was too late.

The truck smashed into something massive which came out of nowhere, blocking the entire street. The impact crumpled the front of his vehicle hard enough to deploy airbags if he owned them, which he did not. The seatbelt stopped him short of ejection but also trapped him in place while the engine crushed through the cab forcing the steering column into his chest crushing his sternum and ribs with a disturbingly loud pop.

Glass shredded his face as he went unconscious. When he came too, he could not move, found himself draped awkwardly over the reconfigured steering wheel. He understood instantly death was riding shotgun because he felt an iciness unrelated to the night air as blood took leave of its human host.

One of his headlights miraculously remained lit

illuminating the strangest of visions. How could something that big appear across a dirt road in the middle of nowhere? Jeff mumbled the last words he would ever speak.

"Is that a house?"

ROOTS OF EVIL
PREVIEW

E arl Hawkins sang along to the country song on his truck radio much to the chagrin of his dog, Butler. Butler was of the mutt variety as were Earl's last two wives he would joke to any who would listen. Most did not. That was just fine by him. The general population did not enjoy Earl's company much and Earl didn't like theirs either. Truthfully, he preferred his alone time.

He had plenty of like-minded friends online, people who still appreciated a long night of drinking interrupted by bouts of porn which was God's gift to the internet Earl also always said. Earl always said a lot of things, repeatedly. It had been decades since he added any new sayings to his repertoire which left him what one would call, 'set in his ways' at sixty.

Earl loved country music because most songs played out as odes to his personal biography. Every honky-tonk bar shenanigans song, every failed relationship, every been done wrong scenario, fit him to a bold, italicized, capital letter *T*. At least he could say, at what he considered the midway point of his life, (because *misery lives forever)* that he had his dog. Except if his dog had the ability, Earl reckoned, Butler would have divorced him long ago over the singalongs.

Not only did Earl not care how it bothered his canine companion, he thrived on singing loudly right in the beast's face. Leaning into Butler he gazed into those puppy dog eyes which all but begged the man to stop as he enunciated words at a high volume. To call what came out of his mouth singing would be an insult to auto-tuned pop phenoms.

"*I'm not big on social graces, think I'll…* shit, don't know that part, *oh, I've got friends in low places…*"

Butler howled in protest suggesting actual pain. There were ambulance sirens, then there was this guy singing, probably a draw Earl thought when he considered which bothered his furry friend the most. Earl smiled at his mutt, stopped singing while Garth Brooks carried on.

"What is it But Face? Me or garth Brooks? You don't like the song or is it my singing because I might take that personal, short-change your dinner later and all that. Which is it? Oh, wait, here we go… *I've got friends in low places!*"

Earl continued crooning to the dismay of his traveling companion while they navigated an ornery pothole filled dirt road on his way home. The back road was a good way in and out of his town but a bitch on vehicles which was why locals used it most often whilst they had an open container between their legs as Earl did. Cops did not frequent the road since it required a department policy car wash after use. The locals knew it was the safest way home if one had a few too many (which was just the right amount where Earl was concerned).

Trees lined the dirt road on either side where branches reached out like witches' spindly hands desperate to grasp anything passing by. The massive trunks gasped last seasonal breaths under fire colored leaves which the tourists flocked to Maine for. Fall foliage they called it. Locals called it, "shit, winter's coming."

Potholes were abundant yet unavoidable given the narrow lane locals called a road. The largest of the bunch caught Earl off guard despite his having navigated the route for what some people would be a lifetime of years.

"Shit on my Aunt Petunia's shingles!" Earl cursed as half his beer found his lap. He chugged the last foamy remnants before tossing the bottle into the backseat, then looked at his dog. "Why didn't you remind me about that dip? I'm three sheets to the wind, what's your excuse?"

Butler replied with a tail wag. It was clear anything that stopped the cacophony of noise that was Earl's singing was just fine with Butler. Earl twisted a cap off another beer, looked his dog in the eyes before belting out words in a key far different from the one related to a new song on the radio.

"When I taste Tequila, baby I still see ya..."

Butler growled, low at first, then louder. A solid whine (minus any cheese) was what his furry friend usually harmonized along with, so the growling caught Earl off guard. He fluffed Butler's head.

"So, you're an old country versus new country dog? I get that. That Blake Shelton is a little too pretty if you know what I mean. And these 'Tequila' guys, don't get me started on them. Good song though."

Butler bit Earl's hand mid pat, hard enough to break skin. Earl yanked his appendage back, cradling it under an armpit while looking shocked toward his pet.

"What was that, But Face? I was kidding about your dinner earlier, but you think you're getting anything now you're crazy!"

Butler growled deeper, verging on a full bark. Earl looked to his beloved pet, noticed the dog's focus aimed outside the truck. Earl tightened his legs against the bottle of beer to prevent a spill then leaned forward, eyed the road ahead. He squinted, checked every direction as Butler grew more frantic.

"What is it boy, I don't see anything."

Wham! Butler slammed his head against the passenger door window.

"Oh no, But, tell me you haven't gone rabid."

Earl noticed a whine layer into his dog's antics, an animal frightened.

"It's okay But, it's…"

Butler slammed his head again, hard enough to crack the non-tempered window. The action drew blood through the fur on his face.

"Oh Lord, stop it Butler, what's wrong?"

Earl finally hit the brakes. Having never earned enough to get one of those trucks with fancy window controls, he leaned over his dog to roll down the passenger window. Crackle and pops from the damaged glass filled the cab as he rolled it halfway down.

That was enough for Butler who forced his body through the small opening where he squirmed free before falling ungracefully in a heap onto the road. The dog quickly rolled back on its paws and trotted away, favoring a leg cut during his escape. Once Butler cleared the truck and reached the edge of the forest, he turned back to bark at Earl.

Earl noticed the dog appeared to resort back to the role of a protector, but protect from what?

"I don't understand, boy. What is it?"

Suddenly the truck jerked so violently Earl's fresh beer rocketed to the floor. The turbulence grew even more severe than the pothole moments earlier.

"What the…?"

His truck bounced into the air even though it was not

in motion which made no lick of sense. Earl grabbed the wheel as the ground rumbled. In the rearview mirror, he glimpsed a spray of dirt shoot upwards where a massive crack in the road opened heading straight towards his vehicle.

He hit the gas, tires spun in the dirt almost sending him off-road, but he compensated, shooting forward, narrowly avoiding the fast approaching destruction. He watched in awe through his rearview as a massive sinkhole swallowed the street behind him.

Turning his attention back forward, he found an even larger hole waiting. With no chance to brake, Earl vanished instantly.

***

If you enjoyed this preview of Paul Carro's new novel ROOTS OF EVIL visit:

https://www.paulcarrohorror.com

for updates on the release date and other upcoming projects.

ABOUT THE
AUTHOR

Paul Carro is a long-time fan of horror and the supernatural. His love of the craft began at an early age in his hometown of Windham, Maine. In fifth grade he had a short story published in an anthology of Maine authors alongside one of his iconic horror idols.

Paul attended Hampshire College where he majored in film/TV with a minor in literature. For his senior thesis he contacted author Jon Cohen to obtain rights to adapt and film a short story from Twilight Zone Magazine titled, *Preserves*. Horror flick director Rolfe Kanefsky served as his DP on the project. The video became a calling card for Hollywood writing and producing for film/TV. Paul resides in Los Angeles to this day.

Recently he returned to his literary roots writing his first novel, the Young Adult superhero book—*Nolan Walker and the Superiors Squad*.

The House is his debut horror novel, with the next, *Roots of Evil,* coming soon.

Made in the USA
Coppell, TX
25 July 2021

59471911R00208